THE STRANGE WOMAN

by

Stephanie Shields

First published in Great Britain by The Sheep Shed Press 2020

Cover image and illustrations: Jacky Fleming

Typeset by: 2QT Limited, Publishing

Printed and bound by: IngramSpark

A CIP catalogue record for this book is available from the British Library.
ISBN: 978-1-9998182-2-7

To Ben and Siobhán

Acknowledgements

I would like to thank the following people.

James Nash, Poet and Writer, for his invaluable editorial advice and encouragement.

Jacky Fleming, Artist and Cartoonist, for creating the magical, iridescent crow, the beautiful flowers and the plump, dark bilberries.

The Courthouse Writers of Otley, West Yorkshire – past and present – always my kind yet honest and critical friends for over a decade, especially Victoria Hannam, for sharing her extensive library with me, and for introducing me to Nicholas Culpeper.

My colleagues from the early days of the Washburn Heritage Centre, for all their encouragement. Being part of the centre's oral history project proved an inspiration. I was the eye behind the lens for the interviews with people born in, or associated with, the Washburn Valley. I thank each of our subjects for sharing their precious memories and stories. These have helped inform the character, the spirit, and the mystery of the valley as it appears in this novel.

My first readers, Andrea Byrom, Janet Fox, and Alison Lumley, for their encouragement, suggestions, and support.

My family and friends, who have smiled, sometimes inspired, and bestowed the gifts of their time to read my work, for their encouragement, and their sound advice.

Contents

Part Two - Girl in a Hole

Part Three - No Turning Area After This Point

Part Four - The Good-Morrow

Part One

The Strange Woman

1

Meeting Margaret

She beckons you.

As you cross the moor, you might think you glimpse her. A silver shape, a form in mist-knit pearl. Then reason takes the wheel. You'll chide, persuade yourself sternly that you are mistaken. An outcrop of rock, a blasted gorse twisting in the wind, a cairn, a tumbled shooting butt or a stone stoop. A floater or a blip on your peripheral vision.

But no, you are right. It is her; it's Margaret. She beckons you.

She's beckoning you to Timble, the hamlet hub for a web of footpaths lacing through the Washburn Valley. It's said that a great ley line crosses close by, and that once there were witches here.

To some, Timble and the valley are enchanted, mysterious, almost mystical. To others, just plain misty, for these others are born without that inner eye, that intimation of the past, that sixth sense.

To find this place from the south, you'll cross the rolls and rises of the moor. There's Askwith Moor to your left and Snowden

Carr right. Across these, the westerlies bend the heather and baffle the broken bronze bracken. They kiss, lick and sometimes bite the boulder carved with cup and ring – the Tree of Life Stone. This was the scene of many a May Day service over the centuries, and the Beltane bonfires.

There's a large rough-surfaced car park near the top. Many slow down, are drawn in, even switch off their engines. Go on, join them. Enjoy a rest. Wind down your windows and taste the sweet air. Turn your head. Take in the infinity of the north.

Fly tippers, beware – she'll get you, will Margaret. Have a care. You desecrate enchanted ground. You will not prosper. This is her patch. She will see to you; she won't hesitate.

Some folk park here for trysts, liaisons or casual sex. They flatten their seats behind smoke glass windows. They can't hoodwink Margaret and she's beyond shock; she's seen it all before. If you sense dark eyes beyond the privacy glass, and it is her, then don't worry. Or, it could be the local constabulary. If so, again, beware.

A breath-taking panorama spreads before you, an expansive landscape of valley, water, hill, moor and sky. Its mood can be changed by a sharp shaft of sunlight, an inverted sea of turbulent cloud, the spears of distant rain showers. You may well be blessed with a full or double rainbow, for this is the valley for rainbows. The rainbows may chase you across the moor if they're in a capricious mood. To be thus picked on is pure privilege.

On a clear day, looking east from here, you might pick out the White Horse at Kilburn and the escarpments of the Hambleton Hills. Margaret has ridden that horse, bare-back and not alone.

In early August the moors will blaze mauve. Heather will sweeten the air for miles. Come February the moors will just blaze, the air tinged with acrid smoke. All for the sake of shooting birds, an indiscriminate slaughter in the name of sport, and for money, of course. Margaret frowns on this practice; be assured. She can't be doing with cruelty or greed. In her time, she has been victim of both.

You will be a challenged spirit indeed if you won't concede some wonder. Your eye may bridge the valley towards Sword Point beyond. To the north you can count the turbines and then pick out the white balls of Menwith Hill. There's the dam at the end of Swinsty reservoir. If the sun comes out, the surface will spangle in dancing light.

Snowden Carr dips down in front of you. It is on this spot, between the Tree of Life stone and the Death's Head rock, that Margaret has risen in flight with Asmodeus, every year since the early sixteen-twenties. A curious ritual, think those who can discern them? Like necking gannets, they begin their rhythmic winding, binding, bodies locking, bills knocking. And off they fly. Enough of this, for there's more to come.

Margaret is waiting; let us go on. Up and over. Down the hairpins of Snowden Bank. A hazard in icy conditions, but this is July. Take a righthand turn at the Timble sign at the top of the hill and keep left at the next fork in the road.

Nigh on four hundred years ago, there was a lot of talk in this valley. Women from Timble were to be charged, as witches, and taken to the assizes at York. There were tales of demons and dolls, pin pricking and possession, and of the death of a Fairfax baby at Newhall, Fewston.

It's 1622, and for those so inclined, a very good year for a witch hunt. Come, for she waits in Middle Ridge Woods.

2

The bird with the bilberry beak, Middle Ridge Woods, near Fuystone, in the County of York, in the year 1622 A.D. – the month of July

The crow swayed with the thin top branch of the ash; his sharp dark eye scanned the stony path that wove through the trees from the Besom Inn. Beneath him, lying on the mossy bank, Margaret Hall rested her own crow dark eyes. This bird knew her well; he knew she did not sleep. He knew she would be plotting; she would be finding the right words for her encounter with the man in black.

The bird was right. Margaret was taking a break from picking bilberries to order her thoughts, to petition for a favour, for support. This would not be a purely intellectual encounter, Margaret knew that. She would line up her arguments, then she'd underpin logic with something more carnal. And the man would come, sooner or later. She would wait, and he would come. She would have him.

Margaret felt hot. She'd hoiked up her skirts over her knees then further, to air those parts beneath the girdle. She stroked her fingers in slow caress, lingering on the sweet velvet mound. The crow cocked his head sideways to regard her better. She became one with the soft moss bank. The breeze fluttered her lustrous hair, cooled her brow and brushed her cream neck and soft shoulders. Her senses were aroused. She was rising to the challenge.

Beside her on the bank a basket of plump blue bilberries brimmed. A second basket was filling fast. She snuffled the damp moss and peat scents of the woods and summoned their spirits. She would need all the help she could muster.

Margaret believed in bilberries – whortleberries to some. In these three brief July weeks she would pick as many as she could. The woods were teeming with them, this year. This was a good spot, these woods by Middle Ridge. Here there were easier pickings than on the moor, fuller fruit, soft and succulent. These plants were kissed by the flickering sun through the tall tree canopy of this sparse wood. They were not thrashed by the westerly winds, nor sodden by the rain. The plants cascaded over rocks at an easy hand height – less bending for her, less back ache. She would pick until her fingers were stained purple blue and sore. When she wearied, she clawed her stiffening fingers into a rake, and dragged her splayed hand through the bushes. But she preferred to pluck to keep the precious berries intact.

Each night she would light the fire under the big pot and witness the transformation, the alchemy of the berries. Cordials, glisters, laxes, pilles, posits, potions, tinctures, salves and syrups. She would press, boil, reduce, sieve, mix with pestle-trounced herbs, bottle, pot, flask up, shape and sometimes set in sticky blocks to solidify.

Margaret had been initiated into the wonder and way of the bilberry by her mother, Pegi. Pegi had taught her about the restorative properties of the plant – a cure for all ills. Well, most of them. Mother Pegi knew the limitations. But she believed in the potential – from the greene sickness of the young girl to the woman's travell in a difficult birth, to womb blething, swound, the strangled heart, fits, flux, griping of the guts, mystiness of the eye, the black sickness, the purpels, wind collick and vomiting. Stiff joints too and inflammation.

The women of her family had looked to cure through herbs and plants for generations. Pegi would make no claims for her cures against the devouring canker, that black crab, the eating worm or wolf, or against the foul disease, but she had some success with her tonics against the fenny vapours of melancholy and the terrors of the night, and gloom, that lowering of the soul. Her pills had vanquished worms in the mind and in the gut, gout, palsie, rheum, spleen, cramps, blens and boils.

Pegi had rehearsed with the young Margaret the words to say as she stirred the pot. None of this was written down for these were women who had no writing, no reading. They kept these secret things, spells and charms within their heads. And passed them on to their own. Chanting, repeating, weird and wonderful mnemonics and incantations.

Margaret too knew the limitations of the bilberry. Like her mother, she rejected all meat cures – such nonsense as the luring of the wolf from the tumour with steak or chicken flesh, then knocking it on the head, when it broke surface. As if. And she could never countenance cruelty – boiling live swallows for a potion for the cramps or baking an owl for gout powder. How could a creature's pain and suffering cure or alleviate pain and suffering in another? Such silliness, such stupidity and ignorance.

Margaret had acquired a reputation for the efficacy of her cures, especially the balancing of the four humours. Women and men felt better for visiting her rough shelter beneath the jutting rocks on Snowden Bank. She built on the knowledge of her ancestors. She liked to add a little more, a certain something else, a secret ingredient, a twist. A little belladonna, a touch of hemlock helped you fly. Lemon balm relaxed both mind and body. Valerian and chamomile soothed the mood too.

Margaret's tonics and pick-me-ups were popular. Amongst the local women her bilberry passion potion was legendary. They fondly termed it the Timble Tingle because of its powers of arousal. Rumour had it, this preparation had led to several visits to the altar and saved marriages grown worn.... But even Margaret would concede her potion may have wrecked a few, too, along life's way.

On rare occasions, she had seen fit to turn down a client. She had her own code of ethics, a singular morality. She was there to cure, not to harm another, abet a harm or feed an addiction. She had been known to decline a commission. If her suspicions of intent were aroused, she would say no. There was a time that this had cost her dear, but she would never speak of this. She feared a recent refusal was about to do her harm again; she had a fear of powerful men ...

Ah, movement. Three caws from the bilberry stained black beak above. Margaret opened one eye. Three more caws. 'Coming, is he?' Margaret shifted slowly and with purpose. She righted her mud stained russet red petticoat, straightened her ochre blouse and covered herself with her rough grey wool shawl. She coaxed colour into her cheeks with a brisk rub and smoothed her wayward fronds of plum cum gunmetal hair. She retied the cross-cloth round her head. Like the crow's bill, her own lips were already bright with bilberries, for who could resist the plumpest, softest and juiciest? She kneeled, stretched towards the bilberry mass and resumed her task plucking the fruit quickly with her long nimble fingers.

The man in black had come.

'Why Margaret, is it? Well the day. You've been busy, I see.' A kindly voice. A pleasant man of middle years and middling height. But for his priest's robes you might pass him on the road and merely note his cheerful countenance, his warm dark eyes and optimistic demeanour. You'd bid him good-day, and a few moments later be unable to recall anything about him.

'Mister Smithson, yes, 'tis only me. A hot day, Sir. Will you sit awhile by me and take a drop of my own bilberry cordial? You look mafted. It's a long walk from the Besom to Fuystone. Souls to be saved there at the Inn, I suppose? Come, my cordial will refresh, I promise you. It's said to be the quickest of my pick-me-ups.'

'I think I will for I am parched. Saving souls is thirsty work.'

Today's occasion had called for hemlock – a sly pinch from Margaret's pouch, sprinkled and shaken.

Mister Smithson settled himself beside her on the bank and adjusted his long black cassock. He took the small stone flask she offered: 'Thank you, Margaret. So very warm.'

She averted her face from his and focussed on his muddy boots. He smiled, placed his left hand on the top of his Canterbury cap and lifted the flask to his lips with his right. She looked back at him and smiled slowly, tentatively, yet clearly anxious.

'Wonderful stuff this, Margaret. Beats buttermilk.' He licked his lips, burped discretely and handed back the flask. Margaret flicked through her memory for flatulence potions to recommend but decided this could wait for another day.

'Something of interest to you, Margaret – back there along the path, where it draws closest to the beck. By the very water's edge, I found some sanicle. A rarity for these parts.'

'Indeed, it is. I have looked for sanicle, to no avail, of late. It shows a likeness to a fat wood anemone, with clusters of white pompoms. These flowers come in June and the seed is ripe shortly after – about now. Some of its leaves are cut like crows' feet. My mother called it butterwort. I will go down and seek it out, for it has no equal when it comes to treating diseases of the lungs and throat, and mouth ulcers too. I make a decoction of leaves and roots in water and honey. It can heal some afflictions of the privities too, err, or so I am led to understand …'

Margaret broke off, and smiled, nervously, feeling she might have spoken too freely. Mister Smithson was not at all abashed.

'I will record it in my catalogue of wildflowers and herbs of this valley. This study proceeds quite well. You must let me know if you come across any unusual plant for these parts, and where it is to be found.'

She nodded, smiled: 'I will be pleased to do this, and to show you.'

Then her brow clouded, and her demeanour changed: 'I'm glad to have met you, vicar. There's something I need to talk to you about. Folk have been saying things. They say the women and me will be taken and then worse. They say we'll go to York once more, and this time, they will do for us. Again, they name Mister Fairfax as our accuser.'

Nicholas Smithson frowned and nodded gravely:

'So, you've heard, Margaret? I see from your eyes you are sorely troubled. You are right to be so.'

Margaret, with increasing urgency:

'I am not the thing he says, Sir. You know I am not. There are no marks upon my body, no suck of a familiar. I have harmed no child, no woman, no man. There is no sixth finger. You know 'tis true. You baptised me, sir. You have recommended me for work to good families in the valley. I have given proper service. You have never spoken against me. Please, speak for me now.'

'Edward Fairfax is a powerful man, Margaret. He insists you have done his daughters harm.'

'Indeed, he says that of all of us. He claims that the valley is full of wit.... We are women, no more nor less. We are neither bad nor good but are not the thing he says. His girls have been with us, yes, true – Helen and young Elizabeth. They have followed us whilst we worked for him in his house, on his land, at his corn mill. They have joined us on our jaunts. They chat and prattle. We have laughed with them. He says we have taken them to the moor to dance, to dance round fires. He says we have caused them to have fits, to fall, to see things that are not there. He says we have pinned their clothes and pricked their dolls.'

Margaret paused for breath. She struggled to calm herself. She stroked the mossy bank, and continued: 'Why is he saying these things? How shall we answer him? What can we say? He says we have caused the death of little Anne. What kind of man is this?'

In the tear pooled eyes of Margaret, Mr Smithson saw a truth. She was a woman, no more nor less. But something in that moment changed. The trees stretched high to heaven, the path and rocks pressed in on him, he saw the big black bird at the top of the ash tree and felt his body begin to rise and sway with the bird. He pushed back down against the moss and felt his youth, a rising, a stirring. Slow at first then faster, gaining momentum. He was up and off. He felt he was flying, and it was weird. He felt elated, flying with a woman as he never had, and he could see for miles and yet no further than her fathomless eyes. The air rushed by them. And then his very body pulsed and shook, and he sank back down to the bank still holding her. He slept the sleep of a child, exhausted yet replete.

When he awoke, he couldn't credit what might have happened between them. Margaret was sitting primly, chastely even, on the bank beside him.

'Mister Smithson, I hadn't the heart to wake you, you seemed so done in. So, I've stayed to watch over you.'

'I had the strangest dream, that we flew together and were one!' His voice was hoarse, his eyes wild. The colour drained from his face. He sought to collect himself.

He stood, straightened his cassock, smoothed his tippet and righted his cap. He rubbed his hand across his mouth, deep in thought.

She seemed to blush. Her eyes still played on his: 'Ah the heat can play such tricks, Mr Smithson. I'll walk you to the road and then we'll take our separate ways. Perhaps you can carry one basket so far if you will?'

They parted at the cross. He shook her hand with great formality and passed the basket.

'We will drop the veil. I will not speak against you Margaret. Nor will I speak against the women of the valley.'

'Now I know you will not, I thank you, sir. The veil is down.'

'Indeed, I will speak up for you all.' He nodded, deep in his own thoughts, then turned away.

Across the tops of the trees the crow had tracked their progress. As the black figure of the vicar disappeared towards the church, the crow cawed three times. Margaret looked up to the bird and smiled. The bird descended and landed squarely on her head. He selected fronds of her hair, teasing them gently through his beak and releasing them from the cross-cloth that was failing to restrain them – an intimate and comforting gesture. In this way, together, they walked the path towards Snowden Bank. The smile broadened on Margaret's lips.

Certainly, Mister Smithson would not speak against them.

3

The Vicarage, Fuystone, later in that day

Profanenesse in my head,
Defects and darknesse in my breast,
A noise of passions ringing me for dead
Unto a place where is no rest;
Poore priest thus am I drest.

Aaron – George Herbert 1633

'Husband, you look all in. Are you ill?'

'Susannah, forgive me, was I dreaming?'

'It's not like you to nap before your meal. Afterwards, indeed. But you have been snorting, juddering and rearing like a soul possessed. What can it be?'

'I cannot tell. But be assured, I am quite restored now, if not refreshed. Have the boys returned?'

'They have and Mary waits to serve us. Please, draw to the table.'

Nicholas Smithson raised himself slowly and stiffly from his armchair by the empty grate. No flickering fire – just boughs, this being the summertime. He loved their dry, almost aromatic, grassy fragrance. He inhaled, paused, then sighed heavily, recollecting. He was still challenged to know what had really happened in the woods that morning. As he slumbered, visions of Margaret, and the strange, wondrous sensation of levitation, and desire, had returned to him. It came in waves of sensuality. He longed for more, but he knew he must banish such thoughts forever. Temptation came in many forms, he reflected. He felt the Lord had been testing him, and he wasn't sure he'd passed.

'Far meadow's shaping nicely, Father. We'll cut it in two weeks, with your blessing, of course. It should make a fine green hay if this weather holds.'

'I defer to you, Robert. So long as the curlews have fledged, is all I ask. You and your brothers are closer to the land than I, these days.'

Reuben, his youngest son, barely seventeen, had been studying his father's face.

'Saving souls is great work too, Father. But are you alright? You look proper hag-ridden tonight.'

'Reuben, we do not use that phrase, ever, but especially in this house, in this valley, now.'

'Forgive me sir, it was merely my concern for you. I forgot myself.' Reuben's face expressed anything but contrition. He smiled impishly.

'So, talking of ha – witches, will you be back to York, Father? We had great sport the last time. Can we come along with you too?' pressed Robert, also supressing mirth. At thirty, he was the eldest of the four brothers.

'You've seen enough of York, my boys. You stay. Concern yourselves with the farm, getting in the hay and tending the beasts. You've quite enough to do – this place will save you four from further mischief.'

Nathaniel and Joshua, the twins, enjoyed Robert's play on 'sport' and laughed too. Twice Smithson's three older sons had been involved in fisticuffs against Tom Herryson, over rush-bearing rites. Twice they had appeared before the Archdiocesan Court in York because they had forcefully resisted this pagan custom.

Nicholas continued: 'You led me astray, my sons. But fine sport it was with Herryson, to be sure.' The vicar began to chuckle, until he met his wife's reproving eye. He pretended to clear his throat.

Nicholas had been involved in, and charged over, the second incident three years earlier. What was more, he had to face further charges for having openly criticised King James' Book of Sports. He had claimed the king's work was contrary to the law of God.

Reuben returned to the witch trial.

'You will support the women, won't you Father? I like them all, especially Margaret Hall. She has such a way with her. A certain something?' Reuben's eyes twinkled and his tongue ran along his top lip.

'I think it better if you don't encourage her, Reuben. You would not be the first to follow Margaret's beckoning smile – into the mire. Reputations are easily tarnished, and never regained.'

'But Father, you know she is no witch.'

'She is a woman, no more nor less.' The words were out before Nicholas could stop them. He was back in the woods, in his head, and he coloured in confusion.

'Husband, you have taken another turn?'

'I tell you I am quite well, Susannah. We'll have no more of sport or witches here tonight. The papists are making inroads enough, without marring a pleasant meal. Pass me the pottage please. Yes, more of that bread too.'

The meal over, Nicholas withdrew to his study to read his bible. This dog-eared volume would be waiting for him, open on the desk. It was his oldest friend and confidante. He liked to fill its margins with his thoughts. Tonight, he would edit these more carefully than was his custom.

After he had left the chamber, Reuben turned to Susannah:

'Do you fear witches, mother?'

'I do not believe in witches, Reuben. It's witch-hunting that frightens me, and what it does to the minds of men, and to some women too.'

Susannah checked that Mary, the servant, had also left and then spoke earnestly to her sons. Her tone was hushed:

'I worry for your father. He is not himself. I believe him to be more fretful about these accusations of witchcraft than he is prepared to say.' Susannah started to rub her hands together and tried to find the right words. She picked them with caution and care:

'Edward Fairfax is a powerful man. He has friends in high places. Why, the king himself is disposed towards Fairfax. The king loves Fairfax's verse, as does Charles, his son. And it has pleased the king to sanction the death of so many innocent women – on trumped up charges, be assured. These are dispiriting, vexing, troubling times indeed. Dangerous times for us all.'

'Why does a king need to pick on poor women – the lowly, weak, old and vulnerable?' asked Reuben, genuinely baffled.

'Because they are just that, my son. Easy pickings. And Edward Fairfax, in making these accusations here, will please the king.' Susannah paused: 'This will not be Fairfax's sole reason, I am sure, for he commands respect, and in most ways appears reasonable. But to gain power, influence, prestige – strengthen patronage – all of these may well be in his mind.' Susannah sighed heavily.

Robert took over: 'Fairfax is convinced the women are guilty. He tells each who will listen that he has more evidence, new and damning evidence. To drag them back to York again, fettered and haltered and thrown into gaol...' Robert breaks off in exasperation: 'Why it was only this April...'

His mother tutted in agreement, then she shook her head in sorrow: 'I wonder at Dorothy Fairfax. I once held hopes for her as friend. Surely, she could have made her man see reason. Surely, she could have talked some sense into those wenches of theirs. But a child neglected will cook up fibs for love. She's never had time for those girls, and nor has he. Helen Fairfax is simple. Lizzie, the little one, is as wick as a lop. And young Maud Jaffray, the other child accuser, is away in the head.'

Susannah's brow furrowed further, as other thoughts flooded into her mind. She still missed Dorothy, but Edward Fairfax had put an end to their friendship.

'I fear Dorothy Fairfax is not the only woman in this valley who will turn against these poor women. There's a fair few who have it in for Margaret Hall.'

Susannah was not done. She continued: 'For what is a witch? A woman bold enough to rail against life's unfairness. Lewd and licentious? I think not. Just poor. Why, if my belly was empty, if I had Margaret Hall's looks, would I not do as she? She is me – and there but for the grace go I.'

'Mother!' Reuben's jaw dropped. He found it hard to credit what his mother was saying. Susannah would leave him no room for doubt:

'Look you, Rueben. I saw you lick your lips for Margaret Hall. Know this, you are not on your own. And she will never walk alone. She has power with her potions, cures and notions. And she has power over men with her sand-glass form and her deep, dark eyes. They say she is a law unto herself. That's the real reason the powerful cannot abide her. They want her in her place, wrapped in wool, sprinkled with clay and covered with clods.'

There was a long silence as the four sons digested their mother's words.

'But it's not just about the stuff Margaret and the other women are accused of, is it, Mother?' said Joshua, the rougher, more down to earth of the twins: 'It is what lies beneath. The fences creep the common land, the stone walls rise, and new hedgerows are set. The fine families want the poor women forced from their hovels, off the land and gone. They don't want them gleaning after the cut. They can't stand them scratting round for twigs and wood. A hanging or two will clear pasture for fleece and mutton.'

Nathaniel nodded at his brother's point: 'There's faith issues mixed up in it too. Religion again, as ever... Fairfax believes our father to be a puritan. Father would not deny he leans more towards the godly, but the parishioners know him as a good and caring vicar. It is a dangerous thing to be too godly in these times.' Nathaniel paused and shook his head: 'Fairfax places himself in the centre. He says he does not look either way. And yet the papists hold increasing sway.'

Susannah added: 'The king himself swings either way – whichever way to suit himself, to divide and to rule. He's supposed to be a Presbyterian. There are papists amongst the rich and powerful of the valley. Only a small number of the lowly tilt that way.'

'Father says he can see no evidence in the bible for witches. He cannot accept these accusations. He will defend his parishioners.' Reuben was proud of his father's stance – all the boys were. But Susannah feared the price they might have to pay. Her tone hushed further:

'Your father's preaching against that odious Book of Sports prompted strong charges against him – sedition and subversion as well as assault. An offence against religion, it was termed. We do not need to provoke further criticism from the Church. We will be watched. We are being watched. We will be judged.'

She sighed again and continued:

'Henry Graver has agreed to speak alongside your father. Henry is a good and honest man. Rough, but fair and never bought. Your father, brave though he is, will draw strength from

Henry's support. I ask you to pray for them both, and for the poor women of the valley. We know them to be good women, innocent of the charges. Their only sin is, as you yourself said, Reuben, their own vulnerability and their poverty. Without your father and Henry, who would defend them?'

'Do you reckon many will speak against them?' asked Joshua: 'Things being as they are, I can't see our women getting off this time.'

The brothers nodded – their faces grim.

'Folk don't think like father, here,' said Nathaniel. 'He's the exception. He's rational. They don't see through the whole sham of it. Indeed, the shame of it. They believe there's witches in the woods cooking up their spells, that hell hounds and headless foals haunt the solitary ways, that demons stalk the dales, and good people get possessed. The only thing we can be sure of is this – through the length and breadth of this land, middling, papist or puritan, most folk don't think like us.'

'Then please, God, have mercy upon those poor women,' whispered Susannah. The candlelight danced in her dampening eyes.

*****

Later that night Susannah retired to the bedchamber and prepared herself for sleep. She loosed her hair from the cap, combed out the silver strands through her fingers, and put on her night gown. She knelt to say her prayers then pulled herself up, stiffly, by the bed post. She eased herself into bed.

Nicholas was not long in following her. He blew out the candle and turned to his wife. She felt his leg nudging, then scaling her right thigh.

'Nicholas? Dear me. Nicholas, what are you doing? Well. This is a surprise … I thought you'd long since lost the path.'

Nicholas stretched back, reached and released the heavy drapes between the four barley-sugar bed posts.

Reader, we'll leave them there, their subdued, but fruity chuckles lingering in the air.

4

Fallen Angel

Were there a second paradise to lose,
This devil would betray it.

The White Devil, Act 111 Scene 11
John Webster 1612

Margaret's work was done for the evening; the table scrubbed, the pot wiped clean, her own long fingers pulled across her apron, backwards and forwards, this way and that. The purple stains would take some time to fade. Her besom brushed the plucked, then discarded leaves across the earth floor and out of the door. The fruits of her labours surrounded her – her potions and preparations stored on every inch of rough shelf space, even down on the floor of her hovel. These had been prepared from the pickings of earlier that day.

The fire was dying down but the ash still glowed. A fire too hot for a July night, too hot for her to stay inside. Margaret stretched and pulled the cloth loose from her long neck. Her shoulders ached, her back stiff. She had not rested since that morning, waiting for Nicholas Smithson. That meeting had stretched her powers, sapped her, tripped her wits to the point of exhaustion. And then there were the bilberries to deal with too. All those bilberries. They should always be cooked on the day of their picking. She could never countenance waste.

She would walk up onto the moor to feel the breeze upon her brow. She took a flask of cordial to test. To this, she twisted a pinch of her mix, mugwort, wormwood and thyme, and shook it right. She would catch the setting sun beyond the stone of The Tree of Life.

Reaching the moor, she raised the flask to her lips, repeating the words Pegi had taught her. First sippings were a celebration, a rite.

She saw him then, sitting high on the Snowden Crags. A well-dressed handsome man in with a long black cape. He hailed her as a friend, a familiar. He stood so tall. He moved towards her, slowly, limping. A black leather boot on one foot. The second was a scaly claw, grey and dark pink. Crow claw.

'It pleased me to watch you fly this day by Middle Ridge, Margaret. You have squared Smithson, but what of the others?'

Margaret was shocked. Both her confidence and the colour in her cheeks drained.

'The others? Which others? Who are the others? Smithson told only of Fairfax.'

'No. Think you back. You said Fairfax. He did not say. Come Margaret. Do not think that Fairfax wants for friends or funds. Smithson may not speak against you now, but what of all the other folk in this valley who will – like the Robinsons of Swinsty Hall – rich, persuasive folk? Mrs Robinson has you marked as witch woman. You know that. She's seen your type before. She's seen the way her husband looks at you, his tongue turning between his lips; she isn't happy. They all have you down as a consorter of cunning folk, a disciple of our Devil.'

'Asmodeus, we cannot, must not die. My friends, the women, are innocent. They are just women, no more nor less. And me, I am guilty only of the lore of herbs and fruit, a low magic. It is only the alchemy of the plants I practise.'

'Really? You tell that to the Justices at York Castle, my dear.' Asmodeus laughed, and continued: 'They will see you hanging, your lovely well-turned calves paddling the air. Those shapely ankles, hmm. Mark me, there'll be no flying there. These local worthies will testify you have dabbled in the occult forces. They'll tell. Have they not benefitted from your own hedge-witchery, and more?'

This he delivered with a smug knowingness – the satisfaction of power. His smile was grim and dark. His eyes alight and flickered green – she thought she glimpsed the livid worms writhing within his skull. Margaret raised her hand to her throat:

'I want to live. Asmodeus, I do not want to die.'

'Why?'

'I love my life. I love this place, the plants, this heath, the moor, the valley and its streams and river. Do not let them place a strap about my throat and drop that trap. Don't let them take my breath. Breathing's what I do best.'

'And what would you give to live, sweet Margaret? Tell me.'

'Anything. I beg you. I would do anything.'

'Then dance with me, here, now, 'twixt the Tree of Life and the Death's Head rock. You will not be the first. Cast your clothes and come beneath my cape.'

'We may be seen.' Her hands drop from her throat to her breasts.

'Cast your clothes. Come, Margaret, catch my bill. You'll be beneath my cloak. We will be invisible.'

His voice had dropped to a whisper.

The dark figure rose slowly off the ground. Margaret, caught in indecision, desperate yet still distrustful, rubbed her brow. Her hand dropped to cup her mouth. Asmodeus hovered. His arm appeared to lengthen, reaching down.

'Come.' His command was soft, seductive. His hand beckoned closer, sharper. 'Come now, Margaret, come. The strap around your gullet, or life. Devest and dance with me, now. Let me fill you.'

Gradually she began to tug, then tear her clothes from her body. Her glinting hair caught by the lowering sun fell from her thrown wrap. The freed fronds cascaded over her smooth shoulders, now peach in the evening's declining light. Her petticoats dropped to the ground. She pulled her shift over her head. Naked, she stretched her arms to him. He took her right hand and slowly, certainly, he hauled her up off the ground. As she rose, she became a thing without weight. She levitated. They floated separately for some moments; their eyes alone locked. She was within his reach, yet freely drifted towards him. He lightly steered her closer, closer. Then he clasped her to him and tucked her under his spreading cape. His clawed foot raised to haul her home and secure her. They folded together, pulsed, then locked in mutual rapture, they flew.

And as they flew their bodies became as birds, a feathered force conjoined. They followed the valley down. She faltered only once, unused to flight. The pair dropped down, lingered on the parapet of the Dob Park packhorse bridge. The music of the Washburn soothed her senses, the leaves above her rustled to calm her fears. He watched her intently. Her breathing steadied.

'Ready? Come again?' he whispered. His beak brushed her. 'Now we'll truly take to air.'

They tracked the waters down to places where other rivers joined, rose and rushed, and then slowed, broadened, then became the sea. She became air and water, life and death. He sucked the life of her, took, then gave her strength.

Later, or earlier the next, as the first rose tints of dawn started to split the darkness, she lay beside Asmodeus by the stone of The Tree of Life. Their journey over; their passion spent. He assumed the shape of man, and she herself again. A chill breeze wrapped around them, shook the livid bracken, the greening heather, kissed the clusters of cairns.

A single blackbird brought in the dawn, full-throated. She grasped her shawl around her. And yet her body ached for him still. She longed to fly once more. He watched her, watched her breathe. He watched the rise and fall of her breasts. He traced the space between them and followed further down her body. He knew he had her now.

'I will not die now; I need fear no man; my sisters will be safe?' she murmured these questions between sleep and wakefulness.

'The women, your sisters as you call them, are of no consequence to me. They are just women. Yes, they will be spared, acquitted by the worthies.' He paused and grinned: 'But you, you will live for a long time, my dear one. You have bought your time and bought it dear. Four centuries. That is the limit of the time I am at liberty to bestow. For eternal life you'd need to take the beast of many faces, Satan himself. But we have made our bargain, you and me. Each year, we will fly together, as we have now. But there will be a last time. Then you will be mine forever, I will suck you in, and .... Ah, you do not need to know. Don't trouble your head, my sweet.'

'Will we fly again tonight?' She turned to him, eager.

Asmodeus was no longer there.

5

The Magdalene

It was the Sunday following his encounter with Margaret in the woods up by Middle Ridge. Since their meeting, Nicholas Smithson had been preoccupied. Susannah had noticed, and so had their sons. He had spent a great deal of time with his trusted friend, his bible. A scratching of parchment was heard from his study. They caught him muttering to himself, as if in earnest conversation with another.

The vicar was preparing his sermon with a lot more thought and care than was his custom. Sermons had been a sore point for Nicholas Smithson. At an archidiaconal visitation in the year 1613, the absence of a monthly sermon had been formally noted. The matter had been taken up with him by the Archdeacon, and he, Nicholas Smithson, had agreed to make a sermon, every month, from then onwards.

Nicholas Smithson really preferred to devote the Sabbath entirely to God. But he did set store by high quality preaching. This sermon was going to be very important to him, an opportunity to set the scene. He had chosen the Magdalene as his subject, her feast day falling on 22nd July.

The church was cool for the season. Sun flickered through the leaded lights, casting sage, lilac and white shimmering, lozenge-shaped shadows on the motley congregation. There were people of quality present, as always – the Fairfaxes, the Robinsons, the Gravers – this final family a little less eminent but quality, nonetheless. There were the ranks of the lower orders – farmers and their families, the tenants, house servants, the labourers, the ditchers, the rough, the itinerant and the downright low and scruffy. The women accused were all present, for it was more important than ever to be seen in the church. They did not stand together, but in their own family groups. Except for Margaret; Margaret stood alone.

Since Pegi's death, Margaret had no family. Her beloved cat and her crow were her companions, and the church was far beyond their territory. Margaret positioned herself as near the front of the congregation as was acceptable. She wished to be seen. She'd dressed herself in her decent clothes. Her top petticoat, a pale, bilberry-tinted wool. She could have dyed it a darker shade, she had the skill and would love to have done this, but she dared not fall foul of the Sumptuary Laws. She was in trouble enough. Instead she settled for a red cross cloth head wrap, from which she had teased some plum wisps and ringlets, and a pink shift. She had dabbed a little lavender oil behind her warm lobes. This sweet scent suffused the space surrounding her.

Margaret drew admiring glances from Reuben Smithson, and many of the other young men, and some of the not so young men too. She smiled cheerfully back, as if oblivious to her own charms and their impact, and to her own precarious position. She pulled her kerchief across her breasts. She projected a cracked piety.

The quality families were cooped and protected in their boxes. They shielded their noses from the effluvia rising from the less savoury worshippers. They held their posies and kerchiefs. They found it hard to conceive that all were equal in the sight of Our

Lord.

Nicholas Smithson waited for silence – for the coughs, snottings and snorts, throat-clearings, spitting and conversations to stop. He then began:

'What do we know of the Magdalene?' His question was delivered in a clear, authoritative voice.

It was met with silence. The vicar had not anticipated an answer. The congregation united in tension. Fairfax, who had been deliberately avoiding looking at the vicar, swivelled his head towards Smithson and glared. Every sinew in his body tautened. What was this, he thought? What new outrage? Confound that wretched man.

Smithson continued: 'Today is the Feast Day of Mary Magdalene. We will consider the Magdalene and what she stands for in our faith.'

Henry Graver's wife nudged her husband and in a loud whisper queried: 'Her was the guinea hen, weren't she?' The Graver girls began to giggle.

'Hear the man out. You might learn some'at,' shushed Henry, all attention. This was going to be good, he thought. Things could get interesting, and he loved a scrap.

'I have combed my bible for guidance, for clues, for evidence. I've looked carefully at the texts. Certainly, in the past, the church regarded her as a sinful woman. It's said she was a woman of low morals who anointed our saviour's feet and wiped them dry with her flowing hair. But now, we see there has been confusion. Characters have been conflated. Judgements have been made in the past, through ignorance and assumptions.'

Nicholas Smithson paused, looked up boldly and met Fairfax's eyes. He continued:

'What I have found is this. Mary Magdalene and Mary of Bethany have been merged into one being. We need to go back to the bible to help us. The most reliable evidence is to be found in Mark, Matthew and Luke – the gospels written in the first century.'

Dorothy Fairfax was sitting in an uncomfortable position in the family box. The seat was hard, certainly, but her discomfort was largely in her head. She dared not turn to her husband. She could feel his fury. She could not look at her daughters. She would not look at Susannah Smithson. She could see and feel where all of this was going and she wanted to force her way out of the oak box and run, run and run. She wanted to run down the valley and then strike east, back home Copmanthorpe.

She had been happy there in her earlier life, her girlhood. She had been happy at home – before him, before all this hateful business.

'What do we actually know about Mary Magdalene? We know that she came from a fishing town on the western shore of Galilee called Magdala. She was a devoted disciple of Jesus. She was probably a woman of wealth, for she supported Jesus with her own resources. She was witness to Jesus' crucifixion, and to his burial. She was first to witness the empty tomb and to testify to the resurrection of our Lord. That much we know.'

Nicholas Smithson paused again; this time his eyes were drawn involuntarily to Margaret's. He continued:

'For centuries the character of Mary Magdalene has been corrupted by the so-called learned and devout. A confusion, indeed, arising from the gospels of Luke and Mark. Both briefly referenced Christ casting out seven demons from her. But it was Pope Gregory 1, in 591, who linked the seven demons to the seven deadly sins, without any basis for his surmising. A fine leap of faith! Thus, Mary became guilty of lust, pride and greed. Imagine this grave injustice to a good and loyal disciple of our Lord!'

The families of the accused were nodding, grunting with agreement and barely concealed indignation. Fairfax went puce. Nicholas Smithson leaned forward and took in the whole congregation: 'A woman's reputation tarnished for centuries.

Century upon century. A woman most loyal to our Lord. This Mary was not a woman of low morality, a promiscuous woman. She was not a repentant sinner. She was the first of our Lord's female followers. Yet, thus have we treated her. Jesus respected women and we should follow our saviour's example.'

Susannah looked at her husband. She knew there would be repercussions, but she felt a surge of pride at his courage. He would fight for these women with every weapon in the chest, she knew that. But he had not finished.

'A final thought from the Sermon on the Mount, Gospel of Matthew, chapter 7, verses 1 to 5: We know it as 'The Mote and the Beam.' Smithson began. The familiar words, the warning about judgement and about being judged. He held the congregation. Not a cough, not a mutter, all eyes were upon him. A pause stretched, and then...

The vicar concluded with a resounding: *'Thou hypocrite...'*, fired directly at Fairfax.

Nicholas Smithson led the procession out of the doors and waited to bid farewell to the congregation: Fairfax stormed out after him:

'You steered well clear of the foot washing episode. You ducked that neatly, Smithson. The senses are the devil's playground. And you are playing with fire. You are a gullible fool. There'll be a reckoning!'

Dorothy scurried along after her husband Edward, with her eyes cast to the earth. Nicholas thought he caught the word 'sorry.' He wasn't sure. Helen and Elizabeth walked past with their heads held high and their eyes averted, as if he were of some lower order of being. He beamed broadly and blessed them. They seemed to shrink from his benediction.

Susannah came to stand by his side. Margaret approached.

'Thank you, Mister Smithson,' said Margaret, and took his offered hand with both of hers. She squeezed his hand tightly: 'Thank you for those words.'

Susannah recognised Margaret's shift as her own cast-off and complimented her on how well she had patched it: 'I wish I had looked half as good as you in it my dear,' said the older woman. Susannah chuckled.

'I enjoy wearing it so much. I feel so fine. I wished to mention to you, I have boiled some fine lichen dye and wondered if you wanted any cloths staining? I have done shades of green, from pale sage to deep holly. I have some russet colour too.'

'I'll take you up on that Margaret. I have some flax linen I'd like in the pale green and some winter wool in russet.'

'Bless you both, and you too, Master Reuben.' Margaret turned to leave them. 'A fine young fellow you have here, Missus Smithson.'

'Indeed, Margaret.' There was a hint of ruefulness in Susannah's voice.

'He'll break some hearts, I fear.'

'Mine first, I imagine, my dear.'

Then Susannah drew Margaret to one side, laid her hand upon Margaret's wrist, and spoke discretely to her.

'I understand it is to be very early this next month that they will come for you. We know of your innocence, and there are those here who will speak up for you.'

Margaret's eyes brimmed. She seemed to shrink in stature, her confidence draining. Fear, shock and resignation fought within her.

'I knew it would be soon. But so soon?' Margaret's breathing became shallow and ragged. Her hands moved up to her throat.

Susannah nodded and wrapped her arms around Margaret.

'Be strong, my dear.' The pair seemed to sway. Margaret was the first to break the embrace.

'That man. That hateful man. What is it with a man like that?'

'He is eaten from within. There is a worm inside his head.'

'You've seen it too, the way he is?

'I have, and it frightens me. I think his wife, Dorothy, does fear it too.'

'How could she not?' Margaret continued: '"The strange woman" is what he calls me. He will not even say my name.'

'If there is a strange woman to him, it is our Mother Nature, not you, my dear. He fears, I know not what.'

'Missus Smithson, if I have ever done you wrong, forgive me, please.' Margaret's voice was urgent, her eyes wild and casting about.

In a calming voice, Susannah answered: 'Margaret, no wrong. You have never harmed me or mine. Your mother brought my boys into the world. She tended me and cared for them and brought us safely through every time. And you and me, we have been, and are, friends. We will be friends. I will say this again – my husband will speak for you and for each of the women. He will vouch for your characters. There are others too who will step forward. Know that; be assured of it. Our vicar can be very persuasive, indeed.' Susannah smiled – an inward smile: 'We are with you, whatever.'

The two women held each other one final time and parted.

'I'll be by to collect your linen and wool,' called Margaret, looking back: 'I need to be doing something, or else I fear I shall go mad.'

Susannah watched Margaret take the steep path down to the river, leading west towards Middle Ridge. She had tried to buttress Margaret's confidence. She feared for all the accused. She feared Fairfax.

6

The Unfortunate Traveller

He called himself coachman. This was a stretch of his own imagination. The coach was but a cart, at kindest view, a covered waggon drawn by four. But he liked 'coachman'. It carried status over the local carriers and carters.

The staging inns were spaced for change of horse. His passengers' comfort was never his concern. Getting them there was all.

His waggon was of squat and solid build, like the man himself. The roads were rutted, rough, with puddled holes. Wheels came off; axles snapped as a matter of course, and the waggon would tilt and creak. The wind whipped the tattered canopy up and sometimes off. The rain found its way to the passengers, soaking them thoroughly without fail. Such were the common hazards.

It was his custom to carry women, and people of the inferior sort. This day he had been sent for seven witches, to fetch them to the assizes at York.

He would have like to have made more on the trip out, but few of the rough sort wanted to travel the full way from York to Fuystone, and he couldn't be drawing up all the time, for time was a factor. When his eyes fell on the place, he could not fault them. What sort of folk live here, he asked himself? A god forsaken hole if ever… He shook his head.

He was not the one who fetched them the last time; he had been warned they had been taken once before – this April just passed.

'They'll not get off this time, that's for sure. Your efforts will not be in vain, carter.' Those were the words of the assistant to the clerk at York Castle. 'Twice to the assizes and your number's up alright. Bring them safe and swift.'

Carter, indeed! Safe, and swift, huh, he mused – on these roads? Safe – well what was the point if they were going to swing anyway. But at least they were likely to pass unmolested by the highwaymen; they would have little time for wenches such as these. Sparse pickings indeed. There were no jewels here, no fat pouches of golden coins, silver, even, no secret rings dangling on strings of pearls, dipping into that sweet groove between the breasts. He licked his lips. No, he had never been troubled by highwaymen and brigands. Most were better off than he was. The bastards.

Swift, huh – five miles an hour at the most. And then the stops. Two days from here to York at best. He would not go the straight way back. The journey out had been horrible and hazardous. Floods and mud, stones and shifted boulders strew the way. August my arse, he thought. The waggon had sunk and stuck. He'd take the slightly longer way back, by Tadcaster. He liked to see the inn keeper's daughter there, a pretty wench, not tight with her favours. The beer was good too.

The women were grouped and waiting by the church gate, guarded by some local, trusted men. Fairfax's men, he'd been told. He'd had to collect the warrant to take them, from the clerk, signed and sealed – for anyone could pick them up and rescue them. Whisk them away, but to what?

The coachman's eyes scanned them. This was what a coven of

witches was like; he took the vision in. Some had their families with them. Folk were upset. Kids were crying, snotty little brats. You never think of witches with a bairn, he thought. One woman stood alone, a handsome lass, mid to late twenties, difficult to tell. She held her head up.

He saw their wrists were tied. Their dear ones wrapped the shawls around their shoulders, tried to comfort them. Brushed the hair from their eyes, the tears from their faces. But not all cried.

'Time to go,' he said. His voice lacked any charity. Some of the family members shuddered. There were fresh tears and cries and sore laments. He blanked it all. He was doing his job, he told himself. He was neither judge nor hangman; he was only the coachman.

'Everyone on,' he approached the single woman first, the one who stood alone. It was Margaret. What he could do with such a wench, he thought. A shame to see such a one swing. A waste of a fine body.

His face loomed up close to hers, a gurning gummy leer. What stained, snapped and broken teeth and stumps remained could not stem the saliva that trickled down with his filthy thoughts. His breath testified to his love of tripe and onions, last night's supper. A scrofulous cluster peeped out beneath the kerchief wound around his filthy neck.

'A York necklace on t'lad,' observed John Dibb, in high disgust. 'He looks as if he could do with a muck out.' Then he turned away from the coachman to Janet, his mother. 'I'll be following mother. We'll be with you.' Nonetheless John placed coins in the palm of the coachman, as did some other family members, to try to ensure the safer passage of the women; to try to secure some little kindnesses. They hoped. They did not know the depths of the man.

A little late, and clearly flustered, Susannah Smithson joined the party, just as Margaret was about to be lifted into the waggon by the coachman. She ran to Margaret's side, and hugged her. There were tears in both women's eyes. The coachman pushed Margaret on. Susannah caught his breath and recoiled. Still she spoke up:

'God bless you Margaret. We will be praying for you all. If there is any justice in this world, we will see you all soon.' Susannah handed a basket of farm provisions to the coachman for the women. It was an act of faith, unrewarded, for he would be the beneficiary. He licked his lips – nice stuff in there he thought, as he tweaked back the covering cloth revealing fruits and muslin-wrapped cheeses and fresh-baked bread.

Three of the armed men remained with the group. They were to accompany them to York Castle, to ensure the party was safely handed over. The coachman asked these men to help him get the women on.

'That lies outside our orders. We are not to touch these women. It is the code laid down by our sergeant, and even if it wasn't, these are witches. Only a fool would take a witch's touch. That's how they mess with you.'

'You call me fool?'

'You make that leap. It is your job, for which I'm sure they pay you well. Where is your companion, carter? We were told you were to be two.'

'I am a coachman I'll have you know. My companion was unavoidably detained in York. In his cups, he was, and a fight broke out the night before we were to leave. Some argument about a wench I heard tell. I left him sleeping.'

'In his bed?'

'The riverbed; the Ouse carried him off.'

The coachman began to load the rest of his cargo. A flickering guilt released his nervous tick – an intermittent spasm that suggested to the passengers he was marshalling them to the left. This led to confusion.

'Come on, on we get lasses.' He grabbed the women by their

waists with his big broad hands. He thrust them up and forward roughly. They had no hands to steady themselves, their wrists being tied. They stumbled and staggered, and tried to help each other.

'There's a bench on the right too, you dim bitches.'

His language deteriorated. He lacked any delicacy. He appealed to the saints, and angels – even the fallen ones, in graphic terms. When he swore on the virgin, the anatomical embellishments bordered blasphemy.

This loading performance would be repeated often throughout the journey for the chosen way was also mired with flood and mud. The two days took closer to three. The first night they had rough lodgings at the Hand and Whip public house. Word got out, and when they left in the morning, locals, peasants, farm labourers and travellers had assembled outside, and along the route, to jeer and spit. The second night he kept them in the waggon. He wouldn't eat any further into the allowance he'd been given against their accommodation.

On and off the waggon. The women didn't like the way he grabbed them from behind, to load them.

'Take your hands off me, you filthy fuck,' Margaret Waite's daughter let fly. 'Much better men than you pay good money for a feel of my arse.'

He laughed and leered. Her mother told her to hold her tongue for all their sakes. Margaret Hall took it all in. She was thinking. Things would not go well for him.

At a safe distance one of the horsemen led the coach, and the two others tracked it. They watched, guarded and engaged in no further talk. The coachman called them: 'the Shadows'.

The women had to walk through rough and broken parts of the road to lighten the load on the waggon. The coachman tethered them together to the back of the waggon, in two pairs and a three. It was hard for them not to trip over each other. Occasionally, one would stagger or tumble. There was no way to escape the puddles. The mud sucked their hems and stuck. Their skirts were heavy with rain and dirt and dragged their ankles. Their ill-clad feet were clodden.

Nearly there. The Tadcaster Road. The coachman stopped the horses and swivelled in his seat towards them. He laughed and pointed.

'Knavesmire – the York Tyburn. That's where you'll be leaving us, lasses.' He pointed across the rough, quaggy ground to the gallows. The stout ropes and nooses jigged in the wind.

'They call the gallows the three-legged mare. It's from the way it's put together – see the shape of it there. They'll have to do you in batches.'

This thought seemed to delight him; he continued:

'Folk love a hanging. It's a grand thing to see. I've been to view one or two in my time. Great sport. Robbers, thieves, murderers – all sorts of wrong uns. But I've never watched a witch dangle. I'll be able to say – I knew them women, I brought them here. The last I saw hang was a fine man, a George Bell, attorney, no less. Last day of March it was, just passed. A Leeds man; he forged the will of a man from Halifax. Not so clever, eh, after all? They brought him here – to the Tyburn, "without the Micklegate Bar". Then they took his body back to Leeds. I suppose we'll take your corpses back to Fuystone. That will be a merry trip indeed with all your loved ones waiting. Won't they be pleased to have you back?'

He smiled: 'When they drive you out from the Castle to the Tyburn, they bring your coffins alongside, you know. You'll come out over the Bridge. I'll show you where, as we pass by. Micklegate's steep. The horses will labour up that one, there being seven of you and your boxes. There will be crowds along the way to cheer you on.'

The seven women stared at him, silent.

'Aye, this place, surely, will bring an end to your gripes, plaints and blethering. These ropes will stop your throats. They like to show you off, once you have passed. Folk will want to come, look, touch, feel,' he moistened his lips and guffawed, 'and marvel. They will pay a penny for the privilege.'

He shook his head and concluded: 'So, behold. This is what awaits you.' He paused, then enquired of them with a mock civility: 'Like you not the view?'

The women remained silent; their eyes never left him.

Elizabeth Foster made to smooth her skirts with her hobbled hands.

'We'll know you again, sir,' she said, prim with pride and yet there was a confident edge to her voice that clearly troubled the man. He was superstitious, for all his lewd, cocky, one-way banter. These were witches after all.

The Shadows made it clear their patience was thinning. The leader had had to double back. He set out again, waving them forward with a sharp hand gesture.

Margaret was proving a poor traveller. Throughout the journey she'd been retching. Mornings were the worst. At first, she begged the man to stop the cart, but now, exhausted, she lay, face and shoulder over the side, and vomited freely as the need arose. She had passed the point of dignity and caring, like a novice sailor, new to sea. She left a pool of puke adjacent to the hanging ground.

'What ails your friend?' asked the coachman. 'She's been chucking up well and proper. No stomach for the gallows?' he sniggered. 'She should have behaved herself, then. But coax her to keep breathing. I will incur a penalty if I lose one of you.'

Silence.

Eventually this bedraggled group arrived at York Castle gaol. They gazed up at the fat stone walls and the tight barred windows.

A soft, sweet voice reminded the other women about the rewards for the persecuted righteous. This beatitude was barely audible above the clamour round the castle walls. The words came from the lips of Elizabeth Foster, who had inclined her mouth closer to Elizabeth Dickenson's ear. Elizabeth Dickenson was weeping silently.

The coachman pulled up through the main gaol gates. He threw the women down; final gropes and fumbles for the comely ones. He only enjoyed brief contact with Margaret because she stank of stale vomit. For a foul-smelling man, he was unaccountably squeamish.

The Shadows saluted the gaolers. The gaolers took over the group. The coachman bid the women 'farewell and safe journey' and thanked them for their company, laughing raucously as he left them. 'Until we meet again, to take you to the Tyburn.'

A fine jape indeed, he mused.

But no, the women were not to meet him again, this coachman. He drove his waggon off, crossing back over the ancient bridge towards Micklegate. He was heading for his lodgings behind the tannery, not far from the river. A far from salubrious area he dwelt in, with a perpetual stench from animal skins, of death and putrefaction. Breathing the air there was choking. He numbered amongst his neighbours, chimney sweepers, jakes-farmers, dirt-daubers, vagrant rogues and labourers.

He followed a route along North Street. He was seen to greet several acquaintances of the low sort, as he went. They shouted abuse at each other in a jocular manner and made vulgar signs. Then he turned the waggon left down Tanner Row.

He had taken drink, it is true, and stopped at hostelries between the castle gaol and Tanner Street. Low and squalid dives. What happened next was unclear. When they found him in the morning, he was still sitting upright on his waggon seat, straight and stiff, with his hands locked around the reins. The kerchief round his neck was a little askew, true, but no more than a cough's twist. The scrofulous cluster had burst, oozed and seeped his frayed shirt. Next to him sat Susannah Smithson's basket of provisions, the cloth pulled open. There sat a half-eaten piece of bread along with a cheese already encrusted with eager flies.

The horses were fully harnessed and still standing, but not in the best shape. People were unwilling to come too close, to check for any signs of life. They were repelled, disconcerted. His face wore a ghastly grimace, a 'demonic contortion' as it would be recorded. A grinning eyeless corpse. The whispers spread like plague: 'The Devil needs a coachman. He's his man. He'll need no eyes for that.'

'The crows must have had 'em,' said the constable, less susceptible to superstitious speculation. 'They always take the eyes first. A soft sweet nibble. A bit like fresh oysters.' No felony was suspected, that is, no human intervention. But given the look of the coachman, not one who beheld him could hand on heart conclude he'd died of natural causes.

*****

The seven accused were pushed along a tight corridor, then down the well-worn stone steps to the dungeons below ground. They were to be held together in the same cell. It was tight, damp and grim; the smell was over-powering. The floor was earth which soaked up most of the urine, but it was covered in excrement; there was no sanitation, not even a bucket. No light penetrated.

All the cells were thronged. The gaol was used for holding prior to trial, and the closer it was to the assizes, the more folk were taken in. By the eighth day of August, the morning of their trial, it was quite a crush.

When they first arrived, they could just make out what seemed to be a bundle of rags dropped in a corner. Only the glint of a pair of terrified eyes lit by the gaoler's torch showed there was a human presence – these and the chain leading from the bundle to a rusty ring in the floor. She was barely more than a child; a young girl charged with infanticide. They didn't hear her tale for she was mute – mute and terrified. She wept. They tried to offer what comfort they could to her. Their gaoler muttered that she'd been there since middle May – she just missed the Lent assizes, otherwise she would have been hanged by now.

The seven women too were chained to the worn and rusted rings on the wet stone floor. The cell bolts were pulled back only once a day. A meal was pushed in – sparse stale bread and thin gruel – and a head count done for each cell, of the living. Those that had passed were pulled out, roughly.

The women didn't have long to wait for their trial. This time Fairfax had just caught the Trinity assizes and their case had been included on the list. They were grateful for this mercy. Otherwise they would be incarcerated until the following February, for the next northern circuit visit. They prayed the judge would get to them before the end of the session, whatever the outcome.

So little food was provided in the gaol, the women's families organised some supplies to be taken into them. They shared what they had with the young girl. She was famished but she could only be coaxed to eat a little.

On the seventh of August it was the young girl's turn. They tried to make her look as respectable as they could – combed her hair with their fingers, gently pinched her cheeks and straightened her clothes. They traded some brought-in food for extra water from the gaoler and tore some cloth off their petticoats. They wiped her face. She could barely stand.

The girl did not return to the cell that night.

The seven had tried to anticipate what the judge would ask to them. This proved impossible. The charges made were based on two young girls' and a young woman's 'say so'. How do you deny something that happened in another's trance, vision, dream, for that is their dream? If they say you were there and did such awful things, and made such threats, how do you counter this? How can you say you were not there and that you never sought to possess anyone? How do you make it clear you are innocent? Round and round they worried all of this and tied themselves in knots; they were sorely troubled. This puzzle became their preoccupation.

On the morning of the trial a little more water was secured. The women straightened themselves out and tried to make themselves look modest and pleasant. It was hard. Their clothes were muddy, dirty and carried with them the stench of the cell. Shit, piss, sweat, stale menstrual blood and rotting food. The guards came for them and took them up. The seven women blinked into the light.

7

The king's mouth takes breakfast

'Fairfax again, eh? Fairfax and his bloody so-called witches.
New evidence is there?'

The judge was not in the most serene state of mind. He feared
he had taken a chill on the long ride up into the northern circuit.

The journey had been wet and unseasonably cold. His party
had crossed the county border in a squall of summer hail. They
had halted at the county line for a change of serjeant. The wind
that had nudged them gently in their backs as they set out, now
shifted round to the north and bit their left ears.

The hail had caught them on open moorland and the party
lacked even a copse for shelter. Rain seeped through their cloaks
and saturated them right down to the skin. The judge harboured
dark thoughts about the north:

'Chilled to the marrow! Call this the sodding summer? What
desolate place is this?' the judge had railed.

'It's the main road to York, Your Lordship.'

'I did not expect an answer, fool! My question was rhetorical.'

The serjeant bit his lip, shrugged and looked hurt.

It had been more clement in late April, on the judge's last

visit for the Lent assizes. He'd imagined the Trinity assizes to be bathed in sunshine.

On a fair day the judge enjoyed a journey on horseback. The movement helped his constipation and piles, something to do with the repeated gentle jolts and occasional friction between his breeches and the firm leather saddle. It helped to balance the fare offered by the lodging house landladies or the homes of the quality into which he was often invited. The cooking in the north was not poor, by no means. Plain, honest and sustaining fare. But it lacked the delicacy of the capital. And it took toll on his guts.

The judge travelled with his servant and two common law judges. They were always accompanied by a serjeant. The judge came to hear the pleas and 'deliver gaols' at the castles of York and Lancaster, the two centres of the northern circuit. The 'Northern' was allocated the shortest span of days. Nonetheless, it seemed to the judge interminable. Perhaps this feeling related to the challenge of the long and sometimes hazardous journey from the capital to the north.

His role as the 'red judge from Westminster' was broad and complex. He was, as justice, *a latere Regis,* the king's mouth, and accountable only to him. As well as mouth, he was the king's ears. Over time, he had become well acquainted with the leading gentry and county magistrates. The gentry would visit the him at his lodgings. He had a fine-tuned ear to the nuances of gossip, rumour and small talk. He was acutely sensitive to the political overtones and he got a feel for the way things sat in the north.

Local dignitaries clamoured to dine at the judge's table. Sometimes he was invited to dine with them. He had a sharp wit, an elegant turn of phrase and was a fine raconteur. In short, he sang for his supper. It was of mutual benefit – to influence and be open to influence. This was the way things worked. This way he gathered his information informally.

The judge was astute; he sifted swiftly fact from opinion. His antennae detected lies and falsehoods. He knew when there was an attempt to manipulate him and he would not be duped. He learnt most by listening and prompting further. If he wanted more, he would summon a member of the gentry, or a magistrate, for private questioning, and more detailed discussion. And when he had garnered as much information as he believed he needed he drew his own conclusions.

Thus, we find him, this morning of the eighth day of August 1622, taking breakfast at his lodgings within the city walls. He and his fellow judges were enjoying a simple breakfast: platters of cold meats carved from the roasts from the dinner of the previous night, mustard, relish and pickles, a capon, a cheese, braised kidneys, some freshly cooked fish caught from the river early that very morning by the landlady's son, breads still warm from the oven and modest goblets of ale.

Two trusted local gentlemen had been invited to take breakfast with the judge's party. They were filling him in on Edward Fairfax. The first gentleman spoke:

'A fine old noble family, the Fairfaxes. We all agree. But we note a subtle distancing from the man by the main family down at Denton. Edward Fairfax is a natural son, you know. Fair play, family members have been up his home, Newhall, to question the girls and to witness this possession. Ferdinando knows this branch of the family well. They all vouch for Edward's skills as a tutor. As a poet, some reckon he stands alone. But as a father, there may be, err, deficiencies. The words the family members use: 'simple', 'gullible' and 'artless'.' The speaker shrugged.

The judge grunted – the sort of grunt that seems to say: 'Surely not?' He was doing battle with a sinewy piece of game meat. He couldn't swear to the bird. He thought the offending object in his mouth was the bit that attaches wing to breast. He picked it out with a grimace of distaste, and a slight shudder of the upper body. He lodged the offending item on the table and subjected it to scrutiny.

'This poor soul will never fly again, alas.'

All eyes were on the small pile of half-chewed gristle as the second gentleman seized the moment and took up the flow: 'Those words describe the man himself, not the daughters. In short, the family say he takes every word the girls say as gospel – God's own truth. If he can be faulted, they say, he lacks that healthy scepticism that oft accompanies fathers when listening to children's tall tales.'

The first gentleman added: 'It's true. He has become their scribe. He writes down each of his two daughters' demonic encounters. It's said that the elder wench rules the house with her fits, visions and her lurid tales of possession.'

Then the second gentleman elaborated: 'They have honed this method for capturing each tranced encounter. Fairfax observes a daughter in fit. He writes down every utterance. But he can only hear her words, her part of the conversation. When she comes to, she tells him what the demon or witch has said to her. The testimony is pieced together in this way. Extraordinary. It works for both of his daughters.'

The first gentleman endorsed this: 'It seems the household witnesses some violent exchanges, but only one side. The girls are seen to hit out, and struggle, but the assailant is invisible. It must be terrifying for the onlooker.'

'And whilst this is going on, the father writes it down? Hmm?' The judge found it hard to contain his incredulity.

'Oh yes. It's the mother and the servants, and the other sibling who try to restrain and to comfort the afflicted child,' added the second.

'Hmm? And you say the Fairfax family stands apart? Hmm? Hmm? And what of this vicar, this Smithson? What do we know of him?'

The first gentleman laughed: 'He's known to be an honest man. What you see is what you get. A little too much leaning towards the godly, it is said, for our current thinking. The diocese had him over rush bearing. Twice in fact. Well over a year ago, and way back in '95. He has a thing about pagan practices. Doesn't hold with them at all. Bit of a hot head – fisticuffs, you know. Him and his sons. They beat up the rush bearer!'

The second gentleman seized back the reins: 'More serious – this recent intervention carried the accusation that Smithson had publicly criticised of our king's Book of Sports. Star Chamber heard that one, February '21. In fairness, there was a fair bit of controversy up here in the north, about that book. It didn't go down well with many sound and sensible folk, for it opened the floodgates to all sorts of idiocy. Drinking, dancing and indecency. Licentious and libidinous behaviour, don't you see. Give 'em an inch and they'll go off a'fornicating, those lower orders.'

The first gentleman again: 'Smithson was also involved in a tithe-related libel case – back in 1604. He was the defendant. I can't remember how that fared, but the point is, he stands up for what he sees is right. He's got guts. But since this latest rush business, I think he's kept his head down. Until now, that is.'

'And what of his parishioners? What do they think about this honest fellow?' asked the judge, lavishly spreading soft butter on his bread then reaching for the honey.

'They hold him in high regard, by all accounts.'

'Hmm. I see. Well gentleman, time waits for no-one. I hear the church bells chime the hour.' The judge licked his fingers. 'We must adjourn and ready ourselves for the day, put on our red robes and proceed to the assizes. Work to be done, judgements to be made, sinners to be sorted.'

The judge looked up to the opening door: 'What Mistress Annis, the coach has arrived already? Thank you. Excellent fare, as always. Such a meal should sustain us through the longest day.' He tapped his belly with satisfaction and seeped a belch from the corner of his smile.

The judge's servant had his lordship's robes laid out in

readiness and his wig dressed and sitting on a stand. As the servant prepared his master, the judge took on a different, more thoughtful demeanour. But the breakfast conversation had been noted. The judge would have cause to recall it later in the day, and on the next.

A pair of dapple greys drew the coach that was awaiting him. The serjeant and the additional two judges emerged from the lodgings first and stood to the side as the judge in his full ceremonial robes emerged. The breeze blew the judge's robes around his ankles. A better day, he thought. The two judges joined him in the coach. The serjeant clambered on the rear to guard the way. The coach driver, in livery, and with whip aloft, gently set the horses in motion. They took the road to York Castle at a brisk pace.

Crowds were forming early to cheer the judge on his way and encourage him to take a firm line with the witches: 'Hang the bitches!' The case had been discussed in every tavern in the city, fuelled by the reports of the coachman's mysterious death.

'He were't coachman who bore that coven 'ere!' Every low type had an opinion. The prospect of seeing so many witches swinging, choking and gagging on the gallows had drawn folk from all over the city, and beyond.

Two liveried trumpeters awaited the judge on the steps to the Castle Court entrance, the elaborately carved arch of an ancient stone gateway. They sounded a fanfare, to prepare those in the courtroom. On this occasion, the seething roar of the crowd had already alerted those inside.

Today would have been a good day for a deer hunt with his hounds, mused the judge. He was missing his wife, his sweet daughters and his home comforts. The girls always spoilt him. Perhaps his chill was making him feel this way? Instead, before him stretched a long day of unfurling of parchments, reading and examining depositions and questioning witnesses. All of this within a stuffy, stale and packed courtroom.

The judge heard a raw and raucous bird call as he alighted. His eyes cast up to the castle battlements. Was that the voice of a raven? No, a crow most certainly, he concluded. Too small for a raven, too big for a rook. This lone bird seemed to be addressing him with its repeated caws. How strange; how odd. A weirdly insistent bird. What could it mean?

The thronged court hushed. His arrival was announced. All stood. He made his way with great pomp and dignity to the bench. He settled himself and then indicated all could be seated. Except of course the accused. He scanned the scene. He saw the women. For some inexplicable reason he heard the bird again. The crow couldn't have entered the courtroom he thought, so it must be in his head. A revisited memory or something like that. And yet so vivid. He hoped he wasn't heading for a fever. Perhaps he was working too hard? This day was drawing close to the final days of this stage of the current circuit. How glad he would be when it was over. Nothing more until next Lent, early in the following year. Yes, he was ready for home. He felt he'd been too far from his family for far too long.

A sea of faces rolled before the judge. He cast his eye over the grand jury, chosen from the quality of Yorkshire society. Families had fought for observers' seats. They wore their finest clothes – stiff ruffs for the men, intricate lace collars for the ladies. Tall feathered hats, bonnets and caps. Fine fabrics dyed bright and rich.

The word had got out, and a witch trial was as good as a murder. This was better than the theatre; this was real life entertainment. And not just one witch, but seven. A veritable coven – just as the king had described in his *Daemonologie*. And this was a case brought by quality, well more precisely, middle gentry. Girls possessed. It was no mystery that this courtroom was thronged. Some had been turned away, downcast, despondent and deprived of the spectacle.

Order called. Preliminaries and prayers.

'Let the indictment be read.'

The indictment was unfurled with due gravity, pomp and ceremony and the charge read out.

For several moments, the judge scrutinised the seven accused who, bound by hand and ankle, stood in line before him. The Fairfax coven had returned. He asked for their ropes to be untied from their wrists and ankles. He said there were guards enough to restrain anyone wishing to leave without his consent. His fellow judges were surprised at this uncharacteristic act of kindness. Other eyebrows were raised too. Then the judge asked each to confirm her name.

Janet Dibb, the oldest member of the group, was the first to speak. She spoke from the throat. The judge reflected to himself that such a voice had been wasted on a woman. It rushed like water over gravel, always deep and sometimes soft and sweet. She was powerfully built, stout, her shoulders square, and although her eyes were bright and kind, she had the ferocity of a chained bear. Her thick grey hair was drawn back from her proud forehead, revealing a perfect widow's peak beneath her cap.

You would not find such a woman as this in all the southern counties, thought the judge. But something in her demeanour touched him. He smiled to himself realising he'd warmed to her immediately. He estimated that this woman would be of a similar age to his dear wife. And more than this, he divined within her a rare quality, integrity. A formidable honesty beamed from her eyes.

The next woman in this line was Margaret Hall. Pale, green around the gills, but here was a true beauty, thought the judge. So, this was Fairfax's 'strange woman'. He'd seen her so called in the Fairfax deposition. Hmm, he considered whether such a name fit the thing in front of him. He wondered what that abundant head of plum locks looked like when unleashed from the cross cloth that was barely containing them. She was humbly dressed in the muted colours of the lower orders, but something within her blazed, lit up the courtroom. Such dark eyes were exotic, not of the north. She carried within those eyes the promise of the sky on a warm summer's night. He enjoyed a vision of infinite navy shot with strands of apricot gold. He felt a little light-headed. He noticed there was a musicality in her voice, and yet a caution. He thought she was the sort of woman a man could never truly know, elusive, evasive … But then it was a crow not a nightingale he thought he heard; he tapped his ear.

The judge looked her up and down. Her muddy petticoats brushed her ankles. Such eloquent ankles. He imagined the turn of her calves, her knees, her soft inner thighs. Again, he was brought back to the scene by the insistent cawing of the crow. He would need to study this one further. Early stages, he told himself, for at present, she was a closed book. A strange woman indeed, he pondered.

Margaret Waite sat next to Margaret Hall. The judge understood that her husband had died at the hand of the executioner, for stealing. In his deposition, Fairfax had recorded that the couple had brought with them a reputation for witchcraft when they moved into the Fuystone area. What he saw before him was a small, neat woman with sharp features, thin lips and a shrill voice. Her head was half-concealed within a hood. He needed to study her countenance. He would request she pulled back her hood when it was her turn to make account of herself.

Margaret Waite was overshadowed by her daughter, again called Margaret. Young Mistress Waite was far more attractive than her mother, being taller, sandy-haired and more prone to smile, not that there was much occasion to smile. A rash of ginger freckles crowned her nose. Her blue-grey eyes were framed with long dark lashes. She wore a bum roll to emphasise her already comely hips, and a rush-boned bodice to lift her breasts to a pleasing tilt. The judge's eyes rested on the parting between her breasts, barely concealed beneath her kerchief. Clearly, thought the judge, this young woman was aware of her charms and made the most of them.

The judge found the daughter's voice easier on his ear than her mother's. In his deposition, Fairfax had accused this Waite daughter of lewd behaviour. The judge saw that this was a possibility for she would certainly not be short of visitors. He made a note to probe further.

The fifth along was Margaret Thorpe. Daughter of Janet Dibb, this young Margaret was but a shadow of her mother. She lacked a little of each of her mother's qualities. She was by no means fierce, nor stout, but carried with her a gentler air. There was a sadness about her, an air of melancholy. Again, she had been widowed early and clearly, concluded the judge, this may well have affected her general demeanour, leaving her sorrowful.

Two Elizabeth's followed. The first was Elizabeth Fletcher, locally known as Elizabeth Foster, 'Foster' being her deceased mother's name. The judge had seen from the Fairfax deposition that it was the mother who had a reputation for witchcraft. The petition from the local people referred to this Elizabeth as a skilled, kind and successful midwife. He saw she wore a relic on a chain around her neck. He needed to find out what this was. She was comely, and apparently, caring. She sat and frequently held the hand of Elizabeth Dickenson next to her, who was visibly upset by being in the courtroom, and on trial.

Elizabeth Dickenson was mousey and diminutive. She spoke quietly and the judge notice how expressive her hands were. She flexed and stretched her fingers again and again. Sometimes her hands came together in prayer. Then they covered her mouth. Her fingers played with her full and pouting lips. He wondered if Elizabeth Foster took her hand to stop her fidgeting and flexing, as well as to calm and re-assure her.

Strange women all, the judge concluded, but were they witches? They would each be taken down, examined and interrogated. Pressure would be applied. The truth would be squeezed out of them.

The judge thanked Edward Fairfax, as the accuser of the seven women, for such a thorough written presentation of the case against them. Rarely, if ever, had a case such as this been supported by such a detailed deposition, he conceded. A veritable diary of possession, but more than this, a complete evocation of the impact of the perceived possession not only on his two daughters but the whole Fairfax household at Newhall, Fuystone. The judge drew his hand, palm uplifted, in a sweep across a table buckling under the weight of scrolls of parchment. He nodded in appreciation:

'Your efforts have not gone unnoticed, sir, nor unread, and no one can doubt the energy you have expended in the support of your two daughters here present.'

A ripple of approval ran through the courtroom. Fairfax inclined his head in acceptance of this tribute.

The other two judges and the members of the grand jury were asked to confirm that they had read and carefully considered this meticulous documentation.

The judge then turned his attention to the alleged victims. First, he called the eldest of the three, Mistress Helen Fairfax, to give her testimony.

Helen stood up and took the position indicated by the judge. The judge appraised this young woman, in her early twenties, very carefully. She was of medium height, demurely yet well-dressed, in shades of blue – a pale blue shift with petticoats of darker blues, good fabric – a white lace collar and matching cap. Her fine flaxen hair was drawn back to reveal an open, artless countenance. On close inspection the judge noted she had a waxy complexion, not typical, he thought, for a young woman raised in the countryside. Where there might have been bloom, she was, at best, plain and pallid. Her features lacked refinement. She looked more like a girl than her twenty-one years might suggest, for she was well beyond the cusp of girlhood to womanhood.

Helen was her father's child, the judge noted, for Fairfax too was pale and waxy, with fine and thinning flaxen hair. In Edward Fairfax's case his shoulders were stooped from scholastic application at his desk, no doubt, although he now claimed to be a farmer as well as scholar. In truth, farming had leant no ruddy glow to his complexion. Perhaps the pallor shared by both father and daughter was the result of prolonged preoccupation with demonic possession, reflecting on it, and recording it to mutual satisfaction. An unhealthy alignment indeed, the judge reflected. He thought with some distaste, what a waste it would be to share so much time with one's daughters in the pursuit of witches. Give him and his girls a deer hunt any day, in his beloved shire, with their fine pack of hounds.

The judge noted that Helen held her own bible in her left hand; for comfort, protection or effect, the judge could not tell which. She certainly projected an air of quiet and youthful piety. Was the image she presented one of wronged innocence, he wondered to himself?

The judge's demeanour towards her was avuncular; he helped her to begin:

'Mistress Fairfax, Helen, I see from your father's deposition that you began this period of possession on the 28th of October last year, being the year of our Lord 1621. During the evening of that day, being a Sunday, you fell into a deep trance and in that time, when your family feared for your life, in your apparently unconscious state, you were attending a church in Leeds and hearing a sermon by the celebrated preacher Mr Alexander Cooke, the vicar of Leeds. This might be seen by some as a wonder and a privilege rather than possession.'

'Punishment more like!' suggested one of the lower orders who had managed to infiltrate the gathering. The guards grabbed him roughly and evicted him.

A ripple of laughter ripped through the court.

'Order! Order!' insisted the serjeant.

Still sombre, the judge continued:

'This was followed by a succession of trances during which state you conversed with your siblings who are dead, and there was additionally an incident with a white cat which caused you to vent copious amounts of blood.'

'That, Your Lordship, is the truth,' said Helen, in a quiet voice.

'Speak up my dear. We are all eager to hear what you have to say. For my own and for the members of the jury's benefit, I want you to move us directly to your first significant encounter with the Devil.'

There was a collective gasp in the courtroom.

Helen began her testimony, hesitant at first, voice high and squeaky, but then gaining in confidence. She related, in fact almost relived, the encounter. She set the scene and transported the courtroom back to her bedchamber at Newhall:

'He comes to me. It is as if I see him now. He comes to me with great civility. He sweeps a low bow. Such show to one as me? He is young, as young as I. Very brave, I would say, and bold. He wears a hat with band of gold, and a ruff of the latest fashion. He does salute me with a compliment, the very same as does Sir Ferdinando Fairfax when he salutes my mother.'

'Are you saying, Mistress Helen, that this thing, this devil presents to you in the form of Sir Ferdinando Fairfax ?'

Ferdinando, present, in fact sitting on the front row in his family group, shifted with great unease. His father, Sir Thomas Fairfax, half turned to regard his son with astonishment. Ferdinando shook his head, shrugged his shoulders, and looked appalled. Helen noticing the reaction of both father and son thought she may have over-stepped the mark.

'Oh no! It is not he, your Lordship. I mean this devil presents itself with the fine manners and words of Sir Ferdinando. That's my meaning.'

Sir Ferdinando's shoulders dropped a little. He remained

disconcerted and uncomfortable. To have his name linked to the devil was not to his liking, not at all. There were nudges and prods in the Fairfax group, and low mutterings. For a man in his mid-thirties, Ferdinando still feared his father's disapproval.

'Please continue your testimony, Mistress Fairfax,' said the judge.

Helen slipped back into role, or roles, for she did the two key players in different voices, adding gestures for dramatic effect:

'This man comes to be a suitor unto me. He asks me most courteously: "Be you minded to marry me, sweet Helen?" He presses me further: "Can you ever like me?"'

'And how do you answer this devil, Mistress Helen?'

'I ask him what he is. He tells me boldly: "I will make you Queen of England if you will but go with me." "No", I say. I ask of him: "In the name of God what are you?" And when I say this, his demeanour became less civil. He says to me, "You must not name God".'

'Pray, go on Mistress Helen.' The judge was leaning back in his seat, regarding Helen with great interest and objectivity. 'How did you feel?'

'I was suspicious, as any pious young maid would be. I told him plain: "You are no man if you cannot abide the name of God, but if you be a man, come near and let me feel you. Come!" I beckoned to him and tried to take his hand.'

'Mistress Helen, were you not afraid to ask to feel this thing that you now believe to be the devil?'

'My father taught me well to fend off evil spirits that I suspected with this test of touch. Father told me it was the best way to tell. If you can feel them, you know they are real.'

'Had you ever had the need to use this test before?'

'Indeed not, Your Lordship, for the devil rarely presents in Fuystone.'

Laughter from the back of the courtroom. People of quality restricted their reaction to a strained and ironic smile.

'Order, order!'

'How did the thing respond?'

'He would not let me feel him. He said, "This is no matter for feeling." I told him once more, "You are no man, but the devil and thus a shadow".'

'And then did he leave you?'

'Aye, only to return with his wife!'

Again, there was laughter at the rear of the court.

'Order, order!'

'This creature he calls wife is dressed in rich attire and far fairer than me. But he says, "If you will but come with me, Sweet Helen, I will leave this woman!"'

'Was that the end of the matter?' The judge sighed for he was rather hoping it was.

'No, back he comes with a knife and urges me to kill myself. I tell him roundly I will not. Then he offers a rope. I reject this for again I see his intent is for me to kill myself. Then he tells me "Take a pin from your clothes and put it in your mouth." I tell him straight there are no pins within my clothes for they are sewed. He says I am wrong, and that there is a great pin in my petticoats. I tell him there is no such pin, and yet when the fit had left me, I found I had such a pin.'

'Was that it?' The judge wasn't sure how much recounting of these incidents would be appropriate to the case for the girl's testimony was following so closely to the words of her father's deposition. This he had already studied. It formed a long and meticulous account, wherein Edward Fairfax had recorded each incident. The judge reflected wryly that if the victim was suffered to take the jury through each demonic encounter, they would all be sitting there until the next assizes.

'No, Your Lordship, for he tries to get me to go to the beck with him to fetch water. I see he still intends me harm. I tell him not to tarry for my father and brother may come upon him and that they will deal with him. He says, "Your father and your brother are naught to me." I send for Mr Cooke. The devil calls him, "Lying villain!". And then in comes Mr Cooke, with a parchment and begins to read a prayer. This tempter then goes. He leaves at speed.'

There was a silence in the court. The judge was writing a note. The three judges conferred, six eyes on Helen.

'Hmm. You resisted his attempted bewitchment, Mistress Helen, and showed yourself a match for the devil?'

'I hope so Your Lordship; indeed, I truly believed I did.'

Three bewigged heads together, in further conference. The judge rubbed his mouth and chin in thought. The judges were marvelling at the eloquence and assurance of the witness who had been described by her own father as "slow of speech", "hard to learn things" and "not knowing much". These terms seem hardly the measure of the young woman standing in front of them.

The witness drew herself up, emboldened and unbid. Her head tilted, sharply, to the right. She spoke as one who falls into a deepening daze:

'He pulls a horse into my chamber! A red horse. There is a green saddle on the horse's back and fine trappings. He says, "pray mount!" I ask him: "Dost thou carry folk to hell on horseback? Well, let them ride to hell who will, for I will go on foot to heaven!" But then he's cutting off its head. I question him: "Is it usual to ride on a horse without a head?" He swears he'll set the head back on if only I will please to ride… He becomes the beast with many horns …'

Helen's breathing became ragged. Her eyes were distracted, unfocussed, as if in a state of trance. Her whole body began to rock. She turned very slowly to the seven women. Still she clutched her bible in her left hand. She held the bible over her heart. She raised her right arm, forefinger outstretched towards the accused. Her body stooped and leaned forward, as if to shorten the distance between them. Her face contorted into a fearful grimace, lips tightening, revealing teeth. Eyes wide and wild, she pointed at Margaret Hall. Her voice deepened to a guttural growl. This evolved into a roar as she spewed forth a gush of blood upon the floor. She retched again, vented more blood and staggered as if to swoon. Court officers rushed to her side and tried to support her. She was as heavy as a dead person.

The judge's eyes followed as she was taken up: 'Yes, yes, take her from the room, do. We do not require a first-hand performance of possession. This is neither hospital nor theatre. This is the courtroom I'll remind you all. Where's the mother?'

Dorothy Fairfax stood slowly, clearly in a state of shock at such a public display by her daughter. Her hands trembled. Her fingers danced over her mouth. She had been singled out by the judge…

'Go with them, now. See to your child.'

Then Margaret Hall, visibly shaken by the incident, started to sigh most piteously. She turned her fine dark eyes on the judge, in a sweet supplication. The judge read bewilderment, sadness, sorrow. Certainly, he reflected, a prettier sight than that loopy lass of Fairfax's. The judge heard again the raucous cawing of the crow. He tapped his ear, once more, as if trying to dislodge wax.

'A chair for that woman,' he snapped, 'and give her water. We cannot afford to lose another. I will call a break in proceedings for the courtroom to be cleared of this carnage.'

The judge turned to a court attendant: 'See to it, and sharp!'

With an imperious wave of his hand in the direction of the blood and vomit, the judge, followed by his fellow judges and members of the jury, swept from the room.

*****

One hour later.

'First, Mister Edward Fairfax, might we enquire about the condition of your daughter, Mistress Helen? Is she well recovered?'

'Indeed, Your Lordship. She is herself again and is now able to join us in this courtroom.'

'Hmm. Why yes, I see her now. A little pale, but back with us, nonetheless. Know this Mistress Helen, you have my permission to leave the room at speed should you feel another turn coming upon yourself.'

Helen Fairfax inclined her head demurely, in acknowledgement. The judge continued:

'We may now turn our attention to the two other witnesses who have alleged possession. I call Mistress Elizabeth Fairfax.'

The judge greeted Elizabeth. Before him stood a young girl of almost eight years. He noted how unlike her elder sister she was. This child had restless, intelligent blue eyes. She had a knowing look for her years. She fidgeted with her cap and wound her ringlets round her fingers. She smiled as she looked around the courtroom as if enjoying the fact that all eyes were upon her. She raised her head and looked directly at the judge. Her mouth was rarely still, as if suppressing a torrent of question and comment.

'Mistress Elizabeth. We did not meet previously at the Lent assizes?' The judge was very kindly in his address for she was but a child. The child responded boldly:

'No, Your Lordship, I was left behind in Fuystone. Father and Mother came with Helen, and Maud was here too, but not I; I begged to join them, but my father told me roundly I could not.'

'Why do you think he left you at home?'

'Because he says I talk too much, too fast and without consideration. And I do not. He says the words flow faster from my mouth than the beck in spate.'

There was laughter in the courtroom. Elizabeth smiled, pleased with her newly found popularity.

'Order, order!'

The judge smiled benignly:

'But this time you will take your time for me, think carefully, and tell the truth?'

'Oh aye, as I have sworn, so shall it be. You will see.' She nodded gravely.

'I sincerely hope so, child.'

The three judges exchanged amused glances.

'Now tell me, Mistress Elizabeth, when did these strange things start happening to you?'

'It was Christmas time Your Lordship. People, my parents' friends and neighbours, had come to our house. About forty folk in number, I think. I was standing in front of the fire, warming myself. I like to stand before the fire, but my brothers and my sisters all complain because they say I block it out, but that's where I was standing, when it all started.'

The judge's brow clouded a little; a hint of impatience. This looked as if it was going to be a long tale, he shook his head and wished Mistress Elizabeth had stayed at home this time too.

'Please continue, Mistress Elizabeth and just try to tell us about when the bad things started to happen.'

'This woman who I did not know came directly to me and took me up. She lifted me and carried me under her arm, a little distance from the hearth, then set me down again. She was smiling, laughing, as if it were a game. I might not have thought this odd, for my brothers often do the same, just to be rid of me and to let some warmth into the room. She took up my place before the fire, and hoiked up her petticoats high behind her as if to warm her bottom.'

There was some laughter from the lesser orders. Elizabeth was encouraged by the reaction, and continued:

'But I could see my sister Helen was alarmed, and my mother too. It wasn't that the guests might see her bottom, which would indeed be rude, but that she touched me. That was what they were concerned about. You see, they take you by touch these women do. That's how they do possess you. My mother said that if this woman, this Bess Foster she called her, was a witch then

I would soon be ailing.'

Dorothy's brow clouded. She was having difficulty remembering this incident.

'Do you see this woman now, this Bess Foster?' asked the judge.

'Your Lordship, so I do. She stands there amongst those bad women yonder, the eldritch ones my sister calls them.'

'Will you point her out to me?'

Elizabeth lifted her arm and pointed with confidence to Elizabeth Foster.

Elizabeth Foster shook her head in disbelief and mouthed the word "No".

'This was she who lifted you?' he asked, nodding towards the accused.

'Yes, My Lord.'

'And did you become ill?'

'A week after she touched me, I began to see a wraith, a ghost boy, in different places in the house.'

'A ghost boy, a wraith?'

'That's what we called him, Helen and me. Papa says a wraith comes to tell you that you'll surely die and soon. He said he had it on the king's very own say so.'

'Comforting words indeed from your father?' The judge's bushy eyebrows lifted: 'Hmm? A wraith, eh? And Mistress Helen saw him too?'

'Oh yes. Then the next day when I sat on our servant Elizabeth's knee, that's Elizabeth Smith, I dropped into my first trance. And this same wraith boy came to me and said he would take me away from my family and drown me. Later, in another trance the wraith boy came again to me and offered me a black, dead creeping thing.'

'If it was dead, how know you it crept?'

'It had many legs.'

Stout guffaws filled the courtroom.

'Order, order.'

'I'll remind you all this is not a theatre. You are not here for the entertainment.' The judge then softened his tone for the child: 'Please proceed, Mistress Elizabeth.'

'Helen and me, we both started having many fits from this time. Helen saw the three-headed monster again, dripping blood, with tail of a worm, but she wasn't in a trance to see this, on this occasion. And truly, she did see it, for then I saw it too, when I was playing with the Smith children at their house, and again when I came home. That very day Helen saw a shimmering silver apparition, and this thing showed itself more than once.'

'And you and your sister discussed the apparitions you have seen?'

'We did, we do. We talk of little else.'

'I see.' The judge stared intently at Elizabeth.

'We frighten each other half to death,' said Elizabeth, nodding with enthusiasm.

'And have you ever talked to Mistress Jaffray, Maud?'

'Indeed, we have, for, as father says, there is a comfort in the community of the possessed. That's what my father tells me. One day at our house we three went into trance together and shared the same vision, apparition. We three talked to an old woman, and she told us that Henry Graver had hired her to bewitch us. Shall I point him out too? He's sitting over there. That's him, sitting next to Vicar Smithson.'

There were gasps in the courtroom. Henry Graver in the third row, started to raise himself to his feet, but he felt the restraining hand of Nicholas Smithson. He resumed his position, but his brow furrowed, and he puffed out his ruddy cheeks in deep indignation.

'Lies, damned lies,' he muttered to the vicar. The vicar squeezed his arm and nodded in agreement.

'Whilst we three were in this trance, the constable brought thither Margaret Thorpe and Margaret Waite's daughter, and we could answer them in our trance, but could not hear anyone else. We told them they were witches – and they too are standing over, err, over there…'

Something strange had crossed the face of Elizabeth, as she tried to point to the women in question. Then she struggled and clutched at her own throat. Her face seemed to crumple, her confidence was routed by terror and she began to simper in misery. Then she doubled up and vomited copious amounts of blood and bile. Helen rushed to her side to give assistance but was also taken by a sudden and similar affliction. She froze momentarily, began to retch, and fell into a fit.

Along the front row Maud Jaffray sprang to her feet and bounded three steps forward towards the two girls, staggered and tripped, then fell to the floor, her feet thrashing in a fearful frenzied flailing. She too started to retch blood and bile and appeared to lose consciousness. Maud's parents rushed to her side to restrain, then revive and comfort her.

The judge regarded the scene with profound dismay and distaste. His fellow judges were similarly appalled. This was not behaviour befitting the courtroom. Mutterings from the jury. People sitting on the front row raised posies to their noses. A strangely pungent stench of old stale blood was hanging over the pile of prone witnesses.

Any formal expressions of concern for the girls belied a shared recoil, squeamishness, and mild revulsion. The judges and jury had not expected all three to embark on a collective demonstration of their afflictions.

"The community of the possessed." The phrase had stuck in the judge's mind. Hmm, he pondered. Perplexity, distaste, and something akin to suspicion registered on his face.

The seven women had looked on gravely as this scene unfolded. They shared a beaten-down bewilderment. Surely such a display would seal their fate, they feared, for who on the jury would not hold them responsible for the girls' fits?

The judge glowered: 'Clear the courtroom. Bear them away. Let them recover somewhere away from here. We will take up the interrogation of these witnesses in private chamber when they are sufficiently recovered and sensible. In the meantime, we will subject the seven accused to a detailed examination of their bodies for signs and take from them any other evidence. Pressure can loosen the tongues of both the witnesses and the accused. We will reconvene on the morrow. Guards – bind the prisoners and take them down directly.'

The judge and his party left the courtroom, ready for some refreshment and sweeter air.

*****

When the court reconvened the next morning, the judge declared that he was ready to begin his summing up. Helen and Elizabeth had taken up their seats either side of their father. Their mother sat the other side of Helen, who still appeared unwell. The mother placed her arm around Helen's shoulders to support her.

The Jaffray family, father, mother and Maud had not appeared. Those who noticed this concluded that Maud remained indisposed.

The seven women were brought up and seated. This day the judge asked not for their ties to be removed. They sat, bound by hands and ankles. Again, those who were seated in a position to notice, took this as an indication that the women would be convicted.

When order was established, the judge began.

'This has been a most perplexing case. We have heard the indictment, a charge of the utmost gravity, the charge of witchcraft, directed at each of the seven women before me.

I can now report that each of these seven women carry none of the usual signs and indications that they are witches. Their naked bodies have been subjected to meticulous examination and nothing was found upon them.

Additionally, myself, my fellow judges and members of the grand jury have been able to interrogate these seven and, even under pressure, physical and of the mind, we have been unable to extract any confessions from them relating to maleficium, or of performing any act with the intention of causing damage or harm to these girls.

In the defence of these women has stepped forward Reverend Nicholas Smithson, the local vicar, who has known them well, and most of them for many years too. He has spoken with great sincerity, conviction, passion I would say, and has assured me and my fellow judges and the jury members that these are not witches. "Women, no more nor less" is what he insists they are: "Local women of good character". What is more, he insists that no reputation for witchcraft has ever attached itself to any one of them, to his best knowledge.

Mr Henry Graver, yeoman, and Mr Robinson, gentleman, have also spoken up for these women, again with great fervour. Two most powerful testimonies from trusted local men of good character. More than this, Henry Graver has collected a petition signed by many in the locality insisting on the innocence of the seven here before us.

From the accusers, the two Fairfax girls, Helen and Elizabeth and Maud Jaffray, we have witnessed their alleged possession in a display rarely seen in a courtroom, certainly, within my own experience. We have been hampered by their afflictions because Helen has remained too unwell to be further questioned. Her younger sister was subjected to much pressure, both physical, and under questioning, and she held true to her testimony.

Alas, the same cannot be said for Maud Jaffray. This girl was reluctant to answer any questions. However, under more strenuous interrogation and physical pressure she broke. She claimed that her father had told her that she must support the Fairfax girls and endorse their testimonies. With such a confession as this, I have instructed John Jaffray to be taken into custody to await sentencing.'

Members of the public were shocked; they were taken aback by this revelation. The balance of the case seemed to be shifting in front of them. There was much muttering and whispering.

'Order, order!'

The judge took a sip of water and held the silence. Then he continued:

'I have been impressed by the testimonies of both of the Fairfax girls. They are of good family. I have been convinced of their sincerity. There is no doubt that Helen has been most genuinely afflicted by a mysterious illness. In the case of Elizabeth, our expert physician, in attendance during the careful examination of the girls, believes that she may well be suffering from a sympathetic malady, a reaction to her older sister's illness. This is not uncommon in siblings who are close, he assures me. It can be brought on by grief and anxiety.

Of Helen's affliction, our physician has said he cannot rule out some demonic possession but that he is more inclined to believe she may have some disorder of the mind, 'the Mother' or some closely aligned malaise. He suspects a disease of an inflamed brain – a humour that lies sometimes in the substance of the brain, sometimes in the membranes and tunicles that cover the brain, sometimes in the passages of the ventricles of the brain, or veins of those ventricles. He recommends a deeper investigation for the well-being of the young woman.'

Fairfax's astonished gasp was quite audible to the court. The judge addressed him directly:

'In support of these allegations, you, Mr Edward Fairfax, have presented us with parchments of prolific and persuasive prose. From a great poet we would expect no less. You have spoken to the these with immense fervour, sincerity and conviction, as one who both records your own daughters' alleged possession by the devil, demons and seven witches and their familiars, but also bears personal witness to the daily impact of your two daughters' sufferings on the household at Newhall. The power of your testimony cannot be denied. The meticulousness of your daily diary has impressed us all. For this we thank you.'

Fairfax tilted his head to thank the judge for this acknowledgement. But he was not happy. He felt the cold hand of anxiety squeeze his vital organs.

The judge took another sip of water.

'However, my learned friends, I remain puzzled, bewildered, confounded even. Hmm. Bear with me and consider this carefully for what I touch on here is central to the outcome of this case.'

The judge paused, his eyes resting on each member of the grand jury in turn.

'Are we here addressing things that happened in this world, in Fuystone, deep in the Forest of Knaresborough, in the County of York? Or, are we looking at things that happened in the minds of two girls, or rather, a young woman and a girl? This is strange territory when it comes to admissible evidence. Listen to me and think carefully.

Here is the typical scene. The father sits by the bedside and records the utterances of his daughter whilst she resides in fit, or trance. The girl awakes from trance and tells the father what was happening and what was said by her tormentors whilst she was in this unconscious condition. There is a matching process happening here. The father can only hear the girl's words and see her movements whilst she experiences the demonic visitations and encounters with witches. The father can only hear the girl's explanation when she comes out of trance. The father trusts the daughter, two daughters, without reservation. Their explanations are recorded, allegedly verbatim. The question is this. Does the father's written account constitute admissible evidence? Or is this ...' Here the judge breaks off for effect, his hand sweeping the table loaded with parchment: 'Is this a sophisticated form of hearsay?'

The other two judges nod sagely. Members of the jury look baffled and then one or two begin to nod slowly, as if seeing a lantern's light gradually penetrate a dark passage. The judge continued:

'Consider the position of the seven defendants. How might these women answer the accusations? How might they defend the actions of their imagined selves? Hmm. Nay, even deeper goes the problem, when they themselves have not shared these encounters? Basically, how can we be held accountable for our behaviour in another person's dream?'

There was laughter from the body of the courtroom.

'Order, order!' cried the serjeant.

'This is no realm for mirth,' rebuked the judge. 'The fate of these seven women shackled before us hangs in the balance.'

Silence. The judge glowers, and then goes on:

'In this court, the seven accused have been confronted with testimonies from two girls, nay three, who claim to have been accosted by themselves, the girls' own lowly neighbours, whilst in fit. The girls have described how these women have possessed and persecuted them. The girls have given us detailed accounts as to how they have stood up to these women who used maleficium – how they repelled them, rebuked them and sometimes physically beat and fought them off.

The women have denied the accusations. Of-course they have. They say they weren't there. Nor were they. The perpetrators are the phantoms of these women who appear in the minds of the Fairfax daughters.'

Edward Fairfax stared intently at the judge. His face was a study in profound dismay and rising anger. He battled to maintain his composure. The judge cleared his throat.

'Mistress Helen Fairfax claimed she became possessed almost ten months ago. She fell deep into a trance and attended a sermon by Alexander Cooke. This young woman, described by her father as slow in her learning, takes on an eloquence that is out of character. Hmm. In her next trance she meets the devil himself dressed in the style of, and with the fine manners of, Sir Ferdinando Fairfax . He then proposes to her. Let me ask you to consider this, members of the grand jury. What if Mistress Helen Fairfax had claimed it was Ferdinando Fairfax himself in this guise? What if she had claimed he was the devil himself, or the devil's agent? Would Ferdinando Fairfax now be making an eighth in the dock?'

There were gasps of horror and incredulity echoing round the courtroom, along with loud rumblings from the Fairfax contingent. Ferdinando Fairfax raised his hand to his chest, his mouth gaped open in disbelief and he shook his head. The judge took another sip of water and proceeded:

'How would Ferdinando Fairfax defend himself? He would say he was not there, that it was merely a figment of the girl's imagination or her feverish state of mind, her illness. How could he prove it? Should he even be asked to do so, eh? Hmm?

We have heard such tales of possession from these girls that is way beyond my experience. True, Helen and Elizabeth have conveyed their anguish, terror, physical pain, mental torment that equates to any torture met out in dark dank rooms within these castle walls. There is no doubt in my mind that they have felt all that they describe. But was it inflicted by the seven before you or by phantasms modelled by their imaginings on these neighbours of theirs? These are girls whose society is a narrow and confined one. On which others should they model their imaginings or fix their fantasies? Who else do they know?

We have been shocked and amazed to witness the violence of the girls in the throes of this alleged possession. We had to have them carried from the courtroom. We are more used to being confronted with depositions, written testimony and reports. I will reiterate; the courtroom is no place for performance.

Performance. Hmm. I use this word carefully, and with

caution. Practiced performances of possession? Can these be called up for the benefit of the jury? Is it not in the very nature of such trances to be beyond the control of the victim? And yet all three, I include the discredited witness, Maud Jaffray, here, were visited in front of us by their tormentors, whilst in trance. And this at a time when we saw these alleged tormentors sitting physically before us. Could these accused be in two places at once?

Are seven women to be sent to the gallows on the fevered imaginings of a young woman and a girl?

Jury I ask you to consider all of this very carefully. May I remind you that it is your responsibility to find on the facts of the case. May I emphasize to you that very word: 'facts'; facts not phantasms.

My role is to determine the law as it applies to this case.

We will withdraw to enable the grand jury to deliberate.'

The judge withdrew and the court was cleared.

*****

It did not take the jury long to reach conclusion. When the judge returned to the courtroom, he declared that the facts of the case did not meet the statutory requirements to determine guilt. He declared that the burden of proof had not been met and the case was dismissed.

The judge took the opportunity to say to Edward Fairfax, before the packed courtroom, that he should take his family home, look after his daughters and to pay them more attention. He made it clear that he did not believe Edward Fairfax was in any way duplicitous or out to deceive, but that if he had a fault, it was to have allocated too much credence to the tales of his two daughters and that he should, in this respect alone, distance himself from them. He had been naïve, said the judge. He, Fairfax was their father, not their scribe. The judge's last words to Fairfax carried a subtle rebuke:

'Cherish your daughters. Pay them attention. Love them. Enjoy their company.'

On hearing this, Dorothy Fairfax's face was a study in cold containment.

About the verdict, there was a muted surprise in the courtroom, rather than shock. The more perceptive had predicted the 'not guilty' verdict from the judge's summing up and his clear steer to the jury. For many of the lower orders there was a strong sense of disappointment, for they had been looking forward to a hanging, and a coven of seven would have been a fine spectacle, indeed. A swinging at Knavesmire was always a spectacle, carnival time. The crowd had been denied their fun, frivolity and festivities.

It was the women themselves who seemed the most shaken. They turned to each other, silent, and as if in slow motion. Their moistening eyes were eloquent. It was too much to take in.

Meekly, the seven gave their wrists and lifted their ankles to be untied. They rubbed their weakened limbs, coaxing life back into them. Then they held each other, taking deep breaths. These women would not be released from custody until their bill for accommodation and food had been met. This would be settled for each of the women by John Dibb, Janet's son, with generous contributions from the purses of Nicholas Smithson, Henry Graver and Mister Robinson. These four men would also organise the waggon home.

Smithson, Graver, Robinson and the families of the women present, gripped hands and embraced.

Fairfax held his head low, his crossed arms resting on his knees. He watched a black beetle cross his buckled shoe. He would not, could not, look up. Helen fainted in her mother's arms. Elizabeth tried to stroke her father's hand, but he shrugged her off. He was vaguely aware that Dorothy was giving instructions for the removal of Helen from the courtroom. Dorothy was unable to look at her husband.

'What shall we do with this lot?' asked the clerk to the clerk, indicating the high pile of parchment.

Fairfax could hardly speak. Elizabeth stood up slowly, still stiff and sore from the prolonged interrogation she had been subjected to. She ventured that they needed to take it all home to Newhall and that it should be packed carefully and placed in the coach.

8

Edward Fairfax

Poor man, thou searchest round
To finde out death, but missest life at hand.

Vanitie – George Herbert 1633

The fetters are untied from their heels, the halters unloosed from their necks. They are untrussed, released. They taste their legs again and flex their fingers.

And I back from the dark glass. I dare not look through, face to face with mine own self. But I know how I am known.

I know I am mocked. Smithson nods and smiles. Graver whoops. Robinson claps them both on the back and glad hands every man who passes. Families embrace the wretched women. But their eyes are upon me. They believe my wits have been a wool-gathering. And now they wish me worse than harm.

I watch my girl go down again. I try to say the words: 'Yes, carry her to the coach. I will follow directly. Take her now, make haste. Go with her, wife. Take your child. Servant take those scrolls.' But nothing comes.

The wife's face is closed to me, but she is not. She walks as one who dwells within her own domain where disappointment and despair do reign. I do not wish to enter there.

The judge left me sparse shreds and tatters of respect. He deemed me simple, a fool rather than a felon, no wicked person out to deceive. At least the judge left my integrity intact, whilst shaming me a gull ... For that I suppose I should owe him gratitude. I hope he roasts.

The judge believed me duped by Jaffray and his family, who drew my daughter Helen in, and she the little one. This may preserve me from the charge of defamation, I trust. They have taken Jaffray into custody. And I, the good innocent, believed all that I heard to be true, not feigned. This is what the judge was saying. Had he seen what we, the family, have endured these long months of suffering. Had he but seen the fits, the possessions, my girls left insensible and shadows of their earlier selves. Had he but tasted even one day of their sufferings.

He did not. And now my Helen descends once more. When will this business end?

We are not over this yet. No. It is not over.

I will not be as they see me. I dare not see myself, not yet. There may still be time to stop *the strange woman's* mouth.

9

Helen Fairfax

In these brackish waters, my picked bones will be the house of eels, tench and pike. There is darkness and silence on this soft bed of mud. The shroud of slimy weed presses upon me, sucks all sense from me and staunches all sorrow. I am rocking on the bottom, nudged by creatures of this deep. And yet I do believe this rocking is the coach. I come and go, rise and sink, surface only to drown again, and again.

It ended abruptly. A coach driven blindly into this deep dark lake. A broken road, a bridge blown. If some survive, I will not be amongst their number. I will never get to shiver on the bank, a wrap around my shoulder. My fight is over. I am sunk.

Who will mourn for me? Not my family. Where have I led them? I never meant things to come to this.

The courtroom fades. I think my mother speaks to me for I can see her soft lips working, as if she chews. She reaches for me, holds me. I cannot make the words I want to say. My jaws are tight and how they ache. I see my father sitting, hunched and broken. I think I have made him sad. I trust I have not turned him mad.

Someone is pushing me, I believe. I feel a pinch. A person passing. In contempt.

The judge believes me sick. He says they need to see to me, that I have an affliction of the brain and that my father has been duped into believing in my fits, fevered fantasies and imaginings. I have taken him down with me deep into this lake of creatures, mud and misery.

I thought my father wanted me possessed. I did believe it; I had reason. It has been during these long months that he has turned to me. We two have been on a journey. He said as much. But I will lose him now, I know. I see how it will be; I see that Eliza will take him from me.

Darker, deeper, down. I neither see nor hear. Have I died already, oh sweet release? Yet these fishy depths cannot be heaven?

If I think hard, I can remember that last trip home. They waited for me at Harewood, the women. *The strange woman* jigged and capered along the bank top, gloating and goading, laughing she was free. She pointed at me. And free again, now, she will be.

The strange woman – it is she who has taken my eyes, my ears, my flesh, my father. I think she dwells within my father's head. Sometimes, in my bedchamber, when my fit is finished, and I return to myself, I have found him by my side, his eyes tight shut and whispering things, not to me, but to conjure her. Truly, I think he should not say the things that I have heard him utter. He has made brisk movements with his hands. Unseemly jerks and judders, sighs, gasps and groans. These have distressed me, frightened me. And I have prayed for him, for I saw that he too was possessed, like me.

And still I want her gone. Is this wrong?

Please God, bring my family peace.

10

Beltane, May Day's Eve, in the year 1623 A.D. – Timble Gill, beside the beck

He slithered on his front across the damp grass and moss; he did not think to save his coat. His body flattened the massed bluebells, squashed the last of the anemones and violets, and crushed the ramsons. The heady mix of sweet scents, under-layered by garlic, passed over him; he was impervious. He pushed himself against the ridge's edge. From there his head came slowly up.

What would he see, this peeper on the Gill's rim? This furtive form, this Mister Fairfax, lying flat, spying on the women in the Gill. He'd had no rest, these long cold months, could not accept the verdict of their trial, their alleged innocence. Was this justice? The verdict confounded decency. He would track them still, these hags. He could not stop. He'd stalk them, stake them out, watch and garner further evidence. He'd have them yet. He would not let them be.

The spot the women chose was by the beck. A flat space, like a beach but grassed almost to the water's edge. A narrow strand of silt, like a fine ochre sand. A balmy night for the birth of May. Unseasonably warm. That evening the beck was rippling and rilling brightly over shale. The beck could rise in moments in a storm, and tear the leaves from the wild garlic, sweep the bedrock clean and bite the bank on the other side, but tonight it felt benign. The trees crowded, fussed and arched over, to form a vernal chamber. A great green hall for the Beltane Feast. A double celebration, for the women had waited long for this night.

They put up a rough trestle table – boards across two bases. A cloth of sack was spread, and rough-hewn wooden plates and clay goblets, some knives to carve and cut. Each of the women brought a dish. Margaret, big of belly, had bought a flagon of last summer's bilberry wine. Candles were lit. A pretty sight it was. Seven women gathered there.

There would be music after, for Mistress Dickenson, Elizabeth, had brought her pipes.

Janet Dibb, as the eldest, took the table's head. She smoothed the cloth with satisfaction. A kindly, stout and homely woman in her later years. Her eyes were merry, and her voice was deep and raw:

'Sweet gossips, can you yet believe they let us off? Twice tried and twice acquitted.'

The others shook their heads in disbelief and wonder:

'I was certain they'd have us the second time,' the other Elizabeth, Mistress Foster, gasped; the wonder of their freedom was still fresh with her too.

'Those Justices were honest men – real gentlemen. And Smithson too. And Graver and Robinson. Not like that bastard Fairfax,' said Margaret Waite, the widow.

'We knew Nicholas Smithson didn't hold with witches, or any of the auld ways. Quaint customs, eh? Remember that rush bearing business two summers since. He would brook no performance in his church. He and his lads lay hands on Tom Herryson and trounced him, proper roughed him round. Smithson, a man of the cloth, eh? And as for Sport on Sundays, dancing and revelling. What is the world coming to?' Janet tutted and shook her head in mock disapproval.

'But we might dance tonight for him?' Young Mistress Waite was all for dancing. She laughed and the candlelight picked out the fine sprinkle of freckles on her nose.

'It's said Mister Smithson is a puritan at heart. He'll get no thanks for that round here, the times being what they are, he'd do better with the other lot,' said Margaret Thorpe.

'The King says sport must be allowed so long as it don't take away from church. King's into witches too. He'd have been after us hanging alright.' Elizabeth Dickenson shook her head in wonder: 'But our sweet Smithson knew this business was a nonsense, a tale cooked up by silly girls.' Elizabeth stroked her pipes. 'I was so frightened. Why, if Elizabeth here hadn't held my hand, I'll swear I would have lost my legs and fallen flat in front of the judge.'

'Those Fairfax wenches fibbed and fibbed. I've yet to meet this black cat Gibbe – and him by my side these forty years, a sucking me body. And me never noticing it? What twaddle spilled from the lips of bairns. That Helen was of an age to know better,' said Janet.

'And what of this yellow bird the bigness of a crow. Tewhit was what those hussies called the thing,' Janet's daughter, Margaret Thorpe chipped in. 'My familiar! Lord, that's what Mister Fairfax called it. First I've heard.'

'By the saints I had a 'familiar' too, a deformed thing with many feet, black and rough of hair, size of a cat. I'd soil myself if I encountered such, ne'er mind give it shelter. A weird friend indeed,' said Margaret Waite. 'I'd rather take in a man, or men. Happen Mistress Fairfax got confused – my dead husband was squat, rough and hairy.'

Their laughter echoed round the Gill.

'It is said Maud Jaffray's lost her mind. She couldn't testify. Something took her tongue,' said Margaret Thorpe.

'Perhaps the devil took it? I've never known that young hussy short on words.' Elizabeth Foster shook her head in sorrow:

'To be fair, the Justices were not kind to her.' Janet frowned: 'They were all smiles and coax to the Fairfax girls, but poor little Maud, barely twelve years old, was put through the mill alright. She looked to me that she would pass with fright. She held her tongue, and she was right.'

'What made them girls do it? It would be nothing to do with family, power and wealth?' Elizabeth Foster smiled, ruefully.

'It's said Maud damped the rushes down,' giggled young Mistress Waite: 'She weren't alone in that. I left a pool. Them Justices, they came on strong.'

Her mother shuddered: 'I bet there weren't one of us that didn't pee ourselves or worse. Indeed, the Justices scared me half to death. I heard Maud laid it on her father and mother. She claimed to be doing their bidding, telling tales on us. It seems John Jaffray was committed to prison. I hope whoever paid him, paid him well.'

Margaret Waite then noticed Margaret Hall:

'Margaret, you're quiet. This is not you, lass. You're normally a'bubble and busting at your seams.'

'As bubbly as the big pot she boils her bilberries in!' said Janet. The women laughed again.

'Come on lass, we're free. Shape yourself. They'll be dancing tonight. No one dances like you, you big, beautiful besom, you.'

'Janet's right, we're here to celebrate, Margaret. What's wrong? You look as if you're sick?' asked Elizabeth Foster, her eyes fixed on Margaret's belly.

'I've had enough of dancing. I cannot eat tonight. 'Tis not just the size of me. The bairn within me rolls and kicks. I feel the cramps so bad.' Margaret's voice choked back bile.

'Heal yourself, Margaret. You have the potions for all ills.'
Janet was looking carefully at Margaret. She continued: 'Perhaps it was the journeys, lass? You stopped the cart a lot. We heard you griping, gipping, chucking up. Three day's in an open cart, those days in that foul cell, and two days back. Those roads so rough.'

'That was nigh on nine months back. Time enough to get over it,' sighed Margaret Hall.

'Them cells so cold, damp and cramped. 'Twas too much for you, my girl.'

'I have the gripes and pain again. This sickness comes upon me quick.'

'You cannot retch,' put in young Margaret Waite, eager to start the feast. 'Why Janet's killed a capon; she wrung its neck. But ours are all safe. Janet shall roast the fowl for our feast. Elizabeth has made a pie. Men would die for a piece of her pie.'

Lewd laughter, but not from Margaret.

'I think I'd better go. I must not spoil my Gossips' fun.'

Then Janet spoke: 'Are you due, Margaret?'

'I think I'm close.'

'You look to me as though the child has fallen down and is ready,' said Elizabeth Foster. 'Look at the shape of you.'

The women fell silent. They regarded Margaret intently. Janet spoke again:

'What man has sired this bairn? You niver said.'

'I cannot say.' Margaret hesitated, her brow troubled, as if weighing the costs of conflicting indiscretions. She appeared to reach a decision, the least of the evils.

She spoke with caution: 'I dare not speak his name. I met him on the moor. He was not from these parts.' She added: 'I cannot even call him man.'

'I see.' Janet's face grew stern: 'Tell more. What was he?'

'He flew me to the sea and back. We danced through air. He took me in his cape.'

'This was no man, Margaret. Say his name.'

'I will not, must not.'

'Say his name.'

'Do not make me, I beg of you.'

'Say now; we need to know. We are your friends.'

'Asmodeus.' Margaret's voice was soft and low.

The women froze. They stood as still as statues, their eyes intent on Margaret, as they took in the enormity of what Margaret had done. Finally, Janet spoke:

'Then you bought us our freedom. You bought us our lives?'

'I could not see us die. He said we'd be acquitted, if I would but fly.'

'And what of you?'

'He granted me four hundred years, to linger in this Gill. Each year I am to dance with him, and fly. We do stuff when we fly. I see such things.'

Margaret pauses. She shudders, flinches in contraction: 'It is not unpleasant, what we do. I long to fly again. But then, as after that, he did not say …'

'Then we must stay with you, until that time … that last time he will come.'

'You cannot bide with me for four hundred years; it don't make sense.'

The women ignored her, nodded to each other. A slow chant evolving:

'*We have not hanged, nor will we die.*' The momentum was forged from resolve.

Janet signalled them to stop. She went on: 'You have bought us our lives. It is agreed. Come, be of cheer, we'll have some fun, we'll watch over our own, our lines to come. We'll look out for them through these long years before us. We'll see them prosper, help them if we can, once our natural span on earth is done.'

Margaret Waite took over, warming to the vision, clasping her hands together:

'Aye. We will become these trees and breathe a sweeter air with our leaves. Lichens will creep over and cover us. We will laugh with the grasses, the fog, the bent and bog, take the time of day with finches, tits and crows when this life's done. We will not leave our Margaret – for paradise, for us, is here.'

Margaret Waite's daughter continued. A strange look came upon her face, a calm distraction, as if in trance. The others listened intently. Her voice had changed:

Each of us will choose our tree, a sapling now, and that will be the one we'll be, for what may seem eternity. Margaret will take the red oak yonder. She will perch above us all, and wander further, until we fall.

Elizabeth Foster nodded slowly: 'We all agree. Shall we now feast, give thanks to all who would not see us hang?'

They pour the bilberry wine into each goblet, to the brim:

'To Smithson, Margaret, and "her Man".'

Margaret smiled slowly, reviving, her spirits rising. A sudden cawing from a crow made her turn her head to the ridge above the other bank. She saw the head of him she hated, backlit by the waxing gibbous moon rising, up beyond the ridge. She pointed, clutching her huge dropped belly. The women's eyes followed. Then with loud, savage voice she spoke:

'And a curse on you, Fairfax, and your friends and kin who took against us. May fire take your grave and the rising Washburn waters drown your very house.'

The women joined her in a chant: *'Curse you, curse Fairfax! Fire and water bring you down.'* They moved as one in his direction.

Fairfax, so absorbed in what was happening below him, had not seen the moon come up from behind. Horrified at his sudden detection, he took in their curse. He saw the furious faces of the women, under-lit by flames and candlelight, their features flickering grotesquely. He saw them coming and, in a great terror, he rolled away from his perch on the ridge. He staggered to his feet.

Pointing down to Margaret, he screamed: 'Whore!'

'If I am that thing, then you shaped me so, from first you came. You made me save myself, and these.'

A rush of anger, a writhing, seething clamour was rising from the group beneath him. Fairfax was overcome with terror and fear for his own safety. He broke into a sprint, west along the ridge and crossed the beck higher up-stream. He stumbled and tumbled, trying to race along the bridleway called Lady Lane, towards Timble, then over the footpath towards Swinsty Hall. He was sweating profusely, and enduring great stitch in his ribs by the time he reached Newhall.

Once home he pushed past his wife, Dorothy, and climbed the stairs to his study. He would write down every detail while it was fresh in his mind. He trimmed his quill, dipped his nib and started to scratch and scrape across the parchment.

That whore Margaret Hall carried a demon's child. She'd copulated with a fiend. On her own say so. He, Fairfax, would have her now.

*****

The women did not pursue Fairfax, as he had feared. It was his own terror and imaginings that chased him, made him quake, tumble over clods, bang into trunks, take on bramble bushes and tear his fine clothes.

A shriek from Margaret ceased the chant. A trickle of water seeped the silt below her skirt and found a channel to the beck.

'My waters ...'

She doubled up, clutched her belly, began to pant and perspire. Her eyes flashed wild. The women saw her time had truly come. They cleared a space in haste, moving food, rough goblets, wooden plates and knives. The sack cloth was left. It became her birthing sheet. They helped her onto the table, gently guiding, then lowering and steadying her body. Two of the women lifted her slightly, cradling her lower back to the birthing position. They plied her with more bilberry wine to dull the pain. Elizabeth Foster handed her a relic to clutch, a crude crucifix, with two sticks bound with some ancient cloth fragment. She believed this shredded piece of cloth to have been part of the robe of Saint Raymond, the patron saint of midwives, women in labour, and the falsely accused. Margaret Waite gave her a stouter, twisted, knotted cloth to clench between her teeth.

The birth was hard, the baby's head was large, the shoulders wide. The bairn seemed stuck. They plied her with a potion taken from rye fungus, tried and tested to hasten labour. At one point they thought to fetch the hook called the crochet – the device to pull out the dead baby. It was not necessary.

The women had no sweet oils to lubricate and work in massage, no precious oil of sweet almonds. New butter sufficed, to relax the tissue. The baby tore her but was, after some time, delivered safe. These women knew how to best assist, when to act and when to wait. This was not their first birth, although it would prove their strangest.

The baby's eyes were as dark as the midnight sky, and wide open on entering this world. A silence descended, the only sound, the rippling of the beck. The women watched, stunned, in awe of what they saw. It was a boy, fine and strong, but something odd, something wrong. The child was well-formed, but for one foot, turned inwards; a scaly, darkened thing it was, more like a claw.

The women tied the navel string with a loose yarn tugged from a shawl. They chanted a charm during the rough cutting. They wrapped the stump of the cord attached to the bairn, with a strip of cloth torn from a petticoat, once the pulsing surge of blood had ceased.

To start his breathing, the child needed to be swung, to gulp the air in shock. The women hesitated to take it by the heels – claw cautious. Margaret, hair matted with sweat to her head, righted herself, hauled herself up with Elizabeth's help. She took her bloodied baby boy and swung him by the heels like a new-born lamb. A piercing scream, he gasped for breath.

Margaret stooped and bathed the baby's body with water cupped from the beck. She wrapped her child within a sack shawl, and made to take herself back to her place, to tend to him and to herself. Elizabeth Foster took the rough rocky path in front of Margaret, lighting her way by lantern. Janet held her arm around Margaret's waist to support her. Another took her some sustenance, some oat bread, from the feast, in a coarse woven basket, and some water. Two women trailed after her to assist and settle her down. This slow procession was tracked by a crow whose persistent caws seemed to sooth the new-born boy. He turned from wails and cries to coos and echoing caws.

When order was restored, and mother and child left comfortable for the night, the women began to return to the Gill. Elizabeth Foster, last to leave, asked Margaret if she had a name for the bairn. Margaret called her back and beckoned her down to her cot. She fumbled in her pocket underneath her petticoat and handed Elizabeth back her relic of Saint Raymond.

'I thank you and Saint Raymond for the strength you gave me and for the safe delivery. I call my son for you, Elizabeth. I call him Foster, Foster Hall.'

'Foster Hall. It's a fine name. May he be the first of many.'

Elizabeth bent and brushed Margaret's brow with a kiss and left her.

*****

The Beltane feast resumed, without Margaret. Before they ate the women took each other's hands in a close and closed sisterly circle. Then they loosed their hands. Each raised a forefinger to the lips. A collective *hush, hush, hush*.

The child's deformity would never be mentioned. It was not safe to ever tell of it, they knew. They owed that to Margaret, along with their lives and total loyalty.

11

Margaret and the midwife – dawn, May Day in the year 1623 A.D.

How soon doth man decay!
When clothes are taken from a chest of sweets
To swaddle infants, whose young breath
Scarce knows the way;
These clouts are little winding sheets,
Which do consigne and send them unto death.

Mortification, The Temple – George Herbert 1633

Soft pink pearls of light from the east above Jack Hill. Spring dawn. Some penetrated the hovel, peeping through the tattered window covers. The sun wasn't up, but it was expected soon. May Day, it was.

Margaret saw the light; she felt rough, sore and strange. She had a pounding headache; a surfeit of bilberry wine. Her lower parts felt as if she had been torn in two. And, her thoughts stalled. She was aware she was not alone. There were sounds coming up from beside her: a snuffling, a sucking, a tiny gurgling noise…

The events of the previous night began to creep back into her resistant consciousness. She would force herself to look, to crane over the side of her settle. She knew what she would see. A baby. She sighed from her soul. No, she wasn't alone – not anymore, not like the day before. Foster, she'd called the baby Foster. Foster Hall. Elizabeth's face came to her. She'd called him for her, Elizabeth Foster, her midwife. Elizabeth, Janet, all her friends – they had tended her.

She would look. She did. He was there in his basket, with some cloths around him. He was alive. She was alive. They would live for each other. They had to, surely?

His eyes were wide, and what eyes. He had the eyes of his father. She prayed people wouldn't notice, join the two of them in their minds. No sensible person would imagine …

Could she love this bairn? Should she love him? Had she any right at all to love him? She looked down at him. His eyes met hers. His sounds changed, more insistent now, for he was hungry. She pulled herself up, righted herself, then bent over and picked him up carefully. She raised him to face her and then snuffled his head. The very smell of him was core, essence of herself. She lowered him and placed him tentatively to her breast. She had assisted so many new mothers to do this, this simple act, yet why did it seem so hard for her?

How that man had taunted her for the smallness of her nipples. The teats of a ten-year old – that's what he'd said. Inadequate in every way, he'd screamed at her. She blotted out his image. 'A body fit only for copulation, gratification, never procreation. The body of a slut, strumpet, whore.' A vile whore he'd called her, and yet he had come for more, again and again.

She coaxed her bairn carefully, whispering to him to try to suck. Gradually she felt a pull, still barely perceptible, as the life began to flow, slowly, between them. She snuffled his head again. A down mossed crown of dark hair. It was damp. It was her own tears that had moistened the baby's head.

'What will you think of me, Foster? I am supposed to be the one you look to and all I can do is weep? I will love you; this I vow.'

And as he sucked a little of the milk from her she felt a shifting in her soul. She had been spared for this. And yet that thought released more tears. Now they sprang freely from her eyes.

'An earthly bairn,' she whispered, 'and you will one day die, and I will live on. I'm locked into a demon's deal which will separate me from you, my own mortal child. Oh, shame on me, what did I do? What bargain have I struck? Was my life so worth preserving? We both should have died in York. Then we would never have been separated. With you locked in my belly; they could never have taken you from me.'

Propped up on the settle, sorrow overwhelmed and engulfed her. Foster slept, bound to her breast by her arms. His mouth drooped open, dribbling a little of her milk and he was content – with so very little. In this state, Margaret dropped into that light sleep that brings distraction and visions. She saw a line of Fosters to follow, a vision of the generations to come as the centuries unfolded before her. Then there was darkness, shadows in the Gill as the beck flowed on. The demon comes, a desperate young woman strangely dressed in the hands of …. No!

The draped sacking at the entrance was pulled back. Elizabeth entered.

'Margaret, how are you and baby Foster? You're a feeding him at sunrise. Good. He's a fine boy. I've brought you bread and milk. But first some warmed water to wash you down – the both of you.'

Elizabeth Foster had arrived with pail and sack, to fulfil her duties as midwife. She brought with her a sense of purpose, a briskness and cheerfulness. She threw back the window coverings and let in more of dawn's pearl light. Elizabeth took in Margaret's swollen eyes, puffed-up lids and matted hair. She made no comment. Margaret broke the silence:

'How can I feed him, Elizabeth? I have milk a plenty, but

tiny tits.'

'Well we fed him off you last night alright. We held him on to suck. You were too far gone on your own bilberry concoction to notice. Easy, it was. Come, when he wakes, I'll watch you. There are tricks for them with small nipples.' Elizabeth smiled at her friend: 'Come, hush yourself. Do you think you are the first new mother with such?'

'But I was told I was a freak.'

'Who on this earth said such to you?'

'A man who liked to visit here,' Margaret bit her lip. She'd started to speak of forbidden things.

'What sort of man was that? To condemn a woman for the breasts the good Lord has given her. Why this man's words condemn himself. What women are put upon by men, some men! It beggars belief.'

Margaret calmed a little; her breathing became more regular. She regarded Elizabeth carefully. Her tears began to ease.

'Margaret, my friend, you will soon feel more yourself. I fear you have the lowering of the spirits that besets many a new mother. Just at the point they should feel so triumphant, having created a new life, they turn in upon themselves. You have something of this. It was not the easiest of births. You are overwhelmed, exhausted, but this will pass. Know you have friends, and that we are nearby. Now let's look on these shelves and see if we can find a 'pick-me-up.' You can teach me a thing or two about these, I think. Isn't it generally our custom for me to come to you for a potion?'

Margaret found herself smiling. She took Elizabeth's hand, stoked it then kissed it. Her spirits were rallying fast.

'Something with bilberries?' suggested Elizabeth with mischief in her eyes.

'Christ no. Stop it, or I shall chuck again. I think I will give the bilberry a rest awhile.'

The two women laughed. Margaret thought for a moment,

then continued:

'Feverfew will do – a herb ruled by Venus to succour our sisters. It's good both for the melancholy and the privy parts. I have a decoction – this herb, boiled in white wine with mace. Over yonder. Yes, there.'

Elizabeth set about finding the tonic under her friend's direction. She soon located the flask.

'I'll take a little of it. You can add some to the water too, for it is also good to bathe the torn area below with it. If I am slow to heal, we can apply the herb, boiled but still warm to the wounds of birth.' She paused, and then thought on: 'Later today, I may take some Lady's Mantel Tea. Feverfew is my first choice, but Lady's Mantel has its merits too.'

Elizabeth began to wash Margaret, and then her baby. Once made comfortable, the baby needed feeding. Elizabeth watched intently, offering advice.

'Remember, it's not the nipple, it's the larger part the bairn latches onto. Press that area with your thumb and finger. Push some milk out first to make it easier for him – that's it. Give him the taste. Just like freeing up a maiden ewe, a first time lamber. Unblock the tit, then work the milk. Good. Very good. And rub your nipples regularly, for they say it helps over time. Pull 'em, rub 'em and tweak 'em. Sharp and brisk. Make 'em stand up for themselves.'

The two women watched as the baby start to suck with increased confidence and appetite.

'Feed regularly; feed often. Don't let the milk build up for it will swell and tighten your breasts. Then it will be harder for him to latch on. And remember, be patient. It may take a little time for you and him to get it right. The two of you will learn to work together.'

Elizabeth took some victuals from her sack for Margaret. A thought occurred to her:

'I tell you this. Big teats are the worse, indeed they are. A bairn with its tiny mouth and a mother with big nipples – you've got a proper problem there. Sometimes the wee bairn can't take the teat at all. There's a wench up beyond Wydra bridge, with her teats so big her poor wee bairn boked and choked. They had to put the babe out to nurse. It was like a curse. Such a waste, for she had milk to fill a churn.'

Margaret started to giggle: 'There's always some poor creature worse off round here. You only have to cast around.'

She took a bite of bread and a portion of cheese and chewed eagerly. Elizabeth grinned:

'I think you're coming round, my sweet. This is more the girl I know. Now I think he's done, so let me have a hold of young Foster.'

Elizabeth took Foster from his mother's arms and started to rock him rhythmically, gently, softly patting his back and humming an old melody to him.

'You were named for me, my boy. Foster. Foster, I will see you right.'

Margaret watched transfixed. She would always remember this moment. She felt an unconditional love for her boy, and a surge of gratitude to the woman who now held and soothed him to sleep. Elizabeth had taken charge the night before, that much Margaret did remember clearly. Elizabeth had led the women to aid her son's birth. She was the last to leave and here she was at dawn the following morn, the dawn of her new life. Margaret felt indebted, but more than that, she felt a surge of sisterly affection and trust.

'And now the both of you will need some rest,' said Elizabeth, gently lowering Foster to his basket. She straightened the cover over Margaret.

'I'll return in a few hours.'

Margaret didn't answer; she was already drowsing, descending deep into sleep.

12

Fairfax after the feast –
May Day in the year 1623 A.D.

E dward Fairfax came to consciousness – a slow process.
    Eventually, he woke himself fully with a snort and a judder, that nerve reaction in sleep by which the sleeper lifts as in a levitation.

Edward's dawning unfolded like this. First, he felt a dampness on his cheek. He feared he had dribbled in his sleep. Dorothy was in the habit of administering a sharp jab to his side, to encourage him to roll off his back when he snored, as he so often did. On this occasion, he had no sense of Dorothy's presence. This unsettled him.

Something of the previous night came back to him. He realised he was at his desk, still, and not in his bedchamber. He remembered entering the house, barring the door, pushing his wife roughly aside in his haste to record all details before they were lost. Dorothy had begged to know what was wrong. He had run up the stairs two at a time, and crossed the great chamber at speed, to reach his study. He turned the key against interruption.

Fairfax's right eye opened slowly. His left eye lid seemed

melded onto his left forearm. His neck hurt. His left shoulder was sore beyond endurance. Through his right eye he saw all was darkness, ink black.

Black ink it was. When his right eye focused, he made out a trimmed nib, a quill, a lipped inkwell on its side, and the parchment he'd been working on, spoiled by the spill.

Fairfax pushed himself upwards off the desk with his right hand. He had no feeling in his left. Had he had a seizure, he wondered? He tried to call his wife. Then he bethought himself. Take time to think, he schooled himself. Think. Remember. Had those women done for him? Had they done this to him?

Gradually, from pins and needles, some element of feeling returned to his left side. He straightened his stiff back and groaned. Sheets of scribed parchment lay across the desk, most ruined by the spillage. Ink stained his right hand. He saw himself darkly in a burnished silver plate and saw that ink was on his face too. It lent him a diabolical look.

He stood up, slowly and in pain. His eyes dropped to his coat and shirt, and to his knees. His whole front was stained with grass, moss, mud. He smelt of fox shit – an unmistakeable, sharp stench.

The enormity of what he had witnessed rolled him like a wave. He could not speak her name. She – *the strange woman*. She had coupled with some demon. On Snowden Carr. On her own admission. He would have her now.

Fairfax summoned his wife. He gave her short instruction. Dorothy called for the servant:

'Master must have this sorted and quick. New parchment, more ink, trimmed quills, clean it all up, now. Freshen the rushes.'

A force-field of fury surrounded Fairfax. His wife was afraid.

'Edward, what ails you? Shall we take your clothes?'

'Whore!' he screamed, bent over and vomited on the rush strewn floor.

Dorothy stepped back, horrified at her husband's rudeness,

his address to her, in front of the servant, and his daughters present. She was terrified he had become afflicted like the girls. She suspected he too was now possessed. What if he should turn on her, denounce her?

'Not you, you fond thing,' he feigned affection. '*The strange woman* – she who entranced my daughters – that's who I bewhore.' He seethed as he muttered this, battling to take possession of his rage.

'Master's not himself.' Dorothy said, briskly. But then she wondered who in her household was these days. Was this all part of the spells, the possessions, the enchantment, the vile curses?

Edward burst out of the study, stomped down the stairs, out onto the yard and across to the barn. He looked north-west up to the church. A bell tolled. A small, solemn procession passed his vision. Another death. Smithson, dressed in his black cape, robe and habitual Canterbury cap, led the coffin, followed by the mourners.

'Traitor!' screamed Fairfax. 'Call yourself a man of God? You stupid, ignorant sod. You odious, godly bastard, you, you …'

His words faded and fell to ground, just north of the river. Smithson and the mourners didn't break their sombre, stately stride.

13

The Chatelaine

She watched him from the upstairs casement. He brimmed with intent and the potent rage of his own righteousness. She watched him storm across the yard towards the barn. She saw him look up north west to the church, his body tensed in fury. He cupped his hands to his mouth. Would he vomit again? No. He was writhing, stooping and shouting. What he said she could not tell. He made a clenched fist and shook it. What could he see? Who or what was he bellowing at? What sort of man had he become, her husband?

Edward disappeared into the mistal, only to emerge beyond. Dorothy's eyes followed him again, as soon as he came into view. He walked briskly across the fields, up towards the church. He parted corn, trampling it down: he clambered walls as if they had been built for his own inconvenience. He walked with a halo of fury.

She had concern he had not taken up his jacket, for it was only May, but in the face of things she let the thought flit idly from the casement. Let him catch cold and die, if it be God's will. A blessed relief, she reflected. She supressed a smile. For her, certainly.

She noted beyond, on the higher ground of the churchyard, a burial, bowed heads, dark garments and a shroud of solemnity, broken only by the furze of bluebells. She was far too distant to hear the earth soft sprinkled on the wool-wound corpse. She could only make out Smithson, because of his distinctive cap. Edward could not have been shouting at the mourners. Could he? At the corpse? Unseemly. At Smithson? Most likely. She sighed heavily. Did she once fancy she loved this man, this thing?

Her eyes caught up with him. She saw him intercept a man about his labours. It was Henry Graver, struggling with a well-ricked ewe. Her husband offered him no help but took him brusquely, roughly by the arm and pull him along with him. He seemed to apprehend their neighbour.

Dorothy watched this pair, one crazed with intent, one reluctant. They disappeared into the church porch, and then she lost the sight of them.

Dorothy lingered in her husband's study. She rested her forehead on a small cold violet-tinted glass pane held in a diamond came of lead. She was aware of the activity around her. The servant and daughters Helen and Elizabeth were working to right the mess and sort her husband's desk. They spoke to each other in subdued tones, clearly shaken. Not one of them durst break her thoughts. She kept her place by the casement, her back towards them. She fingered the wooden frame.

He'd called her whore. He then bethought himself; he changed his mind. Who was the whore? Smithson must be involved. She knew the two men continued sore divided over this witching business. Smithson's stand had greatly provoked her husband's wrath. Edward had hoped for better.

Dorothy tried to banish the coagulating fear from her mind, again. It followed her like a familiar. It lay in waiting in the recesses of the great chamber. It lingered on the cold, worn stone stairs. It forced itself upon her upon her in her bed.

She feared her husband had gone mad.

And at what point, she wondered, at what point might she be absolved from her vow of obedience? She had promised to love, but love had evaporated like the ground mists that clung to the waters of the Washburn – that teased and told of a clear day, and soon burnt off. Long ago she had ceased to love him. She had promised to honour. That one was easier, lip service. She remembered his birthdays, humoured him, kept him fed and clean. In sickness and in health. Yes, she had done all of that.

What's more, she managed the corn mill, kept the accounts, chased the debtors, ran his household, bore his children and bit her tongue. Got up, shook herself, and did it all over again. Certainly, he ran the farm, dealt with drainers, but to spend the greatest share of his waking moments, listening to their dim daughter, dull Helen, prattling on and on, and scribing her preposterous tales of misadventure. Lord give me patience, she thought. And then the young one, bright Lizzy, had gone down too.

But to obey? That had already cost her dear. She summoned Susannah in her mind.

'Mistress come see here. A thing of wonder…'

'What on this earth is it Elizabeth?'

'A thing most strange. A rarity.'

Elizabeth Smith, the servant, was pointing at the parchment. Dorothy knew that Elizabeth could not read. She knew no lurid confidences would be revealed.

'I swear it is a corbie – a perfect corbie's head made by the spill – and look below, a claw. A wonder, is it not?' Dorothy saw Elizabeth wore a vacuous grin of fascination.

'She's right, I see these creatures all the time. I see the corbie's eye. It follows me. The corbies fill my head,' said daughter Eliza. 'Sometimes their cruel cawings score my mind. They fly betwixt, from ear to ear – a portent of doom!'

Dorothy shook her head in exasperation.

'But Mother, they are both right. I see the bird too. It's horrible – crow and crow claw. Err. Are they coming for us again, sister?' asked Helen.

'No such things,' barked Dorothy. 'Corbies, claws. portents of doom, my arse. I hadn't you down as a fanciful, Elizabeth. I thought you had more sense. As for you Helen, we all know about you and your visions. But I thought you were over these. Elizabeth Smith, you must not encourage either of them.'

Both girls had started to sob and tremble.

'Now look what you've done. You've set them both off. God preserve us. Why don't you go over to John Jaffray's house and see what havoc you can start there? Must I always dwell amongst idiots, imbeciles and mad folk? Two daughters and a servant, and each as loopy as a wolf!'

Dorothy took up the parchment and screwed it into a ball.

'Don't do that. It's new evidence,' said Eliza, her hands clasped over her mouth in shock.

'Hush your tongue, child. And no word to your father or I'll swing for the both of you girls. You too Elizabeth, not a word to the master. He has already too much on his mind, and most of it is thanks to you, and your demon drivel, Helen. I'm out of patience with you all, and him and this very household.'

'Father should see it; he'll be cross you are destroying it, Mother.'

'Shut up Helen. He won't be cross because you will keep your thin lips corked. The three of you will finish off here. Truly, I have had enough. This household would try the patience of a swarm of saints. I shall try to compose myself. I'm going down to the corn mill to check the ledgers. I advise you – I will not brook interruption. And remember the rushes. Change the rushes. Burn these; they stink of his sick. This I find distasteful, even if you three do not.' Green sick, she reflected. What had he been eating? Where had he been last night?

Dorothy left them to linger in silence and shock. She swept

down the stairs, called into the kitchen, then strode across the yard, taking a different route to the one her husband had chosen. She followed the path by the river south east. But she did not go to the mill. On this rare occasion she took time off. She needed to dwell in her own thoughts awhile.

The black crow image on the parchment had seared itself upon her mind; she could not deny the remarkable likeness. She had taken up the parchment and cast it on the fire in the kitchen grate. She stood and watched the crow's head curl to ashes, the eye the last to go. How had the fire resisted that odious eye?

By the bank, she turned her head and looked back to Newhall. She now hated this house. Nigh on four years she had dwelt here. This valley, this spot, such a pleasant place, seemingly benign on first acquaintance, felt so dark, damp and dire.

Newhall was jostled by the surrounding hills; Dorothy could swear they were coming closer. It was throttled by trees, a tangle of leaves, branches, vines, ivies, hollies and brambles. It sat at the nadir of the valley. There was no aspect from the front of the house. The house was served by no road. It could be reached on foot, for there were pretty primrose paths. Some of the foot paths were blind, and expected guests failed to arrive, on time, or ever appear at all. A rider on horseback might pick the way through, but a cart posed challenges for these paths were narrow. Moving in had been a caper indeed, she recalled. Its isolation, appealing to her husband, had made her sad. She often wondered what the state of mind had been of the person who commissioned such a building in such a spot.

Many was the night she dreamed of trailing tendrils taking her breath; she gagged on the inescapable greenness.

Perhaps the absence of sunlight and the layered lowering of generations of spirits had contributed to the gloom that hung about the house on the brightest of days. For whatever reason, bad luck permeated every crack in Newhall. Dismay settled like dust – impossible to dispel with a flick of a cloth.

Had she brought this on them all, Dorothy wondered? She had been a dutiful wife – willingly, once. But, it's true, she had not wanted to come here. Occasionally, before they moved in four years ago, they had had brief periods in residence. She hadn't taken against the place in those earlier times, but when Edward said this was to be their permanent home, she had been unaccountably disturbed, distressed even. She could not tell him why, for she didn't know herself. It was as if she had a premonition, at least a feel, for the troubles to come.

The family had also spent a brief time at nearby Scow Hall, in Ferdinando Fairfax's absence. That had been a sweet time. She smiled as she remembered the kitchen, with the great slow semi-circle of a stone, inglenook fireplace, the whole wall's width. She'd nurtured the garden to the front, south east facing also, yet always warm. She'd planted herbs and lavender and the plants had thrived. The back of the house nestled under the hill and was saved from the westerlies. Scow had a good atmosphere – her memories were filled with the children's laughter. No tales there of possession, demons and visitations. She might have been happy there.

But Newhall, she believed, had some elusive quality, something like a presence, if not sinister, certainly not benign. It was as if the house itself mocked her. It felt as if it was seeing how far it could push and prod her before she snapped and cracked.

There could have been a life at court. Her husband's poetry had won admiration at the highest levels. Why, the king himself loved Edward's work. His translation of Torquato Tasso's *Jerusalem Delivered* was deemed better than the original. It was regarded as art on its own merit, something beyond a translation.

She'd watched her husband immerse himself in his subject – the first crusade by Christian knights against the Muslims, during the siege of Jerusalem. He'd lived and breathed it. Had he carried the battle on in his head, she wondered? Had he transferred the crusade to this valley and taken the local women for the foes? Why should he do such a thing, unless he was not well in his head? This was what she feared. Was this place Jerusalem doomed, not delivered, she wondered?

What had happened? Was it not in the South that their troubles had started? There had been issues, rivalries, jealousies. He had not seemed himself down there.

She remembered his clever friends, so witty and worldly. He seemed to change. These men had been dabbling in their youth. He had dabbled too. She knew they had taken things together at first, to give themselves ideas, he had said, inspiration. There was some talk about Discorides and his *Materia Medica*, she recalled, an ancient text. She'd listened to them by the door. Substances to make you sleep, help pain, and more. Potions to let you see things, imagine things, visit places you had not been. Then he continued to take them alone, locked in his study. He'd called them his herbals. A jar of green ointment he kept locked beneath his oak writing slope. Once, in an unguarded moment, he said the stuff released his muse.

Well as far as Dorothy could see, his muse had long left home. Her husband could have written more poetry, surely? He could have taught the sons of the wealthy, and not just the sons of the Fairfax family. But no, he would not take up a place at Court. They could have lived in the capital. It would have afforded such better opportunities for the children, and for himself, for he was revered by the best minds, the intellectuals, the academics, poets, men of literature. True, Ben Jonson had been rude about Edward, but then the playwright left few of his fellow writers with their reputations intact. But many said that as a poet her husband was superior to Edmund Spenser. High praise indeed. She smiled wistfully at the pride she had once taken in his achievements, and her joy at being chosen by such a man.

Oh yes, she could have had fine gowns and jewels. Her daughters could have been well-bedecked, painted and portrayed to advantage. They might have secured wealthy suitors. A talented artist could have made something of Helen's face, possibly? But it was not to be.

Dorothy's thoughts rushed on – what made her husband hide himself in this infernal, vernal hell? And sweet Anne their baby daughter – dead. Their sons sent off for education, when they could hardly afford it. Two of their three remaining daughters had been possessed, by something, at least. Many of their neighbours ostracised them, the Smithson sons took steps to dodge out of their way on the lanes. And Susannah ...

Dorothy's thoughts thronged further. Forget London, for now she'd settle for Leeds. She might well prefer it, for they had spent their early years of marriage there. Leeds was a place that would present less temptation and risk. She did not really need the Court. Indeed, she'd happily slip into a life back in Leeds. But no, that was not to be either.

Edward had become increasingly solitary, disturbed, obsessed with hunting witches, naming them and pointing the finger of shame. He had become possessed by lurid notions. Now he was engaged in a battle that could only be resolved by death.

What curse had descended on their household? She had no-one to turn to. If only she durst approach her erstwhile friend Susannah ... But how should she ever dare approach Susannah again?

Dorothy thought of the women, the seven accused by him, and felt a sharp stab of shame, and yet it was a shame she could hardly bear to acknowledge to herself. Helen, that dull, plain lumpen daughter of hers had turned her father's head with her dreams, her visions, her accusations and visitations. Elizabeth had similarly succumbed. Now her husband? And where had he been the night before, coming home smelling of fox shit and covered in mud, his eyes wild and his best jacket snagged and shredded. Throwing up green puke. What the hell was going on here?

Her thoughts clung on to Susannah. Oh, the hopes she'd entertained for Susannah Smithson. If ever she had needed a friend, it was now, and it was her – Susannah. 'A sister-in-waiting,' said Susannah. 'Count on me,' she'd said. So very sensible. Susannah was bright and balanced, mother of four fine sons. Edward took against her on the instant. He went on to discourage their friendship, frowned on their growing familiarity.

'She wields the whip. It is not seemly in a wife,' growled Edward.

It was true, Susannah had an independent mind. But her boys revered her, that was quite clear, and her husband Nicholas hung off her every word. She was his rock.

And then the chill set and smiles were tightened.

There had been a falling out.

It started with familiars. Edward had declared the crows that Margaret Hall fed from her palm were familiars. Helen had told him this. Helen had also informed her father that Margaret had a spirit in the likeness of a white cat which she had kept for twenty years. For some reason unknown to Dorothy, Margaret was referred to, by both her husband and Helen, as *the individuum*, or *the strange woman* and never by name although they both knew it well.

Dorothy had challenged the 'familiars' notion. She had already discussed the subject with Susannah. Susannah had explained that she had given Margaret her cat four years ago, after Pegi had died. Susannah had thought that Fillie, the white kitten, would be company for Margaret. Susannah had presented Fillie out of kindness.

Susannah had explained that Margaret was born into that old tradition of caring, for people and for animals and birds. Pegi, Margaret's mother, had tamed the birds from the trees with seeds and suet. The birds had afforded her great pleasure and affection. Margaret too was often seen with a crow on her shoulder, or on her head. It had always been that way since she was a child. Dorothy had tried to put this case to Edward.

'Husband, she just likes to feed the birds by hand.'

'You fool. Can you not see the devil in his different guises?'

Susannah happened to be with Dorothy at the time and added:

'Come Mister Fairfax, those crows are no devils. Margaret has a way with all God's creatures. She has tamed the wildest and cared for many an injured thing.'

'Mistress Smithson, her power to do this is not natural; her intent is evil. She imposes her own will. She has no right to do this in the sight of God.'

'Her mother Pegi brought her up another way …'

'Witches both,' he snapped.

'I think you should be careful with such words. There are no such things.'

'No such things? Are you insane? Or are you a member of their coven, woman?' His face loomed towards Susannah. His expression was one of menace.

'Edward Fairfax, how dare you?' Susannah was mortified not only by this accusation but by his clear intention to intimidate her.

Fairfax continued regardless: 'You are obliged to listen to your husband I suppose?' He smirked. 'I would expect no less a heresy from him. I've heard about his actions over rush-bearing. He should have a care. He spoke out against the king. A foolish thing indeed.'

'I know my own mind. Neither me nor Nicholas believe in witches. As for Margaret and Pegi, God rest her soul, and Janet and Bess Foster – fine midwives they have been to all of us in this neighbourhood. Pegi brought each of my sons into the world. These are wise women. They have enquiring minds. They have tried their remedies and know what works. How can helping and healing be wrong? For the poor amongst us, where else can folk turn for help?

'White witches are the more dangerous – they still follow the devil under a different guise. Where do you think their power comes from, and all their special skills? These women have taken you in, that's for sure. They are seductive. This is what they do – how they win people over, and then corrupt their souls.'

'Because these women have the temerity to take on the Grim Reaper you condemn them?'

'I do. The poor should know by now, that all their miseries and their experiences in this life are fleeting and of no importance. Their rewards will come in the next. They should draw comfort from that. It is enough for the lowly. That's where our good Lord placed them.'

'Edward, I'm not sure…'

'Silence wife; hold your tongue.' Fairfax's voice was one of intensifying menace.

Susannah shot one look at Dorothy. She turned on her heels and returned to the vicarage. Susannah was a woman who would not conceal her displeasure. She did not suffer fools. Dorothy knew Susannah would treat Nicholas, her husband, to a blow on blow account of the interchange. She also knew that her closeness to Susannah was over, and her heart was heavy and sore.

That night Edward called her to his study. There Dorothy received her formal instruction not to entertain their neighbour again.

'You will bar the door against that woman.'

'But we have daughters. The Smithson boys would make fine husbands…'

'There will be no mingling of our blood with theirs. You will not see her as a friend, ever again. And any scheme you two might have been cooking up to unite Helen with one of the Smithson twins you will now abandon. Do you understand?'

'I fear Helen already will have deterred any suitor with her tales of possession, visions of vileness and her talking in tongues.

A fine dowry! Find me a young man in fifty miles of here who would take on such a wench. She's knocked her own chances on the head with a mallet without you laying down the law, husband.'

'Enough! And you watch your tongue. Susannah Smithson's plain-speaking habit has already turned your head. Gossips and scolds the lot of you. Have you joined this secret society of local women, this rebellion of peasant folk, this odious conspiracy of abortionists, healers, nurses and midwives, with their old wives' tales and their simples and spells. To hell with them all! And to hell with you if you go on down this path. You'll swing in York with them.'

'Husband! Have you forgotten yourself? And I will remind you, our Queen Elizabeth defended such women as these to collect their simples and work their cures for the poor.'

'King James does not. He knows a witch when he sees one, and so do I. I've said enough. You will forget her. You will obey me. Muter Libis wife! This book is shut. Now get you out this room.'

*****

Dorothy felt the warm sun on her face. She heard the ripple of the Washburn over the shale, rocks, stones and boulders. There were May blobs on the bank in full flower. Wild garlic bloomed in the damper gullies and crevices. Violets, birds' foot trefoil and bugle – a furze of violet, white and blue. She looked beyond to a thicket of silver birches and a carpet of bluebells. A hatch of flies, swallows dipping, curlews calling. A kingfisher flashed along the water. A gentle leaf-ruffling breeze.

A paradise marred by the seeping stain, a broadening blot. The mighty pen in the hands of a mad man, cutting down the innocent, plotting for them to swing. The fires of his fury fuelled by feeble-minded girls desperate only for his attention.

Yet still Dorothy felt the sting of humiliation at the words of her husband, as she remembered them, along with her too familiar fear about the state of his mind. He and his daughters had locked her out of this lunacy that was their present life. They had slammed the door. There was no place for her, nor would she have claimed one if she could.

She fingered the keys hanging from her girdle. Had she no eyes, she would know these keys through touch alone. That big rusty one for the corn mill, this slim one for the desk to secure sugar cakes, raisins and treats, the small yet sturdy one for the money chest and the substantial metal one for the house, Newhall, itself. How sweet, she thought, how sweet to lock her husband and her daughters in that house and cast the last key in the deepest river pool and see it sink. Or to watch it tumble over stones and rocks, taken by the surge. Or hurl it high in the air, to be caught by a magpie and carried off. How well it would be to be rid of them. And how she would love to walk with sweet Susannah through the wildflower meadow and laugh and talk as once they had, arm in arm, heads together.

Dorothy turned back towards Newhall with a tightening clamp around her heart. The wind had risen, changing direction. It was coming down from the North. A chill creeped under her shawl and held her heart in its grasp. The rushes rattled along the River Washburn. The bluebells bowed their sweet arching heads as she passed.

She looked up at the house, square in front of her. Her attention was caught by a lone yet insistent buzzing. She spied the bulge and stain of a dormant wasps' nest tucked up under the eaves. The buzz distracted her but for a moment. A torpid insect wakened by the sun's early, capricious warmth. She wondered if she was to die in this green hell, and when? She wondered if she had already passed. She felt fear, and yet was quietly resigned. What did it all signify? And what did it matter?

They would be waiting for her, Edward, Helen and Elizabeth. Elizabeth would tell their father about the ink crow. Of this, Dorothy was certain.

14

The Strange Woman

'I tell you I saw and heard it all! With my own eyes, my ears, as God is my witness.'

Mister Smithson sighed. Henry Graver shook his head and sank down heavily onto the wooden bench. Henry was beginning to find this whole witch business tedious. He couldn't afford the time or cost of another trip to York, a third trip, not to mention the sheer discomfort. It played havoc with his cramps and gout, and he'd got the farm and the family to think about. His wife and his girls needed him home. He'd had enough.

But for the three, the church was empty. A cold place even on the warmest day. The corpse was barely in the ground before Edward Fairfax had burst in on the vicar, pulling Henry Graver along with him, by the arm. He'd found Henry in the fields, checking his stock. Henry Graver stood up again and took up his position, leaning heavily upon the altar, which was placed sideways in the sanctuary. His hands were filthy, and his shirt stained with mud. His wore an exasperated expression. He'd just pulled out a ewe tangled in some briars and needed to tend his own cuts and grazes.

The vicar lifted off his soft black cap and ran his fingers through his grey and wiry hair. He spoke in a firm yet kind voice: 'Edward, I beg this of you, it is time for you to let this matter rest. You must know this, for the sake of your own sanity and for your family. Bury it now.'

Henry burst forth: 'Twice you've dragged them there women to York. Let 'em be, for Christ's sake. Even the Justices found them innocent. Witches my arse. I've known most of 'em all me life. They are just women.'

'Henry, please, this is the house of God.' Although Mister Smithson's tone carried a mild reproach, he agreed with Henry's sentiments. The vicar spoke calmly:

'Let's go through your latest testimony, Edward. Let us think how it will sound to right-thinking people. How will it sound to the Justices? You are implying that Margaret Hall ....'

'Don't dare speak that vile woman's name in church. She is a monster of depravity!' Edward's voice was high in register, almost a screech.

'Edward, please be calm. How shall I call her?'

'*The strange woman* – that's what my poor girls call her.'

'I will not, for shame. Margaret is one of my parishioners.'

'She's a witch, a whore and she's a consorter with demons. I didn't catch his name. Let's call him 'the man in black'. He's been at her.'

Mr Smithson looked away, perplexed, anxious, troubled. He rubbed his neck.

'She said she flew with him, in her skin.'

'Lucky him!' Henry licked his lips. He'd paid for the pleasure, one night, a few years back. What he'd trade now for another.

'Henry, please, this is not helpful.' Mr Smithson had recovered his composure, but he was looking unusually pink. He continued:

'Bear with me Edward. Consider this. How will people look on you when you tell them that on the night the women chose to celebrate their safe return to the valley, their deliverance from death, you, their very accuser, was drawn to spy on them. Clearly you anticipated or knew there would be celebrations. They had been spared a hanging. But no, you could not rest. You left your home with the very intent to ferret. What do you think folk will think of you?'

'Aye, Mister Smithson's right, Edward. What was you doing lurking at night on the far bank of Timble Gill, watching them women? Don't look good Edward. You a Peeping Tom indeed. And sure, they would be celebrating. They'd got off, and it being Beltane. A double reason for a feast.'

The vicar turned on Henry: 'Our parishioners do not celebrate Beltane, Henry. No pagan rites and rituals here.'

But Edward was driven beside himself with exasperation:

'She carries a demon's child! She's sold herself to save those women.'

'On your say so. We don't know.'

'Henry's right. We don't know the father of the bairn. But careful there, Edward, for are you not a natural son yourself? Some would lay the charge of hypocrisy at your door.'

'It's you who should take care, vicar. Don't you dare dip there. My father was a great and powerful man. Do not cast aspersions against my siring or you'll be the one who's boots are dancing in York, and your quaint cap nodding along. Be warned. Vicar or not, I'll have you.'

'You'll do no such thing. I fear you've lost your mind, Edward Fairfax. Our vicar speaks the truth; you cannot threaten him for that. And you can't deny for all your wealth, long poems and learning, you're hedge-born. In short, you are a bastard.'

'You dare to …'

'Henry, please, this will not help resolve this matter. Edward, we merely try to warn you how you will be regarded by others. After all this is over, you will have to learn to live with your good neighbours. I will be frank – they are already well out of patience with you. Has it ever occurred to you these women might be innocent?'

'Innocent! And good neighbours my arse! And whose child is it then?' screamed Edward.

'She will not say, nor need she. Let her well alone.' Mr Smithson delivered this with a such a level of vehemence that Henry shot him a glance.

'Man in black?' Henry wondered, but said nothing, raised an eyebrow and smirked to himself. Fair play to old Nick Smithson, he thought. Susannah Smithson would have his guts for girdle ribbons if she ever suspected.

Edward seethed: 'I see I will get nowhere here. You are either ignorant, or under her spell, enchanted, the both of you. Who can tell which? Be assured I will take this to a higher authority than you, Smithson.'

The vicar and Henry watched Edward walk towards the door, half open. Dappled sunlight was flickering in from the porch. He stopped and turned abruptly:

'She cursed me and mine. You understand that? You understand what it means, a witch's curse? She cursed Newhall. She said that fire would take my grave and the Washburn waters take my home.' By this point Fairfax's voice had become a croak.

Mister Smithson and Henry Graver shook their heads slowly, exasperation tinged with resignation.

Edward turned back to the door. He turned once more, looking back to them, but saw them not:

'He'll be back for her. Know you that. Four hundred years on, and the demon will be back. And I'll be there.'

Mister Smithson and Henry Graver sighed, both bewildered at the state of Fairfax's mind.

'Ah, well happen we'll miss that spectacle, Mister Fairfax, and so might you. Don't be getting your hopes up now.'

'Melancholy? A terrible affliction,' sighed the vicar.

Edward slammed the heavy, iron studded, ancient oak door.

The church felt colder. Colder still. The three would never speak together on these matters again.

*****

Edward Fairfax returned to Newhall, entered his study, and took up his quill once more. As he started to write, he was determined to complete the record and in vivid detail. He wanted to add this latest episode to the history of the events that began with his daughter Helen's first fit on Sunday, 28th October 1621, when William, his son, had found her, that evening, in deadly trance by the hearth in the parlour at Newhall.

Fast forward. Visions of the celebratory feast in Timble Gill pulsed through his head. A powerful finale; grounds indeed for a third trial. Surely? He had been right about *the strange woman* all along.

Fairfax wrote without interruption. When he had finished, he sat in silence for a while, an hour at least, the time spent in deep thought. What was he to do?

The charge of voyeurism had stung him. The distaste etched so clearly on the faces of Smithson and Henry Graver haunted him. He feared that his diligent surveillance, what they saw as snooping, might reflect badly upon himself. Graver had named him 'Peeping Tom'. This cast him in a poor light and might undermine his whole testimony. His daughter's testimony, both daughters in truth, he corrected himself. Should this come to pass, it would be beyond endurance, far worse than even the second dismissal of the case.

Fairfax was reaching his conclusion. True, he had felt cleansed for committing what he had witnessed to these pages. But …

Stiffly he stood, straightened his body and descended the stairs. He carried the latest sheaves of parchment, hesitated, hung onto the newel post on the turn of the staircase and then descended with greater purpose. He cast the barely dried parchments onto the kitchen fire.

He watched the sheets collapse and crumple in on themselves. He saw the odd word squirm and capitulate to the flames. Like so many martyrs were his written words. This act was sacrifice. It pained him. He felt it as keenly as burning a baby. Then, he felt a lifting, a release, relief almost.

'Mother cast the crow in the fire, too!' said Elizabeth. She was watching him from the kitchen doorway. Out it all came, the gabbled account by a garrulous eight-year old.

Dorothy was called to his study and was asked to explain why she had chosen to destroy the ink crow. She remained silent but gazed at him as she might stare at a stranger whose face, she thought, she could almost place.

Dorothy felt the dismal spiral of her existence coiling lower and lower. Was there to be a nadir, or just further slippings and sinkings? Misery infinite?

*****

The burning of the final chapter is the reason why Fairfax's account broke off at the end of the entry for 11ᵗʰ April 1623. The abrupt ending was noted in 1882, by William Grainge, the Harrogate antiquarian and author. It was Grainge who wrote the Biographical Introduction and 'Notes Topographical and Illustrative' for the *Daemonologia*, when it was eventually published. He remarked that it was as if some portion of the work had been lost, or the tale had not been fully told. Both were true.

Edward Fairfax would never forgive the Justices at York. The judge had told the jury the evidence presented did not reach the statute. He dismissed the accused and gave the women back their liberty. But Fairfax himself would never be free.

When Edward Fairfax was satisfied with the final draft of his *Daemonologia: A Discourse on Witchcraft*, it enjoyed private circulation only, and to a largely hostile reception. Ridicule and incredulity will reverberate through four centuries.

Fairfax lived on for twelve years. In the long, cold, damp months, the flickering lights and shadows from the fires in the hearth set demons dancing on the walls of Newhall. In the short, midge-plagued, sweaty summers, Fairfax heard bones crunch and babies squeal, beneath the part-dried rushes.

The worst time for Fairfax was always late October, that period running up to All Saints and All Souls, and the start of the beginning of the Celtic winter. It linked in his mind with the anniversary of Helen's first fit.

The eve of Samhain, October 31st, summer's end, was the time that the souls of the dead were permitted to return to their earthly homes and haunt those who had inflicted harm on them in life. For Fairfax, a living ghost came along with them too, for still *the strange woman* lived in her hovel beneath Snowden Craggs, and still she haunted his mind. He couldn't keep her out.

Through the flickering flame-forged dancing demons, she wove her way, softly. Her eyes accusatory, but a newer quality, triumph, shone forth.

'Begone!' he held his temples and snarled: 'Is it not enough you won, that you still breathe and feel the warmth of the sun? Begone, you whore!'

'I shan't be gone for centuries to come.' She taunted with her laughter, blew a kiss and yet, she beckoned.

He would still have her. In his mind, he tracked her, intent on revenge. He slipped back to the earlier days at Newhall, reliving that doomed day, the 28th day of October, in the year of our Lord, 1621.

15

The White Devil

A rape! A rape! ... Yes, you have ravish'd justice

The White Devil (3.2.278) – John Webster 1612

*

Her breasts were naked for the day was hot.
Her locks unbound waved in the wanton wind;
Some deal she sweat tired with the game you wot.
Her sweat-drops bright, white, round, like pearls of Inde;
Her humid eyes a firey smile forthshot
That like sunbeams in silver fountains shined,
O'er him her looks she hung and her soft breast
The pillow was, where he and love took rest.

Godfrey of Bulloigne, or the Recoverie of Jerusalem
Edward Fairfax's translation of Torquato Tasso's
Gerusalemme conquistata 1600

Newhall, 28th October in the year 1621 A.D.

Edward Fairfax was struggling to shake off gloom, grief and despair, the legacy of his little daughter's death. He felt his breast was torn in shreds. Barely four months old she was – baptised in June and buried on the 9th of October. He had lost other children, but Anne? Gone. The brightest and the best.

In the two weeks since baby Anne's death, Fairfax and his wife had barely spoken. Their sorrows and grief they could not share.

He needed to lose himself, to write again. He longed to return to the rush of ideas, the surge of fancy, the ferment and the flow. Was it too soon to shrug off the cloak of gloom, too soon to shake his feathers, preen and flex his wings?

Fairfax prepared his desk to write. The parchment on the pad, the sharpened quills, the ink well brimming. All he lacked was inspiration.

All? The tumultuous surge of creativity had stemmed since Tasso. His juices had caked along the surface of his brain, his muse shrivelled to a withered crone.

Had his genius grown and shown too soon, blown like a flower? Had it burned far too brightly, too early? Was he a mere shooting star, so swiftly spent, to fade and die in a constellation of ever brighter bodies? He likened himself to the nightingale who dies of shame if another bird sings better. Like this bird, he believed he was languishing and pining away in anguish of the spirit. Was he but a translator, clinging onto to the tail – at best, barely able to ride on the back of the true poet – Tasso. Was his writing merely an exquisite echo? And so soon to be forgotten?

More dark torments coursed through his mind. These thoughts were of a different nature. He had long entertained a fear for his health. He had contracted the Clap in his younger days. He cursed that unlucky alignment of his own sexual activities and proclivities with the alignment of the stars.

Fairfax had prided himself on being so careful. He and his friends, fellow writers and drinking companions, knew about these things, the perils and protections. Had he not practised hard pissing in the whorehouse, for the flushing out of those harmful bodily fluids, after the act. He had even procured a soft yet tight leather sheath to hold that which he fondly termed his sword. He secured it for the sole purpose of protection, for visiting the stews, but he had found this cumbersome barrier less than satisfying. He couldn't swear he'd always used it. It also caused the whores to mock him. Their ribaldry irked him: puns on stewing in his own juice. He'd left it somewhere, but he knew not where.

On the first appearance of the pox sores, the younger Fairfax had been rubbed with mercury, even his genitals, and, on more than one occasion, sat in the steam barrel. He'd downed mercury solutions too. Earlier in his marriage he had gone to the trouble to secure for Dorothy *The English Housewife* for the management of their home. Furtively he'd noted down the salve for French Pox. He now knew the cure by heart. His choice, his favourite for the ease and convenience of securing the ingredients, went along the lines: *take thee of capon's grease that have touched no water, juice of rue, fine pepper powder and mix to a paste. Apply around the sores with generosity, but let it come not into each sore.* The remedy promised, in time, to dry them up.

This chosen and oft applied paste might have dried up the ulcers, and then the pussy lesions that inevitably followed them, and the mercury might have helped reduce the groin swelling, but what about the restoration of the balance of his body's humours? He needed something more to push away the darkening.

Fairfax felt that he had been so unlucky, for one who had tried to balance risks with precautions and cures. And yet, so many risks he'd taken in his wilder, later youth, believing himself to be above and beyond retribution. Had the piper now named the price – the enduring cost of his promiscuity? This would be a price too steep to pay, the loss of his beloved muse.

His *Jerusalem Delivered* readers had expected so much. He had failed them and fled. It was not shame alone that made him bolt. As well as admiration, his work had sparked envy, rivalry, hatred, rumour. There were detractors, and those who ridiculed his work. A blow with a word strikes deeper than the sword, he reflected, and he bore the scars of calumny, bitter jest and satire.

The price of fame. The flame went cold. He retreated north to Fuystone in the county of York. He chose this spot, the lowest in the valley, a house hid from any highway, to hide from them all, and to escape from himself.

And yet he longed to fly again. He would find his muse. This very morning, he would call to her, seek her out and coax her back to him. Surely, she would show herself.

Furtively, Fairfax turned the key in his study door lock. He lifted the carved oak box onto his desk. He retrieved a small silver key dangling from a thong around his neck, unlocked the space beneath the writing slope and took out the jar. He stared for some moments, musing, his head tilted to one side. A beam of sunlight fell across the jar. It seemed to radiate a deep warmth, a promise. He took this as a sign, an omen.

The livid substance contained therein was no cure. The green ointment, the precious unguent, was his sole inspiration. This had unleashed his muse. In case of discovery, he had labelled the jar: *Leg Balm*. A subterfuge – a sly nod to its properties and propensities, for it gave him wings.

Fairfax feared that Dorothy might find it, or even Elizabeth the servant. He mis-labelled it and congratulated himself on his cunning. He had, at certain times of year, been prone to rashes and irritation on his shins. But who would see this jar? And if they did, who would suspect? Nonetheless he kept it locked away.

Fairfax prepared himself for application. He began to remove his clothing. Suddenly a wild clamour at the door. Bangs and calls from servant and son. A tup, ready to be put to the ewe flock, had leapt a hurdle in the mistal and was now amongst his own progeny, his gimmers. The hands needed help. Fairfax dressed rapidly and ran to intervene.

Later, on his return to the study, he froze, paralysed with horror. It was as if he had been punched in the chest. His breath eluded him. His daughter Helen was bent over at his desk, her foot lifted, perched upon his desk chair. Her petticoats were up above her bare knees. He saw she massaged the ointment along her shins and thighs.

Generally pallid, his countenance had been rendered pink from the exertion of the tup chase and ensuing struggle with the beast. Now all colour drained from his face. He took three paces, then:

'Helen, what in God's name,' he croaked: 'What are you doing? What have you done?'

'My shins were so itchy. I've scratched and scratched and made them bleed. I thought I'd try this stuff of yours. I saw it sitting here. See I can read the label!'

'Dear God, no, no.' His voice was one of choked back panic. 'Go, now, and wash yourself. Go to the river and bathe your legs. Go. Do this immediately.' His voice was hushed, fearful and urgent.

He bethought himself and called her back: 'Not a word of this to your mother. To anyone. Understand? Now go.'

'But Pa, the river's cold. The water's deep with rain, and fast in flow.' Helen was shivering with fear. She keenly sensed both her father's alarm and displeasure.

'Enough! Now take yourself down to the river; go! Bathe yourself and well.'

He should have known, he oft reflected, that she would not venture in – just splash a little water on.

Fairfax saw her application had not been sparing. Inadvisably liberal. His precious green unguent was sorely depleted.

He feared for his daughter, true. He had no way of telling what … But, more than this, he feared for himself too, for without this potion he would sink to mediocrity. How could he replenish his ointment in this God forsaken place?

That afternoon he set about his quest. He made discrete enquiries amongst local folk. The best local herbalist? Did anyone dabble a little, in potions, cures …?

All fingers pointed to the wench who dwelled beneath Snowden Craggs, one called Margaret Hall.

Later that afternoon, he took his near emptied jar along with some gold coins and placed them in his pouch. He crossed the river, paced his way with purpose past Swinsty Hall, and then up over the fields. He touched only on the edge of Timble, and took the way down Lady Lane, over Dick's Beck Bridge, and clambered up the Carr.

The jutting rocky outcrops towered and loomed above him. A dark and northerly aspect, even on the fairest day. A rough hovel indeed, he thought. He had surprised her. He saw she was afraid. This pleased him. He had her at a disadvantage. He told her what he wanted, showed her the remains in the jar. She took the jar from him and held it close to her nose. She inhaled, took her time. Her brow clouded, frown furrowed further, eyes narrowed. She repeated the inhalation, deep in thought. Her eyes avoided his.

He told her what he believed it contained but confessed that he did not know the quantities.

'What you ask, I will not do.' Her voice was calm yet emphatic.

'What? Why ever not? I will pay you well.' He started to count out his coins.

'Why do you want stuff such as this?' She spoke with marked distaste.

'This stuff, as you call it, is the key to poesy. The casement pushed wide. Imagine this, woman – to stride the surf of an un-swum sea, to catch a comet's tail and fly the bridge of the firmament and to not look back. Such things it brings to me, or takes me there, for though my mortal body will not stir, my mind will roam wherever; where ...'

'Please place your money back and take this, Sir, take it away from me.' She held out the jar, her face etched with distaste.

'No, wench, you seem not to grasp the fact. This is not a choice I'm offering to you. You will do it. You will, or you will have good reasons not to do as I instruct.' His anger was rising. He seemed to grow in stature. She held her ground. His face loomed big into hers.

'Perhaps I can prepare a lighter potion?' She kept her voice low and calm. She would not show her terror. 'There are less poisonous, dangerous ways to fly. Take mugwort, wormwood and thyme. These plants infused in oil for three moon cycles, then strained ...'

'Foolish woman. Some light titillation? Your stuff won't take me to the unknown shores; it won't let me fold the firmament around my head. I'd barely make the Humber estuary with that. Pathetic, silly potions.' His laugh was sinister, jeering, sneering.

'Sir, I know this potion that you seek. I know what it is. This is the flying potion: seeds of henbane, belladonna, grated mandrake root, monkshood, water hemlock and, and ....'

She broke off, shuddered, then collected her thoughts: 'Each of these, alone, can make a man mad, each can kill, if wrongly taken. If the balance of the mix is wrong, the effects can be most terrible.'

'You have these plants?'

'No.'

'But you could get them?'

She nodded, swallowed hard, then shook her head emphatically: 'Seeing things that are not there, hallucinations, they call them, feelings of reckless flight. Elation and wonderment soon to be replaced by phantasms and horror. These things will turn your head to madness, reduce you to babbling, delirium, trance, and death, a screaming death, a true hell.'

She added: 'I would not give my enemy this stuff.'

'You'll make me your enemy if you don't; do not do this lightly. I warn you.'

She continued in a soft, reasoning voice, trying to divert him from his purpose: 'A little of each plant, alone and well placed, and mixed, in a base such as bilberry, perhaps. In the hands of a skilled person, only. A little can arouse the senses and desire. A pinch for pain alleviation. Perhaps a little more. But this, never. I'll not do this.'

'You have some reason you are not telling me. I see you choose to keep something back.'

'Sir, I try to cure, not to condemn. I will not harm. I will not hurt a living creature or abuse a dead one. And I will not plunder a corpse.'

There was a prolonged silence.

'What is it you are saying, woman? You are one who babbles.'

'The base of your potion must be the blubber from a baby's cheek. It is the fat from the body of a murdered, unbaptised infant. That's what you ask me for. Now get you gone. I am no witch.'

'Witch you are indeed. Your sensibilities are mere quibbles. You have access to such material. You and your friends, your gossips, scolds, wet nurses and midwives. Don't tell me you don't murder bairns.'

She had started to cry. She was horrified, mortified and sorely afraid for her own safety.

A sudden shift. He raised his arm and caressed her neck with his hand. His voice softened to a sinister wheedling: 'Please, take me to the walls of Jerusalem again; this you can do for me. You can fly with me. I'll fuck you further than the firmament. We'd both like that. You know you would.'

'How can you suggest such a thing, such a travesty, with your own wee bairn, Anne, so recently buried? Have you no heart, no feeling as a father?'

'Whore! Shut your mouth. Don't dare mention my dead daughter's name. You are not fit.'

'Please get you gone. Get you back to your wife. Now! I shall have none of your money. Go.'

She had not seen it coming. She felt the sand shift, sudden, in her head; she dropped to her cot. She tasted the blood in the back of her nose. Her eyes had closed with tears and more blood.

His furious face loomed into hers: 'I'll have you. You may be sure of this. I'll have you, and your friends, your crones. I'll have you swing, the lot of you. It will be my pleasure.'

'I'll tell on you.' Her voice was barely audible. Her vision was closing.

'A witch against a Fairfax? Sure! Blab all you want you slut.'

'My name is Margaret Hall,' she whispered, for she was fading fast into oblivion.

'You?' he sneered, 'you have no name at all. Enjoy your scruples. Taste your fear. This time next year, you won't be here.' He was now addressing an unconscious woman.

'I will call you *the strange woman* but first, here is a taste of it means to refuse me.'

*****

Fairfax fled the hovel, and descended the bank, adjusting his clothes, and smoothing his stringy flaxen hair as he set off down towards Timble Gill. Where Lady Lane crossed the beck he stopped, sat on a low stone and cupped his palms into the water. First, he swilled and swished to get the taste of her out of his mouth. He spat back into the beck. Then he washed the blood and other substances from his hands. He then relieved himself hard and washed those parts, fearing for further infection.

How he hated her. How he hated them all, these carriers of contagion. Whores and painted strumpets, women of the night, wet nurses, even the wife … plucked roses, eaten from within by worms. Was it not mortal women that had driven away his muse?

The fairer sex? He scoffed at the very conceit. Yes, a woman's body was a breeding ground for disease. They lured, they snared, then sucked the life-force from a man. Their brains were in their boxes. Pot-boiling witches and pox carrying bitches all.

*****

This would not be his only visit to Margaret's hovel. Desire has no rest; there is no respite. He returned, and on a regular basis, until the July of the following year, always with the intention of persuading *the strange woman* to make up the flying potion. That's how he justified these repeated visits, and his behaviour to the woman, to his conscience. It was how he soothed and settled down the better part of his mind.

Margaret continued to refuse his commission. She tried to fight off his most unwelcome advances and his inevitable conquest. She took his threats to her friends and neighbours seriously. He repeatedly reminded her that he was a powerful, well-connected man, a pillar of local society. He was a Fairfax.

Occasionally, Fairfax tried to dampen his obsession with *the strange woman*. He'd taken holy thistle to calm his drive and yet he was mastered by an urge, an itch no hand could soothe. Was she not there for the covering? Each visit ended in the same way, with what became, for him, an almost ritualistic bathing and cleansing in the beck, and a cursing of all women. The more *the strange woman* disgusted him, the more he desired her.

Following this first encounter, Fairfax took the flagstone path to the north, leading to his home. By the time he crossed the Washburn River he was ready for his supper.

The clamour at Newhall reached him before he entered the door. His son was in the porch; he had been seeking him.

'William, what is it?'

'Thank God you are home, father. Helen's been taken ill. I found her lying by the fire deep in trance. We've carried her up. Mother is by her side. Helen is quite insensible and has been so for an hour, at least. I feel compelled to prepare you father, for I fear we might not recover her.'

'I will to her side, immediately.' He took the stairs two at a time.

Fairfax sat at his daughter's bedside. He took her hand. Remorse and fear tormented him. He could barely force his eyes to gaze upon her. Her moon countenance was ashen. She had already taken on the waxy look of the nearly dead. He struggled not to weep. What had he done? What had he, in his own arrogance and stupidity, inflicted upon his innocent child?

He was joined by Dorothy, and William, whilst Elizabeth hung back and watched intently from the doorway; nothing escaped Elizabeth. There was no comfort for any present.

'Anne, and now Helen,' sobbed Dorothy: 'It's more than a mother should have to bear.'

He scowled at his wife. How might she like to bear the load he carried, he thought, and he could find no words of comfort for her.

Helen lay inert.

After several hours her breathing gradually began to revive, her pulse thready, but there. Her breaths came stronger and then she spoke.

Helen astonished them. She claimed she had been at church in Leeds and that the Reverend Alexander Cooke, the acclaimed yet controversial vicar, was giving a sermon. She gave a fair account of his preaching, and the subject of the sermon, in which he had taken on the papists again.

Many such trances were to follow. But swiftly, Helen turned her attention to the demonic. She was beleaguered. She told of visitations by the devil, his demons, temptations, confrontations with witches, violent encounters, out of body experiences, and bizarre occurrences. She was goaded to destroy herself by knife, by rope and by water. She was even offered poison.

She chose Newhall and the valley for her battlefield. She described the local landscape in a new and terrifying way. She took lowly neighbours as her foes and tormentors and saw these women's pets as their familiars. She dealt with what she knew but transformed her daily life into a compelling narrative based on her perceived battle against evil.

Helen believed she was fighting off those who would possess her soul. Her weapons were her words, tricks, tests and even sticks and fists. Frequently, in trance, she physically attacked her assailants. Above all she fought with her faith.

Edward Fairfax was astonished. Something indeed had happened to his daughter. He rejoiced in her metamorphosis from dull and bulging caterpillar through the chrysalis of trance, to a creature testing her bright new wings for flight. How sweet to see such a slow mind thus transformed, a tied tongue loosened to eloquence, a vocabulary once limited rising to new heights of sophistication. A beautiful, virtuous, vegetable mind.

Through the state of trance, Helen's wit and powers of reason had transformed. Her character too, for she had become brave and bold, a young woman who would not even flinch in the face of the devil himself. And she was not insensible to her new-found powers. There was a confidence, a knowingness, perhaps even a slyness in her demeanour that she carried into her life outside of trance.

As Edward Fairfax spent long hours by his daughter's bedside in the early stages of her affliction, he came to a momentous decision. He would be her amanuensis, scribe and aide. Through this task he would bring his own creativity, his genius with words and all his wit to bear, and thus create a unique account of possession and witchery in the Washburn Valley. He would call it *Daemonologia*.

Fairfax had found his muse. The precious flying potion was

not to be wasted after all. He would travel with his child through this local hell. He would sing of her battles and triumph, for triumph she would, and so would he. She would lead him back to greatness. Together they would take on Satan himself, and his followers.

In the silence of Helen's chamber, in the first hours of the morning, whilst she was in an early trance, he sat alone beside her. With great solemnity he made this vow to her unconscious body:

'Sweet Helen, Muse, I will follow thee, where 'er you choose. You will restore my poetic soul. Make me lie besides you in these green pastures, lead me further besides the still waters of the Washburn. These are the places the witches abound; you will reveal them for what they are, and thus they will be known. Take my hand, child. Together we will walk through this valley of the shadow of death. We will fear no evil, for thou, my child, art righteous and have proved thyself so. How can I fear evil if thou art with me; thy rod and thy staff will defend us both. You will smite these witches and goad the demons. We will purge and purify this place, and we will dwell together in the house of the Lord, forever and ever, our world without end. Amen.'

Helen's possession would be his means of vengeance on *the strange woman* who wrecked his sleep for the very wanting of her. And her filthy coven of besoms, scolds, friends and neighbours. Helen, his virtuous, virgin daughter, would be their undoing.

Fairfax shared this scheme with no other person.

In the early days of Helen's illness, Dorothy Fairfax believed her child to be afflicted by a disease called 'the Mother', a peculiar female complaint believed by physicians to be an atrabilious humour, and treatable by the plant Motherwort. Her husband played along at first, for it suited his plan. Gradually, through his subtle persuasions, the idea of the daughter's possession became implanted. The family and servants became convinced.

Elizabeth watched. How she envied her sister's new role

within the family. Helen enjoyed such status as "the possessed daughter". Was it in sympathy or in envy that the younger child was drawn to imitation? Fairfax pondered this, for Elizabeth had applied no flying ointment, and yet her trances and fits became as compelling as Helen's, and her accounts equally as lively and as violent. She lived the role and grew within it. The sisters drew closer.

It was a gradual process, the taking in of a lie and transforming it to truth. The alchemy of the mind. Over the period of the possession Fairfax began to convince himself that both his daughters were genuinely possessed. His servant Elizabeth was entirely taken in, and William his son too. Only Dorothy stood apart. And if the girls were possessed, thought she, then so was her husband.

*****

Fairfax's mind deteriorated further, following the second trial. He became relentlessly reclusive, haunted, and out of step with his neighbours, and some say, with his own family. Certainly, with his wife, who maintained a sullen silence, for her own spirit had long fled the house. Dorothy was a husk.

Towards the end of his life, Fairfax took some consolation from the fact that Nicholas Smithson would not conduct his funeral, for the vicar died three years before he did.

Fairfax died at his desk, delusional and demented. He was buried at Fewston Church, on January 27th, 1635. It is said a fine marble monument was erected.

The monument, along with the church tower, was destroyed by fire in 1696. The poet's own home, Newhall, passed outside the Fairfax family to other owners, in 1716. In 1871 it was subject to a compulsory purchase order by Leeds Corporation and was demolished completely in 1900. The plot of Newhall, by the old course of the River Washburn, now lies beneath Swinsty Reservoir.

Fairfax's two daughters, Helen and Elizabeth, both recovered from their strange affliction. Helen was the first. Her father records on 19th of November 1622, following the second trial, and her resulting illness, and deafness of many weeks' duration, she returned to full health.

Helen retained no memory of her possession by the witches. Elizabeth's continuing trances amazed Helen and she wanted to know what was wrong with her young sister. After Christmas of that same year, 1622, the appearances and trances reduced for Elizabeth too. Fairfax had continued to record further details of Elizabeth's possession until 11th April 1623, at which point his account ends, abruptly.

William Grainge, Yorkshire antiquarian, poet, historian and publisher, gave details of the daughter's later lives:

> *"Of the daughters, the victims of the spell, Helen married a certain Christopher Yates in 1636, the year after Fairfax's death; the others persons of the name of Scarborough and Richardson, apparently obscure and rustic people; and it is observable as a sign of the female education of the period, that of these girls, the children of the translator of Tasso, one signs her name in the rudest fashion, and another affixes her mark to the parish register."*

(Biographical Introduction (to the Daemonologia); giving an Account of Edward Fairfax, his Ancestry, Family and Writings by William Grainge 1882.)

Fairfax had eagerly bestowed his full attention and credence to two of his daughters' tales of witches, apparitions, bizarre dreams and enchantment. He had given far less attention to their schooling.

Dorothy Fairfax was buried on the 24th January 1648. She outlived her husband by thirteen years, which was time enough to rekindle her friendship with Susannah Smithson, a later life relationship with so many tales to tell by the fireside, and so many reflections on their lives and the times in the valley. Susannah had been her sister in waiting.

Nicholas Smithson remained vicar of Fewston Church until his death in 1632, aged sixty-seven years; his reputation remained intact as an honourable, respected and reasonable man, a man of piety and integrity. Of his four sons, two outlived him, Joshua died in 1666 and Reuben in 1667. His neighbour, Henry Graver died on 12th February 1641, mourned by his doting wife and devoted daughters.

After the birth, the seven women grouped tightly into a protective circle around Margaret and Foster. Elizabeth the midwife had swiftly alerted the others to the darkness that lurked in the depths of Margaret's post birth moods. More than this, each of them sensed the danger, the dark presence, demon or man, that threatened their friend. They watched out for the mother and son in so many ways.

In time, Foster was taken on as farm boy to one of the families and brought up in the ways of the shepherd. This family helped him start his own flock. He farmed and prospered. He began to build Black Crow Farm in the year 1644.

Each of the women accused, then exonerated, went on to lead a quiet life in the valley. In those days, no-one was there to record the lives of the poor, the trials and tribulations. History was in the hands of the literate. These women were poor and illiterate. Their story was recorded only by their persecutor.

Be assured, things settled back. The seven learned to take delight in small things, cherish the common day wonders of life. The women worked their ways to keep food on the table and their families clothed. They washed, cleaned, mended, tended, cooked, raised their own and the children of others, acted as midwives, cared for the ailing and laid out the dead. They continued to work for the rich households, to freshen the rushes in the chambers and wash the fine linen down in the

River Washburn, pouring over kittles of boiling water. They guarded the items of laundry from chancers and passing thieves and watched the washing dry on warm days. They rubbed up pastry, preserved fruit, pickled eggs, thickened sauces, and ......and they never forgot. Of course not.

Trusted, they were. They gave no cause for doubt. Each was silent on the trauma of the trials, and the aftermath. Not one broke rank. As each reached the end of the natural span they died in peace, mourned by their friends and families who paid due respect at their passing.

Janet was the first. The trials and trips to York had done for her. Her heart had not been strong, but her courage never faltered. The others followed, a sombre succession.

The valley was less for their passing. Or was it? The women were accorded Christian burials and their bodies laid to rest in the churchyard. But rest was not their intention.

On death each became a chosen oak down in Timble Gill.

And the waters of the beck rose in spate, and then abated; the winds of time blew on. The seasons turned, the years churned, the centuries flew through civil war, war on war and sometimes peace.

And now the year, the month, the week, the hour approaches fast.

Four hundred years on, and a reckoning there will be. You will see.

Part Two

Girl in a Hole

1

Fast forward four hundred years

Down the hairpins of Snowden Bank again. Go right at the Timble turn. This time choose the right fork and make directly to the village centre. Just like the valley that tries to contain it, Timble wears its past in its pockets. Deep and stuffed pockets they are too.

Strip out the white golf balls of Menwith Hill, decant the string of reservoirs back into the old River Washburn's course, topple the wind turbines, and you will see a landscape largely unchanged for four centuries, and certainly since the enclosure of the Forest of Knaresborough, in 1778. Many of the small field patterns predate this time and go back to medieval times and earlier. Then, each field was given a name based on a quirk, a feature, a singularity. People knew their land. They knew their sheep and they called their sheep by name too.

In these earlier times you would have seen many more small farms, field barns and cottages, hovels on the common land, dispersed settlements, with clusters of compact fields, closes, garths and in-byes.

Timble never and always changes. Twenty houses and no

shops nowadays. The last bus left in 1962. The hamlet sits high on a ridge, a line of stone houses capping the rising sweep of small fields patchwork-pinned and tacked together by dry stone walls, hedgerows and wood and wire fences.

Turning its cheeks from the westerlies, Timble looks down the valley. It hunches its shoulders and lifts its collar against whatever the north-east and north-west can throw and blow. It's only when the breeze comes softly from the south and smoke rises straight, that Timble drops its shoulders and lowers its guard.

At the fork in the road, you might see sheep silhouetted against the sky as you turn your wheel. These sheep seem stretched and magnificent, for they graze banks that are higher than the road. Look up to sheep. They are worthy of your attention, for this is still sheep country.

From the single-track road approaching the village, you will lose sight of the houses for a brief distance. The sparse copse of trees on your right has battled the westerlies for rising forty years. 'Plant a tree for '83' was the well-meant initiative. Fair play to the planters, the trees have survived – but stunted, bent and bowed they are now.

The stone houses sneak back in view. From this aspect they appear to nestle like clusters of fresh sprouting mushrooms in a late August meadow. Brick is banned, for this is a conservation village. There are black and yellow 'Neighbourhood Watch' signs, for Timble folk have always watched their neighbours – rather like their more tooled-up neighbours at Menwith Hill.

Let's choose two of these neighbours in Timble and join them for morning coffee.

2

Girl in a Hole

'Got a lot to tell you, June.'

Ginny watches as June lowers the cafetiere onto the bare pine table. Mugs, side plates and serviettes are set out before her.

'Columbian Reserve?' She tilts her head towards the pot.

June, with an air of mock secrecy: 'No, today, an innovation. This is Columbian Supremo – a dark chocolatey bean – reckoned by some to be even better.'

June places a plate of cakes before her friend. Ginny's hand awaits no invitation. She secures one for her plate and scrutinises it.

'And did you bake these buns yourself? Looks like blueberry and pistachio? My goodness, I hope you're not for saving any.'

'They're friands. Bilberry, actually. Local – Middle Ridge Woods. Foster passed me a bowl of them. He's been picking again. You can take him a couple of these for his tea.'

'Ne'er mind Foster.' Ginny peels the brown paper baking case off the cake and takes a first, appreciative bite: 'Talking of that waster of a brother of mine, like I said, I've got some 'goss'.

Foster's found a lass!'

'Oooh! On the internet – Tinder, or whatever it is they do now?'

'No. He found her stuck down some hole. I told him. I told him straight – something funny there. Are you going to pour, or what? No, no sugar – you should know that by now. Got to think of my girth. You know, it's as if his antennae were snipped off at birth, along with his umbilical. He was born without the alarm bells the rest of us are granted – steady with the milk. – and it's a mercy that we are too. Talking about alarm bells, the boiler man's due anytime soon.'

'Ginny, I don't want to sound like a bore, but let us recap. You said, Foster found this lass down some hole. Please, this calls for further explanation, surely?'

'It's just like I said, she was stuck down some hole.' Ginny breaks off to lick her fingers. 'Do you remember, about six or seven summers ago, yes, 2015 it was because that seemed significant – VJ Day – August 15th, 1945 – making it seventy years? It's Princess Anne's birthday too. Where was I?'

'You're telling me why the girl was down some hole.' June wants to hear the tale, but her tenacity is being challenged. Her imagination has been fired with images of a daring subterranean cave rescue.

'Right. Forget Princess Anne, for she is of no relevance here.'

'Virginia, let me remind you, it was not me who introduced the Princess Royal – you did.'

'Don't get snarky with me, June.'

'Please, Ginny, do proceed.'

'Well, as I was saying. Foster wanted to mark VJ Day with something special. He's into war and that sort of stuff – Help for Heroes, Invictus Games, you name it. His dad – not mine – it was our mum who was common – well not common as in 'cheap' – not like her – our girl in the hole. What I mean is, we share the same mum but have different dads. Well his dad was on the

Burma Railroad, but there hangs another story … '

'Another story for another day, Ginny.'

'Hmmm. These buns are scrumptious.' Ginny reaches for a second, then continues:

'Okay. Right, well we've had this massive stone – one of the ancient gate posts – lying at the top of the far field above Timble Gill since either of us could remember. Foster's getting the wall repaired – proper job – working along-side Diddy Kex, the waller from Otley. Diddy's the man to call if you ever have a fall.'

'Why are you telling me this? Am I facing a fall?'

'So,' Ginny glowers across the table: 'So, I said that the big stone would make a nice seat for walkers – picnics and stuff, or just to sit and enjoy the view – right down the valley, and up to the top of Redding Hill. Great spot to reflect on things, as we all need to do. The public footpath runs just by it, you know.'

'Nice thought, Ginny.'

'Well, Foster and Diddy thought so too. So, they build up a stone seat snug into the corner and then they asked Midge from top of the village to come down with his old Fergie and bucket, to lift this stone, and pop it on the top. Lovely job. I took down refreshments and we did our own little celebration cum commemoration – on VJ Day – 70 years on.'

'Ginny? Girl in the hole.'

'Oh aye. That's what I'm coming to. Well as we sit Midge starts to reminisce, as he is wont to do. It's age that does that. The oldsters lose the track. Sad. Well, he was saying he was a young boy in the war – he remembered a doodle bomb in the valley no less....'

'Ginny?'

'Bear with me.' Ginny flaps her crumby fingers: 'Midge says the government made 'em plough up the fields in the war to plant spuds and root vegetables – totally unsuitable land, being boulder clay, but that to get the ploughs in they had to take the stone gate posts out. They dug them up and just cast them aside.

That's the reason there's so many big stone gate posts lying on their backs round here. So, there is a connection.'

'With the girl?'

'No, the war.'

'What about the girl?'

'Right. Well the long and the short of it is this. Since doing the seat in the corner, Foster himself has taken to sitting on it. He calls it "his" seat – I'm sure he thinks it was all his idea! Well, I let him away with it – I'm good like that. This is what men do, isn't it? Nick a woman's best ideas?'

June nods, and deftly supresses a yawn. Ginny fails to notice this and takes up her thread again:

'Anyway, he takes his flask down, squirts some thistles from the knapsack sprayer – terrible stuff that, you need a mask – Europe's going to ban it – then he breaks off for a breather. He says there's even a place for his mug – the hole where the gatepost used to fit in. You know, there's even a mug-holder on his new red sit-on lawn tractor. Mug-holders must be all the rage. Well he's sitting there and can see there's something – just stuffed down his mug hole.'

Ginny pauses for breath; she has now recaptured June's lapsing attention.

Ginny goes on: 'You know Foster – he always feels the need to investigate. He sticks his fingers down and pulls it out.'

June's mouth prunes in distaste: 'Well I wouldn't have touched it. It could have been anything – a crisp packet, an empty sandwich bag, even a doggy bag – a full one. They leave them everywhere you know, the dirty buggers. Err, mucky, ooh, no – or a used condom. Urgh – litter. Not nice. Okay. So, what was it?'

'It was a card with a message.'

'Go on.'

'On one side it said **'Izzie woz 'ere!'** Slang like, in scruffy biro handwriting. On the other, printed all nicely: **'Can I help you** to Make do and Mend?' Then she, this Izzie, lists her services: 'alterations, hemming, mending (including darning) new zips, small curtains. Upcycling – new from old? Tell me your idea and I'll see if I can do it.' The minx has given all her contact details, phone, mobile, email and website. Bold as you like.'

'Proper little Busy Izzie, isn't she? Makes me think of Sooty and Harry Corbett – "Izzy, Izzy, let's get busy".'

'Actually, it was "Izzy Wizzy, let's get busy", June. Do you want to hear this tale or what?'

June nods mutely, and Ginny continues. 'Well Foster reads this and decides it was meant.'

'Meant?'

'They were meant for each other, he meant. He believed this to be a sign, that she, this Izzie, would mend his poor heart.'

'Really? With a new zip? Sorry, it's not funny. Bit of a stretch though, a leap of the imagination or a leap of faith?'

'More like a leap into the abyss. Proper loopy if you ask me. But you know, he's not been himself since Letty left. Truly, she broke his heart. People don't think straight in grief. They get superstitious, clutch at straws, look for signs, omens. I told him not to be so soft. "You're away in the head," I said.'

'Did he listen?'

'Did he hell. He rang her – a cold call you might say – and he asked her for a date.'

'Then what happened?'

'June, you'll just have to wait. The boiler man's due and I daren't be late.'

3

Black Crow Farm, Timble

All so my lustfull leafe is drye and sere,
My timely buds with wayling all are wasted;
The blossome which my braunch of youth did beare
With breathed sighes is blowne away and blasted;
And from mine eyes the drizzling teares descend,
As on your boughs the ysicles depend.

The Shepheardes Calender, Januarie
Edmund Spenser 1579

The landscape tilts between the telling and the truth. In truth, there was no cold call.

Foster Hall paces the foot-worn Indian rug. A patina of ash, dried mud and cast hay mutes the flattened tufts of pale sage, a deeper green, cream and pink, so carefully matched by its creator, one continent and half a century away. The rug had been his mother's luxury. But to Foster, now, it is just a mucky old rug.

'*Tell me your idea.*'

Izzie's voice is a soft sultry whisper in his head – a voice that's wrecking his sleep patterns and haunting his waking thoughts.

'Tell me your idea and I'll see if I can do it.'

These words make Foster feel warm and horny; he's brimming over with ideas. His eyes take in the crumpled, once-white bedsheets. His Izzie vision lingers her tongue along her lips, she fingers her brow and her eyes draw his own to the rumpled patch. She throws back the sheets.

'Foster, what are you thinking of?' The harsher voice of his long-dead mother chastises him. 'Whatever you're thinking, stop it!' His mother's photo sits squarely on the dressing table, her eyes ablaze and accusatory. A random query flickers across Foster's mind. Why was she wearing a hat? Then he remembers how she insisted in wearing a hat for chapel. His ardour is beginning to wilt. Other memories flood his fantasies, driving away his siren.

Once, when he was fourteen, mother caught him masturbating. He'd forgotten to lock the door, a copy of Fiesta opened on the floor. It had been so embarrassing. Then she'd told his dad, to make things worse.

'Did I survive the bloody Burma Railroad, so you could toss off in the bathtub, yer little waster.' Then his dad had thumped him.

Ginny's voice now moves into the space in his head: 'This place is a total tip, Foster. Look at it. You've gone to the dogs since Letty left. Letty kept it lovely. Look at it now and look at you, too!'

The women in his life, nagging and slugging it out in his head – one dead, one has left him, one his sister, and yet, the one he hasn't even met is going to be different. He believes this. He intends to meet her. He knows her calling card by heart. It only leaves his breast pocket at bedtime. The card over-nights propped against his cuckoo alarm clock.

There aren't just four women, Foster corrects himself. The female cast is far more extensive. There's Lou his sheepdog bitch, and his beloved Leaper, matriarch ewe of the flock. And coming back to women, there is a significant other – Margaret, his secret saviour. Some might call his forbear a witch, but he always corrects them. He has his retort off pat:

'My forbear, Margaret Hall, was accused and acquitted. Innocent – never a witch.'

He rarely mentions that she still lives down in the Gill with the other women. Once he shared this fact with Letty. Early days, first flush of love, he thought he could trust her.

'Psychotic episodes is what you're having, matey. See a shrink.' And she'd told Ian, his best friend – exposed him to ridicule. Unforgiveable. The cracks, the betrayals showed early, and soon became fissures, into which he would trip and fall. But Margaret had been there for him since his memory first focused. He thinks of her as his faerie godmother, forever young, kindly, benign and always batting on his side. She's encouraged him, protected him, shared his triumphs, few that there were, and helped him shoulder grief and disappointment. Sometimes she points the way, sometimes she shows a path change, a gentle shove in the right direction.

In his own way, Foster has let himself lean on her a little and love her a lot. If he thinks about it, and this might not be often, he believes himself blessed.

Margaret was there for him when Letty left. She stopped him from smashing and trashing their home. She placed a soft translucent hand on his:

'*Wait Foster, wait. You're in a state. So calm and wait. There will be another, well worth this wait.*'

Did Margaret have a hand in the Izzie card business? Foster likes to think so. That means it is more likely something will come of it.

Foster is now scheming how to bring a meeting with Izzie about. He is exploring possibilities. His first ruse was to contact Izzie over a broken trouser zip. He soon concluded that this was too crude, too obvious, especially the bit in the fantasy when a hot-eyed and wanton Izzie suggested she helped him take them off. It was the sort of scheme that makes sense in the night, but in the cold light of dawn appears less sound and shrivels. In your dreams he told himself.

Foster has only one decent pair of trousers – one pair that anyone might be persuaded to touch. These are part of his suit, a dark wool mix herringbone from Spencer's New Year's sale, down in Ilkley. Weddings and funerals, out it comes. He's earmarked it for his own – funeral or wedding – a good suit will be required for either eventuality. Okay, the zip slips down, but if he sheds half a stone, as he intends, this problem might right itself. And if he's stretched out flat on a slab, gravity will keep it in place.

Foster moves over to the window. A sunbeam streams through, split by the two ancient stone mullions. He presses the curtains further apart to let in more light. The edges of both curtains have been heavily blanched and shredded by the sun over the years. Originally a pert singing thrush motif, the bird pairs now seem mothy and semi-plucked.

'Genius!' He mutters and congratulates himself. 'New curtains. New bedroom curtains.' He'll go for a 're-furb'. Letty was always nagging on about a refurb. He's seen the odd programme on the television about what you can do with old farmhouses, and they end up looking like little palaces. And, at least he might get Izzie into his bedroom, if not into his bed.

Foster scans the room. He concedes it is a bit of a mess. He doesn't need Ginny to point this out. He will tidy up, chuck some stuff out, recycle the pile of Farmer's Guardians, yellowing and curling. Then he'll re-decorate and call in Izzie to measure up – perhaps to advise on colour schemes. Ginny's always drooling over a paint catalogue – 'Barrow and Fall' or something like. She says it's one up from Dulux, but his mate, Ian, who works for the Decorator Centre, says they can knock up any shade in the world and they're cheaper.

To decorate? Foster's thoughts fall back to earth at what this might entail. He hasn't painted a room in years. Perhaps it is a case for the professionals – cracks filled, damp work done, removal of the mushrooms. He has got the whole range of old house issues, with perhaps the exception of the death watch beetle. They had those little critters sorted after his father died. He vividly recalls the clicking and the knocking in the countdown to his father's final breaths, then his dad's own rattle drowned them out, as death triumphed over life and infestation.

Decorating – no. He certainly doesn't feel up to this himself, what with the farm and everything. He isn't really in the mind to get up a step ladder and paint between the beams. Tedious and fiddly and the sheer strain of working upwards into the roof space, above and between the purlins. Yes, he'll find out a firm and get them in. Ian will point him to someone good and cheap. He'll go for a fancy-named paint substitute. It'll be one in the eye for Ginny; she'll be proper shocked, he thinks.

Ginny's voice will not be silenced quite so easily: 'And just look at you too.' Her words track him into the bathroom and wrap round his shaving mirror. He hasn't intended to shave this morning. Who is looking – other than Ginny? He sees a shock of deep auburn hair, interspersed with random silver strands. He sees a chin like a blush gooseberry, eyes with drooping dark sacks beneath them and eyebrows that demand the scissors. He thinks he looks wrecked. He used to be considered handsome, at the Young Farmers, a catch even. That's where he met Letty.

Foster bargains with his reflection. He'll tackle the bedroom first, and set things in motion, then address 'the man', but a shave would keep him the right side of civilised. He turns the hot tap on.

Foster, the man with a plan, walks down to Borrins meadow, towards Timble Gill, with a spring in his stride, a smooth cheek and a light waft of aftershave. Lou, his faithful sheepdog bitch is hanging back, tracking him, with suspicion. Lou has detected something unusual, strange even, about her master. Perhaps it is because Foster's had a shower, and even treated himself to fresh underpants. Dogs, especially border collies, are sensitive to such issues. Lou isn't sure she approves. To the bitch, Foster smells fine, just the way nature intended a man should.

This morning the weight of the full knapsack sprayer doesn't drag Foster's back down. He shoulders it with ease. He'll take his break on Izzie's stone. There might be another message even, he wonders. He'll check. He always does.

4

On the footpath to Timble Gill, one month earlier

'Izzie, what are you doing; what are you thinking of?'

Linda watches her friend scrawl a message on her business card. Izzie's balancing her sandwich box, card on top, on her knee, whilst keeping her coffee mug on an even keel. She brushes her spiked fringe out of her eyes. A smile creeps across Linda's face. She's looking at Izzie's millefleur bandana. As Linda sees it, the bandana concept was to keep sweat or hair out of the eyes. Not our Izzie, she reflects. Carefully tweaked, deep auburn fronds have been teased out to frame her face. Vain, no, not really. Just so, that's how Izzie likes it. Style over sense, form over function, every time.

'What we need is a proper recession – a depression even. Whatever made me think I'd get by on "Make do and mend"? The work comes in trickles. It's like a urine infection – you're desperate and nothing comes, well hardly. Just in dribs and drabs, or more specifically, dribbles and drops.'

'But you've got your vintage back-up. That place in Hebden Bridge – Emily's Hot Press – keeps you going with repairs and adjustments. They say your work is brilliant – meticulous. Didn't the manager woman say they could barely see your stitches?'

'Well it's hardly a flood of garment restoration, and they pay sweet Fanny Adams. I want to make my own designs, but it costs me lots more to make things than the on-line chains sell their stuff for, and they give free delivery and returns. Foreign sweatshops, Amazon, eBay, whatever – it's all cut-price. Or it's high end. There's no place for someone like me.'

'Etsy?'

'Hmm, a possibility I suppose, but I'd never get to the top of the list, and I'd take any criticism of my product personally – I always do.'

'So why are you stuffing your card down this old stone's hole?'

'I've never passed this way before. I thought I'd try and reach a wider market this way, you know – broaden my customer base.'

'From a card poked down a hole?'

'Yep. It's like *Message in a Bottle* – old Sting's SOS.'

'Old Sting as you call him never needed to go grubbing round poking his calling card down every cranny he came across.'

'You don't know what he was driven to. He was fleeing English teaching too – just like me.'

'There are more safe and tested ways to attract new customers, surely?'

Izzie bites her lip. Her expression becomes serious.

'I believe in serendipity, happenstance, fate.'

'Izzie, fate cuts both ways; you don't know who will find it. Come on, engage your common sense. All your personal details are on it. It could fall into the hands of a wrong 'un, a stalker, a fetishist. The papers are full of them. And all of those women who read the news – they fall prey to these weirdo types.'

'I'm past caring and beyond caution. If I can't get more customers, I'll have to go back on the supply list, new groups of rabid adolescents on Monday mornings when someone's phoned in sick, hung over or just off-it, or, worse still, having to do team-building for management trainees in tall glass towers in Leeds – I perish the thought of it. Torn 'twixt Bedlam and Babylon, eh?'

Izzie's frown deepens, accompanied by a barely audible growl. Linda's troubled too. The friends fall silent.

Izzie's thoughts spiral back to her mid-teen years, to those times at the white melamine table in the tiny terrace's kitchen. Her mother, Annie, had been an ambitious woman. On a 'one-afternoon stand' as she called it, Annie had got pregnant with Izzie. Izzie often wondered about the conception. At which spot, just off the Rochdale Canal towpath on this fateful nature walk with a lad from her class, had her mother fell on. She had a feel for the stretch between Mytholmroyd and Luddendenfoot; it always gave her goose bumps. Even Annie wasn't sure of the father's name – long since forgotten, or just blanked. She became a mother at barely seventeen.

Annie raised her daughter on her own, along with the grudging and often reproving support of her parents. She had been denied a career through a cruel twist of fate, a hormonal surge and ensuing circumstances. The class she was born into, and the community, tightened the tethers. She channelled her ambitions and her dreams onto Izzie.

Annie desperately wanted her only daughter to have chances and choices. First in the family to go to university, that was her vision for Izzie. True, Izzie was an avid reader, felt a genuine love of literature, but her real passion was art. Annie could not, would not, countenance Art College as a proper pathway:

'You'll go straight off the rails, just like I did.'

'But Mum, you were still at school.'

'Same difference. You'll end up with some idle hairy irk or pretentious jerk. You're soft as shit, you are, my girl. You'll not be able to handle it. But at University you'll meet a better class of boy – there's husband material there alright. Follow the money. And if you don't click, you'll have a proper career to fall back on

– a teacher, a librarian or even the law. You'd like that so much more.'

Izzie had coaxed, pleaded, railed and raged. Tears before tea, tantrums at breakfast. All to no avail. The Deputy Head was on Annie's side, and so was Mrs. Pullen, the careers teacher.

'Hardly worth your mother's sacrifices; you might as well go for a job at the council offices now, for that's where you'll end up.'

The English teacher, Miss Richardson, piled in too: 'Art college? A sheer waste of good mind. When I read Izzie's work, I'm jealous. She has such a way with words. She's the lass in the class who gets it – whatever we are reading. She just gets it.'

Even the art mistress lacked the sisterly solidarity that Izzie might have hoped for: 'You want to sew? Craft work? It's hardly fine art. Izzie. Surely you can think of something with more of an edge. You'll not end up rich on tea cosies, collages and tapestries. You can do all that sort of stuff on the side. Run the church bazaar, if you must.'

Izzie was left isolated by a group of ambitious, older women. Ambitious on her behalf, and well intentioned, certainly, but they seemed to guard the gates of her own chosen way and slammed them shut in her face.

It was with a trailing pen and barely half her heart, she filled in the forms to study a degree in English Literature …

Izzie rests her inner eye on the kind face of Grayson Perry – her muse. He's got more guts than me, she scolds herself in an inaudible whisper.

Linda has been watching, shooting sidelong glances at her, picking the right time to have another go:

'Now what are you thinking? What are you muttering about?'

'Paths not taken, the permissive footpaths of my life. Grayson Perry. I wonder what ever happened to my portfolio. It was always kept under my bed.'

Izzie swallows a sad smile and pushes her card down into the stone's hole. Suddenly she feels a surge of confidence, conviction – almost optimism.

Linda's demeanour tightens again:

'You may come to regret this card in hole business. It's rash. Remember the estate agent? Don't you come whingeing to me when someone shady tries to lure you into a trap, rapes and murders you.'

'That being the case, I'm not likely to report back to you, am I? You'll be denied the pleasure of one of your "I told you so" moments.'

Izzie draws breath and raises a finger to indicate the cessation of hostilities:

'Linda, listen to the birdsong. Look at the view, the trees in the Gill below us, that curious hill beyond with sheep that look twice their size – some optical illusion, I suppose. We're up here in nature, looking down the valley towards Leeds, or over the hill knowing Bradford lies beyond. This is a benign valley, a beautiful place. I put my fate in the hands of the spirit of this valley.'

Linda concedes defeat with some grace:

'Steady on Izzie, from what I've heard, this is the valley where the witches once danced.'

'No way?' Izzie grins with delight. Linda has diverted her friend.

'Yeh, the last time I walked here I talked to one of the natives – a farmer-type. He looked a bit sad but cut quite a figure – his shirt in tatters, open to his navel. What a chest! Grizzly hair – auburn sprinkled with gunmetal over a deep tan. Hmm, nice.'

'He seems to have made an impression on you.'

'Well, it was probably you he needed – his trousers were held up with a belt of pink baling twine. And no, he wasn't making a statement.'

'We'll keep an eye up for him – sounds as if you'd know him again.'

'Oh, I'd know him again alright. Strange bloke. Attractive. Slightly funny walk – mild scoliosis perhaps, or club foot – untreated? But what kind of man hangs dead moles round his midriff?'

'Eer! Disgusting. How old was he?'

'Mid to late forties? Hard to tell these days. Very tanned and lots of lines but that's how they look when they work outdoors all the time – fit, I'd call him, very fit.'

Linda smiles at her memories of the meeting, with a far-away, unfocussed look to her. She shrugs and shuffles her shoulders out of her deep green anorak, and continues:

'I suppose it would be this time last year, about this time anyway; a late spring's evening walk. Like you, I was tired of work. I was tired of the endless talk. The prattle of colleagues, the gossip, the whole idiocy of my workplace. I sought only my own company that evening.'

Linda has Izzie's full attention now. She continues:

'I don't often talk to strangers. I don't know why I don't – you know me better than most; it's my natural caution, I suppose. The signs weren't good. Single woman meets strange bloke. Remote path over wooded ravine. Anyone's guess? And, he's got these bloody mole carcases hanging round his middle. Hardly a come on.'

Izzie laughs sympathetically. Her friend draws breath and carries on:

'And yet, I am old enough to know the pleasure that can be gained from a random interchange. I met the mole-man's eyes and saw no ill-intent, just sorrow. Nice, dark eyes they were. I confess I spoke first, broke my own rule. Just pleasantries. Then, he asked if I'd been walking for long. I told me I was trying to park the cares of work.

I remember saying something like: "You hang your work from your belt."

He told me straight: "I'm a farmer, not a mole catcher."

I asked him why he killed them. I felt so sorry for them. I noticed their almost human, crinkled hands, their black velvet coats and blind, pink snouty faces. I reached to stroke the nearest one. So soft. I was repulsed but fascinated. Then he stopped me in my tracks. He said they killed lambs.'

'What?' says Izzie.

'Yes, they kill lambs, well in a roundabout way. He explained that the soil from mole hills contaminates the pasture, the silage and the cut hay. It introduces listeria. Listeria kills lambs. He said he managed moles to save his sheep.'

Izzie takes it in: '"Managed" sounds a wee bit mendacious. But it's funny, we need to know stuff like this. We go round thinking men like him are savages, primitives, yahoos, and they aren't really, are they?'

'No, not most of them. I asked him what he would do with these moles. I was thinking moleskin trousers.'

'And?'

'He said he placed them on the wall capping stones for the red kites to take. The kites live off carrion. He said the dead moles were always gone in the morning.'

'We should never rush to judge. He's really a hero – saving lambs and feeding kites?'

'Yeh. You could say that. There's another line of argument that says he's tinkering with the balance of nature. Playing god.'

'I suppose we're all doing our best, mostly,' sighs Izzie.

'Well, we walked along the ridge together, with that deep ravine below us. It was a weird encounter – memorable on many fronts. He asked me if I'd ever seen a badger. He then swore me to secrecy because there were those who hated the creatures, wished them harm.' Linda recalls the conversation:

'"Cattle farmers and psychos," he said. "The link, if there is one, is complex – a case of which infects which?" But then he added that he was a sheep farmer and liked to see the badgers play, especially the cubs.

He showed me some badger setts. He told me where to sit to get the best view. You need to check wind direction, you know. They've got a brilliant sense of smell. I'd never thought of that.'

'Well why would you? We don't meet so many badgers in Hebden Bridge,' says Izzie.

Linda blanks this: 'We walked on a little further together for a short while, and he pointed down the steep gill to a sand bay by the beck below. There was this flat grassy area. He said that this was where the Gill Women laid out their table and danced.'

'Gill Women?'

'He meant witches, but he wouldn't call them that. Early seventeenth century it was – sixteen-twenty-something. He said he could trace his line back to one of the women – a woman called Margaret Hall – "Old Maggie" he called her. We sat together in a peaceful silence, then he was gone. I was thinking my own thoughts and had dropped into a sort of silent reverie. Well, I didn't even notice him go. Strange encounter.'

'Knowing you, you'd probably just dropped off, and he thought he'd better leave you to it. So, did they burn them, these witches?'

'No, he said they were imprisoned at York for a while. The women were tried, and they got off. Not like the Pendle women.'

'I suppose we don't go round torching women here. I like to think we've got more common sense this side of the border, if less imagination. Anyway, the lasses were probably just partying,' says Izzie.

'By sixteen-twenty, they would have been hanged, not burned – had they been found guilty.'

'God, it's terrifying. Not many can have got off. These poor women were the lucky ones.'

'Hmm.' Linda looks reflective. 'You do wonder what was really going on, what really triggered the witch hunts. They still happen, you know. To demonise the victims exonerates the hunters. And the victims are largely women. Many fine feminist thinkers see the witch hunts of the sixteenth and seventeenth centuries as an earlier manifestation of the war on women. I'd like to go into this further – the history, the thinking. Stuff like this fascinates me.'

Linda pauses, and continues: 'I do remember a bit of the history. Elizabeth 1st didn't encourage witch hunts, and it certainly wasn't common practice in England in the late sixteenth century. Things were different in Scotland. There, witch hunts were all the rage. Up to four thousand people were burnt to death is what I've read. That said, the numbers need a health warning. It's the way they were 'officially' recorded that is the problem. Sometimes the potential penalty is recorded, rather than the actual outcome of a trial. But then again, many people, women especially, will have been killed because the locals will have acted on their suspicions and taken matters into their own hands. These deaths won't have been recorded at all.'

'I had no idea there were so many...'

'No, it is surprising. It seems James 6th of Scotland became an expert on witchcraft. He became the arch persecutor of witches, in fact. He even wrote a book on the subject.'

'But the numbers are really shocking.'

'They are – especially when you bear in mind that Scotland's population was only around eight hundred thousand in the year 1600. That means half a percent of the entire population was killed, and mainly women. Just to put it in perspective, that's the equivalent of thirty thousand in the UK today.'

'What! That's fucking carnage.'

'Indeed, it is. Three thousand six hundred died in the shootings, bombing and other killings in the Troubles, between 1969 and 1997. That was appalling. What James did was f'ing unbelievable.'

'So, what was his problem?'

'It seems he linked the death of his mother, Mary Queen of Scots, to a witch's prediction, and he also believed that both he and his new bride, Anne of Denmark, had been endangered in a sea crossing through the practices and spells of witches.'

'Right?'

'As I recall, James pushed the thinking further on witchcraft and even made up new angles. Witches working in covens, not alone, was one of his brainwaves.'

'I suppose that helped him torch more women with less trouble and fuss. Economies of scale, eh?'

'Absolutely. And another thing – he drew no distinction between white witches and black witches – the scary sort. And when you think about it, there's quite a fine line between an apothecary, herbalist and hedge witch. Gender might etch this line.'

'I'm not warming to this James bloke.' Izzie's mouth purses in distaste.

Linda continues: 'Once he took over the English throne, he seems to have hit reverse. He swiftly put space between himself and his reputation as a witch hunter. Things were different in England. He found a more civilised, cultured and intellectual climate in his new court, where contemplation of wider philosophical issues was the thing.'

'So, being a witch-hunter wasn't cool?'

'Well, that was the story. But the royal seal of approval had already been given and the belief in witches and enthusiasm for their persecution caught like moorland fire during a hot spell. Most people believed in witches then, even those we would now call professional people – lawyers, academics, "proper doctors" and the clergy.'

'"Proper Doctors"?'

'Yeh. It's funny this, but when I did my midwife training, I found that many of the midwives were feminists. There are many reasons for this, but it also harks back to the history of the period we are talking about, and the status of midwives, herbalists and white witches. These were all lumped together back then and were treated appallingly by "the physicians" – all male, of course. These men were hell bent on stopping them practising. Accusing them of witchcraft was neat – a quick fix. It was easy to deal with them as witches.'

'So, this was about stopping the poor get medical help and advice?'

'Exactly. There's a book I'd love to get my hands on by Nicholas Culpeper called "A Directory for Midwives" or "A Guide for Women". He was such an amazing bloke. He's best known as a cataloguer of wildflowers and plants. "The Complete Herbal" is his, but he also dedicated himself to making medicine accessible to the poor. He was in bitter opposition to the closed shop of medicine imposed by College of Physicians. And alongside all of this, he was a radical republican and an astrologer.'

'I don't know much about him at all.'

'People don't, but he's a fine man from the seventeenth century. A true hero. The world's crying out for a proper biography.'

'Well write it, why don't you?'

'Perhaps, when I retire. I don't think I could do him justice right now.'

'But those poor women – the accused, the witches, the midwives. You can't help but feel for them, and, feel anger on their behalves!'

Bird song. Sunlight. Same place, modern times. Both women are silent for a while. Linda pulls the flower off a thistle, then continues:

'But there's no denying that this place does have a different feel. It has that time-shift gene – the here-and-now and the there-and-gone all seem to rub together. There's a strange and timeless harmony.'

'I agree. It is special, and very beautiful, and it carries its past close to the surface. But my card remains in this hole.'

Linda shakes her head in disapproval: 'Izzie, don't do it. Pull it out. Grow up.'

'Bring it on, whatever 'it' is,' says Izzie. She squints up into the sunlight and calls to the air above her: 'Are you listening sister witches, I'd like some customers. Save me from 'supply.'' Then she adds 'please' as an afterthought.

A face rises slowly behind them. It comes up above the dry-stone wall like a full moon. The penumbra focuses into thick fronds of plum and gunmetal flowing hair. Large dark eyes, a broad smile, a kindly aspect. A young face yet ancient, there, yet not there. Margaret Hall brings her hands up in a cupped benign benediction, over the heads of the Izzie and Linda. She likes these women. She likes what she's been hearing. Soul sisters indeed. She particularly likes the younger, more wayward of the two. She sees a little of her old self in this one. There's something almost familiar about her.

The two women, oblivious to their companion, sit on the warming stone seat in silence. The sun is hot on their faces. They soon forget their minor skirmish over the card. Old friends from way back, they are usually of one accord.

Their eyes are parallel with the tops of many of the trees in the Gill below them. But Izzie and Linda do not notice the slight perturbation of the air – a shift, not quite a disturbance. It starts somewhere between a hiss and a sigh, a flickering of the sunlight as through fine hair, a silvering of sound gathering to faint crystal voices – a slow soft clamouring: *Izzie, Izzie, we hear your call. You shall fall for Foster Hall.* A barely audible chorus of interchanging *Izzie's* and *Foster's* escalates – a crescendo of sweetness tipping into giggles, modulating to raucous cackles.

'What the hell is that, Izzie?'

'Sounds like something in the Gill – a bird alarm call, perhaps a jay?'

'Whatever it is, there's more than one. Sounded to me like those dreadful crows we passed in that last village, Timble. What a racket.'

'It's peacocks that do my head in – they scare the shit out of you at dusk.' Izzie rubs her upper arms: 'I think we'll move on. I feel a bit chilly, a bit funny in fact.'

Linda gets out her iPhone and studies the Ordinance map app: 'We'll cross the beck and branch down to the old turnpike road then up towards Swinsty Reservoir and over the dam. Then it's up to the road, through the woods and the Sun Inn will beckon us. We'll be ready for half a pint and a bag of salted peanuts, and we'll have made space for the calorie hit.'

'Sounds great, but my feet are killing me.'

'I told you – boots not trainers. You never listen.'

'When did you become such an old fart?'

'Piss off,' laughs Linda, and then: 'if you behave, Izzie, I might point out the witches' spot.'

'Lead on, Mac-Linda. I place my safety in your hands, today, at least.'

Six pairs of eyes in the tree-tops and rippling laughter through the leaves follow the friends as they walk on down the track. The face behind the wall turns, to face Timble. Margaret is thinking about Foster and how she might bring about a successful coupling. She hasn't needed to make an intervention like this for a century or two, but time is running out for the Halls, in more ways than one. Time and timing will be of the essence, she reflects. She knows that of old.

5

Black Crow Farm, Timble

'Bloody hell Foz! Have you considered a webcam on that cross beam? You might go viral.'

Ian's eyes follow a large stately spider picking its way across a dense web towards a caught, yet still struggling fly. Above the beams, from the roof cavity, there comes a distinct sound of scratching.

'I've never seen owt like it.' Ian is so stunned he removes his beanie and runs his fingers over his shaved and tattooed scalp. He smooths the feathers of the Leeds owl motif: 'How long's it been like this?'

Foster shrugs.

Ian turns his gaze from the roofing timbers above Foster's wrecked double bed to face his friend full on. His voice softens: 'Look mate, I don't want you to take this the wrong way; I don't want to be personal, but is this why Letty legged it?'

"Appen it may have contributed – aye, she used to call this place 'Cold Custard Farm' on account of having to doss down under that kind of yellowy cream stuff on the wood up there. She never liked it, or them mushrooms either. But it wasn't just the state of this place – we had some personal issues causing her concern too, it has to be admitted.'

'That's not custard – it's mycelium – dry rot to you, and the mushrooms are the same, only more mature – they produce the spores. Fruiting bodies. You need it sorting mate, and quick.'

'It isn't harmful is it?'

'Not in itself, but the damp that's causing it won't be doing you, or your lungs, any good at all. It won't be doing your house any good either.'

'What would you suggest?'

Ian exhales through his puckering lips, blowing something like a raspberry: 'It's out of my league mate. You need a specialist damp firm, but you've got to be wary. Cowboys roam the range freely out there. They'll promise you the earth, rush in, inject chemicals, and never get to the root of the problem. They'll charge you an arm and a leg too. Then they'll declare bankruptcy, making the guarantee worth nowt.'

Foster looks alarmed.

'Leave it to me, Foz. I'll ask around. I won't let you get ripped off.'

'Ta. Fancy a can of lager?'

'Aye, we've earned it. I'll sort your decorating, mate, but at present, it's a wee bit previous. The paint would just drop off, along with your plaster. I suspect you'll need to attack the problem from the top and bottom at the same time. It'll be coming down from the roof, and up from below the boards – I can smell the rising damp downstairs. I've got to warn you – all this is going to cost, mate. Sorry for that.'

The two men settle themselves downstairs and sit companionably at the ancient table. Foster's cleared a couple of spaces, in between the movement certificates, invoices, and veterinary treatments. He's located a big bag of crisps, only just beyond 'sell by'. A desultory discussion about the Championship League and Leeds's likely chances lapses.

'So why have you got the bit between your teeth – this bedroom renovation project – folk will talk Foz?'

'Well, Ginny's been on to me.'

'But that's not the reason, is it?'

'No. I suppose I'm thinking, if I'm going to try and find someone else, I need to do something drastic and soonish. Letty was very forthright – never one to pull her punches. She called this place a shithole. I felt that was a bit over-the-top, myself. A bit uncalled for. Unmodernised is what an estate agent would call it.'

'Yeh well Foz, some estate agent isn't going to walk into your home and gasp "what a shit-hole!" is he? He'd be after your business, his percentage like, and not be wanting to offend you. They call it customer care.'

'Why are we talking about estate agents, anyway? This house isn't for sale. It's been in our family since 1644. It was built by the first Foster Hall.'

Ian sighs; a tactical subject shift: 'Letty's not coming back, then?'

'No, she's gone and got someone else. Seems she's shacked up down in Burley. She met him in a pub. He calls himself Brian and he's in property maintenance.'

'Would he do you a discount?'

Foster's eyebrows meet and greet. Instant monobrow. There are times he can look fierce, ferocious even, and this is one of them.

'Joke mate – that wasn't a serious suggestion.'

Foster's face flicks from anger to resignation. They move on into the bathroom. He shrugs:

'Seems she's even got a wet room, down in Burley.'

'She had one here, mate, by the look of it.'

'If you're going to spend tonight taking the piss you can fuck off now.'

'You never used to be this touchy, Foz. You need to get over 'yourself. Move on.'

'Yeh, I know. And I'm trying. Okay, I might have found someone. But I need to get things right, before I make a move.'

'All this stuff will take time Foz. It won't be done in a fortnight. Will your new lady wait? You could take her to a hotel – push the boat out and give her a "Premier In".'

'I've gone without for a year now, I can wait a few more months. Look, do me a favour, and say nothing to our Ginny. I don't want her to know about the work on the house, she'll be trying to stick her oar in, and it's none of her business.'

'So, is this house all yours, or has she still an interest in it?'

'It was my dad's house and passed to me, along with the farm. When my mum died, her stuff was divided between me and Ginny. Ginny has no interest in this house, technically – like financially. But she likes to keep a close eye on me. We are family, after all.'

Foster softens his tone: 'You see, Ginny's dad died in the war, and then her mother met my own dad, and eventually I came along. Ginny's a lot older than me; she's always looked out for me. As for my parents, it seems there might have been issues around conception when it came them to having me. There was a lot of trouble like that for PoWs. Strangely enough, that was an issue between me and Letty. She was desperate for kids, and it never happened. We never gelled, or whatever you call it.'

Foster draws a gulp from the tin, and continues:

'It was always worse when she got back from the hairdressers.'

'What?'

'Well it was the magazines – stuffed full of celebs no-one's ever heard of. These women were all either heavily pregnant or had a fabulous home, or both. It's not like that up in these parts. I'm a hill farmer. It's a least favoured area. And lying on her back eyeing up the yellow mushrooms might have made it hard for her to concentrate on the matter in hand.'

'I see what you mean, mate.'

'Aye, and she could never be persuaded to climb on top.'

'Some women are funny like that. They miss out on some of life's pleasures.' mused Ian: 'Did the pair of you find out what the problem was?'

'Ne'er – she didn't want any of the hospital stuff, all the appointments and probing. She said her mate went through it and it was far too – hmm "intrusive", yes, that's the word she used. I think it came from some magazine's problems column.'

Foster takes another swig: 'She blamed me instead. She once said that if I was one of the tups, firing on blanks, she'd have got in the knacker man. Stun gun and job's a good un. I'd have been taken off in the back of the wagon. That's what she said.'

'Bloody 'ell! Bit brutal that! It could have been her. Look, I'm sorry mate – I didn't mean to pry.'

'No, you never asked. It just came up. I suppose there's still time for her, Letty – Brian might come good, so to speak. Anyhow, I wish her well. I was no angel. Another tin?'

'Aye, I won't say no.' Ian pulls the ring and then picks at his callouses: 'You never know. You might be better off without her. Doesn't sound as if she oozed sympathy for her fellow man. I've read about the likes of her. Reducing a bloke's self-esteem is the first stage of coercive control. There was a thing about it in the Mail. I tell you mate you are well rid. Her putdowns could soon shift into thumping you. Life eh? Bloody sad, when you think about it. Still Leeds might come good too.'

'To Leeds.' Foster raises his tin. He goes quiet; he's a bit rattled in fact. Something in what Ian has said rings true. Twice, before she left, Letty had hurt him. Foster had been undecided; did she really mean to do him harm? In the first incident, she had caught him unawares. She'd brought a casserole pan down on his head, whilst he was listening to the Saturday scores. Then she'd tried to pass it off as a joke. The second time, she claimed it was an accident as she slipped on the flags and tripped. She was carrying a knife. But it wasn't an accident, he was now certain of this. The bread knife had glanced off his shoulder.

'Leeds!' Ian has perfected the art of the 'articulate belch'. He belches the word Leeds, as clear as a bell. Both men find this trick hilarious.

'Tha's a dirty bugger!' declares Foster, in admiration: 'Now have a go at Harrogate Town.'

'Aye, they're doing well. I'd better get practising.'

'Better still, Accrington Stanley.'

'But I've never supported them?'

'I know that. I just wondered if you could get your throat round the longer club name?'

'Well, at a stretch mate, but I might need the full force of a chicken biryani first. Ammo like.'

The two will part later, after Match of the Day, ever the best of friends. The following morning, they will both wake worse for wear, but more than willing to be paying the price of a night well spent.

6

The Damp Man calls

A canary yellow van with bold black lettering draws to a halt in front of Black Crow Farm. The Damp Man – that's what it says on the side and there's an image of the Damp Man himself. He's a proper superhero, raw-boned, taut muscles and a well-turned calf. Damp Man sits somewhere between Spider Man and Captain America. Well, that was the original concept, but this macho vision is undermined by the wand between the fingers of his right hand – think Tinkerbell, or Simon Rattle.

In truth, there had been a tussle over this detail of the image. Richard E Sough, the van's proud owner, had felt that The Damp Man should be holding a damp meter – a prime tool of the trade. Michael, the designer from Harrogate, favoured a light sabre, referencing Star Wars, the power of Darth Vader and the notion of the quest to eradicate damp and pestilence from the home.

'Wow, it would be totes apocalyptic!' claimed Michael. But Wendy, Richard E's wife, won, as always, and rammed home her victory with a wand and a trail of stardust. 'He spreads his magic everywhere; obvious or what?'

The script on the van's side goes on to describe The Damp Man's services: Woodworm, Wall Stabilisation, Waterproofing including Basements, Wet and Dry Rot, Damp Proofing, Infestation, Rodents and Pest Control. This list is terminated with a perfunctory 'Zap!'.

Unlike the cartoonish illustration, Richard E is not wearing tights. Instead he wears a smart turquoise nylon over-all. He sits for a while on the driver's seat, in mobile contact with Wendy, who trebles as his administrator and secretary. The signal is poor, and it takes a moment or two to realise that the strange soft, yet insistent, hammering is, in fact, coming from outside the van window, and not from a poor connection.

'Here Richard, err, might you move the van along a bit – like outside next door. I don't want nosy neighbours to think I've got damp.'

'No probs, Mr Hall, Foster, if I may. I can see where you are coming from, mate.'

'Actually, it's my sister. She'll be straight in here if she thinks it's me. She means well, but she'll want to know what's going off, the ins and outs of everything and she'll have an opinion. Talk, she never stops. I'll get the kettle on.'

'Cheers, mate, be in in a minute.'

Richard E is close to Wendy. Together they run a good business – friendly, reputable, fair. Their customer satisfaction ratings on-line are high – lots of likes, thumbs ups and smiley faces. It was Wendy who came up with "The Damp Man". An honest and good-hearted woman, she foresaw no possible innuendo. His mates took a different view and he was soon Damp Dickie to them.

'Adolescent humour. Over-grown schoolboys – that's what they are. Anyway, you've always been Ricky. No-one has ever called you Dick or Dickie, love. They are just being silly. They're jealous because you've got a nice new van, a lovely home and … me. You're my superhero, sweetie.'

Richard then made the mistake of sharing Wendy's reaction with his mates. Well he shared an edited version, omitting 'the superhero bit' but it was still enough to cause further mirth. She was immediately rewarded with the Wet Wendy title, which was further corrupted to Wet and Windy when Richard wasn't with them. A digression.

The Damp Man moves his van, but it's too late to stem the gossip. Diddy Kex and Midge happen to be standing by the red telephone box opposite the farm. They see The Damp Man emerge and disappear into Black Crow Farm with his box of tricks and a stout pair of step ladders over his shoulders.

'By heck it must be right bad. Fozzy Hall's got the deepest pockets this side of the A59.'

'Tell me about it. He's still to pay for that walling job, with the seat.'

The two men move over to get a better look at the van.

'That's one hell of a fairy,' marvels Midge, pointing at the cartoon character.

'Bloody 'ell, have you read that list?'

'Which one's Fozzy got, I wonder?'

'Trouble down below, I shouldn't wonder. Old house like that, 1600s and it's still got its cellars. He's forced to have basement issues.'

'Happen he'll be having 'em filled in with concrete. There's springs springing up all round here you know. We could be lifted off the street at any moment by a geyser.'

'Which geezer? He'd need to be a strong one.'

'You daft sod. Morning Ginny!'

'We were just saying, Ginny, your Foster's gone and got The Damp Man in.' Diddy points to the van by way of explanation.

Ginny has come round from Back Lane to call on Foster to check if he has a shopping list for her. It's Friday, her shopping day in Otley. She smiles at the men and affects nonchalance:

'Show me a place round here that couldn't use some of those

services.' But Ginny's thoughts are furious and mutinous. How dare Foster get in a work man without consulting her? What's going on?

She passes the time of day with the men, light touch and cheerful, then in she steps through Foster's front gate. As always, the gate comes off its crude hinges as she unlatches it.

'Foster?' she calls up from just inside the front door, trying to supress her indignation.

Ginny can hear the muffled murmur of men's voices upstairs, but they sound distant. She mounts the first five steps, stepping lightly to avoid the creaks, and listening intently. Foster and The Damp Man are up above Foster's room, the main bedroom that had been her mother's. From what she can make out from the slithering sound they are crawling along the narrow roof void above the purlins. Both are coughing, fighting for breath. She keeps on up the stairs, silently, cocking her ear to catch what they are saying. She peeps round the door into the bedroom.

Foster's left foot dangles down though the hatch. She knows it's his because of the scar above the ankle – an old biking injury from childhood. The foot itself is about eighteen inches above the step ladder's top platform.

'It's bad this, Foster, it's spread right across.'

Ginny sees flashes of a strong torch beam above the hatch.

'Some major work here mate. And the damp in the walls is off the meter. You've got flashing issues, and missing tiles. Okay, I've seen enough up here. Let's have a look at your cellar.'

Foster's leg starts to paddle the air, trying to locate the step ladder's platform. Ginny backs out, unseen, except by her mother in the photo frame. Their eyes meet. Ginny can sense her mother's presence and indignation.

'He's let it come to a pretty pickle mum!' Ginny mouths silently to the photo 'I don't like this at all.'

When did Foster get so furtive, so secretive, she thinks, as she scurries down the stairs and back out of the front door?

'Essential maintenance,' she calls breezily to Midge and Diddy, who are back by the red telephone box: 'Always better to keep top side of it.' She disappears, briskly, back along the lane. She does not look back.

Ginny isn't the only one to have noticed the arrival of The Damp Man. Margaret has emerged from behind the stone wall opposite Black Crow Farm. She is studying the van's emblem with great interest. She thinks it's male because of the muscle structure. This figure seems to be flying. More than that, it's waving a wand. Margaret feels uncomfortable with this. A male magician perhaps, a cunning man, a warlock, whatever. She's going to keep a close eye on developments. She'd watched Black Crow Farm being built centuries ago, for her own son, the first Foster. This is the home of the Halls. She'll be watching alright.

She'll share her caution with the women down in the Gill. She hopes it isn't Asmodeus, in a new guise. They're going to need all their strength for this one, she's quite convinced.

7

At an Otley supermarket

'Ginny!'

Their trolleys clash gently on the tea and coffee aisle.

'Oh. June.'

'Ginny, are you alright? You look - you look really down.'

'I'm fine.' Ginny looks back to the Yorkshire Gold: 'On special offer this week, to card holders. I might invest in a couple.'

June sees the moisture accumulating in her friend's eyes.

'Come on Ginny, there's always time for a coffee. I'm going to push the boat out and treat you to a warm croissant, butter and jam. Follow me. Throw caution and the calories to the wind.'

They skirt the fresh cheese and deli counter. June notes the rotating greasy golden chickens on a spit, suppresses her saliva and makes a mental note to return to secure one later. She mouths 'save me one' to Samina on the deli, who nods 'message received'. Samina knows June will want the one with the crispiest skin.

'Now sit down here and I'll get us a tray.' Ginny watches June at the counter. This is what friends are for she muses, and it will help to talk.

The two friends settle down and arrange their cups, plates and napkins to their satisfaction.

'So? What about you? This is not the Ginny I met a week ago. What's gone off?

'Foster.'

'What, with that Girl in a Hole?'

'No.'

'You never told me what happened there?'

'Don't ask me. Did she ever exist? Was she just a smoke screen to stop me asking about Letty? I don't know anything anymore, and I'm not going to be told. He's made that quite clear.'

'You've had a falling out?'

'No. If I had I'd be able to sort it. But this is different.'

'So, what has he done?'

'He's getting The Damp Man in.'

'Who?'

'You know, a bloke who fixes damp. A big yellow van with Superman on the side.'

'Really? Right. Well what's so bad about that? Haven't you been going on to him about sorting his place out? You said that's why Letty left. Less than complimentary you were, Ginny.'

'Yes, I know I did say some stuff. But I did expect to be involved in any developments. It was my home too. I lived there from childhood. I always look on it as my home, and him – my brother. I didn't expect this.'

June squeezes down the plunger of the cafetiere and then pours. She looks kindly into her friend's eyes:

'Ginny, have you considered why he isn't consulting you – his reasons?'

'I had to find out from Diddy Kex and Midge. I had to pretend I knew. It was awful, shaming, humiliating. Oh June, we used to be so close.'

'I think you need to stand back a bit. You need to consider what he's up to. So often, these things are not as they seem. I've had to learn when it is, and when it isn't about me. This may not be about you, in fact I'm certain it isn't.'

'Well, who or what else might it be about?'

'Think about it, Ginny. You've been on to him for a while about Letty and why she left. He's suffering a broken heart – you said so yourself. Perhaps it all became too painful? Too personal?'

'You're saying I was cruel?'

'Not intentionally, Ginny, but perhaps you should have held back a bit – be there for him, but not onto him?'

'You make me sound awful – an interfering bully; that's what you're really saying.'

'No, your intentions, I know, will have been the best. But you might have forced him underground. Perhaps you have stung him into action and he's too stubborn to acknowledge it?'

'I think I see. Yes.'

'Perhaps it's all about trying to get Letty back, and he's too ashamed to admit it?'

'Ahh, yes, that could be it.' Ginny's bottom lip stabilises. 'So, me thinking it's about me – yes – it's about him realising I was right, but not being able to admit it?'

'Yes, something like that.' June isn't quite sure that was exactly what she had been trying to tell Ginny.

'But following my instructions, nonetheless. Gorgeous croissants June. Very fresh and flaky. So glad our paths crossed this morning. Pour again?'

'Give him a bit of space, Ginny. What's the old rhyme? "Leave him alone, he'll come home, wagging his tail behind him."'

'Was it wagging – I thought it was waggling? Still, these oldsters knew a thing or two, June. Perhaps he will come waggling back?'

*****

Ginny drives slowly over the Wharfe Bridge, heading north. She likes to try to spot the swans. There's a breeding pair with cygnets. No luck today. As she accelerates for Billam's Hill she confesses to herself that she's feeling a lot more positive, optimistic even. Thirty miles per hour here; she checks her speed.

June's reasoning and her words of advice echo around Ginny's mind. Why couldn't she see it, she asks herself. Perhaps she had been too preoccupied with feeling the sting of not being consulted. Well, she can see it now. It's all about her being right, and him wanting to do all the improvements Letty wanted. He's desperate to get Letty back. Of course. Obvious.

And so, Ginny begins to plot. She'll write to Letty, keep her in the loop. She still has her email. She'll fill Letty in. And, when Foster's project is reaching fruition, she'll invite Letty up for coffee and then, take her round – to inspect, approve. Envy. Desire!

Ginny's scheme requires for Foster not to be at home, the day of the visit. Easy, thinks Ginny – market day, especially the auction mart at Skipton. The ram sale – perfect. He's never been known to miss one.

Ginny is growing into the role of fairy-godmother; she wants to be the one who sticks the couple back together. And, as she warms to her theme, timing couldn't be better. It's nearly a year now since Letty packed her bags. Just long enough for cracks, reservations, frustrations to show with the Burley builder.

Letty never suffered fools, reflects Ginny. She always prided herself on skewering male imperfections. She had Foster where she wanted him. Eleven months – just long enough to introduce a glimmer of doubt. First flush of romance over, passion thinning, evaporating in the chilling light of daily life. By the time the improvements are done, Letty will be desperate to come home from the suburbs, surely?

Then a darkness descends on Ginny's brow. Unless there is already a baby on the way? Ginny exhales, audibly, and sucks her bottom lip. She takes the Timble turn at the top of the hill, swings right, and pokes the disagreeable thought away. Letty was the far side of forty. She might not be able to drop on quite so quickly, no matter what the magazines claim these days. Ginny hopes not. Her smile returns, along with her confidence and resolve.

8

Black Crow Farm, Timble

The birds awakt him with their morning song,
Their warbling musicke pearst his tender eare,
The murmering brookes and whiskeing winds among
The rattling boughes and leaves, their parts did beare;
His eies unclos'd beheld the groves along,
Of swains and shepherd groomes that dwellings weare.

Godfrey of Bulloigne, or the Recoverie of Jerusalem
Edward Fairfax's translation of Torquato Tasso's Gerusalemme
Conquistata 1600

The song thrushes are tuning up for the dawn chorus. Light filters through the tattered curtains warming the room and brushing Foster's folded brow. He loves to wake with the kiss of light. He loves this time of year, especially if the ground is dry. He feels the joy surge. He can name each one of the wild birds, imitate the song of each. Then there's the clamour of his guinea fowl – they too have names but of a different order. There's Ruby Tuesday, his familiar, his main girl – the matriarch. She always gives him a piece of her mind. Then there's Janine, Camilla,

Dolly Divine, Baby Love and the rest.

'Bloody 'ell, you make it sound like a brothel – you and your girls. Foz.' Ian was wont to tell anyone who'd listen about his "hill-shit best mate" who lived with a dozen females. If only, thought the now celibate Foster.

Foster wakes Lou the bitch for her early morning walk. Lou, still warm and drowsy in her box, shakes herself, stretches and bounds around her master before squatting down for a long pee by a birch tree. They walk across the north side fields to take in the changes and check the stock. A fox has passed through overnight. There are the remains of a sparrow-hawk's kill, grey feathers, blood, a part of a wing not worth the picking. Foster takes in everything – the foliage, the scents of the morning, the light on the white golf balls of Menwith Hill, the dew and tracks through the grass, the webs on the walls, the sharp cool of the places yet to be reached by the rising sun. And always the swelling song of the birds.

Foster feeds Lou her kibble and tripe. His own breakfast will be a modest affair. No smiling, cheerful and chubby, aproned wife waits for him – not that any aspect of this description would have matched his wife. Since Letty left, Foster sorts himself out. He likes to fry an omelette and sandwich it between two rough hunks of bread. Just a little salt and pepper. He's never understood why he enjoys an omelette but could never face a fried egg. He spoons a piling mound of instant coffee into his mug and tips on the boiling water. He'll take a little milk and sugar.

This morning Foster leaves the upper half of the kitchen stable door wide. He hears the slamming of car doors outside. It must be Sunday. The Methodists are parking up for chapel. His mother had been a committed chapel woman. His father had other ideas, like Foster himself. Both were of "the Gill". Neither of them had ever discussed it – they just knew and understood that there is a belief beyond the book, a spirit who walks and

185

stalks, even talks to you if you are lucky, a spirit in green, felt and rarely seen, and only then by the privileged few.

Foster smiles as he hears the full force of six Methodists singing *Lord of the Dance*. 'Keep breathing,' he offers this as a blessing to the elderly chapel goers. Their voices swell with the organ, and he feels his prayer has been answered. Rising and falling voices – just like the birds, but only once a week and later in the morning. There's something about Sundays, he reflects – serene and satisfying. He's poised to dump his pots in the sink and take Lou to the southside when he hears the phone ring. He picks up the receiver. It's the Damp Man – a call he's been expecting.

*****

Foster glowers at his own enraged face in the mirror.

'Meer, rargh, agh!' He is clinging onto the washbowl rim, roaring. He is showing some teeth.

'Let it out, Foster.' A soft, sweet, sympathetic voice, archaic in intonation. This is a different presence smiling over his right shoulder into the shaving mirror, but not one unfamiliar to Foster.

'You can fuck off too, Margaret,' snarls Foster.

'Fucking off is what I do. Come on, my boy – splash your pretty face. Think hard, think wise. It can be done; it shall come to pass. Think canny, my lovely. You can win this lass.'

'How? I don't have that sort of cash. What's the term – asset rich and income poor. Poor's not the half of it. I'm up to my ears in debt. Hey. Now where have you gone? Margaret? Margaret, come back. I didn't mean to be rude. Come back here, please. I need you, Margaret …'

A crystal disappearing laugh echoes round the bathroom. Then it is gone.

'I'm losing the plot. That Izzie lass has done for me. I'll never get her. I could never get my hands on that sort of sum.'

Glum Foster moves back into the bedroom and throws himself on the crumpled bed. He closes his eyes. Izzie, blonde and curvy, in dishevelled diaphanous negligee, is waiting for him. She suddenly pulls the silk wrap across her ample bosom and unwinds herself from the bedclothes. She stands. She's waving now. She sweetly raises her fingertips to her lips and blows a kiss:

'Bye, bye, Foster. Nice knowing you,' she simpers.

Foster emits something close to a whimper. She's going too. She's leaving me. 'Izzie, Izzie, come back. I'll do anything... Stop!'

'Tootle pip, honey bun,' lisps Izzie.

'Fuck off the lot of you, then.'

Foster, in despair, throws himself back on the bed, his head flops on the pillow and he drops slowly into a deep doze. As he descends, he relives the Damp Man's call:

'How much? How much did you just say? You're having a laugh, you are.' He's shouting at the ceiling.

Foster had stared bleakly down the phone, as if trying to persuade it to re-adjust the sum. His plans, his dreams, were falling apart. It was as if he had been winded.

'Are you still there Mr Hall? Mr Hall? Mr Hall, have we been cut off?'

'I were just pulling up a chair to sit down.'

'Would you like me to take you through the itemised estimate, or shall I call in tonight? I do such calls on Sundays. You will, of course, appreciate it covers extensive work. There may be stages – we can undertake a phase at a time. I'd be happy to tackle it in this way.'

'My mate Ian said you didn't do Harrogate prices. Sounds like a bloody shed load of money to me.'

'It's fair and reasonable for the work to be undertaken.'

'Happen you'll have to leave it with me for a bit. I'll need to see.' Foster switched off his mobile and stared out across the

Main Street. He could see all too clearly. There was no way. He felt anger and despair surge up inside him and he climbed the stairs slowly.

It's an hour later and Foster has re-surfaced from his bed. There's sheep to be attended to and Lou needs to go out. Why is it, thinks Foster, that when you finally feel cheerful, hopeful and optimistic, why is it at that moment of serenity, your world comes tumbling down?

The fields have lost their glow for Foster. The jaunty walk of earlier has transformed into a heavy trudge. Lou looks up for affection, but Foster can't even manage a pat on the head or a tweak of Lou's silken ears:

'It's not your fault old friend,' concedes Foster, his shoulders slumping in misery.

Lou's heart aches for her master; she knows all is not well in his world.

*****

Later that morning Lou and Foster descend to the Gill on the quad bike. Down at the bottom of the hill, Lou leaps off and settles on the grass. Foster paces along the line of sheep netting and wire that separates the lowest field from the steep gill itself. Foster is testing every post, wobbling each one for rot and possible replacement. Lou is watching her master working his way along the line. The bitch's head is cocked to one side. Suddenly her ears are up; she's on alert. Foster is still engrossed in levering out some stubborn staples. Lou growls a warning. Foster turns.

An elderly man is climbing over the netted dry-stone wall. Capping stones are falling both sides, rumbling as they fall. This man cuts a curious figure. He's wearing immaculately tailored country clothes – camel coloured plus fours, elegant brown woollen knee stockings, stout leather walking boots and a tweed Norfolk jacket. His accent is Yorkshire posh – Pathe News in the north.

'You there! Where's the ruddy path?' There's a distinctly accusatory tone to the man's voice. It was as if Foster had, in some way, failed in his duty of path provision. The man continues:

'No signs. Absolutely nothing to support the walker. Safe in your bloody hands – I don't think so. Disgraceful!'

Foster's jaw drops. He is unused to being addressed like this – on his own land, his territory. Walkers usually fear farmers; that's the way he likes it. Foster is so taken aback he holds out his hand to steady the man down from the wall. No word of thanks. The man pulls his hand from Foster, the moment he is steady with both feet on the ground.

'So where is this ruddy path; where has it gone?'

Foster points wordlessly up to the gate at the top of the hill.

'And where does that lead?'

'Timble.'

'Tut.'

Lou rears up and places her two front paws on the man's chest, by way of a greeting. The bitch is batted down sharply with a map.

'Keep your bloody dog under control.'

'Down Lou.' Foster speaks softly to her. He feels keen indignation on both his own, and on Lou's behalf.

The man walks off up the steep field. Foster watches. Halfway up, the walker starts to open a small side gate into the next field.

'Not that gate. It's the one at the top you want,' shouts Foster, his patience thinning further.

The man, half-turns, appears to wave either in acknowledgement or irritation and then proceeds up towards Izzie's seat. The man then disappears from Foster's view. That was quick thought Foster. He turns away and continues with his post work.

'Funny bugger,' reflects Foster to Lou. 'I wonder if he's got that there dementia, they all have now. You see Lou, you have to help old folk, no matter what irritating fucks they are, and even when it seems they don't want any helping.'

Lou nods; she didn't like the man at all, and her snout was still smarting from being blipped with the map.

Time comes to take a break and the pair approach Izzie's seat. Lou bounds ahead and then appears to be investigating something on the ground.

'Bloody hell!' Foster stares down to the ground. There, right in front of Izzie's seat, is a pyramid of excrement. Pushed neatly in the top, like a sandcastle flag, is a scroll of pink tissue.

'The dirty old bugger!' Foster gags and starts to unstrap his shovel from the back of the quad. He scoops up the offending pile and carries it off to the field boundary of his land. The sanctity of his sacred seat has been defiled.

'Dirty, dirty bugger!' Foster reiterates. The day had begun so well. He hoped it wouldn't keep on deteriorating. God knows what depths he would have reached by tea-time.

Foster and Lou do not linger by the stone seat today. Foster is praying for a sharp squall of rain to cleanse the whole area. As the quad chugs back up the fields, he notices the same man. This time he's walking away from Timble down the Lady Lane bridle path, towards the Gill. The man is walking in a distracted state, like a person possessed. It is as if he is being pulled by some strange force. Foster hears laughter on the wind.

'Steady girls – have your fun, but nothing fatal.' Foster is remembering the ancient tales of a man called Wardman, murdered in the Gill – struck dead with the butt of a gun – allegedly. Wardman's ghost haunted the Gill, terrifying travellers who passed the spot of his death, after dark. A catholic priest was called into exorcise the spirit, by means of prayer, a bell and a lighted candle cast into the beck. Foster shuddered. He didn't like that tale. He frequently found himself in the Gill at dusk, if not after dark. He knew it was not a place to linger.

It does flicker across Foster's conscience that it would be the decent thing to do, to follow this man down and lead him back to Timble. But the toilet business, as Foster would later recount to Ian, put him off any further intervention. He feels he's done quite enough. He's had his own problems this day.

As if things can't get any worse, Foster reflects. Approaching the edge of the village a familiar face pops into his vision. A head is sticking out between the blackthorn bushes. It is the familiar, strangely beautiful face under a cross-tied cloth, with fronds of plum and gunmetal grey hair hanging down in tendrils.

It's Margaret and she's trying to get Foster to stop. She smiles her most kindly smile and beckons him to follow. Foster turns to Lou. The hairs on the back of the bitch's neck are standing up right. She's staring at the apparition, emitting a low, whimpering growl. Margaret is beaming at Foster, leaning over the wall of the paddock, a small one-acre plot belonging to Foster. She appears to be gesticulating down towards her groin area.

Foster is frightened Maggie's going to lift her skirt: 'You can cut that business out now. I'm not interested.'

To be propositioned by his forebear would be the last straw, thinks Foster. She's never tried that on before.

'But Foster, come, see …' Margaret is quite insistent.

'What do you want with me?'

She smiles, smirks, points down at the ground.

'*Ransom!*' she says.

'What? Like kidnap someone for money? Get a grip, Margaret.'

Margaret, patient, shakes her head slowly.

'*No Foster. Think. Ransom plot. Cash in on what you've got. Sell this land to win her hand.*'

A chorus of airborne voices join with Margaret's:

'*Sell, sell, then who can tell?*'

It's the Gill Women.

A realisation reverberates round Foster's brain: 'You clever old twat. Mags, you're a genius.' Foster leaps from his quad, grabs hold of Maggie and dances round the paddock. The two are whooping, high-kicking and twirling each other round. There is a cacophony of cheers, squeals and delight from the sister Gill Women. These have appeared from Lady Lane.

Mrs Kearney, the new owner of The Grange, is adjusting the drapes in her extension. She is shocked to see Foster Hall embark on some frenzied jig – a solitary bizarre dance round the paddock, watched only by his dog who sits in a state of terror on the back of the man's quad bike.

Foster Hall has got to go, she thinks. That man has got to go. What will he be up to next? Local colour is one thing, but this behaviour is bizarre. And he could park anything on that land, deposit a huge muck heap, build some sheep shed, keep pigs – anything. He's got to go. These hill folk, she concludes, are loopy. They're all in-bred and bonkers. What on earth has got into that man? What makes a man like that suddenly cavort round the paddock like a man possessed? What's he on?

Mrs Kearney, Androulla, resolves to instruct her husband, Raymond, to go round this very night and make Foster Hall an offer no sane human being could ever refuse. Well, to ring him up at the very least. Otherwise, they will have to move. She feels distinctly vulnerable with that man prancing round, doing funny dances and cackling to the air. My God, he's unstable. Why he might reveal himself to the children. Buy him out – worth £100K, no £150K of anyone's money, even without planning permission. But with planning permission … Mrs Kearney sees there's a killing to be made, and the profit will be hers.

*****

It's later in the day when the telephone rings. Foster isn't sure whether to pick up the receiver. The day has been mixed, a day of extremes, a sequence of lows, but seeming to end on a high. He doesn't want any more trouble. Margaret and her scheme over selling the ransom plot has fired his thoughts. As he sits at the old table, wondering how to go about it, he realises he is a long, long distance from the goal.

Foster sees the code is local and thinks perhaps it is a neighbour saying the stock has broken out. The locals are good like that, even if they don't have a clue about farming. He lifts the receiver.

'Foster Hall?'

Foster doesn't recognise the voice. The man sounds posh, authoritative.

'That's me,' says Foster, with caution: 'Who are you?'

'It's Raymond Kearney from the Grange. We haven't met, not yet. I think you know my wife though?'

'I've done nowt to your wife,' grunts Foster, alarmed.

'No, my man, I'm not accusing you of anything. I have a proposition for you. You own the paddock next to our house. I'd like to meet up to talk about it. I wonder if you might consider selling it to me and my wife? We'd offer you a good price, you can be sure of that.'

'Well,' Foster pauses, thinking quickly. Not too keen, he cautions himself. 'I'll have to think – I've never thought to sell it. The paddock has been with t'Halls for four centuries.' Foster tries to supress a smirk. How has Margaret pulled off this one, he wonders?

'We'd both need valuations. Of course, we'd pay for yours, as well as our own, and your solicitor's fees. No worries for you there. It's just that Androulla has a vision for the landscaping of the grounds, and the paddock would increase her options, and the size and scope of her project, no end.'

'I can see how it might.'

'She's set her heart on a gazebo. She's seen one in the RHS mag. Can't live without it now. You know women and their needs.'

'Mine's fucked off…'

'Yes, I heard. Sorry for that. We'll, let's try to keep mine on side, and on site, eh?'

Silence.

Raymond continues blithely:

'I can't expect you to give me an answer now, but I'd like you to consider it carefully. It will be an offer you won't get every day.'

'Mr Kearney, I will.' Pause. 'I'll need to take advice. If I was thinking of selling it, I would have put it on the open market.'

'Well, I'll offer you £150K to settle now.' There's a hint of panic in Raymond's voice. Why, he was reasoning to himself, on the open market, someone else might buy it. Better the devil you know.

'And you'll pay costs on top?' Foster feels the man has lost his faculties.

'I said I would.'

'Alright. I'll sell.' Foster spoke without apparent enthusiasm: 'Done deal.'

'Good man. I'll write with all the details you'll need. All you need to do at this stage is to provide me with your solicitor. It'll have to go through the land registry, naturally.'

Foster replaces the receiver and starts to laugh. Winning the lottery couldn't have released such mirth and incredulity. Lou regarded her master with caution and concern.

'Margaret,' calls Foster, into the air: 'Margaret! Thank you, my precious!'

But the river never runs smooth for long. As Foster checks his emails, he opens one from the North Yorkshire Police Department. It's part of the NYPD community messaging facility. He likes to check the theft alerts and whether there are suspicious vehicles in the area. Sheep rustling, tractors and quad-bike thefts, kerosene thefts – all these worry him. This one is about a missing person. Foster scrutinises the details. There's no mistaking the description – age, gender, height, clothes. It's the man he met earlier. A vision of the pyramid crowned with a pink tissue flag flickers across his mind.

Foster experiences a sinking feeling, a heady mix of revulsion, guilt and shame. He could have stepped in and guided the man up to Timble and to safety. Now the police are searching for him. The man's daughter has reported the man missing and believes he might be in the area. He has a medical condition Foster can't pronounce and needs regular medication. The elderly man is prone to bouts of deep confusion, sometimes dementia.

Foster feels wretched. He decides he must respond. He rings the police who are grateful for the detail of Foster's sighting. The officer asks him if he would mind walking the Lady Lane bridle path to check and they will meet him down at Low Snowden, below Snowden Carr. Foster agrees readily, takes out his strongest torch and collects the reluctant Lou. He calculates that it will be dark in about an hour.

Deep dusk is falling as Foster crosses Dick's Beck bridge. The helicopter is out, making a tremendous racket. Its strong beam lights up the sweep of Snowden Carr. An officer, known to Foster by sight, greets him and thanks him for his help. Suddenly there are voices, lights flashing and a call over the officer's radio: 'He's here Sir, he's okay, breathing at least. He's down on the ground by this strange pitted stone.'

Foster and the officer clamber up the rough ground and approach the scene. Foster recognises the man immediately. He's clearly confused and lacks any of his earlier assurance. He's calling for his mother, in the voice of a child.

A lady arrives with another officer. Her joy and relief are tangible: 'Dad, what were you thinking about, going off like that?'

'Them bloody women – they are everywhere. They've led me a merry dance; they led me here. They scarpered when that thing came along. I don't blame them. I'm not getting in that sodding whirlybird thing!'

'Dad sees people who aren't there,' says the daughter to Foster and the officer. Then the elderly man focuses on Foster and Lou:

'Not you two again, you ignorant buggers – keep your bloody dog under control.'

'Dad, this farmer has just saved your life. You'd have been out on this bank all night and be dead of pneumonia in the morning, for sure. You just be grateful that there's some kindness and decency left in the world.'

'Kindness my arse. Watch that dog. It wants putting down.' Lou looks indignant.

Foster is relieved the man is still cantankerous. It means his condition is not too serious, and it also makes Foster feel less guilty. The man is persuaded onto a stretcher, strapped in and is hoist up into the helicopter. He shouts, rails and argues every inch of the way. The daughter turns to Foster and hugs him:

'Ignore him. You're my hero. I am so grateful. He's a grouchy old sod these days, but he hasn't always been that way out. He's not well you see, and I'm not sure how long I can look after him at home. Sometimes he's delirious, sometimes in dementia, and then some days he gives me the slip and off he goes. Like today …'

The lady's eyes fill with tears.

'I'm really sorry. You know, there comes a time those closest are not the best to look after a relative, not when the person is ill. You need to think about yourself, and your own family, if you have one.'

The lady reaches up to Foster and kisses him lightly on the cheek: 'Bless you for saying that, and for all you have done for Dad. I will always remember your kindness.'

One police car takes her to the hospital. The other conveys Foster and Lou to Black Crow Farm. As Foster climbs into the car, he thinks he sees a shimmering figure dodging behind an outcrop. He also thinks he can hear strange laughter on the air.

*****

And thus, begins the period of upheaval. These will not be the most comfortable of times for Foster. He is a creature of habit and has always resented anyone, or anything, ruffling his nest and disturbing his routines. But he is now filled with a sense of purpose he's never experienced in his life before.

Bring it on he thinks. And in comes the Damp Man, the bathroom and kitchen re-furbishers, the plasterers – a veritable army of specialists and their work teams. Vans galore. Each night there is progress. Each night, something to check, admire and to always, always, anticipate the day he will be able to approach Izzie.

The stately turbines turn on Penny Pot Lane. Days and months pass. Eventually, cometh the hour.

Part Three

No Turning Area After This Point

Licence my roving hands, and let them goe
Behind, before, above, between, below,
Oh my America, my new found lande,
My kingdome, safelist when with one man man'd,
My myne of precious stones, my Empiree,
How blest am I in this discovering thee,
To enter in these bonds is to be free,
Then, where my hand is set my seal shall be.'

Elegie XIX: To his Mistris Going to Bed
John Donne – probably late sixteenth century

1

Foster crosses the Wharfe

It's a rare thing for Foster to cross the Wharfe at Denton Bridge, unless he's pulling a trailer, early, to the abattoir, full of forty kg finished ram lambs. He's not dressed for the abattoir today. He's swapped his green rubber waterproof bib and brace trousers and jacket for his dark wool mix herringbone suit, the one he keeps for weddings and funerals. Foster has a date.

Date is stretching it, he checks himself. He's meeting Izzie in a café in Ilkley. It is their first meeting, that is, the first time he's met the real Izzie. He spoke to her on the phone two days ago.

Foster parks up in the supermarket car park. You get two hours free and he can pick up some cheeses after the meeting. He has a passion for their Lancashire cheese, but keeps this under wraps, because most of his mates are addicted to Wensleydale. Old loyalties die hard. He takes the zebra crossing and walks along Leeds Road. There is something about Ilkley not to his liking. He always feels out of place. Otley is a working town, and more to his taste. Ilkley has a different feel.

Ilkley exudes things alien to him – money, success, sophistication, a Yorkshire preciousness and pride. It makes his hands feel too big and too rough. It makes him feel rough too and second rate. He lowers his brow and scowls. Then he re-adjusts his face and tries to smile. He's about to meet the woman of his dreams, his bed sheets' companion. He needs to look cheerful. He practises a winning smile in Walton's window. His new expression is framed by preening peacock wallpaper. He throws back his shoulders and stretches into his five feet eleven and a half inches.

Foster has googled the café that Izzie proposed. She said that she would book them a table, to talk business. He's looking for somewhere called Legume. He passes a cinema – he didn't even know there was one in Ilkley. Why perhaps he and Izzie … No, he stops himself. Don't jump the guns.

A bit further along, and there it is, Legume. He runs his fingers through his hair and tries to think optimistic thoughts. A pleasant looking lady with a ponytail greets him. Is this her, he wonders, surprised she's wearing a pinafore?

'Table for one, sir?'

'No, it's a table for two, booked under the name of Izzie Blair.'

'Foster, you must be Foster?' A soft voice calls over from the seat in the side window alcove.

'Is this your first date?' asks the ponytail lady, beaming with interest and enthusiasm.

'Just a business meeting,' says Izzie, beckoning Foster to join her.

Foster follows, transfixed. This is not the Izzie of his bedclothes' reveries. This is not the lip-licking, centre-fold siren of the early hours. This is a pretty woman in her late thirties, with a spikey fringe, a halo of deep auburn curls, large, dark, wide-spaced eyes and a pale complexion. Everything about the real Izzie is neat, cheeky and challenging, not louche and dirty. She is wearing tight pale denim jeans, plum velvet knee boots and a pink over-sized jumper.

'So, Foster is it?' She talks in a cheerful way. She sizes him up, looks him up and down quite boldly: 'You never did say how you found out about me?'

'I found you in a hole?'

'You what?'

'I pulled your card out of a gatepost hole above Timble Gill. I was having a rest. I saw the edge of your card sticking up.'

'I see.' Izzie's tone, her demeanour changes. There is a shift. She looks uneasy. It is as if someone has walked across her slab.

'Are you alright? You look worried?'

Linda's words flood back to her, something like "it could fall into the hands of a wrong 'un, a stalker, a fetishist. Think of all of those women who have fallen prey to weirdo types."

But she herself had argued for serendipity, happenstance, fate. Was this fate? Her first impressions are positive. He doesn't seem like a predator or pervert. She looks him in the eye:

'Yes, I left it there. I never imagined I would reach anyone. I remember the moment I stuffed it in the hole. How extraordinary.'

'You reached me. You've sat on my table for months. You see, I've been having a renovation and I think I might be able to use your services. Curtains, advice, things like that.'

'Were you hiking when you found it?'

'No, I live up at Timble. It's my land. I'm a farmer.'

'Ah, a farmer. Wow. Well, that makes sense then.'

Foster suddenly feels self-conscious. She's looking at my hands, he thinks. She's having Ilkley thoughts.

'What made you do it?' He needs to distract her eyes from his hands, bring them back up to his face.

'What?'

'Stick your card in the hole?'

'I was walking with my friend Linda. I wasn't getting much work. I thought I'd drop my card in some unexpected places, just to see. Marketing, like. Promoting my business, trying to reach new customers.'

'Well, it's worked. Here I am. Job's yours if you want it?'

'It did work, didn't it? But don't you want to discuss terms?'

Izzie suddenly breaks off. She hears something strange in her head, like a call of birds, a clamouring. She raises her hands to her temples.

'Are you okay, Izzie?'

Izzie likes the softness of his voice, his concern, the worry written in his eyes. She feels she can share things with him. She says:

'I'm okay, yes, but I'm remembering the strange sensation when I walked along the side of the Gill, after sitting on the stone seat.'

'That would be the Gill Women.' A casual comment. Foster acknowledges to himself he is being unusually frank.

'Who?' Then Izzie remembers Linda's tale about the farmer she'd encountered. She continues:

'Gill Women? Tell me some more.'

'I hear them all the time. You learn to live with them. They are okay, but sometimes, if they are in an odd mood, or bored, I just get hell out of it. They like to mess with your mind.'

'Really?' Izzie is fascinated. She hadn't imagined a farmer would entertain such odd ideas.

'Hmm.' He smiles in such a way she can't tell if he is being serious. Foster is now eager to change the subject. He doesn't want her to think he's mad. He continues:

'Anyway, to the matter in hand. I need your advice. My damp has been sorted. I'm re-plastered now. De-humidifiers are working over-time. It'll all soon be dry. I'll be needing some new curtains, blinds perhaps, colour schemes, stuff, whatever, and I haven't got a clue.'

'I'd love to see your place. I can do concept, colour schemes, you name it. I'll come and look and measure up.'

'I'm what you might call a blank canvas. I'll be looking to you.'

'Ready to order yet, or would you like a minute longer?' The

Ponytail has returned with her pad.

'Give us a moment, luv,' says Foster.

Foster and Izzie scan their menus.

'This is my favourite café ever. I'm going to go for parsnip soup and a panini with roast pepper, hummus and olives. It's brilliant.'

'There's no meat option?' Foster's jaw drops.

'What bit of Legume don't you get, Foster? Did you think it was a leg of lamb?'

'No, I know what legumes are. I'm not thick. Some farmers swear by them for forage, but…'

Foster pauses. He hesitates to open a subject still sore to himself, and perhaps indelicate to Izzie, for he knows nothing of her circumstances. He searches for the right words: 'But, there are fertility issues for ewes, especially with the red clover. There's a lot of research going on around this. Thinking changes all the time.' This Foster delivers this with a new tone – erudite and informed, with only a hint of a piss-take.

The Ponytail has been rivetted by the turn in the discussion. She's wondering if she should warn the café owners that the name might imply a contraceptive ingredient. Could this be a culturally sensitive issue? She frowns.

Foster turns to her. He's anticipated her line of thought:

'You wouldn't want to be peddling prophylactics, would you?'

The Ponytail shakes her head, mutely. Silence.

'Sorry.' Izzie says the word as if she meant it. She looks a little shame-faced: 'I wasn't casting doubts about your brain, Foster. But this is a vegetarian café, for human beings who cannot countenance meat.'

'And some of us are carnivores – individual choice is important. So, where is the meat option?'

The eyes of the Ponytail meet Izzie's. A smile plays around the corners of Foster's lips. Izzie sees that Foster is laughing at them. She will not rise to the bait.

'Try something new Foster. It may not be what you ordered, but you might like it?'

'Indeed.' Foster looks into Izzie's large amber eyes and finds his anxieties are evaporating. He has a vision of this petite auburn-headed woman in her over-sized pink jumper and plum velvet knee boots kicking the big buxom blond off his bed and out of the door.

Izzie's thoughts are tiptoeing off along another path. She's worried. The Legume incident has unsettled her. She has a real problem with the type of person, usually male, who reacts irrationally and unreasonably to words like vegetarian, and more especially vegan. She's thinking of farmers, and people who feel their world is under attack from metropolitan, city-based, intelligent, liberal folk.

She's hoping Foster isn't the sort of man who denies climate change, calls walkers 'anoraks', deifies Boris Johnson, worships at the feet of Jeremy Clarkson and hangs dead rooks on Chris Packham's gateposts. The "safe in our hands" brigade. In short, she hopes he isn't a wanker.

Izzie bestows a disintegrating smile across the table to Foster.

No, she hopes Foster isn't in the wrong camp. She'll be watching him.

Izzie repeats her order.

'Make it two. Perhaps we'll have a bit of cake to finish off?' adds Foster.

'The carrot cake is to die for.'

'Again, make it two. A pot of tea?'

'Yes please.'

'Builders' or Earl Grey?' asks the Ponytail.

'Whatever?' says Foster. He feels he's made enough fuss. Izzie, in a conciliatory mood, orders Builders. She prefers it anyway.

The two sit and smile, and then don't know quite where to look. Something is registering with Foster, an alien sensation. It is the first time he can recall a woman ever saying sorry to him.

'I hope you are not an arse.' Izzie breaks into his musings.
'What?'
'I said, I hope you are not an arse.'
'That's a fine way to extend your customer base.'
And they both start to laugh.
'I only take commissions from people I approve of.'
'I see.'
'Tell me about your farm.'
'I thought you'd sacked me.'
'Not yet, but you are on a probationary period.'
'I'd better be good then.' Foster doesn't know what to make of this woman. But he feels disposed towards her and wants to find out more.

Foster clears his throat and begins: 'Well, it's been in the family for almost four centuries. Generations of Halls. I'm the last, a bit like the Last of the Mohicans. It's called Black Crow Farm.' He has a fleeting vision of himself, dressed as Chingachgook from the film, standing on the summit of Redding Hill. He's smirking to himself, enjoying the thought, but then notices Izzie looking anxious. She's raising her hands to her temples again.

'Is there something wrong, Izzie?'
'It's the big bird sound again – like a clamour of calls.'
'I hope it isn't that there tinnitus. Me dad had that. Drove him daft, it did. He was depressed anyway, but that broke the oss's back.

'No – I'm okay again. I'm sorry. You were saying, the Halls of Black Crow Farm? Do go on …'

*****

Izzie and Foster arrange to meet one week later. Izzie is going to come to Black Crow Farm for her initial consultation. She needs to get the feel of the house, she says, and Foster has told her so much, she's eager to see the farm, the land, the sheep. She's eager to see him again too, although she'd be hard pressed to admit to herself why.

Between the now and the then, Foster finds it hard to contain his excitement and anticipation. He is a-buzz. Even the funeral of his old school friend Alfie Waite can't subdue his spirits.

2

Losing his religion

Alfie's coffin enters to Albinoni's *Adagio in G minor*. The music is piped into Fewston Church from a CD. This had been one of Alfie's favourites. Alfie wasn't deeply into classical music, but they'd played it as funeral music in The Sopranos, and so Alfie had chosen it for his own. He wanted to come in to Albinoni and go out to Mazzy Star's *Look on down from the Bridge*, also on the Sopranos. That one made him think of the Packhorse Bridge down at Dob Park. Sandwiched in-between these are some prayers, nice words about Alfie from the vicar, a sweet and moving tribute from Wynsome, Alfie's sixteen-year-old daughter, and hymns. *Hills of the North* is the first hymn.

Foster loves *Hills of the North*. As a small child his thin sweet quivering descant had risen and fallen with visions of the landscape around him. It spoke to him as no other hymn could. It spoke of the valley. He still loves the hymn now, almost fifty years on. Foster lends his fine tenor voice to the faltering few. Later he engages the vicar, by the church porch:

'Alfie put that one in for Pan, Rev. You should have it more often.'

The Reverend is having no truck with the Old Religion.

'I'm sorry Foster. You need to go back to the words on the page. It's not about your lot doing funny dances at dawn.'

'Ah well, Rev. Damn good song and a cracking tune. Powerful. Wasted on the worthy, eh?'

'It were our Alfie's favourite too, Foster,' says the tearful newly widowed Miriam. 'Do you remember Miss on the piano? Shame they ever shut Fewston School.' Miriam leans forward and grasps Foster's hand.

'Thank you for coming, Foster,' she whispers. Foster has bent down his head to catch her words. He thinks he catches brandy on her breath. What's more he's convinced she's just reached up to suck his earlobe – nibbled it, almost; sucked it, yes. He finds this disturbing. He's further disconcerted by Wynsome who is pouting and posing for a selfie in front of her dad's coffin.

Foster had dated Miriam once, many years ago, before she started going with Alfie. Cheese and onion crisps. That's what Foster remembers as the deal-breaker. He'd bent to kiss her goodnight on that first date and that was enough for him.

This latest earlobe business is way out of order. He's poised to follow Alfie's box to Carlton Crem, to watch his old mate rattle off behind the velvet drapes. Now Foster expects Alfie's head to pop out and bellow 'hands off you dirty bastard.'

Foster makes his excuses and leaves to retrieve his car, parked a way up the lane.

The stretch of the A59 from Blubberhouses to Skipton is reckoned to be the most dangerous road in the country. That said, there are sections of it that could claim to be the most beautiful. Foster loves the pass through Kex Gill. He's still humming *Hills of the North*, as he negotiates the hairpins, through the deep canyon with its sinister rocky outcrops. He's stuck at the temporary lights.

'Yea though I walk through the Valley of the Shadow of Death,' thinks Foster. Chilling stuff. Poor Alfie, barely dead and she's stretching up to his old best friend and sucking off his lobes. Cheese and onion crisps, and now this. Alfie gone to meet his maker. Letty gone too, but to the Burley builder. How might it be with Izzie, if they ever become an item? Whose lobe would Izzie be licking, with him still warm on the slab? Or would she be doing a selfie for her followers? He visualises a long line of thumbs ups, stretching off the page.

Doubt turns Foster's thinking back, away from passion and the profane. It's more along the lines of the meaning of life, the 'why are we here?' question. Churches always make him uneasy, queasy, reflective and restless, especially Fewston. Fewston troubles him. It's as if it's waiting for him, that it knows what he doesn't. Sometimes he feels the thick walls breathe.

When had he finally lost his religion, Foster muses? Why didn't that stuff seem to matter anymore? It used to. Both his parents' ashes rest in the north-west corner of the yard. What would they have said to him? Well, his mother at least, for his father had all the makings of a pagan, a cunning man, as they used to call them.

Then he remembers that Christmas Eve over a year back. His first Christmas without Letty and he'd felt lonelier than he could ever recall. He'd sought refuge, and company, in the church. Then the app priest had arrived for Midnight mass. They'd beamed him in from God knows where, this stand-in priest. Foster relives that night, in his head.

The weather was blasting in from the north-east. It sharpened the icy waste of the reservoir. Billowing white robes and a halo of snowflakes. The man trailed slush puddles up the flagstones to the altar from his black Doc Martens. The church warden shook her head. She was thinking Health and Safety, but mainly – that someone, like herself, would have to mop his mess in the morning.

Priest mounted the stone steps and turned to face the congregation. His right hand fumbled through a slit in his cassock into his trouser region. The congregation's collective eyebrow raised. Foster was thinking about all the dodgy priests that had been in the news, and that the congregation didn't know a thing about this one. In these remote parts there was a tendency to distrust strangers. They all read the local papers. Leeds and Bradford came over like Naples in the crime series 'Gomorrah'.

Finally, priest pulled it out and the fumbling stopped. His iPhone. Relief fast followed by horror. A flying vicar with the service on his iPhone. Baby Jesus are we come to this Foster wondered? What was in the man's head? No-one can get a signal up here, at the best of times, whatever network. The hills, the trees, the thick stone walls.

Well, the hills closed in, in curiosity, the trees teased, the waters of the reservoir rolled with mirth. The congregation sang the Christina Rosetti, the only one they could remember by heart, four times. App vicar wouldn't let the wardens distribute the books. Since when had God gone paperless?

After the service Foster crunched up iced North Lane, the back way to Timble. He went to check the flock, the in-lamb ewes. He sat on the cold hard hillside.

Margaret glimmered and shimmered up and sat down next to him in companionable silence. Slowly the ewes surrounded them too, settled, snuggled up, steam breath rising in the clear star-studded moonlight. They watched the firmament together. Early hours, Christmas morn.

Yep, that was the year I finally lost my religion, thinks Foster, and found my God.

3

Measuring up

Your pretie mouth with divers gifts,
Calen o Custere me
Which driveth wise men to their shifts:
Calen o Custere me
So brave, so fine, so trim, so yong,
Calen o Custere me
With heavenlie wit and pleasant tongue,
Calen o Custere me

A Sonet of a lover in praise of his lady –Unknown –
first registered as a broadside ballad in 1582

The knocked-about pine table stretches almost the length of Foster's kitchen. Bills and newspapers, unopened brown window envelopes, junk mail – garish adverts for cut-price pizzas and curries and factory outlets, The Watchtower magazine and a can of WD40 slug it out with a half-full milk carton and an empty can of beer. Foster has tried to tidy, but he must have been distracted. Izzie is welcomed into the kitchen and she gasps.

Izzie blanks the clutter. Instead she sees the original stone floor, the inglenook fireplace with its rackan crook, the rusted ham hooks hanging down from a span of ancient beams and the sunlight shining in through the grimy mullion windows, picking out the muted colours in the tapestry fabric of the tattered window seat cushions.

'Foster, I know you said this house has been in the family for four hundred years, but I never imagined ... It's quite beautiful; in fact, it's bloody brilliant.'

Foster drops his shoulders and lets out a long exhalation of breath.

'It's listed, you know.' He pauses, then he confesses: 'I thought you'd hate it. Even though I've had the work done, I've been fretting about what you'd say. My mates have always said it was a shithole. As for their wives ... As for my ex-wife ... Don't go there.'

'More fools all of them. I love it.'

'I've always been well suited with it too. Tea or tour?'

'Tour! I'm bursting to look around it – I want to see it all. Then you can make tea, and I can sit and think.'

'Come on then.' Foster bows formally to Izzie as she walks through to the central hall. Elaborately carved and spiked wooden bannisters skirt the foot-worn stone stairs – gothic in style.

Izzie does the tour in an awe-inspired silence. So many visions; so many possibilities. She tells Foster how it is essential to retain the original character, but to enhance, simplify, be more minimalistic ...

'Tidy up a bit, you mean?'

'Well, yes, but more than that. With a bit of organisation, ingenious storage solutions in wasted space and voids – but Foster, you have so much space here, and so many delightful rooms. Your windows are amazing – why, everything is.'

'I live in the kitchen, sleep in the bedroom and use the bathroom as necessary. I sometimes think I'd be better off in a flat.'

'I think you need to look to your creature comforts a little more.'

'But there's the dog, and the ailing lambs come in, in early spring, and so much mud and shite.'

'A little more discipline Foster,' Izzie teases, 'and a drying/ cleaning area for mud and boots and wet clothes. You've got a utility room with a fine Belfast sink. They've gone back to calling them boot rooms now in the house-style magazines. You seem to have used that excellent space just to dump stuff. I think I can get you sorted.'

'Will you take me on then?' he gazes in disbelief at Izzie. 'So to speak,' he adds, a little embarrassed in-case he's over-stepping the mark. Instead she just nods, as if it is a done deal. And in Izzie's head, it is becoming one. A bit like Elizabeth Bennett seeing Pemberley for the first time, Izzie has decided she will most certainly take on Foster Hall, should the opportunity arise. In truth, she feels she's finally come home. She's feeling a surge of anticipation for her new commission. Izzie senses this might become more than just another job.

Foster brews a pot of tea and retrieves some ginger nuts from the pantry. Izzie has followed him in.

'What an amazing space! A brilliant pantry. You don't see so many nowadays,' says Izzie in admiration: 'They tend to knock them into the kitchens. Estate agents call them larders; they've become a status symbol, you know.'

Foster's brows join in perplexity. Boot rooms and larders? What's wrong with these people, he wonders. Haven't they got enough to think about?

The two sit down together, side by side, at the table. Izzie has brought her bag of brochures, catalogues, colour charts, fabric swatches. She's thinking Arts and Crafts meets minimalism. Functional or beautiful, and preferably both. Occasionally their heads touch. She steals the odd glance at his neck, his frayed plaid shirt collar, the way his deep plum and silver hair curls inside it. Occasionally she catches the scent of him and finds it very appealing. At one point he inhales and says: "You smell great – you're sweeter than sileage.' Then he's embarrassed and apologises. Izzie smiles:

'I'm glad you like it – Rochas' Femme. It's the only perfume I've worn since I was nineteen.'

'Well, I'm just not used to women smelling as good as you.'

They are both suddenly uncomfortable. Foster doesn't want to frighten Izzie off by being too forward. He proposes going down to the Gill, to the stone where he found her card.

'A sentimental journey?' he says.

Izzie's eye's flash with delight: 'Yes, let's walk down.'

'Walk? I was going to take you on the back of my quad. Farmers avoid walking anywhere if it can be avoided.'

'I've never been on a quad, ever.'

'Time to try, come on.' He leads her through the utility room to the back courtyard.

Perhaps Foster hasn't thought it through. Perhaps he has. To take a passenger on a quad bike requires a level of intimacy Izzie has not anticipated. She affects nonchalance and throws her leg over the seat, gamely.

But something is about to come between them.

'Can I put my Lou between your legs?'

Izzie has not expected such a proposition, and so crudely couched. She feels her colour rising, her cheeks exceed her blusher – apricot to crimson. She forms words, reforms them and falters. Her quest for a suitable response is brought sharply to a conclusion by the piercing blast of a whistle, a whistle which appears entirely lodged in Foster's mouth, although secured round his neck by a type of lanyard. Then, a wild projectile of fur, white, grey and black, rears up in her face, swivels and plonks itself down right between her inner thighs.

'She'll settle – no need to hold her. Just budge your arse back a bit. Give the lass some space.'

'It says here,' Izzie points primly to the safety instructions printed on the side of the red quad bike, 'it says here, don't carry a passenger. It says it can destabilise the bike!'

'Well you and Lou make two passengers, so that should even things up.' Foster is pleased with his response.

'This dog smells a bit.' The words are out before Izzie can check herself.

'Bitch.' says Foster.

'Hey, steady on ...'

'She's a bitch, not a dog,' qualifies Foster quite oblivious: 'they can give off a bit when they're in season. She's just about to come out of hers.'

By the time Izzie adjusts herself to accommodate Lou, Foster has straddled the barrel of the quad bike, engaged neutral, activated his engine and the bike is moving forward in second. Izzie reflects that she had never shared so intimate a position with a relative stranger, with only a furry bitch between them. She feels in shock. This outstrips Linda's warnings.

The quad jolts. Izzie finds herself pinching her skinny buttocks against the seat for stability. She's never been on a motor bike before, let alone a quad. She's seen adverts for 'The Quad Bike Experience' in Nidderdale, on the Ilkley Chat. Here she is, experiencing this one for free. She strokes Lou's soft silken head and is rewarded by an enthusiastic lick on the ear. She is determined to enjoy the ride.

Halfway down Back Lane, where the main line of houses stop, Izzie notices a sign nailed to an ancient free-standing stone gatepost. A white square with bold red letters:

No turning area after this point

Izzie thinks about this, but only for a moment or two.

So be it, she decides, as Foster gets off-then-on the bike to open the gate onto his top field. Yes, so be it, she thinks.

They pass over three fields, through three gates and he stops. There is the seat:

'Izzie's seat!' calls Foster, to her. Lou, sensing the special moment, leaps up onto the stone, jumps up towards Izzie's face and licks her enthusiastically. 'Down girl! Lou, what has got into you? She's taken to you alright.'

'So, have I passed the test?'

'You've certainly been awarded the Lou Paw of Approval.' Foster sits on the stone.

'And what about Foster's Seal of Approval?

'Jury is still out,' laughs Foster, tapping the stone for Izzie to come and sit with him. He continues: 'What about me? Am I still in my probationary period?'

'Hmm? We'll see. But I'll tell you this – you are so lucky! This beautiful place, your farm, even your dog adores you.'

'Everything but the girl, eh?'

Izzie sees the sadness behind the mirth and changes the subject.

Her eyes follow the path down to the Gill. The recent rain has been heavy, and the beck is pounding through the steep gulley. He follows the direction of her eyes.

'No,' he says softly. 'We'll take the path, just behind us, through the other gate, and down to the right. There's a place I want you to see.'

Lou bounds ahead. Along the edge of the trees down by the Gill, Izzie sees the gate. Beyond this, further down, the beck. She gasps at its beauty. Foster leads her down a rough path. Lou is waiting.

'Throw her a stick and she'll be your mate forever.'

Lou plunges into the pool. She starts to swim. The pool has formed at the base of a low waterfall. The bedrock has been worn away over the centuries. The bank arches up on the far side, creepers barely covering the hollowed-out cavern. Foster's side has a beach and shallows, leading down to the pool. This is where Foster's land ends. It is a perfectly private and secluded place. Izzie feels the enchantment, the magic, the shifting. She says nothing to Foster, just sits down on a large smooth stone and starts to remove her shoes.

'Watch for thorns – it would be easy to get a cut. The stones are sharp.'

Foster's words fall on deaf ears. Izzie is like a child first seeing the sea. She peels off her top and then her jeans and enters the pool in her bra and pants.

'I'm still decent!' she calls to him, by way of reassurance.

'I wish I could say the same for my thoughts,' he calls back.

'Well, rather than standing there having dirty thoughts, come in and join me, and we'll see how the moment takes us.'

'Jees Izzie!'

'Come on in. It's cold. I need a warm body like yours.'

Foster was never good with buttons. In the end he pulls his shirt over his head, kicks off his boots, totters out of his trousers and socks, and goes in in his boxers. Neither Izzie's bra and pants, nor Foster's boxers survive for more than three minutes.

'Come on Foster, consenting adults and all that.'

'This wasn't listed on your card, my girl.'

'Optional extras – I've plenty of those you know.'

'I can imagine.'

'This must be what the Sunday supplements call wild swimming. Bear Grylls?' calls Izzie, above the sound of the tumbling stream.

'Bare arse more like. It's certainly wild, Izzie, but my feet at least are still on the bottom. Now what are you doing? Oh, good god lass!'

But our bathers are not alone. The trees are arching over. It starts as a rustling of late summer leaves, twigs and branches. A hissing of approval, encouragement in the breeze. Delighted, whispered mirth. Bright eyes are everywhere.

We'll leave them there, for a little while.

4

Come live with me and be my love

Come live with me and be my love,
And we will all the pleasures prove,
That Valleys, groves, hills and fields,
Woods, or sleepy mountain yields.

The Passionate Shepherd to His Love
Christopher Marlowe 1599

It's a weary trio that chugs back up the four fields on the quad.
Some subtle shift has happened. Lou now teeters on the back
board. The bitch has relinquished her space with good grace.
Izzie's arms are now wrapped around Foster's waist.

It's as if we are on a ship, muses Izzie, as she feels the early
evening air rushing by her face and ears. A land ship, of course.
But the land itself rolls and dips like waves.

The trees and the hedgerows are blushing in the early evening
sun light. Some leaves have started to turn, just; the purple sloes
are formed on the blackthorn, too soon to pick, and the red haws
showing in the hedgerows. The pale mauve-blue harebells nod
as Izzie passes, so fragile, she thinks. Izzie feels an indescribable

oneness with everything around her, especially the man she hangs on to. She feels invisible and yet so there she can't quite believe the turn her life has taken or even trust her reactions.

She laughs softly to herself. Foster half turns his head. She brushes his ear with her lips, lightly. This time Foster doesn't mind at all. Izzie banishes the ghost of Miriam. Izzie is seeing off Letty too. She fills his head, his heart and his senses.

And so, begins their new life. Paint cards, swatches and sex, so much sex. Foster feels himself blessed.

Three days into what they now call the project, Izzie arrives with a full car. Her sewing machines, needlecraft cases, bathroom bag, clothes in a case and cat in a basket. Foster had suggested, and Izzie agreed, that it made more sense than the daily commute to and from Hebden Bridge, the traffic being what it is. Foster said she should empty her fridge and mothball her small terrace. Instead she let her newly separated friend, Jenny, move into it.

'Just keep it aired and clean,' asked Izzie, 'for I don't know when I'll be back.'

'If you'll be back!' protested Linda. 'I've never seen you like this before.'

'Love?' asked Jenny,

'I suppose.' Izzie started to laugh. Her friends couldn't help but notice, she looked almost tearful.

She hugged Linda, who whispered: 'Take care, I'm going to miss you loads kid.'

*****

The first Friday after Izzie has moved in, Ginny pops round for Foster's shopping list. Foster makes a formal introduction.

'My sister, Ginny,' he says to Izzie, and to Ginny: 'Izzie is my interior designer.' Foster makes no attempt to explain further. Ginny notes the sewing equipment, and her suspicions are in no way aroused. When she asks Foster if he has a list, he says that they will be going into Harrogate to look at some fabrics, and that he'll be able to pick up some things there.

Ginny confesses to herself that the Izzie of her own imagination, the Girl in a Hole, is a far-removed thing from the real-life Izzie.

'Definitely not Foster's type,' she confides in June. 'I'm so relieved. And I've seen her in action on her machine. She certainly knows what she's doing. I might get her to run me up some curtains too, before she disappears off the scene. She's quick, neat and very competent. It seems she's in high demand by some of the local amateur dramatic groups and theatres, even as far as Leeds. She does garment restoration – vintage as well as alterations. Quite a useful girl to know about.'

'So, is the place looking better, Ginny?'

'My God yes! You'll have to have a look. Nowhere near finished. By no means. But so much better. I've only seen downstairs, but if upstairs is anywhere like it, I could move back in myself. This Girl in a Hole has good taste – I have to hand it to her – and style.'

'You might have to stop calling her that, Ginny. You might get yourself into trouble.'

'Don't be silly. I'm not going to call it to her face. I'm not daft.'

June looks anxious. There had already been talk in the village. Clearly it hadn't reached Ginny, but Diddy Kex had seen Foster and the woman together on the quad – 'So close up I'm surprised she could catch her breath. Huh! She might catch some 'at else if she don't watch it. Poor bloody dog's pushed out onto the back shelf.'

'Aye,' said Midge. 'No fool like an old fool.'

'Lad ain't that old, is he?'

'Whether or not, a lass like that could give any fella a new lease of life.' The men guffawed.

June had bid them both a curt 'Good day.' She is now troubled because she knows that Ginny will only notice what she wants to see. Her friend will not want to see something growing between her half-brother and the so-called Girl in a Hole. June wonders if she should warn Ginny about their growing intimacy. But no, she reasons. She doesn't know anything, and she does not wish to be the cause of Ginny blundering in and laying down the law. Leave well alone, June concludes.

5

Let's see what he's been up to …

Busie old foole, unruly Sunne,
Why does thou thus,
Through windows, and through curtaines call on
us?

The Sunne Rising – John Donne 1633

Ginny leads Letty down the front path to Black Crow Farm. She pulls her key out of her pocket. The heavy oak door swings open.

'Are you sure he won't mind, Ginny?'

'He won't mind because he isn't going to know. It's sale day. The girl might be here, but we'll hear the machine going if she is, and I won't say who you are, if that's okay?'

Letty nods. A conspiratorial silence falls. Letty takes in the central hall. She walks into the dining kitchen. Her jaw drops open: 'I don't believe this. Amazing! It's transformed. Granite! Look at those appliances. And you think he's done all this for me?' I wish to God he'd done it whilst I was here.'

'When it's all done, he'll come knocking – you can be sure

of that.'

'Does he ever mention me?'

'No. Too painful, I imagine. He's always been deep. He keeps his emotions well hidden; he always did. Letty, are you really happy down in Burley?'

Letty doesn't reply. If the question had been put an hour earlier, she might have had a more enthusiastic and committed response. Her attention is diverted.

'I just love these curtains. Zoffany? And look at those fittings. And these gorgeous wall colours. This place must be worth a fortune now?' Letty snuffles in the air: 'It even smells different. Lilies? What the hell has happened to him? Since when has Foster ever invested in flowers?'

'A broken heart can concentrate the mind. It has always been a catalyst to self-improvement. Come and see the lounge.'

'He's gone eclectic minimalist – thrown out all the furniture! I saw a programme on this – afternoon telly. Foster's never thrown out anything in his life, not even a sweet wrapper. So, where has the money come from? All this is new stuff.'

Ginny shrugs: 'A little recent windfall, perhaps. Upstairs – shall we go up?'

'New stair carpet? Nice.'

Ginny reaches the top of the stairs: 'It's all nice, Letty. I just knew you'd love it. That's why I invited you up – to see it. Let's see what Foster has been up to with the Girl in a Hole in your old bedroom?'

Ginny throws open the master suite door with a flourish.

Letty steps forward then freezes to the spot. Her ear-splitting, high-pitched shriek settles somewhere between an 'eugh' and an 'aagh'. Her eyes are torn between incredulity and horror; her mouth opts for disgust. Ginny's face looms over Letty's shoulder. Her look is one of mortification.

Before them, on the bed, a tangle of naked limbs and spent lust. Two bodies still fused and napping. The post coital reverie is brought to an abrupt end. Izzie reaches down, and snatches the quilt from the floor, for cover.

Foster's head turns sharply to the door: 'What in fuck's name …?'

The grand tour is terminated. Letty storms down the stairs. Ginny follows, stammering apologies to Letty.

'So, he's done it all for me, you fool! You! You silly old cow!'

'No need for that!' gasps Ginny, in deep shock.

'His bloody designer – schemer more like. Did you set me up?'

Letty raises her hand to silence any response.'

'Goodbye Ginny.' Ginny will never forget the look her former sister-in-law shot her as she opened her car door. Letty speeds off back to Burley, and her newly beloved builder.

Back upstairs, Foster is lying back against the headboard with his eyes locked shut.

'Foz?' whispers Izzie. She's still processing the vision of Ginny with a woman she doesn't recognise, a woman a few years older than herself. She hears the door slam to. She hears raised voices outside, and a car engine starting. Then all is quiet.

'Foz?'

'That was the wife,' groans Foster, 'Ginny and the wife.' Foster still hasn't opened his eyes.

Izzie begins to shake.

'Are you all right love?' Foster feels her body shaking uncontrollably. He opens one eye to regard her.

Izzie is convulsed in laughter; it's infectious. They laugh until they can barely breath.

'It's not funny, Izzie.' More mirth.

'We'll never live it down!' Izzie is beginning to collect herself.

'Ah bollocks. Fancy a brew?'

*****

Margaret emerges from the back of Black Crow Farm. She

has watched the altercation between Ginny and Letty with unconcealed delight. Her eyes follow the car out of the village, and then she watches Ginny make off, in a high degree of agitation, towards her friend June's. Delicious.

Margaret has had a busy morning. The wisdom of foresight, she reflects. Sensing Ginny's treacherous scheme, Margaret engineered a timely intervention. She found a six-inch nail and placed it carefully beneath the back passenger-side tyre of Foster's Defender. This was done in the sure knowledge that Foster would have to reverse out to get to the tup sale at Skipton. Margaret anticipated that Foster would be in no frame of mind to change a wheel so early in the morning. She had noticed he was finding it harder and harder to rise early. The lark was becoming the bat.

Foster's expletives on finding a flat were not as foul as was his wont. He shrugged, went back inside, put the kettle on, and took Izzie a cup of tea. The rest is history.

*****

Later that morning, in June's kitchen, the whole sad saga comes out:

'I've never felt so humiliated in my life! June, it isn't at all funny!'

'I'm sorry Ginny.' June tries to contain her giggles. She clamps her palm over her mouth. Later, as the story sinks in, June will have the odd qualm that she could have made an early intervention about the relationship of Foster and Izzie, to prepare Ginny, but these thoughts only linger for a moment, and she, June, had no idea Ginny was going to try to effect a reconciliation between the estranged husband and wife.

'I should have known. I should have guessed when I found mother in the skip.'

'You what?'

'I found the framed photo of our mother thrown into the

skip. She was wearing her chapel hat with the peach chiffon trim. Mother was always in the bedroom, on the dressing table, watching over him. I should have known he'd gone off the rails.'

'What did you do?'

'I climbed up and retrieved it. I had to fetch my pantry steps. It wasn't easy. There'll come a time he resumes his right mind. I'll pop it back. But I fear there'll be no persuading Letty back.'

'Would you want Letty back? She sounds to have been very rude to you, Ginny.'

'She was. Unforgiveable. Perhaps, in the circumstances, but no – so rude and uncivil!'

'Will you apologise to Foster? Your visit, the house tour, might be deemed a little intrusive, impertinent even?'

'No! Absolutely not. I've always been welcome in his house – to come and go as I please. I put his shopping away. It was my home once. I'll not apologise to him and as for that, that, slut, slapper, whore – that f'ing Girl in a Hole – apologise, indeed! The very idea of it.'

Part Four

The Good-Morrow

If ever any beauty I did see,
Which I desir'd, and got, 'twas but a dreame of
thee.

And now good morrow to our waking soules,
Which watch not one another out of feare;
For love, all love of other sights controules,
And makes one little roome, an every where.

The Good-Morrow – John Donne 1633

1

Moondance

Izzie presses her palms to her nostrils. She slowly inhales the sweetest of scents. It's thick, strong and musky. It's deep and dark, not dirty – well, not entirely. Pheromone, ram pheromone, a secretion to make animals change their behaviour. It is the queen bee substance. It is the essence of a ram. It will make the ewes available, willing to stand, carry the weight of the ram on their backs. And to Izzie, that scent just makes her happy. She raises her hands again and breathes in. You can keep the pine forest, she's thinking, keep the fields of hazy lavender in Provence, keep the fresh-washed cotton in the press. Izzie confesses to becoming a secret ram harness sniffer.

Foster's going to put his tups in early this year. He explains to Izzie that it is a matter of optimising new grass growth in the spring. It's about catching the ewes at their fertility peak, it's about lambing, weaning and ewe recovery, the whole management of the flock. Izzie commits each detail to memory. She's trying hard and quick to learn.

Foster has explained that the planned date for the start of lambing is the pivotal element. Gestation is one hundred and forty-seven days, give or take about three, and the new lambs will be nibbling grass at six weeks of age. Foster shows Izzie the gestation table – the tupping/lambing ready reckoner.

'We will start lambing, give or take those few days, on 9th March, next spring.'

Time, the seasons and the changes they bring. The car bonnet has only just cooled from the September sales, the trailer hosed out and the records entered up, and now they are bringing in the stock rams, sorting their feet, fitting their harnesses, and slotting into each the crayon blocks. Foster explains how they will change the crayons every week through tupping.

'We will start with gold, move onto red and then finish off, hopefully, with blue. Blue on red makes purple and we'd prefer not to see too much of that on the rear ends of our ewes. I always dream of a tight lambing. A protracted lambing means more feeding complications, more chance of mastitis and more broken nights for us.'

Foster tells Izzie that exhaustion at lambing will be cumulative:

'You know, I've sometimes wondered if the ancients cursed their foes with 'God send them a long, drawn-out lambing. You'll be absolutely bollocksed by the end of it, Izzie.'

Izzie is learning the ropes. Foster is giving her a crash course in farming.

On the surface, autumn shows a closing down, the fall of brittle leaves. But, under the earth surface the conspiracy of the rebirth starts early. Time is an accelerating vehicle. October brings this quickening, the strengthening pulse. Life dances to the beat of the unseen heart. The seeds will be sown for the spring crop now.

The cold set in four days ago. The chill in the air nipped and shocked. It had seemed to Izzie, this early autumn, that the warm, hazy, delicious days would go on for ever. The nip in the air was like a pinch from an uncaring employer. 'Work to be done, you, this won't do.' And so, the pair of them set to, with

Lou.

And the cold and the shortening of the days prod the rams into action too. They wake from their summer torpor. Languor and sloth evaporate with the first frost. Izzie finds even fitting the harness is a challenge, for the ram who wanted his belly rubbed and his silken ears tweaked last week is now no longer her darling boy.

She looks at Foster's beautiful stock tups. They are full of the old buck, as Foster calls it, meaning the devil himself, and it makes her laugh as Foster tries to restrain them, one hand beneath the chin and a knee in the flank, for the fitting of each harness. An irritable shake of the noble head and Foster's feet leave the straw. But he won't let go. And neither will she. Izzie's down on her knees, struggling to clasp the harness under the tup's massive girth.

'There's some gorgeous girls out there waiting for you, boys,' says Izzie. She pushes the stiff plastic clasp home. Then, up strut these tups into the trailer, all ready for action. Lou brings up the rear.

If the change of season has stirred the old buck, so has the moon. For all the ruminant males in the northern hemisphere dance to the same beat. Fertility peaks at the Rutting Moon, the second full moon after the autumn equinox, late October.

Izzie looks on as the rams join the tupping groups on the south-side fields and softly serenades them, a snatch of a fond, remembered song – Van Morrison's *Moondance*.

'I'll make a farmer of you yet, Izzie,' whispers Foster, with pride.

2

Hope spears, at the turn of the year

The scanner man rings late on Christmas Day evening. 'I'll see you at 6.30 am – day after tomorrow.' He has a gruff, some might say insinuating, way of talking. But he doesn't talk much. Foster replaces the cream telephone receiver: 'That lad brooks no opposition, so save your breath for the remains of the pudding.'

Izzie stares at Foster in disbelief.

Not just 'you' she thinks, but ewe and ewe and ewe – almost five hundred of them. Tomorrow is Boxing Day, for some a public holiday, but no rest for scanner man, or for Foster and Izzie.

'We'll have to get them in – they're all over the show,' says Foster.

And so they do, droving and driving, jollying and cajoling, with the odd gentle kick up the arse, for some girls would like to savour the neighbours' listing wall flowers, the last flush of autumn roses, the winter jasmine spilling over stone walls. Some ewes rear up on their back legs and peek and juke over the walls – they love to scan peoples' gardens, plan their menus.

The lanes through Timble are strewn with dark pellets – Back Lane, Billy Lane, then past the pub and across Main Street. Too much excitement. Down the track they thunder, hefted to the barn. Girls will do most things for a bag of sugar beet pellets, especially with Lou in hot pursuit.

And when all the in-lamb ewes are comfortable, and bedded down, enjoying the teaming racks of summer's fragrant hay, Izzie can't help but wonder at their fleecy loveliness. Their sweet warm breaths steaming upwards, their sheep fragrance, their trust and companionship. The Leaper, flock matriarch, turns nine this year, and allows her soft silken ears to be tugged and rumpled. Her eyes say neatly done, for she considers herself a key team member. Foster notes her sunken flanks, her parting fleece, once tight as a rug, and he knows this ewe will not go round again; this will be her last lambing, and life the less for her passing, and so much richer for the knowing. He does not share this with Izzie.

Boxing Day is a day of treatments – quality ewe time. Pedicures, foot baths, wormer, fluker, sorting, inspection and general ewe encouragement. In-lamb ewes need reassurance. Foster and Izzie tidy the barn together – lime, straw and sawdust.

Next day, at 6.15 am the scanner man arrives. He brings a lady helper. This pleases Foster, for she has a soft and gentle demeanour, and this makes the scanner man more polite. All hands are involved to set up pens, and a chute to the scanning platform. Scanner man fine tunes his screen. His helper holds the spray canister. The universal code – no mark for twins, one dot on the shoulder for a single, one dot on the rump for triplets and two for quads. God save us from quins, thinks Foster. He had them once and they survived. 'G' is for geld, and 'L' for late – a late lamber.

And through the chute they file. 'More singles than normal for you lot,' says scanner man, 'fewer multiples.'

'It's to be expected,' says Foster: 'This year's flock is younger.'

It's all done by 2.00 pm and then Izzie cooks something to eat.

'Always feed the scanner man,' explains Foster.

They all warm themselves up indoors. When the scanner man and his helper have gone, Foster and Izzie go back down to the barn and start to sort by spots or lack of them. Twins are the biggest group by far. Triplets and the quads go together. They will start to be fed soon. February's feeding regime will be dictated by all these scores. The ewes will remain in these groups until lambing.

Scanning is like the witch-hazel's sulphur beacon to the turn of the year. It is like the hope spears of tete-a-tete daffodils to early spring, it's the unfailing thrill of the first rose of May and the deep depths of dahlias to autumn's darkening days. Scanning says here there is new life – just look at those swirling shapes on that grey and grainy screen.

*****

It's later that day. The log burner is lit. Foster studies the lambing scores with the excitement of the Saturday five o'clock football results. He's noticed during the sorting that the Leaper's expecting a single. Foster sees this as good news – she's always had twins, but this time round, she might just manage to raise a single lamb.

Izzie walks into the room with a bottle of red wine and two glasses on a tray.

'How's it looking?' she asks.

'Pretty good luv.'

'Well, add another one to your list.'

'What?'

'Go on, add another one, a single. But I haven't had my shoulder stamped.'

'Izzie, you can't be saying… Are you telling me…?'

'I'm saying, my sweetheart, touch wood and fingers crossed,

and all the other silly things people say for luck, that come summer, you'll be a father.

Foster cannot speak. His dark eyes moisten. He's battling with emotion. He's never been known to cry, well, only in private. He stands, takes the tray and then wraps his arms around her and buries his face in her hair. They stand together – Izzie motionless and Foster betraying just the slightest tremor of the shoulders.

'Beautiful Izzie,' he whispers. 'We'll have a glass, but from tonight, that's it for you. I'll be drinking alone.'

'I hope you're not going to be one of those silly fussing first-time fathers.'

'Izzie, you can be assured – that's exactly what I'll be. You have no idea what this means to me.'

3

Lambing alone

Science sided with the fussing, first time-father. The day after Izzie shared the news of her pregnancy, Foster delivered a lecture on zoonosis – specifically, the transmissible diseases of lambing.

'Spare me Foster. Shall I ever forget 'the legumes lecture' and their prophylactic properties? I bet that Ilkley lass with the ponytail won't either. You could have closed them down.'

'Science goes hand in hand with good husbandry. You'll be grateful to me. You have to be super-careful near livestock, now you are pregnant.'

'Go on then. What must I do – or not do?'

'Basically, I'm going to ban you from the barn. And, of course, the breeding flock.'

'What? You can't.'

'I have to. There are all sorts of stuff – perils and dangers. It's a huge hygiene issue.'

'From the man who on his own admission, only changes his underpants on Otley Show Day, that's a bit rich!'

'Izzie, I'm deadly serious. Close contact with sheep who have given birth – and that includes those ewes which have aborted – can lead to enzootic abortion or clamydiosis, and listeriosis, toxoplasmosis and even Q fever. You must steer well clear Izzie. I'm not joking. You could damage or lose our bairn.'

'But Foster, I want to help you. I want to be part of lambing. There must be things I can do to help?'

'Keep me fed and watered – that would be great. Help me keep my spirits up. But do not go anywhere near my lambing clothes – especially overalls. Washing my stuff is off too.'

'I'm so disappointed – about lambing, not washing your kit.'

'You won't be when the baby's born, safe and healthy – god willing. And there will be other springs, and we should have many lambings left for us.'

*****

Banned from the barn; for Izzie this was bitter news indeed.

Izzie had fallen in love with the barn the first time Foster took her down to it. It soon became her enchanted place.

When she first went down, she met the resident dunnock. He was always there, hopping a hurdle, high on a cross beam, hoovering a trough, somewhere, caught in the sun stripes.

In the barn, Izzie entered a wonderland. Sunlight, slattered by space board. Swirling particles of soft lit straw dust made small constellations – 'Silky Ways' she called them. Frayed band held hurdles in pens – rainbow hues of blue, yellow, orange and pink. The aisle was kept clear except for the ever-eager Massey Fergusson 135, circa 1966, red with white trim. Foster said it was in remarkably good condition. This tractor had been his father's most enduring love.

Izzie walked through it in reverie. Iron hay holders skirted the walls with fronds of hay still spilling through the wire, along with shreds of torn fleece, for sheep enjoy a rub and a scratch. Troughs were propped against the hurdles in a drunken camaraderie – some on their backs. A limed and strawed floor in gold, grey and beige shimmered beneath.

The storage area was to the right, with random water-buckets, tubs and spent cake-bags. Immediate right – the old chrome tap. Its neck emerged swan-like from straw – a crude attempt to insulate. 'There won't always be sunlight,' warned Foster.

Beyond, winter hay bales were stacked high, along-side great rolls of tightly netted barley straw. And then there was this chair – one of Foster's great grandma's wedding set from 1913 – rustic, cream-painted pine, these days chipped and hobbled. On its seat sat syringes, a drench, a latex glove box, foot trimmers and clippers. Some spent torn mid blue gloves littered its feet. A collection of rams' harnesses cupped last year's crayons hung limp from a hook, along with a fat towing rope. The harnesses smelt of rams. And everywhere the sweet mutton scent of sheep.

Then there was Foster's old red plastic sledge – long left for more worldly thrills – and the orphan lambs' ball – a World Cup Special 1986, deflating further by the year, but young lambs need to play, said Foster. They enjoy its squashy quality; they like to dribble it across the straw, and then flop on top of it.

Izzie will miss the barn this year, at least until it is safe for her to return. Foster throws himself into the lead up to lambing. His activities escalate. He shares the details of the breeding flock's feeding programme – the rising plane of nutrition and how this is dependent on how many lambs each ewe is expecting. This is one reason why the scan is so important, he reminds her. She can tell he's trying to involve her in the whole experience as much as he can, and for this she is grateful.

Whilst Foster's work escalates, Izzie is not idle. She has been getting quite a lot of costume work for the local theatres, and orders for special occasion dresses, alterations and adjustments, as well as curtains and counterpanes. Her counterpanes, originally designed for children, have caught the imagination of adults too. Izzie has re-imagined the eiderdown. Her counterpanes of different fabrics, yarns and textures are cosy, colourful and feature delightful images of flora, fauna and farm. She's experimenting with natural dyes. She now has the space to do all of this.

Izzie realises she can sell as many of her counterpanes as she can make and at a good price too. She's taken over an upstairs room at the farm as her workshop. She has had a huge table installed, along with her machine, and she can leave her work out – a real luxury for Izzie. She can just walk away from it when she needs a break. This room becomes her space. She's a real 'nester' and decorates the room with her artwork, including her newly completed cot counterpane that she has devised for their own baby. Foster is amazed at her talent and her skill and gives her every encouragement.

Izzie can do fittings at home and she installs a vintage chinoiserie screen for her clients to try things on with a degree of privacy. She's developing quite a client list just through word of mouth. The threat of a return to supply teaching recedes by the week, and she is delighted with her new life – and man, too.

For inspiration, Izzie loves to walk through the fields. Sometimes she walks with Foster, but mostly she walks alone. She loves the view down the valley from her stone above the Gill. She's becoming more reflective, more and more tuned in to the natural world. To sit on her stone and take it in – the changes, the age-old landscape, the ever-changing weather patterns, the slight shifts in light, the sounds, the notes.

Tuning in, she thinks. That is what it feels like. Has she become an instrument, or is she tuning herself? The note in her head began like a slow, steady scrape across an 'A' string. She remembers the note from the violin, from orchestra practice at school. The note, the concentration, the peg adjustment with her thumb and fingers. That's what it is like, she thinks. Slow notes, then other notes, tuning gently up and down – a perfect A, then the A and D strings together, then D and G, then a fine-tuned E and A, all in tune.

And now she's tuned she's ready to play – or be played. She

tunes in to the rusting rustling hiss of fallen leaves, the calls and cries of sheep, a distant cock crowing, a clamour of birds in the Gill, the rhythmic, soothing hoot of pigeons.

She learns to taste rain on the air – a storm coming in. She studies clouds and watches them race, or sometimes lurk. She marvels at the intricacy of iced lichens on green stone walls. Alabaster grey lichens, some orange and gold, and the rarer blood red ones.

And gradually, Izzie sees something more. She sees it, especially as she sits upon her stone. In abstraction, she sees the shapes of other things, especially, figures, female forms ethereal. There is sometimes a woman, a strange woman. As soon as her eyes follow her, and focus in on her, the woman is gone. But she senses that the woman means Izzie to see her.

Izzie has no fear. She knows the woman is there. She isn't a threat, more of a fact, a comfort, a pleasant, benign presence. This woman makes her feel safe. Her rational mind would tell her otherwise – that there is no one there. But Izzie knows. She has tuned in, and she's taking the signal clearer and clearer, every day. She will wait. She knows they are heading for connection. Something will happen.

*****

Foster takes in 'the triplets' first, in February, the ewes expecting triplets, that is. Through early March the pens begin to fill. Then a sea of ewes flows in. Foster and Izzie wait. And then it starts.

For each ewe the moment comes – lip-licking, neck-stretching, stargazing, hoof-scraping. Choose the spot, strain and push. Some need help – some don't. The smell is of iodine and birth fluid – iodine the umbilicals, unblock the teats, lift out the afterbirth and bury it. Or what remains of it, for a wise mum takes it back. From mothering–up pens they move onto the mother and baby unit. Lambs' ears tagged, sides are sprayed with mothers' numbers, ewes drenched, feet trimmed – then out to grass. Done, yet never done. This is how Foster relives it for Izzie.

Izzie watches Foster. His knees begin to buckle and his eyes bag. He is bollocksed. But he continues to include Izzie, sharing his triumphs and his traumas.

One morning, Izzie is sitting at the old pine table. She's been feeling strange. Happy, certainly. Content, indeed. But her mind isn't a cloudless sky. It's that softly scraped A string again. Ginny keeps flickering across. Izzie doesn't feel right about the estrangement between Foster and Ginny. In some strange shift she now feels her happiness with Foster has been gained at Ginny's expense. Izzie knows this is irrational, but she feels it, nonetheless.

On two separate occasions she has tried to raise the subject of patching things up, with Foster.

'She's your only sister. She has no-one – no family, that is.'

'Don't care. Half-sister, anyway. Can't see why it bothers you so much. Not after the stunt she tried to pull on us.'

'But when she tried to show Letty your improvements, she had no idea I was on the scene. She just had your own interests at heart. She was just trying to mend things for you. Fix things.'

'Let it be Izzie. Something will happen; it always does.'

'Couldn't you just apologise?'

'What for? For making 'lurve' to the woman I love?' This Foster delivered in his best pseudo-seductive voice.

'Cut that out, creep!' she giggled.

Foster continued: 'Whilst big sister did 'Through the keyhole.'

Izzie was laughing so much, she had to let the subject drop. But it wasn't to be forgotten. She would keep on chipping away, she promised herself.

There is another party keen on reconciliation. Like Izzie, Margaret has been feeling rare twinges of remorse, rare for her that is. Margaret feels bad because it was she who set up the situation that led to the falling-out. She had caused the puncture.

She had sacrificed Ginny to see off Letty for good.

Margaret has a lot of time for Ginny. She knows there beats a golden heart buried in that busy body. Enough is enough, she reflects. Compassion to the fore. Margaret has decided to mend the damage that she has caused. She knows that Ginny is suffering, depressed, and she sees that Izzie is a suitable conduit for reconciliation. Izzie, especially in her current condition, is susceptible, emotional and a little vulnerable. Margaret will work on this.

Margaret keeps peeping through the window at Izzie, planting thoughts. Margaret is adept at telepathic transfer, hence Ginny's recurrent appearances in Izzie's consciousness, and her escalating feelings of guilt. Margaret disappears, abruptly.

Izzie is suddenly aware of a strange silhouette at the window. She turns her head. It's a new-born lamb, the first of the season, and it is waving its hoof and tapping it on the glass. It bleats to her: 'Enya ...'

A peel of delighted laughter bubbles up from deep within her. The child in Izzie is desperate to believe that the lamb is really waving at her and calling to her. The woman in her loves the man the more for doing this.

'You clown!' she calls to Foster. He's carried his first lamb to the kitchen window, held aloft in his arms. He's used his hand to make it wave at her. Foster appears behind the lamb, blows Izzie a kiss, then he hurries it back down to the barn to its mother. It has already taken its first feed of colostrum, but it is essential not to break the bond.

Izzie feels overwhelmed with emotion – love, fear of loss, vulnerability and still – guilt. It all feels so intense, complex, and her cheeks are damp with tears. Foster misses this outpouring. Izzie swallows, blows her nose and composes herself.

Margaret watches man and lamb disappear at speed, down to the barn. She shakes her head in wonderment. She's seen it all now: 'What is he like?'

As she leaves Timble on the air, she thinks to herself, when did men become so soft? And then she thinks how good it is they have changed. Why if I lived now, she muses, I might almost fall for one of the better sort. But then she remembers Mister Smithson and reminds herself that not all were demons then.

*****

No matter how tired he becomes, Foster continues to keep a careful eye on Leaper. Next to Izzie and to Lou, Foster loves the Leaper. More than Ginny, certainly – the beloved Leaper, his favourite ewe.

As a lamb, the Leaper had had a thing about walls and fences; they provoked her. They were there for the scaling, she thought. As a gimmer there was no holding her. She could clear a high, dry stone wall on a whim. All it took was a hint of fresher pasture or a suspicion of a brighter vista, for the valley was hers. The rest of the females in the flock would follow, for she was the matriarch in the making. Now she's nine she's steadied up, a little.

Leaper was born a twin; her sister, 124, was a more conventional beauty, more 'correct' in breed society terms. Leaper has a horizontal straight fringe across her brow which gives her a quizzical scowl. As a lamb, she had fleecy sideburns. Nine years down the track and these have circumnavigated her whole face to give her a fine and feisty leonine presence. Her glamorous sister was more refined, softer, and less spirited. Leaper's sister also lacked the extreme longevity gene. She went a couple of years back. Seven's not bad for a breeding ewe, reflected Foster, secretly relieved it was the sister who went first, and not his favourite. Leaper has lived on.

But things don't always go well with breeding and rearing sheep. At lambing, there exists the finest line between a good outcome, and abject disaster. Lambing brings a lot of dread and loads of trouble. Foster knows this only too well.

For seven years the Leaper had produced twins, big fine twin lambs. This year, if all goes to plan, she will produce her fifteenth lamb, a single. Foster had real worries about her at tupping time – whether to let her go round again. But she had a full mouth of teeth and sound, supple pink bags. He felt, and there were no lumps. He softened, for she was, after all, the Leaper, queen of the flock. He put her to the new tup in early November.

The mild wet autumn seeped into a saturated winter and the Leaper was visibly losing condition. She began to look haggard. Foster was mindful that his Leaper, especially, would need special care and attention in the run up to lambing. He began seriously to question his decision to let her go round this extra year.

*****

It's an unseasonably hot day in March. Izzie comes home from Otley. She finds Foster in the kitchen rummaging in the drawer for the Land Rover keys. She locates them for him immediately.

Izzie sees that Foster is upset.

'It's properly presented – front feet and nose – but it is totally stuck. It's a soft tissue issue. It just won't budge.' Foster looks truly concerned. It's the Leaper, he explains, and she's clearly in serious trouble.

'I'm going to give her one more go and then it's down to the veterinaries.'

Izzie knows that it is a very rare thing for Foster to consult a vet, at lambing. His skills are extensive, but this is, after all, the Leaper.

'I've already rung the vet. She's expecting us,' Foster tells Izzie. 'You can tell from her eyes she's given up or given in. There's this switching off; it is beyond disengagement.'

'Why don't you ring Ginny? You said she was great with difficult cases – that she's got small hands and strong arms, along with instinct.'

Foster shoots Izzie a look.

'The lamb will be dead by now,' he says. Izzie knows Foster feels the need to prepare her for the worst. He also needs to manage his own expectations.

'They'll both be dead,' he says, for an encore.

'Foster, it's been going on too long. Between you and her I mean. Please ring Ginny. Take her down with you. You might be grateful for a spare pair of small, strong hands.'

Izzie watches Foster struggle with his emotions. He has the feeling that he is being judged, and not necessarily by Izzie. He too is feeling Margaret's influence, although he doesn't realise what is stirring his conscience.

'Just one more try,' he says. 'I've got my mobile. I'll keep you posted.'

Foster leaves the kitchen.

Izzie barely waits a moment and grabs the phone.

A cautious voice answers: 'Foster?'

'No, it's me, Izzie. Look Ginny, this is difficult. Please forgive me for contacting you like this. Foster doesn't know I'm ringing, but there's a lambing problem. It's the Leaper.'

'The Leaper. I'll come now!'

'Please, could you pretend you were just calling by to see how things are going? He has always said how good you were with births – your small hands and all ….'

Izzie is cut off by Ginny:

'Leave it to me. I'm on my way.'

Within moments Izzie hears the gate swing open. She watches as Ginny walks briskly down the drive to the barn.

Ginny finds Foster on his knees. He is close to praying and he looks the part.

'Ginny?'

'I miss lambing. I just wanted to see how things are going, Foster?'

'A timely arrival. Leaper's lamb's stuck.'

Ginny executes a quick internal examination and then feels the ewe's belly. She shakes her head, slowly: 'It's massive. Veterinary, I think? Hope it's not too late.'

Foster nods.

Ginny helps Foster 'utch' and shove Leaper out of the barn. He's backed the trailer to the entrance. Together, they manhandle the ewe up the aluminium ramp. Leaper keeps staggering sideways and sinking to her knees. It is not an easy thing to move a ewe who is well beyond the early stages of labour and exhausted and definitely reluctant to leave the familiarity of the barn. Eventually they succeed.

They drive the Leaper up the road and over the moor. The thought of the Leaper lying on sawdust in the back of the trailer, in great pain and giving up the ghost is difficult to endure. Foster feels he has let her down, that he has failed her, and he confesses this to Ginny.

Ginny leans over and places her hand on Foster's wrist. She squeezes it gently. As she does this, the pair of them miss the shimmering, smiling Margaret, standing at the top of Snowden Bank. She raises her hands in benediction, blessing the vehicle, trailer, siblings and ewe and un-born lamb.

'Foster, I wanted to say how delighted I was about the news – your baby. I haven't had chance to say, but I just wanted you to know; I'm really happy for you.'

'Thank you, Ginny.' Foster's voice is choking back emotion. 'It means a lot to me that. I've been a stubborn fool. I should have been around to tell you myself. It was unforgivable. Izzie's been desperate for me to call round and try to make things up with you.'

'Has she?' Ginny is surprised to hear this.

'Yes, she's been on to me for weeks. Look, whatever happens today, can we be friends again?'

'Of course. It was my loss too. I bet you thought I was a silly interfering old bag.'

'No, you weren't. You cared for me, just like a sister should. Izzie said something. She said you just wanted to fix things for me, 'cos you knew I'd been gutted about Letty.'

'Izzie said that? My goodness.'

'Oh yes. She's tried again and again to make me see sense.'

Ginny is welling up now, just as Foster swings the trailer into the veterinary's car park.

People with pets go to the vets' waiting room. If it is livestock, the farmer must keep the animal in the trailer. The young, female vet comes out with ropes. She has the breezy demeanour of someone who thinks there won't be a problem. She doesn't know that it is a rare occasion when Foster seeks help, and, as a rule, that he can be counted on to get the un-gettable.

'She's nine; she's our oldest girl. Head ruled heart,' Foster tells the vet. Then he asks if they can help to pull. She declines, remarking that it is all properly presented, as she slips the cords over the lamb's two front legs and round its neck.

The vet changes her mind about the offer of assistance very quickly. Within moments, Ginny is holding the ewe and pulling her in the general direction of the supermarket over the road. Foster takes the leg cords, and the vet, the neck cord, and the three pull as best they can. The lamb is stuck. More obstetric gel is massaged round the lamb's head. It is very difficult to feel further, yet they agree there is nothing caught – no shoulder obstructing progress. It is the sheer size of the lamb that forms the impediment.

The Leaper is not taking this situation lightly. Her nearly human screams must be startling the Friday teatime shoppers in the supermarket car park, although no-one comes to investigate, or to complain. She makes more noise than childbirth in the movies. Eventually there is movement. Centimetre by centimetre the lamb is tugged forward.

'It'll be dead by now,' says the vet, 'but it has got to come out anyway.'

Out 'sluthers' the lamb, along with a massive rush and gush of blood and associated tubes and bags and birth fluid. The lamb is of monstrous size, swollen, beyond bedraggled and inert. Foster is desperate for any sign of life; he wants so much for the Leaper to have a lamb to rear, this very last time round.

'It's dead,' declares the vet, 'and if it isn't, it's brain dead – has to be.'

But Foster will not accept this. He feels for a heartbeat and finds the faintest flutter of one. He starts to swing the ram lamb high, down, high, holding his long back legs between his fingers. The lamb takes his first gulping breath. Now it is all on to save him. Heart massage, injections, oral spray. Foster works on the mother and Ginny takes over the lamb. Mother and lamb are made as comfortable as possible for the journey home. The vet retreats in back into the surgery. Cats and dogs await her.

As Foster and Ginny drive back over the moor, very slowly and carefully, the fate of Leaper and lamb is still uncertain. Foster rings Izzie to report on progress and says, a little sheepishly and with wonder in his voice, that Ginny is with him.

'I'll have a meal waiting for all of us, that's if Ginny fancies coming for tea?'

Ginny beams and nods. She certainly does.

When Foster returns Leaper to the barn, he and Ginny weigh her ram lamb. It weighs in at nineteen pounds, an exceptional weight for any lamb and certainly a record for Foster. For lambs, like human babies, weights of up to ten pounds are normal.

Izzie is waiting up in the house, desperate to know about the Leaper. Foster gives a blow by blow account, over the evening meal. For Foster, Ginny and Izzie, their whole attention is on the Leaper story, so there is no awkwardness about Ginny's sudden appearance on the scene. Tricky questions are thus avoided, and Foster will never ever know about Izzie's telephone call to Ginny. The three of them will never know about Margaret's telepathic interventions either. Mysteries, these will remain.

'Tales should have good outcomes,' says Foster. 'It's all we ask for in life.' Then he shakes his head. in a mock philosophical way: 'Life eh, you do well to survive it. I'm not sure what the lamb's chances are.'

The Leaper's boy is not brain damaged, contrary to the vet's predictions. He is very slow to get going. Like his mother he is traumatised by the birth. He does not stand on four legs for his first eighteen hours; he doesn't even try. During this period, Foster, frequently assisted by Ginny, will feed him by stomach tube, with colostrum drawn from his mother. The Leaper herself will spend two days dazed, as if she dwells on a different planet. She does not reject her lamb, but she stands apart and abstracted, ignoring everything around her. Foster has penned mother and son together, separated from the rest of the ewes and lambs.

After the first day Foster abandons the stomach tube and holds the lamb up to suck off the Leaper's teats.

'Go on son, you can do it,' he coaxes. Leaper does not seem to mind. She gazes, dull of eye, into the middle distance. After two days something clicks, and her maternal rush begins. She licks her boy, takes charge of his feeding programme, loves and nurtures him. When Foster is sure they have bonded fully, and strength recovered, he lets them out into the low field by the barn. Here Izzie can watch them both at a distance, monitor progress and get Foster to intervene if necessary. This will not be necessary. Ewe and lamb are bonded, inseparable – inseparable until the inevitable separation of weaning. But that's in the future.

4

The devil makes work for idle hands

An unholy alliance evolves rapidly between Ginny and Izzie. Foster is monitoring it, half-horrified, but he must acknowledge to himself, relieved and pleased. He's a bit suspicious too.

Ginny has commended Foster's ban on Izzie entering the barn. She says to Izzie:

'A lambing shed is absolutely not the place for a young woman carrying a child. It can lead to all sorts of problems. I'll help Foster, but there is something you can do to help me, Izzie.'

Izzie has made the mistake of agreeing, before hearing what Ginny has in mind. This is always dangerous practice. The request concerns the annual women's feast in the village. When initial planning began, Ginny was isolated from Foster, and feeling downcast, depressed even. She hadn't joined the planning with her customary zeal.

Suggestions were requested for the Timble Ladies' Spring Barbecue, 2023. Some initial discussion took place, then the Timble women took to the keyboard. Emails had been fired off. First thoughts were the Robinson Library garden, but then the barbecue morphed into a picnic. A dejeuner sur l'herbe, and not too far from the village, but somewhere far enough away for fun, frivolity and loss of inhibitions. Dancing perhaps? Music – definitely. Somewhere away from male eyes.

Suggestions were shared, ridiculed, dumped, revived, rejected again. In her newly enthused state, Ginny came forward with a novel suggestion, a proposal with appeal for almost every woman in the locality.

Ginny reminded the Timble Ladies on the email circulation list that it was a very special anniversary. This was the year of the four-hundredth anniversary of the Timble Witches celebratory feast – the one they had held after they'd been acquitted by the Justices at York. A quatercentenary! The very name had a special ring, a resonance, like 'Quatermass and the Pit' for those who were old enough to remember it. Many of them were.

'In the Timble Witches' honour, we should hold our evening's picnic down in the Gill. A re-enactment. I see wine chilling in the beck, perhaps some fizz, hampers, canapes, cake and gingham cloths. Flasks of coffee, and cocoa for later, and toasted mallows. We'll have to have a bonfire.'

'What if the weather's crap?' asked June.

'It won't be,' said Ginny, and even the god of weather would never dare defy her. 'Anyway, think of those poor witch women. Do you reckon a little precipitation would have dampened their joy at getting off? We are made of the same stuff as they! Why, some of their blood may still course through our veins.'

'Yours perhaps. Most of us are in-commers, and recent ones too.'

The Timble women loved it. Everyone piled in again, each one putting in her own two pennies' worth. But all agreed it was a great suggestion. Well, almost all.

Izzie was reticent, despite her promise to help Ginny. Foster agreed with Izzie: 'Hold back girl, let it run. They can turn, that lot. I'm not sure some of our neighbours, especially our close relation, would get off at York Castle, if the trial was held today.'

'Foster, she's your sister! You are being nice to her now, remember? You've kissed and made up, and she's being fantastic over lambing.'

'Half-sister actually, Izzie. I suppose you are right. But I still don't see why you should find so much forgiveness in your heart. Not after the dirty trick Ginny tried to pull on you.'

'That was before she knew I was going to have your baby, Fozzy. It seems she was very fond of Letty. Ginny's been lovely to me of late. She does keep trying to extend the olive branch to me.'

'Yeh, if only to poke your eyes out.'

Izzie, new to the village, feels she is treading a fine line. Her position is complicated. As Foster's new partner she is still under scrutiny. Ginny has been very kind to her, but Izzie is still haunted by the bedroom incident. Izzie still goes hot and puce when she remembers the moment: 'Let's see what Foster's been up to with the Girl in a Hole!' She'll never forget the two faces as the door swung open.

Foster owns the land – the section of the Gill where the women want their re-enactment supper. His support is essential. He has said nothing so far. Keeping his cards close to his chest, he calls it.

Foster is holding back for so many reasons. The Gill is his special, private place. He doesn't want a load of strangers making free with it. Once they've found it, there will be no stopping them. Also, he is very sensitive to Izzie's position, and more than this, he is worried about Margaret and the Gill Women. Foster himself knows more about the original feast than anyone in the valley. Something else is troubling him.

Shortly after the request to hold the picnic, Foster lingered in the Gill to talk to Margaret, to sound her out about the scheme. Margaret shrugged her silvery semi-see-through shoulders. She'd seemed seriously distracted, down, depressed even. Clearly, she had bigger things on her mind, he concluded.

Foster had judged Margaret's frame of mind well. But he was unaware of the cause.

Margaret had felt distracted when Foster opened the feast subject. It sounded to her as if the re-enactment was going to coincide with the final coming, for Asmodeus was going to be on his way for the last time. The demon would take her forever. Nothing to be done, she thought, but she desperately didn't want to be taken. She didn't want to die, and she didn't know what would happen to her friends without her there to protect them. They might die too. What's more, she didn't want her departure to become an entertainment. Her thoughts led her back down the tunnel of time to Knavesmire, and she shuddered.

Foster reported back to Izzie his anxieties about Margaret's state of mind:

'She's right down, Izzie. I don't ever recall her being so glum and gloomy. Melancholy? It's as if the candle's going out, slowly guttering. It's as if she's fading in front of me. She will not talk about the reason. Believe me, I've asked her, pressed her to tell me. She just shakes her head and looks over her shoulder.'

'Would she talk to me? It might be easier for her to talk to another woman. Since I've been seeing her, she's smiled, waved in passing. I think she might relate to me.'

'You might try, I suppose. Something's up…' Foster became lost in thought. Then: 'Yeh, nothing to be lost. If you don't mind? Put yourself in a position where she might approach you. Why, sit on your stone seat. She'll probably come to you there.'

5

Meeting the family

What are these,
So withered and so wild in their attire,
That look not like the inhabitants o'the earth,
And yet are on't?

Macbeth – William Shakespeare 1606

It takes some courage to deliberately put yourself in the path of a four-hundred-year old woman. Izzie has waited patiently on the stone seat. The sun is warm on her face. It is a hot afternoon for late March. Such balmy days have become more common of late, but they still thrill the soul and raise the spirits, though each such day carries a warning of the recent warming.

Izzie has become strangely distracted. She is re-living the moment she pushed her business card into the hole. That seemed like a lifetime ago. Linda had begged her not to, but she had insisted, and cast away caution. Now she has Foster, and their baby on its way. She's settled in the beautifully refurbished Black Crow Farm. She feels fortunate, and she suspects she owes so much to the strange woman she waits for. Izzie's fingers trace the hole in the stone slab she is sitting on.

Then something. The A string sounds sweetly, as if now played on an ancient instrument, a viol. Izzie raises her eyes. A shimmering on the Gill's edge. A heat haze in March? No. An instability in shape and form, a soft shifting, as if the fabric of the landscape is set loose from its moorings. Then a subtle rift in the trembling landscape from which something seeps.

At first it is like a mist creeping up off the beck itself. Izzie sees the mist twirl and twist over the wooden style. It follows the diagonal path across the field. She is mesmerised. As it drifts towards her, about halfway up, Izzie begins to make out forms, human forms, the shape of women. They come into focus. Women, of different ages, dressed from a different time. Six of them there are. They fall into a single file. Mysterious dancers, led by the stoutest, stiffest, most aged. They skim the surface of the meadow, just brushing the dry winter's end grass tufts. A weird procession they form:

'Izzie, Izzie, be calm, don't fear. Izzie, Izzie, we six draw near.'

'Izzie,' a surprisingly soft voice in her right ear. Izzie turns round, sharply. There, leaning over the dry-stone wall is Margaret: 'I knew you would come; I summoned you.'

Izzie finds it hard to speak. Her left hand holds her side, above the bump of her unborn child. The baby flutters inside her, stirred by her own agitation.

'Don't harm me, please,' whispers Izzie, her earlier confidence sapping swiftly.

'We have never meant you harm. Be calm. It was we who heard your call for help. We have worked for your good. We mean no harm now. Now it is us who need you. We need your help. Hear us out. Do.'

'You need me?' Izzie is amazed: 'How can this be? How can I help? What must I do?'

The women settle on the grass in front of Izzie. Janet, the older woman seats herself slowly down besides Izzie on the stone and takes her hand, stroking her palm with her thumb.

Izzie relaxes. She responds to this gesture, feeling the agitation leaving her. She feels a fleeting desire to lay her head on Janet's ample bosom and fall asleep. Margaret rolls slowly over the wall in an elegant sideways soft vault.

'I will show you,' says Margaret. Margaret sits the other side of Izzie and places a sisterly arm round her shoulders. Their heads are touching.

Izzie is perplexed. She tries to anticipate what will happen. Soon it becomes clear that Margaret will transmit a tableau of images and visions to her. She sits still. So do the women. They share their thoughts in a way Izzie would not have thought possible. It is as if they share one mind, watching a common screen. She knows they see what she is seeing, but they are remembering too. Each adds her own recollections.

Margaret's images come first, scenes from Snowden Carr, the Cup and Ring stone, the Tree of Life, a vision of a tall dark man with the foot of a crow, the cloak, the flight. The "film" loses its focus then and breaks up. Then, back on track, the rough trip to York on the crude waggon, the women passing the gallows, a Judge in court studying a parchment, making a pronouncement.

Then there is the celebration in the Gill. There is a curiously dressed man peering over the ridge. He has wide accusatory eyes and is shouting something. Izzie thinks he shouts "whore". There is something more sinister about this man than even the demon, thinks Izzie. This is followed by the birth of Margaret's own baby with a funny foot. The images flicker through Izzie's mind in a slow succession. She knows that the women's very existence has come at a high price, and that Margaret has been the one who has paid for it, and who yet has the biggest price to pay.

Izzie is made to see that this thing, this demon, Asmodeus, will come and take Margaret away. Izzie has a vision of consuming fire and dire pain and she shrinks with terror. All the women, except Margaret, tremble and turn away too. Margaret is unflinching, fatalistic, almost.

Now the visions have ceased, Izzie realises that she is crying, sobbing for the women and for their troubles. Margaret has taken hold of Izzie's other hand. The women sooth and shush her. They comfort her.

'Husha, tush now. Husha, tush.'

Through her tears, Izzie whispers: 'What can I do? What can I do to save you? Please, tell me, what I can do. I will do anything to stop that thing from taking you.'

Margaret and the women nod slowly and with solemnity. Margaret speaks for all of them: *'We need you in the Gill this night to come. Foster tells us the women of Timble have plans for a great feast there, to celebrate our acquittal. They have chosen May Day's Eve. Well, so be it. Let it come to pass.'*

The women nod, as if to endorse.

'When first I flew with Asmodeus, it was full summer, July, the time of bilberries. The child was born the following May Day's Eve. From that time on, he moved our yearly tryst to that night, to celebrate and to endorse his power upon me, and his interest in my son. He need not have troubled to do this, for I would have flown freely. But this time, I would rather not; I choose not to fly.'

Margaret hesitates, then in a lower, confiding voice:

'There are ways to vanquish a demon.'

Izzie's' eyes widen. Margaret continues, leaning closer to her:

'It will be no mean task. It will require us all to unite and pool our powers – the spiritual and the physical. We need to summon a strength beyond ourselves to vanquish him. We can do it, we can be greater than the sum, but there are rules; there are requirements; indeed, there are ways. We need you to lead the Timble women. Strategy, planning and action.' And then as an afterthought, Margaret added: *'And we will need stout and sturdy ropes and hooks.'*

'What on earth are we going to do?'

'Our course is becoming clearer in my mind. I now know what we might well do. But it is too soon for you to know. You and I will share

my plan nearer the hour. Tell the Timble women only what they need to know and when. Do not tell any man, not even Foster. Lend your support to the feast, work with Ginny – she can be an old scold, but there inside her is a heart of gold. Think of a game, a dance? Teams of women. And together we will need to pull a great weight.'

'Like some tug of war? Then we'll need strong men for body weight?'

'No men! Hecate forfend us! Women have greater strength than men – when it comes to it.'

'No men, no men, demons don't die at the hands of men.'

'OMG! Are we really going to kill that thing with the crow claw?'

'No more questions, for now.' Margaret raises her finger to her lips. The Gill Women do the same. *'Support the feast. Secure the ropes and hooks, teams of Timble women yoked together, and no men. That is all you need to know for now, Izzie.'*

'I understand. I will try.' A fierce resolve formed in Izzie's mind. She added: 'No – I will do it. You count on me.'

And they are gone. Izzie sits on her stone, her mind racing faster than her pulse. And then she feels a rush of adrenaline, determination, of courage. It will be done; it must be done.

Izzie returns to Black Crow Farm and treats Foster to a highly edited, clipped version of events:

'Yes, Margaret has approved the feast. She has asked me to take a lead role in the planning and preparations. And, she has told me to work closely with Ginny.'

Foster raises his eyebrows. He takes a moment or two to think, and then says:

'Well, that makes sense, I suppose. You can control proceedings then. Make sure things don't get out of hand, like keep our Ginny under control. That date though – it isn't giving you much flex with your due date. We don't want you giving birth to our lad down in the Gill.'

'Foster, calm yourself. Two points. First babies are notoriously late and there's easily thirteen weeks between the dates. What's more, we made the decision together not to know the gender. Baby might not be a boy. Has that occurred to you?'

'Hmm. Well we'll see, on both counts. Time alone will tell. You just be careful. I've waited a long time to become a dad. Too long for any stuff like this stupid women's picnic to upset things.'

Izzie knows Foster would have a fit if he knew the whole of it. What is more, she's promised Margaret and the Gill Women. The Timble women are the least of the problems. She has a flash back to the shared vision of Asmodeus on Snowden Carr, and she shudders.'

'Someone walk over your grave, luv?'

'No, it must have been a sudden draught. Did you leave the backdoor open?'

Izzie watches Foster spring to his feet and walk into the utility room to check the door. He is so fussy, so solicitous about her well-being. She realises, to her shame, that this isn't the first time she's kept anything back from him. Her phone call to Ginny remains a secret. Izzie hates the deception. She doesn't like her omissions. But she has sworn, and she is a woman of her word.

The more rational side of Izzie's nature takes over. She comforts herself that it is probably all a load of silly nonsense. Witches and demons indeed. And yet, she isn't at all convinced.

6

Back at the Legume Cafe

L inda has been texting from her table at the Legume Café. She's waiting for her friend. The bell on the door clinks and Izzie enters, bringing with her a draught of cool air. Linda leaps to her feet and bounds towards her. They hug.

'Well look at you. Your condition becomes you, Izzie. Radiant is the only word I can think of.'

'My condition indeed – you quaint old thing, you! I look plump, perky and pink, and if that's radiant, so be it. Even my beloved says I look as big and broad as a boat'oss.'

'Charming – it's all his fault, too!'

'I think we both must take some responsibility, Linda, in fairness to Foster.'

Thoughts of wild swimming flickered across Izzie's mind and her colour intensifies.

'Looks like you are carrying a girl. Boys sit more on the front.'

'Jees, don't tell Foster. He insists on its "maleness". Time will tell. I'm sure he would be suited with a girl, should he be a she. Anyway, enough of this baby talk. I'm famished and I no longer worry about my girth – not anymore. I've got an excuse to pig out.'

'I was thinking about what you just said – "time will tell" – time eh? The changes recent times have brought to you.'

'Don't – there isn't a day I don't thank heaven I called down those witches. Ready to order?'

'All set – tomato and basil soup today, I think, and haloumi panini with hummus and roasted pepper. Filter coffee with cold milk.'

'Me too! Why spoil a winning formula? Keep it simple.'

Izzie starts up again: 'Talking of the witches – oh, and I have to remind us …' Izzie starts to laugh, 'Foster still insists we call them "the Gill Women", on account of their having been acquitted. Remember? Where was I?'

Linda's eyebrows rise: 'I think you were about to tell me about "the Gill Women".'

'I have something to confess. Linda.'

'Oh god, I hate confessions. They terrify me. Whatever it is, wouldn't you rather keep it to yourself? A confidence is always such a burden to the receiver.'

'But I have to tell you. I might need your help, in more ways than one.'

'Oh – if you must, then.'

'I can see them.'

'Who? Who can you see?' Linda looks around the café.

'These witches, I mean Gill Women.'

'Izzie, get a grip.'

'No, please Linda, you understand this stuff.'

'I'm no shrink.'

'No, but you had that background – in your degree, well, one of them.'

Linda shakes her head and takes a sip of her coffee. She doesn't look directly at Izzie:

'When did this start?'

'Just about the time I felt the first flutter.'

'Your heart?'

'The baby you idiot – when it first moved, quickened.'

'Oh, right. Look, just tell me about it.'

'Well, it started with Margaret.'

'Margaret?'

'Foster's forbear – God knows how many greats back. I sensed her before I could see her.'

'Foster introduced you?'

'Don't be daft. I only see her when I'm alone.'

'Does he know you see her?'

'He does now. I didn't tell him at first. I didn't even know what I was seeing, or rather sensing, for sensing it was in the early days.'

'And?'

'He's been seeing her, and has talked to her, since he can remember – as a tiny child – so it makes perfect sense to him.'

'Go on…'

'For Foster, she has many guises. He says that sometimes she's a feeling, as if he's suffused with a haunting presence, like some people can sense a beloved dead dog, years after the dog has left them.'

Izzie checks Linda's eyes, but Linda is still listening, not ridiculing her. She continues:

'Sometimes she is a shimmering form, and at other times she is more tangible – she will sit beside him, or even accost him, as clear and finely described as the days when her mortal self, breathed air. That's when she talks to him in earnest.'

'And now you are seeing her too?'

'Yes, it's just as Foster says. That's exactly how she appears, and her mates.'

'Dear god. Does she trouble you, scare you, worry you? Like, is she malevolent?'

'No, not at all. She's not like that. I've met them all now, the Gill Women. They're the sort we'd choose as friends. They are a bit out of time, but they need our help.'

'Izzie, this is all very silly.'

'No, please bear with me. They are in mortal, or rather immortal, danger. Especially Margaret. Asmodeus the Demon is coming for her. I've got to help her. He'll take her to hell.'

'Soup ladies, and paninis. Coffees coming.'

'Thank you,' beams Izzie: 'I'm ready for this. It smells so good.'

Linda looks around furtively, checking no-one is listening to them.

'Let's eat. Questions are clustering in my head, Izzie. I'm worried about your state of mind. It does sound as if you are having psychotic episodes.'

'You think I'm mad, don't you? Have your soup and I'll fill you in further. Suspend disbelief, please.'

The meal is a strangely silent one. The two friends eye each other with caution, suspicion almost.

Following the last spoonful of soup, and the final morsel of panini:

'Well, go on,' says Linda.

And Izzie does. Izzie fills her in on the meeting with the women above the Gill, the plans for the summer's night celebration and the fact that the Timble women might have a key role to play.

'Come on Izzie. Help me here. A Faustian pact? A demon – this Asmodeus? You've gone native. You've been out of Hebden Bridge for far too long. Most of us keep our demons in our head. He's not going to show now, is he?'

'Margaret thinks he is.'

'This all beggars belief. She's not real, either.'

'But she is. I see her; I talk to her. There are different realities, running side by side. I'm telling you! Margaret needs our support, our solidarity. She needs us there. She needs to be protected, by women, a group of strong and determined women. I'm so worried for her...'

'I tell you who I'm worried for – you! What worries me is that you believe all this crap. You really believe a demon's coming – I can see you do.'

The two friends watch each other, Izzie in frustration, and Linda incredulous.

'Cake and another coffee?' Izzie asks, placatory.

Linda nods: 'Carrot and walnut. An americano – I need a double strength one.'

Izzie turns, calls the waitress and places their order.

Linda sighs: 'Okay. I'll be there for the supper, but for you, not this Margaret woman. Tell me this isn't happening. Pinch me.'

'Well if it is all nonsense, which I assure you it isn't, you can just have a nice night out. A lovely evening in a beautiful place. The great outdoors, eh? And there's going to be music.'

'No worries there then.' Linda shakes her head.

'Well there is one other thing,' says Izzie, with caution.

'What's that?'

'Health and Safety.'

'What?' And then Linda starts to laugh. 'You're plotting the murder of a demon, with your coven of witches, or I should say Gill Women, and… and all you can worry about is Health and Safety! You have totally lost the plot. Izzie, come on?'

Izzie continues, ignoring her friend: 'Perhaps I spent too long in educational institutions. But the Gill is rather steep, and some of the Timble ladies aren't in the first flush of youth.'

'Sounds as if some of them won't see four hundred again.'

'I'm not so worried about the Gill Women, well not from slipping and breaking bones, at least.'

'I give up. Here comes the cake, thank god. Saved by the tray.'

*****

It's a couple of hours later, and Izzie needs the loo rather urgently. She blames the second cup of coffee, and the pressure of the baby on her bladder. They nip into another café, by the car park, and Linda orders a pot of tea for two.

Sitting in the sunny window, watching the shoppers and the tourists pass, Linda re-opens the subject.

'Izzie, what did these Gill Women do? What were the charges against them? This is just an academic enquiry. I'm not conceding their existence. Right?'

Izzie smiles. She can see Linda is being drawn into the plot.

'Well it wasn't what they actually did at all. There were three accusers – two girls and one young woman aged twenty-one. Helen Fairfax, the young woman, claimed the women had put a spell on her. She accused all seven. She knew them all, well, all except Margaret, who she called "the strange woman".' Helen claimed she was experiencing all sort of visions, visitations, trips – all from her bedchamber. She claimed she was subject to the women's spells and their attacks – according to Helen there were some quite violent interchanges.'

'So, it was like Pendle, or Salem?'

'Well sort of, except that, as you know, the Timble women were acquitted. It seems the Fewston vicar, a man called Smithson, and another local yeoman, Henry Graver, along with one or two other men, stood up for them. Smithson was very well respected, but he had to take a stand against the Fairfax family, who were extremely powerful in the valley. It sounds as if he was quite brave.'

'What about the other two girls?'

'Elizabeth, Helen's sister, was aged seven or eight, and there was another local girl called Maud Jaffray. Maud was almost in her early teens. They came forward with similar tales, about being taken up to the moors by the women, about dolls and pins and dancing and bonfires and all that sort of stuff. It seems the Justices at York were far more sympathetic to the two Fairfax girls than to the twelve-year old. They gave Maud a very hard time.'

'How do you know all this?' asks Linda.

'Oh, from Edward Fairfax, the father of two of the girls. He was a poet, well-educated, an intellect. Intelligent, certainly. He wrote it all down in his weird book called *The Daemonologia*. It makes bizarre reading. He was prompted to write it after his youngest daughter Anne died. She was only a baby.'

Izzie continues: 'Helen's first fit happened in October 1621. Fairfax accused the group of practising the dark arts of witchcraft on three of his daughters, Helen, Elizabeth and Anne, and of having caused Anne's death.'

'And he really believed what his daughters said?'

'Well he witnessed Helen having the fits, and then, afterwards, she would recount where she had been whilst unconscious, or in a trance. She gave him information about what she had been doing, who she met and who said what. It makes bizarre reading. It's really detailed and totally daft. And all of this whilst she was under the fluence – the mysterious, magical, hypnotic power of these women.'

'I'm still finding it hard to credit that he just accepted his daughter's version of events.'

'Well, yes. At first, he said he thought it was a condition, an illness they used to call "the Mother" ...'

'Ironic, isn't it – they call some affliction "the Mother" They wouldn't call it "the Father", would they?'

Izzie acknowledges Linda's point and continues: 'It seems it was linked to Motherwort. Like Motherwort was the cure. Motherwort was reckoned to be good for heart symptoms, palpitations due to anxiety. Still is. Anyway, then Fairfax became convinced Helen was genuinely possessed. Eventually, Elizabeth started having similar issues.'

'Sounds like psychosis – delusions, trances, hallucinations. It's not unusual, in young women and girls.' Linda pauses, and Izzie adds:

'Helen hears voices too, and her father describes speech

problems after she has been in a trance, disrupted sleep patterns, headaches and nausea, so yes, it does fit.'

'Do you think Edward, the father, was abusing her?'

'Oh dear. God, I hope not.'

Izzie thinks about it. 'It's impossible to say,' she pauses. 'It is possible, but I really have no idea.' Izzie looks perplexed, then adds: 'He describes Helen as slow to learn. He is pretty rude about her. Most parents don't run down their kids like that. So cold and almost analytical. He describes her as free from melancholy, but not knowing much. Bit rich that – he was a tutor as well as a famous poet. He said something like – she wouldn't know much because she had been educated in his own house! That struck me as odd, for he was the tutor to other Fairfax children – the sons of his legitimate half-brothers.'

'Hmm, he might have felt he had failed her. He might have been ashamed of her ignorance, saw he had neglected her and then felt he was obliged to believe her tales. Perhaps he saw it was better for her to be seen as being possessed rather than just dim. Her stories played into his hands and salved his conscience?'

'She wasn't that dim. She certainly knew how to work him,' says Izzie, then she remembers something else: 'The younger girl, Elizabeth, was said by her father to be very bright and quick. Eventually she is the one to experience the fits.'

'Perhaps it was her turn to be jealous, and she wanted to claim back his attention? Sibling stuff going on?' wonders Linda.

Izzie nods: 'Possibly. I suppose that we shouldn't judge Edward Fairfax all these centuries on. We can only speculate, but I'd love to know the truth of it all. It's funny, but each period has its own take. When you read the introduction to the *Daemonologia* by Grainge, a Victorian, he argues that Edward Fairfax was actually a legitimate son, but it's not very convincing. He also laments the absence of a proper memorial to this great man of the valley.'

'Really?'

'Yeh. You know, I think this *Daemonologia* is a perfect

memorial to the man. It speaks volumes about the bloke.'

Linda nods in agreement:

'I think we can judge him for his behaviour to Margaret and those Gill Women, and we should. He will have caused them immense suffering, even if they did get off. The threat of hanging, the two trips to York, the incarcerations, even the trials would have been horrendous for them.'

As an afterthought, Linda asks: 'Could religion have had any bearing on his accusations?'

'Well, he didn't like the vicar, probably because Smithson supported the women, but in those times, catholic or protestant, most believed in witches. And there was a certain cachet in having a child possessed, whichever way you looked.'

'You're right about that. As part of my research I had to read Robert Burton's *Anatomy of Melancholy*. It came out about the same year as your Timble witch trials. Nowadays it's viewed as the first psychiatric encyclopaedia. What amazed me when I read it was how widely folk did believe in witches and the power of witchcraft – even amongst educated people.'

'I suppose these educated voices would mostly belong to men,' says Izzie.

'Too right,' agrees Linda. She continues: 'For Burton, the possible causes of melancholy are extensive and various. It did make me laugh. As well as grief, he cites over-much study, diet – he's very down on cabbage and most fruit – wind and costiveness, haemorrhoids, monthly issues in women, sexual abstinence in men, too much sex, inhibition or no sex at all for women, too many baths for either gender and on he goes. Even breathing itself seems to bring on melancholy. But the section on witches is huge.'

'Linda, how do you remember all this crazy stuff? Your brain must be clogged-up. It's not a brain, you've got up there, it's a fact-berg.'

'Ha ha! You know how you see things in 3D, being so arty

and crafty, well I just see the page. Once I've read it, it's in there forever, or at least will be until dementia strikes me down. Oh, and by the way, never ask me to make you some curtains...'

'Perish the thought – I remember trying to teach you to tat. Clever but cack-handed, that's what my mother called you.'

Linda sighs heavily, thinks for a moment or two, then says: 'Accusations of witchcraft followed by mock trials and murder, eh. It's still going on, you know. Africa, India, Nepal and so many other places the world over – terrifying femicides.'

'When stuff like this happens, money is often the root cause,' suggests Izzie. 'Money or sex.'

'Follow the money on this one too,' says Linda: 'Economics and capitalism. Women in a subordinate social position to men, punished for any move to independence, and accused of sexual transgressions, vilified, persecuted, and destroyed.'

Linda pauses, then goes on: 'And it's usually the older women, beyond child-bearing, who are first targeted. Old women and children are seen to be of lower status. Your Gill Women were charged with witchcraft at the dawn of capitalism, the time of the enclosures, a time of extreme poverty for many. People were being thrown off the land. They were probably women who had the temerity to be angry, express dissatisfaction, or just be in the way. Women had to be tamed or eradicated. Women were there to obey.'

Izzie takes a sip of tea: 'What you are saying, it all makes sense.'

Linda continues:

'But sex comes into it too. Uncontrolled female sexuality was feared; it was perceived as a social danger. That explains the accusations of lewd behaviour, immorality, prostitution and, frequently, infanticide.'

Izzie nods. She can't disagree with any of this. 'So many ingredients bubbling away in the cauldron, eh?'

'Your Gill Women would have been deemed the terrorists of

their own time. They may have been the women who spoke up for themselves, strong, independent-minded women. Custodians of a dying culture and a lost, kinder community. Custodians of the natural laws. Their being taken and tried would be designed to keep the rest of the women around them in their places. And some local women would have colluded with the oppressors, mark my words.'

Linda holds up her hand: 'I've almost finished. Sorry to rant. Just one more reflection, for you did ask me.'

'Okay,' Izzie always loves it when Linda is on a roll. 'I suppose I did ask for it.'

'I'll tell you what really pisses me off, big time.'

'What?'

'These bloody shops selling witch dolls on broomsticks as toys. Cutesy souvenir shops. I notice they don't do this up where you are. You know, it should be banned everywhere. Instead, where these persecution practices were carried out, there should be statues to the victims. There should be museums to the murdered, the dispossessed. That's the part of our heritage that is often just blanked. Witches should have their own Remembrance Day, lest we ever forget. I jest not, for it seems to me most of us have forgotten. A proper commemoration is required, for if we don't remember, we do forget. That's when it can happen again. Think about it. It could have been you or me.'

'That museum for the Pendle witches gets it right. There, there's loads of information about the accused women, what they were subjected to and the factors that led up to their persecution. And they do good cake too,' says Izzie, 'but it's better to do the café first for it seems a bit disrespectful to stuff down cake after the presentation.'

Linda nods sagely.

'Linda, confess, you are beginning to warm to the cause. You will fight the demon, I can tell.' Izzie chuckles.

Linda sits back in her chair and lets out a long sigh: 'Izzie, what the hell have you got yourself into?'

Izzie glances at her watch.: 'My goodness, I'm going to have to fly – well not literally, but Foster will be fretting about me and my parking is up.'

'It's been great to see you. Well, I think it has?' Linda laughs softly, but her eyes show concern. 'Take great care. I have to say, I'm worried about you.'

'I'll send you the date of the supper,' says Izzie.

'Count on me. I will be there. But it's against my better judgement.'

'Think of it as Timble's Remembrance Day for the cruel War on Women.'

'You watch out for demons. You can't anticipate the shape they'll take.'

Izzie laughs and waves.

Linda, brow furrowing, watches her friend breeze out of the door and disappear into the sea of parked cars.

7

Conspiratorial

The inner circle is meeting for morning coffee. Four women are sitting round the old pine table at Black Crow Farm. Foster has relinquished his kitchen to them; he's enjoying self-banishment with Lou on the south-side fields.

Introductions are being made.

'Ginny, June, this is Linda, my best friend from god knows when.' Izzie smiles at Linda, and nods in encouragement. Linda greets the two older women:

'I'm pleased to meet you ladies, although, I have to say, I'm a bit alarmed too.'

'Me too,' says June, 'I've done some strange things in my life, but this is certainly the most bizarre.'

Izzie pops into the kitchen for the tray, and Ginny brushes aside any doubts:

'Faint heart and all that. Now is not the time for doubt, or panic.' She breaks off: 'Anything we can do out there, Izzie?' she calls. 'By the way, I've baked something to go with morning coffee – one of my special orange polenta cakes. Polenta is so good for you, you know.'

'Oh Ginny, you are a star!' calls Izzie: 'I haven't got round to baking. Shop biscuits aren't the same, no matter how fancy.'

'You should rest more, and not even think about baking, with Baby being so close. I'm so excited, you know. A new generation – a new Hall in the valley! I'm just bursting with it all – I can hardly wait. And, you know what, not only am I to be an auntie, I'm to be godmother! I'm so proud.'

'Ginny, you and Foster are both spoiling me so much, I'm reluctant to part company with it. I want this to go on; I feel so fit and able – a ship in full sail.'

'Well I'm chairing this meeting of the planning committee. What's the latest from the Gill Women, Izzie?' Ginny is multi-tasking. She pours from the cafetiere with one hand and passes out plates of cake and paper napkins with the other, whilst continuing to drive on with the meeting.

'Margaret is fixed on ropes. She intends to lure Asmodeus down to the Gill, manoeuvre him into position, tie him up and skewer him.'

'Jesus!' June chokes on a piece of polenta. Linda springs to her feet to fetch a tumbler of water and prepares for a Heimlich.

Order restored; Ginny begins again:

'Look, you two – you've been invited into the inner circle because you are both trusted. You've got to square up better than this. Demons don't take prisoners. We've got to go down there determined to win.'

'Have you ever met a demon, Ginny?' asks June.

'Of course not, but I can do empathy along with the best.'

'I'm not sure I can go through with this Ginny. I've never been very brave, and I tend to freeze if I'm frightened.'

'June, don't you underestimate yourself. We've got the Gill Women on our side, and Margaret knows who she's dealing with. The rest of the Timble women will be there for back-up. They'll catch the mood of the moment, and there's all sort of professional women – including an ex-deputy chief constable, as well as two nurses – one is psychiatric, three accountants and four solicitors.'

'We'll probably have greatest need of the solicitors and the psychiatric nurse. This is forced to end in litigation, and one of us might go nuts,' reflects June.

'Izzie, you are quiet?' Ginny looks quizzically at her.

'No disrespect to Margaret, but I've been doing my own research on-line. I googled "how to vanquish a demon?".'.

'And?' chorus June and Linda both exchanging incredulous glances.

'Good girl!' chimes in Ginny. 'So, what did this Google chappie have to say?'

'My search led me, eventually, to The Book of Tobit.'

'Isn't that the Apocrypha?' asks Linda.

'Yes, that's the one.'

'Well that's not much use is it? Aren't they the bits they kicked out of the Bible? Meaning, like – they're apocryphal. They didn't happen.'

'Since when did everything in the Bible happen?' asks June.

'Fair point,' says Linda, nodding sagely, then bursting into nervous giggles.

'Linda, June, you two are not helping Izzie, and we need all the help we can muster. Izzie, you were saying?'

'Well, it seems the demon Asmodeus can't abide the smoky smell of frying fish – the gall, the heart and the liver.'

'Oh? I love the smell of frying fish.'

'That's not the point, Ginny. It's Asmodeus who can't abide it, and he's the one we need to see off. And it isn't cod or haddock in batter that works, not even halibut – it has got to be fish organs, from a big fish – gall, heart and liver.'

June, reasonably patient up to this point, interjects: 'Hang on a minute. Are we to believe that Asmodeus is just going to give up on taking Margaret – like: "Oh what a puther, disgusting, I'll give it a miss today, eh?" Just because we've thrown some bloody fish body parts onto the barbie?'

'It's part of our strategy yes, but it's not exactly a quick fix. It's more complex. You need ashes with incense – incense sprinkled on the embers.'

'Oh, I can pick incense up in Hebden Bridge any day – no bother there,' Linda is smirking, raising her eyebrows.

Izzie continues, undeterred: 'In the Book of Tobit, it says that the demon smells it, and goes away, never to return, forever and ever.' Izzie pauses, reflects, and continues: 'Except, it seems that Asmodeus has only gone as far as Egypt. Raphael, Tobias' companion angel, has to follow him there, to bind him hand and foot.'

'Oh, one of the neighbours said he got a real deal on a Nile cruise, but that it was a bit of a disappointment. Sub-standard hotels and I suppose if you've seen one set of ruins, you've seen them all. He said the beggars got on top of him.'

'That sounds awful, Ginny. Was he injured?'

'I think, June, he meant bothered, pestered or accosted, rather than physically attacked.'

'I'll continue, if I may, Ginny?'

'Please do.'

'Just a minute,' interjects Linda. 'How come…?'

'How come what?' Izzie's patience is now being stretched.

'How come Asmodeus has been seen, on and off for over four centuries, on Snowden Carr, flying and messing with Margaret, if Raphael saw him off in Egypt, in the Book of Tobit?'

Silence.

'A tribute act,' shrugs June.

'Hardly,' snaps Izzie.

Then Ginny regains her certainty: 'Never mind all that. This time we'll make a proper job of it.'

'Yes,' says Izzie: 'Last time round there were only two blokes to tackle him. It seems men can't kill demons – Margaret told me. This time we'll be mob-handed, a full female cast and tooled

276

up. Okay?'

Everyone nods.

'What I propose is a multi-faceted plan. We need to draw all strands of attack together. We need ....'

And so, the grand scheme evolves. The shopping list comprises stout ropes from the ships' chandlers down in Leeds, the loan of two 4x4s with tow bars, two heavy duty tractors, as many quad bikes as can be commandeered, in case of an emergency evacuation, first aid boxes, hand sanitiser, barbecues, briquettes, long matches to avoid burnt fingers, incense, fish kebabs and fish body parts in a bag. Alongside all of this were the more regular requirements for dining al fresco: lots of wine, prosecco, sparkly water, disposable plates, serviettes, crockery, cutlery, crisps, canapes, salads, burgers, sausages, chicken breasts, cheeses, vegetarian and vegan options, gluten free dishes, cakes, trifles and buttered bread rolls.

By the end of the meeting, the inner core agrees who will contact who, who should be approached for vehicle loan, and who will collect the rope. Izzie has already paced out how much they will need, under Margaret's strict supervision.

Ginny starts to bring the meeting to an end, then remembers something else: 'I have to say, the fancy-dress element has proved very popular. Usually folk grumble, but they are all up for dressing as witches. The creative juices are certainly flowing.'

'Some of them won't have to try too hard.'

'June, that isn't like you.' Ginny looks at her friend in mild surprise.

'Music?' Linda's trying to lighten the mood.

'Oh yes, I forgot,' says Izzie: 'Wet Wendy, the Damp Man's wife, is coming. I didn't realise she was a Dirty Skirt.'

'What?' asks June, 'What exactly is a Dirty Skirt?'

'It's the Nidderdale Morris team from Pateley Bridge – all-women of course. Seems the purists hate females doing Morris.'

'How dare they?' chimes in Linda, truly indignant now. Izzie continues:

'Well Wet Wendy says she can ask them along with their accordion trio, the Mucky Pinnies. I've heard the Pinnies play and they are excellent.'

'Go for it,' says Ginny.

'Just one more thing, friends,' says Izzie. 'We need to agree a chant. I promised Margaret. She says we need a word, or words, as a rallying call.'

'How about Go!' suggests June.

'Fuck off – that trips nicely off the tongue,' says Linda. 'I've always used it to good effect.'

'I think we need something more formal than either of those.' Izzie tries to recall some of Margaret's suggestions: 'But you are right, it does have to be a command, an imperative.'

'Obliterate – that has a nice ring to it,' says June.

'Okay – team it with Eliminate,' says Ginny.

Then a head of steam builds up:

'Exterminate!'

'Annihilate!'

'Eradicate!'

'Bit weak, that last one – half-hearted like.'

'Power of three?'

'Force of four!'

'Force of four – you win, Ginny.'

'Let's try them together – Obliterate, Eliminate, Exterminate, Annihilate!'

'Love it, we'll trounce the bastard. What a grand chant it is. Let's go for it again.'

The ladies run through it several times, tweaking word order to best effect.

'Eliminate, Obliterate, Exterminate, Annihilate! – trips off the tongue a treat.'

'What are you lot bellowing about?' Foster's head appears round the door. He enters the kitchen. He's shocked and bemused.

'Oh, we're just practising a piece for the Gill supper – for the re-enactment. Don't concern yourself, Brother.'

'Hmm?' Foster is suspicious. Raucous women in his kitchen – whatever next?

'Oh, by the way, can we borrow the tractor, the big one, the flat-bed trailer, the Defender and the quad?' asks Izzie.

'I suppose so. I knew all this business would get out of hand. Any of that orange cake going spare?'

'Of course, Foster.' Ginny cuts him an unusually generous slice and beams at him: 'Double cream, dear?'

Foster grunts an acceptance, then bethinks himself:

'Actually, I'd be well suited with ice cream.'

'Ever the over-grown schoolboy, Foster,' says Ginny, smiling indulgently. She turns to the rest: 'Meeting over. Until next week!'

The women go their separate ways. Izzie begins to clear the table.

'You look a bit peaky, luv. Let me.' Foster finishes clearing the table and puts the kettle on to boil. 'You don't want to be overdoing this silly barbecue business. Are you sure Margaret approves?'

'Absolutely, she does, Foster. Hand on heart. And it'll all be over soon, and we can relax again.'

8

Come fly with me

The cavalcade of farm vehicles, SUVs and women on foot, draws to a steady halt by the gate above the low meadow. Women are sitting on trailers, clutching bags, hampers, bottles and boxes. Chatter and laughter – there's a carnival atmosphere. The sun is slowly declining above the ridge beyond the Gill. As Ginny predicted, it is a fine evening.

Barbecues, chairs and trestle tables were taken down earlier, and set up, by Foster, the Damp Man and Ian. Foster risked life and limb to attach a hawthorn crown around the top of the great oak. Streaming green, white and red ribbons have been secured to this crown for the Dirty Skirts to perform their May dance. These ribbons have been weighted down on the ground with stones, to stop them flying up in the breeze and snagging on higher branches. This activity has been done under the strict supervision of Wet Wendy.

'We dance to wake up the Earth, ready for summer,' declared Wendy: 'We dance sun-wise.'

'How on earth did we ever get by before?' asked a sceptical Foster. 'It's a miracle the flowers could ever be arsed to bloom, in years previous.'

Wendy shot him a dark look. She will not tolerate ridicule.

'And we'll be doing stream jumping, over the beck.'

'What's that in aid of?' asked Foster.

'We give thanks for water, and make sure there is enough to feed the land in the growing time.'

'Well, your lot bloody overdid it last year, luv. It pissed down. So much foot rot. Un-f'ing-believable. So, you go easy on the beck-jumping business, and don't dare squash the ramsons. The bluebells will be at their best too, so watch it.'

At some points during this setting up, Foster harboured malevolent thoughts towards Wendy. He felt a good deal of sympathy for The Damp Man. Letty might have had her issues, but Wet Wendy, he concluded, was the real ball-breaker.

Foster went down to light the barbecues around five o'clock. It was part-altruism, but self-interest was in there too. He didn't want anyone torching the trees down in the Gill. Now, there's a wonderful waft of light smoke in the air.

Foster has also prepared two modest fires of logs and brash – on Izzie's insistence. Bel fires, she called them. These are yet to be lit. A Bel fire was another new idea for Foster. Izzie explained that each of the women has been asked to bring something she no longer needs or uses, to represent something she wishes to be rid of. Foster thought it all sounded very Hebden Bridge, and said so. Izzie had smiled benignly, not rising to the bait. She didn't tell him that this, too, was on Margaret's insistence – part of the ridding process.

*****

A reception party of seven figures emerges from the low meadow and stands at the gate. They salute the Timble women, who fall uncharacteristically silent.

Gradually, whispered comments can be heard: 'Oh my gosh, they look so real. Brilliant costumes. I wonder where they went for those?'

'That place near The Crescent – you know – near Hyde Park, is good. It used to be a garage.'

'There's a good one now in Otley too.'

Androulla's voice rings out above the rest: 'I'd die for a pair of those thonged sandals. Just right for Portugal this summer. Antique leather's gorgeous – a really ethnic vibe.'

Wet Wendy's nose starts to twitch: 'What's that funny smell? It's a bit peaty – a cross between the inside of a plant pot and damp nettles.'

'Patchouli Oil. I'd recognise it anywhere. It was very popular when I was at catering college.' Ginny closes the speculation efficiently with an authoritative snort.

Margaret steps forward from the group. Izzie and Ginny go forward to meet her. Margaret looks moved by the size of the gathering. The three acknowledge each other in a shared silence with a strong sense of sisterly solidarity.

Izzie turns to the Timble women; she gestures towards the seven and begins her part-prepared and much thought about speech of introduction:

'These ladies are from the other side. We will look after them tonight. They are our guests, as we are theirs. Each represents a so-called Timble Witch, whose innocence and acquittal we are here to celebrate. We will remember a night four hundred years ago. In role, these women will not speak. They should not be questioned. I ask you to respect them, and their privacy.'

'You can tell that Izzie used to be a teacher,' says Linda, nodding with pride.

A muttering begins:

'She must mean they come from over the other side of the Gill – Low Snowden, or over beyond Dob Park, or Sword Point? I haven't seen any of them before.'

'Perhaps they don't speak English? Au pairs?'

'The younger ones, possibly. Two of them look a bit long in

the tooth.'

'Asylum seekers? Illegals?' queries Androulla.

'Ours not to question. Respect. That's what Izzie said. Leave that sort of stuff to that lot up at Menwith Hill,' says Linda.

'Fair enough. And now, it's party time girls!' calls June, rubbing her palms together with anticipation. She motions the group towards the Gill.

The cavalcade rattles down to the Gill, and the provisions are carried through. Izzie directs the preparations for the feast.

No one notices Ginny, Linda and June, lingering, hanging back with intent. Two of the young local farmers remain with them. Wynsome Waite and Karysma Foster, both descendants of Gill Women, have been drawn into the scheme and sworn to secrecy.

The two girls together cut quite a presence. Wynsome's taut muscular lower body is encased in Braided Booty Festival Shorts, bought on-line. These have been cunningly designed to reveal rather than to conceal. They allow for maximum movement which surely will be a plus in most eventualities. Wynsome is Prince Henry's School's great hope for the women's heptathlon team, javelin and shot put being her strongest events. The county talent spotters have their eyes upon her. Many of the party goers find it hard to take theirs off her too. Wet Wendy has commented that if it wasn't for the wellies, Wynsome would look like pole dancer. Izzie told Wendy to hush; they needed to keep both girls sweet.

Karysma's outfit is equally impressive but evokes more of 'the Goth'. She's gone for dyed pink red denim studded cut-offs teamed with an open mesh black crop top. Izzie was commissioned by Kary to run these items up to Kary's own specification. Her tanned tattooed midriff features a black crow, apparently descending towards her navel. Karysma's jet black and shiny over the knee rubber boots add a dominatrix vibe to her outfit and this is endorsed by her black leather thigh strap phone holder. Think Honey Ryder emerging from the sea in Dr No.

Both of our girls can handle themselves. These two young women, Karysma and Wynsome, have already been drawn into the inner sanctum, and the mission has been shared. In short, Izzie and Ginny have prepared them for some action. With purpose, they climb into their cabs and begin to manoeuvre the two tractors. Each tractor is positioned pointing up the hill to the north. The ropes are coiled around the girth of the oak, under the ribbons, and then pulled through the netting fence from the Gill. Each is tied securely to the tow bars of the tractors. Then the quads are turned and pointed north for a quick getaway. All keys are left in ignitions.

Margaret has come up to join them. Her eyes take in the vehicles with keen interest and great satisfaction. She nods appreciatively at Karysma and Wynsome; she's spotting family resemblances.

Ginny explains to Margaret: 'The weather forecast looks good, but sudden high winds from the south are predicted for later.'

'I should think they are. I've been summoning Borrum, the wind god, for five days now. He said he'd come. I pray that he shows. We might need a strong nudge from above.'

'Are you ready for it all? Feeling strong yourself?' Ginny looks Margaret straight in the eye. 'We will succeed.'

'We have our chant,' adds Linda, gamely.

'And we've practised it loads,' says June, rather lamely. She swallows hard.

'We'll join the rest and wait.' Margaret leads them off down into the Gill.

The evening brings much merriment, for most. The feast is good, the wine flows freely and the talk and laughter fill the air. Bottles of bilberry wine are produced by Ginny. A treat, from Foster, she declares. Foster and The Damp Man had found this great stash of it in the cellar, during the renovation. Dust and dirt covered clay flagons from heaven knows when. He, Ginny and Izzie had tried some, with no ill-effects, but they decided it probably needed drinking now. Of course, given her condition, Izzie keeps off it, and so do Ginny, Linda and June, for they agree they must keep their heads clear for action. Wynsome and Karysma are both teetotallers; they find their kicks elsewhere.

It has reached the moment to celebrate the Gill Women's acquittal, four hundred years ago.

Wet Wendy has been invited to open this phase with a traditional May Blessing:

> *Oak and May*
> *Upon this day*
> *Will both heed*
> *Those in need*

The glasses are charged, and the ladies toast 'The Halls, our hosts!'

Appreciative sounds and glasses are re-filled. Next toast from Izzie:

'The Women of the Gill! May innocence always prevail.'

All gathered repeat, in great solemnity: 'May innocence always prevail.'

A sudden shadow passes over. A man is emerging from the other side and crossing the beck. A handsome man in black, with a rather lopsided walk.

'No men here,' slurs one of the villagers, 'but we might make an exception for you, honeybun. Dishy, or what?' she hiccups.

'Be off with you!' snarls Wet Wendy: 'I don't like the cut of your jib.'

'This is girls' night out, so you bugger off,' calls another, her ending morphing into a burp.

The tables fall silent, the chatter stalls.

'Margaret,' he says. A strange, gravelly, seductive voice.

Margaret stands.

285

'You were not on the moor. You were not by the Tree of Life; you were not on the Death's Head stone. This is our night. Come.' He raises his hand and beckons.

Margaret is backing up towards the tall oak.

'Margaret. Come. Now.' His voice is more insistent.

'I will not join you.' Margaret's voice is calm and strong.

'Come now, we will fly. You like to fly. Come.' He's beckoning her with sharper gestures.

'I will no longer fly with you.'

'You have no choice. Tonight, you are mine forever. Come.' His voice is becoming increasingly sinister and insistent.

'No, never more.' She is still backing away from him, leading him to come forward.

'You'd break your word? You cannot treat a demon thus.' Asmodeus is now menacing.

'I will not come with you.'

Margaret starts to back up the steep gill. He follows. His head is cocking from one side to the other, like a bird. His body is rocking. His voice is mocking.

'But you like to fly and fly we will. Come take my bill.'

'I'll have none of you anymore.'

'Do these ladies know what you have done?' He turns slowly, and his gaze sweeps over the women.

'We do, and we don't care. You forced her there. You are depraved.' Ginny is on her feet. She points at him in scorn.

'It's true. We banish you.' Linda spits the words at him.

'We're here to vanquish you, Asmodeus, for ever,' screeches Izzie.

He seethes:

'You know my name, woman? Meddlesome fools and whores the lot of you! I'll take you all to hell.'

He lunges towards Margaret. She steps deftly behind the great oak. A strange dance of changing positions begins. Ginny and Linda send Kary and Wyn up the bank towards the tractors, to climb into the cabs, start the engines and await the signal.

The Dirty Skirts take up position, pick up their ribbons and wait, first feet pointing forward. The Mucky Pinnies press the buttons and squeeze out the opening bars of *On Ilkla Moor Baht'at*. The May dance begins. Margaret steps back, and the women, in a brisk, tight two-step begin to circle and to bind the demon to the tree. Asmodeus is diverted by the circling dancing women and the strange music, and it is a few moments before he realises exactly what is happening. Then he starts to struggle.

The party group members are all singing a customised version: *On Snowden Carr Baht'owt* – revised by Izzie for the occasion.

'*Cunts!*' he cries.

'Shut your face, you dirty old sod,' squeals Sally, a local farmer's daughter, and leader of the Dirties' team. She raises a single finger towards him, with a menacing grimace on her face.

Round and round they go, a relentless, dizzying progression. The ties are binding him tighter, weaving him to the oak tree. He squirms and writhes. Know that his language is not fit for print.

A strange chorus of whooshes emanate from the Gill Women. Margaret is now up in the top branches of the old tree and she's starting a dramatic swaying of the upper section.

'*Now. Chant now!*' she shrieks from her high perch. Her eyes are wild, and her skirts are billowing out.

Linda, Ginny, June and Izzie, from four corners start to move towards the demon:

"Eliminate, Obliterate, Exterminate, Annihilate!" over and over. They move like diabolical, mechanical, creatures. Their arms are raised high and their forefingers pointing at him, stabbing the air. Their voices take on an escalating tone of fury. The Timble women find the chant infectious, intoxicating. They all join in.

'Eliminate, Obliterate, Exterminate, Annihilate!'

'Eliminate, Obliterate, Exterminate, Annihilate!'

'Eliminate, Obliterate, Exterminate, Annihilate!'

Asmodeus seems mesmerised.

The four are closing in on him. The rest of the guests are pressing in on him too. The Dirties have done their work and join the throng. Wet Wendy's screechy voice can be heard above the rest: 'Bastard! You hateful bastard, die or else!'

The whooshing is escalating from the Gill Women. Margaret is causing a frenzy in the upper branches.

Ginny and Linda remember the fish bits and incense and sprinkle the contents of the bags over the embers. Suddenly there's an obnoxious and asphyxiating stench.

The whooshing is reaching a crescendo, as Margaret screams: *'Borrum! Now!'*

And blow Borrum does. A sudden bang hits and the great oak creaks. The women step away briskly and move up the narrow path, in an orderly file, towards the low meadow. The two tractors' ropes take up the slack and start to pull. Margaret flies to the crown of a neighbouring tree.

The bound Asmodeus catches the first whiff of fish organs cooking on the incense-infused embers. He gags. His face contorts: *'Disgusting. You whorey fuck-pigs!'* his last words...

The great oak groans in its death throes. It creaks and topples back towards the bank. The Gill's side reverberates as the trunk hits the bank with a thunderous thud. Asmodeus is skewered though both head and heart by its snapped branches. This is certain demon death.

A huge crust of earth and root is torn up from the Gill floor and a vast chasm opens like a great void, as the great oak topples. The remaining women peer down the hole in silence, as if trying to get a glimpse of hell.

The last to leave are Izzie, Ginny, the Gill Women and Margaret. Margaret's breathing begins to steady. She turns her head slowly, upwards towards the far bank. Something has caught her attention. She raises her head, then points. Her whole demeanour is transforming.

Izzie follows the line of Margaret's fore finger. It's getting hard to focus in the gloom. She just makes out a head, the head of a stranger. It is the pallid-faced, flaxen haired man, lying on his belly, on the ground at the ridge top. He's staring over towards them, or rather towards Margaret, for his eyes are fixed solely upon her. His face is a study in rage.

'Seen enough this time?' screamed one of the Gill Women – Margaret Waite's daughter. It was she who had been accused by Fairfax himself of "impudency and lewd behaviour" in his deposition.

'Yes, he's here, he's back to see,' cry the Gill Women in unison. They start to move as one, towards the beck, towards the man, in a practised, menacing rhythmic shuffle: *'Curse you Fairfax! Curse you once again. Fire and water bring you down.'*

Izzie is transfixed. She watches the man stand. He's wearing a strange, dusty black antique frock coat, breeches and knee boots over the top. He has a voluminous shirt with a big, lace-trimmed collar. His countenance is that of a corpse, translucent green, and pocked; she sees the skull beneath the skin. He appears agitated, angry, outraged. Yes, he's quaking with rage. He seems to want to speak, but no words are coming out. His finger points back at Margaret. It's stabbing the air, emphatic, yet impotent.

Izzie wonders if he's been up there watching, all through the evening's proceedings?

'Fairfax – get you back to hell,' screams Margaret. *'You came to gloat, to see me taken. Go get you back to hell.'*

Fairfax finally finds his words:

'No! No! Oh no, no, no! This isn't how it ends.'

Margaret's confidence is sapping swiftly. She has not anticipated this. This was not in the plan. Izzie sees that Margaret has a far greater terror of this man than of Asmodeus himself.

Fairfax, a furious forcefield, is crackling:

'Long centuries have I waited, to witness your departure to hell.

To see you and your demon lover together for the last time, and for him to drag you down. To witness your degradation, wings scorching, crumpling, burning so bright into perpetual night. You, who would take him, the prince of demons, over me. Never willingly was it with me. You chose him over a Fairfax? No, this will not do. This is not how it ends.'

In a split second, Fairfax moves his position. He's now standing there, right in front of Margaret, sneering, jeering, menacing with his spectral hands clawing the dusk thickening air of the Gill.

He finds more words. In exasperation:

'And my line is dead, and yours goes on. My house is drowned, my monument consumed by flame. Don't dare think you have escaped my venom, bitch.'

Elizabeth Foster steps forward: *'Come Mister Fairfax, you were a god-fearing man in your time. Surely you know your Beatitudes. Doesn't it say something about the meek being blessed? Yes? And what happens to the meek and poor folk? They inherit the earth, don't they? This valley at least. And that's what we've done.'*

'Hold your tongue you idiot scum. Don't think I haven't watched what's gone on.'

He shifts again and re-appears right by Izzie's side.

'Well here's one line that I shall cauterise, burn and sear and stop forever. And now...'

He turns to Izzie and prods her big belly with his bony finger:

'You knew the demon's name, our lord of lust and lechery, so you will come with me to hell. You carry the last spawn of these odious Halls.'

Fairfax strokes Izzie's hair softly yet with molten malice. She tries to pull away, to disengage. It is futile; she is locked in his grasp.

'This one, no two,' he laughs with glee, *'will come with me and be mine.'*

Izzie is distraught. Her dreams of her future flash before her.

Never has she felt such love for Foster, and the life she could have shared with him, and will have lost. Her unborn baby? What has she done? What has she risked? These 'whats' point to a longed-for path that now will never be taken. She tries to prise Fairfax's fingers from her arm, but she is locked in bone. There is no give.

Margaret's face registers the full horror of this new situation, this turn of events. This is outside the plan so carefully put together. This is the darkness of her vision, after the birth of her own son. An unborn Hall to be cast into the flames of hell, alongside the bairn's mother. This is too cruel to bear.

Margaret has now to think fast and quickly. She will play on his vanity; she will make her appeal. She will summon her courage once more. Her voice softens to disguise her terror:

'You are wrong Edward Fairfax. You are so wrong. She carries no demon's child, and nor did I. An earthly child isn't sired by a demon, even the prince of lust can't do that.'

'Then whose child is it, strange woman?' he demands.

Silence. Margaret half-smiles – an ironic lift of her left brow.

'Are you telling me...?' Fairfax stands stunned, incredulous. Then he contorts in a paroxysm of even deeper fury:

'My precious seed flows through the valley's peasants? This is the final affront, the last indignity. This is ... unacceptable.'

'Perhaps you should have hoarded your precious seed more carefully?' Margaret doesn't expect a response. Fairfax turns his back on Margaret and faces Izzie: *'Oh yes, slut, you are definitely coming with me.'*

Suddenly there are raucous squeals followed by a bellow:

'Fuckpig Fairfax, here's one from posterity, you vile, wrinkly old prick!'

And down it came, a brilliant aim, a two-pronged steel hay fork hurled as a javelin. No-one has noticed Wynsome and Karysma coming quietly back down the path by the side of the Gill. Everyone's attention has been fully focused on Fairfax.

Wynsome with her hay fork, and Karysma with her iPhone. Wynsome had wanted Karysma to video the fallen tree and crushed demon for her page. And she thought the hay fork might come in handy to put out fires or untangle ribbons to get to the skewered remains. The two had not realised there were new and sinister developments afoot. They did not realise that they would have to take on the persecutor of their own female forbears.

Was it the force of the fork throw? Was it some curious interaction of the solar wind with the Earth's magnetosphere, causing the magnetic field to stretch out onto the dark side? Or was it the fact that on some inspired impulse, Karysma threw her iPhone at Fairfax's heart as the hay fork hit the spectre? One thing is for sure – some profound fluctuation happened in the magnetic field that held the phantom of Fairfax together. Of this there can be no doubt.

'The dirty fucker's pixelating. Look at him! He's breaking up. He's gone and disappeared, that's all. And my iPhone's dropped down that big hole with 'im.' So screams Karysma, torn 'twixt disappointment and elation: 'Still we got the bastard, Wyn!'

'Yeh, we did, didn't we? Sorry about your iPhone, Kary – insurance job – lost in the line of duty. Were all your bank details on it?'

Which of the two can claim his demise will become an irrelevance over time. Big hearted young women, they will each concede to the other. For the rest of the party, it was just sheer relief.

Elizabeth Foster steps forward: 'Child of my child's child's children, dearest of all the children.' She envelopes Karysma in her arms. Both begin to weep.

'Wynsome, we honour you!' Margaret Waite and her daughter hug their plucky and resourceful descendant. 'You have done us Waites proud! You're never to be forgotten.'

Margaret, Izzie and Ginny make a hugging trio too, shoulders shaking and tears for each other's eyes only. They break apart at last. Then every woman remaining down in the Gill congratulates the pair – most admirable young women both.

Margaret turns, lifts her arms gently and shepherds them away and out of the Gill: *'Come my sweet gossips, for now, truly, it's over.'*

She will not look back.

*****

No-one really knew what to make of it all. A swell party it was. An amazing floor-show. Then the tree got blown over in the wind. The rain had started rather suddenly after that, and then, they all went home. That's how they thought they remembered it.

A kind of collective, partial amnesia descended on many of the villagers. Was it the bilberry wine? Perhaps it didn't go with prosecco. Two things were certain, their clothes smelled of fish and they all had splitting headaches the next morning. Some of the guests awoke to tilting floors.

In retrospect, it was deemed the best village do ever, and they all agreed they must do it again. But no firm plans were made. Well, it wasn't the sort of occasion you would wish to repeat too often. Foster stuck up a Private sign on the gate above the low meadow. 'Health and Safety' he explained: 'The Gill is pretty unstable in that area and trees have been known to topple.'

Foster went down the next morning to tidy up. The women had done a good job, and there wasn't much to be done. He was shocked to see the old oak tree on its back. He thanked God for public liability insurance, and then breathed a sigh of relief that no-one had been hurt. This oak was by far the oldest tree in the Gill. He reckoned a full four hundred odd years old, or more – he tried to count the rings, then lost count after four hundred and sixteen.

The only remaining party debris was the sodden tangle of

green, red and white ribbons, woven round the fallen tree. He gave these a half-hearted tug. Given the state of them, he didn't think Wet Wendy and the Dirties would want them back. He started to cut them off and found some of them bloodied along with a handful of blue-black feathers. He couldn't work that one out. It made him feel strange and uneasy. He chose not to mention it to Izzie. He knew that the village women would be upset that a bird might have been hurt. They are sensitive like that, he thought.

The old oak was ringed and then split into logs. It kept Black Crow Farm warm for three long winters, once the wood had fully dried out. Foster said he was amazed the great oak hadn't fallen before – rotten to the core it was. Its time had come, he said. Nothing to be done; nothing is forever.

9

On the last day of July

It's the last day of July 2023, a Monday. Foster has set the alarm early for there is a job to be done. He's taking a batch of cull ewes down to the market at Otley.

He gets out of bed carefully so not to disturb Izzie. He looks down at her sleeping form. Even in the curtained light of dawn he can make out her full silhouette under the lightweight summer sheet. It has been warm, and he has felt such concern for her, carrying so great a burden. She's due any day.

He carries out his clothes in a bundle, and dresses on the landing.

Foster, shouldering his own burden, tiptoes down the ancient stairs. He moves slowly and silently, steadying himself, hand on the bannister. He makes for the kitchen, or more specifically, for the kettle. Once it has boiled, he pours a steady stream of steaming water onto the teabag he's placed in the base of his favourite mug. This features a pin-up of Lou, cunningly captured on its side, a birthday present from Izzie. She's kind and sweet like that, he muses. He still marvels that any woman should ever wish to celebrate his birthday.

He stands at the window. In the early morning light, he spots a hen pheasant picking through the long dewy grass. He delights in the soft, mottled colours of her breast – a subtle spectrum of pale cream through beige to cocoa. He's always loved the females, less showy but so beautiful. Foster declared Black Crow Farm a haven for pheasants and all the other game birds who entered this domain, when he took over the farm from his father. 'Wankers' is how Foster dismisses the people who shoot birds for sport. He sees them as a group whose own souls are already shot through. He suffers pangs of guilt if he accidently clips a bird on the road.

Foster can hear the hen pheasant's confiding chuntering. It's a comforting low noise and he needs comfort this morning. He pulls himself together. He reminds himself she isn't making those sweet sounds just for him. He grabs the keys to his Land Rover, his movement forms that he completed the night before, and his well-worn jacket, and as quietly as possible, locks the door behind him. If it wasn't for the task ahead, he thought, he'd be enjoying a glorious midsummer morning such as this.

Down in the barn a small group of aged ewes is contained in one of the middle bays. These ewes are enjoying some of this July's new hay. The Leaper comes towards him, greets him with a tilt of her head and offers her ears to be pulled. Foster manipulates them and strokes her nose. He speaks out loud, confident in the knowledge that there is no-one there to hear and to mock. But his voice is cracking: 'Come on Old Girl. Time has come.'

He leans over the hurdle and plants a kiss on her brow. She rewards him with a look of trust, but there is something quizzical in her expression.

On the other side of the barn, Foster releases Lou from her run. His bitch leaps up at him with joy and tries to lick his face. She races into the yard for a wee, then bounds back into the barn. He whistles her to his side. Now she knows she's on duty.

The night before Foster had lifted the trailer arm on to the Land Rover's tow bar. This morning, all that remains is to get the ewes installed. He drops the ramp, lifts out the hurdle to form a chute, then sends Lou round the back to drive the old girls on board. Leaper leads them on. She reckons she's going to the southside, thinks Foster. He secures the trailer doors and whistles Lou into the back of his Land Rover. As he makes his trailer check, his eyes meet the Leaper's, through the slit in the galvanised metal side. He makes soft encouraging clucks to her. He sets off sedately and with heavy heart.

The ride over the moor is stunning, and this makes the journey more poignant. He hates to take his old girls to market, but this time it feels almost unbearable. His thoughts turn back to that day during lambing, when he drove Ginny and The Leaper to the veterinary. Now, over four months later, he is taking her down again, without Ginny of course, and not to the vets.

It's part of the deal, he reminds himself. He is a farmer. Leaper is livestock. It is what happens, what must happen. So why does he feel so bad?

Foster has been reading a lot in the farming press about the future of livestock rearing. It has rattled him more deeply than he's prepared to confess. Farming has been his life, but now he is being prodded to view his work as something less than worthy – an environmental issue, a challenge to the planet. 'Safe in their hands' they used to say about the countryside and its farmers. Now no-one is sure. People in wealthy countries are being urged to change their eating habits – to eat less meat and move over to a plant-based diet.

Foster sighs heavily. He looks to the right, over Askwith Moor, a stunning view on a morning like this. A mist hangs over the Wharfe, filling the valley bottom. But the tops are sharp and gin clear, the higher landscape rearing up through the low cloud. Ilkley lies wrapped in mist. He senses it rather than sees it and thinks of the Legume Café. Was that an omen? Didn't the

Legume bring him Izzie and all the joy in his present life? Has he got it wrong? Should he be taking this vegetarian business more seriously? Should he be starting to turn the farm in a new direction? But soybeans aren't suited to boulder clay. Black Crow Farm is on a hill – 'less favoured' according to grant allocations. You might get away with soybeans in the south, where the land is lighter and the summers warmer, longer and less severe, but not up here.

Foster cautions himself; he tells the scowling reflection in his rear-view mirror not to over-react. People are being told to cut back on meat, but not to stop eating it. Okay, he reasons, farm animals produce more greenhouse gases than growing crops, and obesity is partly due to folk getting too many of their calories from meat, but there are other issues to bear in mind. Vegetarian foods, even the avocado, can cause environmental damage too. Eating food that is locally sourced and seasonal is something that can be achieved, thinks Foster.

But Foster knows things are changing and, in many respects, farmers are on borrowed time. He needs no persuasion about climate change. He's seen it, lived it, picked up the pieces on his own patch. He could list the changes in the local bird population. He's seen the swallows disappear and the house martin community under the eaves of the Robinson Library decimated. Not one swift this summer, he's reflected. Bats are a rarity now but quarter of a century ago Foster remembers pipistrelles lacing the air on summer evenings' walks. Losing this life in little deaths – the phrase comes back to him. He's read it somewhere. Is it too late to halt the decline, he wonders?

If he's honest, Foster would have to acknowledge that farmers were responsible for some bad stuff. There must be a point of balance, thinks Foster, between animal welfare, environmentally sound land management and profitability. It's time to put his own house in order and to fight back, he thinks, to show a positive example. He vows to review his own farming practices and try to make them more sustainable and kinder to the environment, for the sake of his unborn child, children even?

Foster slows to join the queue of trailers and then pulls into the market. He hands his forms over to one of the staff, who directs him to a bay for unloading. He'll power-wash his trailer but will not stay for the sale; he cannot stay. The banter of the auction would not be to his taste this day.

It is a hollow sense of loss he experiences as he crosses back over the Wharfe at Otley, and rises up Billam's Hill, towards home. The Leaper, the birds, all the creatures, this way of life, he sighs. He hopes it's not too late – to take some small steps to protect the remaining lapwings, to keep the curlews, to coax all the remaining birds to stay whatever means it takes, whatever can be done at local level.

Foster is so wrapped up in his thoughts he fails to notice six misty yet familiar forms at the top of the moor, their right arms extended, pointing him in the direction of Timble. He fails to notice Margaret, standing alongside the Neighbourhood Watch sign on the edge of the village, beckoning him with some urgency. Margaret gives an exasperated shrug as he passes her and rolls her eyes skyward. What is that lad like, she thinks?

Foster enters the farmhouse and washes his hands slowly. Izzie has introduced anti-bacterial lavender handwash in a dispenser and insists on clean towels. Foster protested to begin with. He's always been suspicious of over-cleanliness. But now, he confesses to himself, he rather likes the scent.

All is quiet. Izzie must have slept in. He'll take her some tea. He walks into the kitchen. There, propped against the candle stick is a hurriedly scribbled note in Ginny's hand.

Waters broken!

I've taken Izzie into Harrogate. I phoned them first and they are expecting her. We've got her case. I'll text you the ward and details asap. You just bring yourself. First babies often take time, but don't hang around, kid. Ginny xx

Lou pushes her head under Foster's trembling hand for re-assurance. She looks up at him. Foster tries to steady his shaking shoulders. He blows his nose, collects himself, puts Lou in her run and sets off again. This time he's driving Izzie's car. He hasn't the time to unhook his trailer.

10

One year on

It's another summer, and a time of joy, not sorrow.

A heavily pregnant Izzie sits with Foster on the stone seat above the Gill. She hasn't too long to go.

The pair watch the sun-silhouetted trio in front of them. Their daughter, Isadora, is taking her early steps, stumbling and uncertain, but cooing with confidence. Ginny is on one side, holding the child's hand firmly and encouraging her:

'Come on little Izzie, you can do it. Best foot forward!'

'There speaks your Aunty Ginny, your godmother,' laughs Foster: 'Go for it, girl! Do as Aunty Ginny says: she'll never lead you astray.' Foster is so proud. He's fallen in love all over again. He's certainly forgotten he ever had any ambitions for a son.

Then Isadora turns her head to the person who lightly holds her other hand. The child smiles up at her, totters, yet is steadier by the step. Another godmother of sorts, or a guardian angel.

'Mar–get,' she lisps, calls her again by name, and chuckles.

The strange woman bends down to brush the child's brow with her lips, in benediction. The trio makes slow progress down to the Gill.

A mist seeps out from the depths of the Gill, over the old stile where the bridge once spanned the beck, before the flood. A once in a thousand years' flood it was called then, but these seem to happen more and more.

This mist takes on a silvering, shimmering substance, or rather substances – first silhouettes, then figures. It is the Gill Women; they dote on Isadora.

Isadora, unsteady on her own feet, is eloquent in her arm movements. Her small, plump arms begin a sequence of waves. She weaves patterns in the air. The women dance to her command. She arm-dances with their spirits and plays with their hearts, as Ginny holds her towards them in her arms.

Izzie and Foster have been watching from the stone seat. Izzie catches Foster's profile.

'Are you welling up?'

'I must have something in my eye – a fly?' he says. 'Or hay fever – high pollen count.'

'A likely tale.' Izzie is smiling. 'It's not a crime, you know.'

'Okay, I confess, I feel – emotional. I mean, look around, Izzie, just look. It took you to open up my eyes to this life; it was you who made me see it.' He takes her hand and raises it to his lips:

'I bless the day I found you in this hole.' He sticks his finger down the stone hole, as if to check. 'Hard to break the habit.' He laughs.

'It's Margaret and the Gill Women we should thank. They did it, Foz. They set us up on this hot date we call our life together. I feel so content – so happy.'

'Perhaps we should give them this part of the Gill?'

'It's theirs anyway.'

'No, I mean these low meadows. Give this sacred place back to nature in honour of Margaret and her friends. Re-wild it, plant some trees, plant a replacement oak for the one that fell. Plant a tree for each of the Gill Women. Let's create a place that's worthy, for the flowers and insects, butterflies, bees, birds and animals. All the things that are struggling to survive. A place of beauty for people to walk through and enjoy. I want our kids to breathe clean air. I want all kids to breathe clean air before it becomes a luxury for the privileged. This might be just the start, but truly, I want to give it back.'

'So, no more spraying thistles with poison, Foz?'

'I promise. Just like our Isadora, I might be taking small, tottery steps, but I'll get there. I see now that nature is as fragile as we are.'

Izzie nods. She squeezes his hand, and kisses him, for sometimes, even words can never be enough.

11

Borrowed time

Izzie strides along Leeds Road, her new baby secured across her front in a floral bamboo wrap. She averts her eyes from Walton's window; she is not in a fine furnishings frame of mind this day. She's making for Legume, and Linda.

Anemones, notes Linda, always Izzie's favourite. Linda is watching her friend's approach. She's sitting at the table in the café front window. As Izzie comes closer, Linda can see the baby's dark, down covered crown, peeping up over the soft sling. This sling has been created from a vibrant anemone patterned fabric. Izzie will tell her friend later that she has styled it herself and has taken several orders – strangers have come up to her and demanded to know where she bought it. A new line; a perpetual cuddle, a natural, hands free hug.

Linda smiles. Inside, she's wondering when it was that Izzie metamorphosised from her old Hebden Bridge self into earth mother. It happens to some, she reflects. Curious, nonetheless.

The door of the Legume Café bursts open, bell jangling.

'Linda, my lovely friend!'

'Look at you Izzie. This is not rude health, it's positively obscene. What's this hanging off your chest?'

'I'll introduce you later, formally. Don't dare wake her up, whatever you do.'

'Where's the holy terror? Is Daddy doing his stuff?'

'Actually, Isadora is enjoying some quality time with her Aunty Ginny. Foster's working on his wildflower meadows. And in truth Linda, next to herself,' Izzie looks down at her sleeping new-born: 'our Isadora is a perfect peach.'

'Good morning ladies; ready to order?'

'Filter coffee and cold milk for me,' says Linda.

'And a lemon verbena tea for me.'

'What?'

'I have to be so careful with this one. You have no idea. She reacts badly to me taking caffeine. Isadora never turned a hair. Sparky isn't the half of it. Wait until she opens her eyes. She'll have the measure of you in fifteen seconds. We are all terrified of her.'

'Hmm. Well, I really can't wait.'

Linda ties to square this vision of sleeping serenity in a sling with Izzie's warning, then she notices Izzie's eyes.

'Hey, what's up?'

Izzie is fighting to maintain her composure.

'Have you fallen out with Foster? Has he strayed? If he's upset you, I'll go up and sort him out. Come on, reveal all.'

Izzie shakes her head and in a barely audible voice: 'I love him to bits. It isn't him.'

'Ginny?'

'No, Ginny's been brill.' Izzie sniffs discretely.

'Margaret and the Gill Women?'

'It's one of the reasons I wanted us to meet.'

'Old Buggerlugs hasn't come back, has he?'

'No! But something has happened.'

'So, are you going to tell me?'

'I will, but it's difficult. I want to tell it right, but it's hard to find the words. I'm still not sure myself – what I witnessed, that is, and what it means. I'm trying to make sense of it all.'

'Cake will help. It always did. I noticed some sticky ginger parkin on the cake counter – ginger curd filling too. Serious times demand a serious cake.'

'You sound like Marie Antoinette.' Izzie blows her nose on a damp tissue: 'I'll never lose the weight if I get stuck into a lump of that stuff.'

'We'll share. Sounds as if you are going to need your strength. Now I'm inspecting you properly, I think you look fair flaky. Go on then; what's gone off?'

Linda catches the eye of the ponytail lady and orders a piece of parkin, two plates and two spoons. She adds a pot of double cream as an afterthought.

Izzie removes the teabag from the cup with her spoon and begins:

'You see, we were waiting for a name for our girl.'

'I'm listening Izzie but please do try not to be tangential. It can be hard to follow you at the best of times.'

'Bear with me.' Izzie strokes her top lip and snuffles: 'Margaret had asked to name the new baby. She had been quite insistent. Foster didn't mind; he never does where Margaret is concerned. I certainly didn't; I was intrigued. But it was the way she spoke that should have raised alarm bells.'

'Go on. I'm getting the feel of something odd, Izzie. Tell me more.' Linda's eyebrow lifts quizzically: 'You didn't like her choice of name, was that it? Bit too trad? Lettice or Tryphena?'

'Linda, please don't try and guess what went off. Let me tell you in my own words and time.'

'Fair enough.' Linda nods and forks a generous lump of cream coated parkin into her mouth. 'God, this is good.'

And so, Izzie begins her tale, with only occasional prompt from Linda.

'We'd gone down to meet them and to introduce our new

girl. They came up from the Gill as usual, Margaret and the women. A little bit slower, dimmer in form and dappling in the sunlight. I had this little one in her sling. Ginny had come down with me, holding Isadora's hand and carrying her when necessary. We were going to let Foster bring her back up the hill on the quad. They both love to do that. He's determined Isadora will take over the farm. You should see them together. He drives with such pride, care and dignity and she clutches the handlebars with her chubby mitts, laughing with joy, the g–force parting her curls.

Well, Margaret sat down beside me on the stone seat. She looked over to where Foster was working, on the far side of the drain. She has, err had, that way of asking a question without saying a word. I told her:

"He's planting flowers for you all, for your wildflower meadow. Seeds and plugs." I said to them. Margaret was baffled by the word 'plugs'. We got round it by saying it was something you stuffed in a hole, and then explained about the small plants he was putting in, especially the orchids.'

Izzie snuffled again and continued: 'They all laughed in delight about having their own meadow. Then they started to choose flowers, but they didn't stop there – they wanted trees and shrubs too ...'

'Well, it seems a reasonable thing. After all, you told them it was their place.'

'To me it was troubling. I sort of saw where it was going. A sixth sense, a presentiment, call it what you like. I was overcome with a sense of pending loss.'

Izzie pauses. 'Janet spoke first, softly, deep and firm: *No need to plant for me. Tell him you'll find me in the ling, blazing bright on a cool wet August day, or lit by sunlight if the weather's fine. You'll find me on the moor or gathered and twine-bound to a stick to sweep clear a cottage floor. Sweet besoms, that's where I'll be."*

And then Elizabeth, Elizabeth Foster, spoke of the violets in

307

the Gill, a flower of modesty, humility, wisdom and faithfulness. She said that violets spoke of the incarnation of Christ and thus would be the one for her. She said that they grew freely there.

The second Elizabeth, Dickenson, went for yellow rattle, for, she said, it made its own rare music when its seeds had dried, hissing, whispering, quaking and shaking in the breeze, and because it encouraged the spirits of the other flowers by weakening the strong domineering grasses that sought to swamp them. As yellow rattle, she said she would safeguard the meadows.

Janet's daughter, Margaret Thorpe, chose a harebell. She said *"I cannot stand the damp, especially after York Castle. I want to lie forever on a dry, grassy bank. Harebells are the flower of grief, and I've had my share of this. I wish to live in sunlight's kiss, forever."*

Margaret Waite and her daughter both chose meadow sweet. *"Well we both must choose again,"* said the mother *"or else we'll squabble, nark and bark our way into eternity and that won't do."*

"So, I'll go for ragged robin, for I thrive in a bog, and yet I'm more delicate and pretty than you," said her daughter, laughing.

"We'll not fall out. What you say is true. I'll be the willow whips on the wayside, noticed only by the few. No matter how I'm cut and reduced, I'll always come back and thrive. Margaret, tell us, what of you?"

"Brambles for me. I'm not one for the bible, but I was told the burning bush was a bramble, the bush that bore the flames of love and yet was not consumed by lust. But I'd like a flower too. Let him plant primroses for me. Let them trail to the Gill, and down to the beck. Primroses for the beauty of women, femininity, new life, youth and new beginnings. And now, before we leave you, let me name this sweet bairn."

Izzie hesitates: 'Linda, I handed my baby to Margaret. She kissed her tiny brow and said she named my child *"Susannah"*.'

'Susannah? Well now, that's not too bad. I like it; yes, indeed I do. It's good enough.'

'Margaret said she had known a Susannah once and that she was a good woman. She said Susannah was a friend who was better than she deserved. She said she had done her friend a great wrong.'

'Go on?'

'She said that she hadn't needed to act as she had and that the woman's husband would have supported her and the Gill Women anyway because he was a fair, honourable and godly man. So, whatever it was, she did not need to do it. Margaret said she had wronged them both and she had carried the guilt of her actions for four centuries. I think she sees the dedication of our Susannah as some sort of … Well, I'm not sure. Perhaps she sees her way to peace lies in this bairn?'

Izzie pauses, then continues, her direct gaze locking Linda's eyes to her: 'She also said that she could see something of Nicholas Smithson in Foster, in his character, his courage, his fairness and in the very look in his eyes.'

'Izzie?' whispers Linda, her brow furrowing.

Izzie holds up her hand for Linda not to interrupt her flow:

'Then Margaret said it was time for us to part. She said that she and her friends were on borrowed time. They were weary of their role; they were flagging. She said they wanted eternal rest in nature, that their appearances in human form were sapping and that their direct interventions had come to an end.'

'Our battle was in vain then? They were going to die anyway?'

'No, don't you understand? What she was saying, I think, was this. Now they had achieved peace, they could leave us. It was their choice. They wanted to go on their own terms, not dragged off and cast into hell. A dignified departure and a good and willing death.'

Izzie pauses: 'It's over. They trust us all to find our own way now.'

'And Foster?'

'He understands, and of course he grieves. He had anticipated it and accepts it. I suspect this is what his preparation of the wildflower meadows has been about. Me, Ginny, Foster, we're all deeply saddened that they have gone. We also know that although they will not be visible, they will still be with us. And when we look at Isadora and Susannah, we will see something of Margaret, them all in truth, in our girls. Women, all of us, no more, no less.'

Izzie blows her nose. Linda places her hand on Izzie's arm. Her own eyes are brimming. The ponytail lady brings them both a second round of drinks and a packet of tissues, both on the house. She's been watching from a discrete distance and has concluded they could use re-enforcements. Both Izzie and Linda marvel at the kindness of strangers.

'And then?' A gentle prompt from Linda.

Izzie continues: 'Margaret brushed Susannah's brow with her lips, made a blessing over her head in words I did not recognise, an antique language long since lost, and then, with reluctance, she handed the baby back to me. Margaret said that through Susannah she would atone for the wrong she had done, and that Susannah would bring her true peace. Then she bent and hugged Isadora, embraced Ginny, and then me. By this point Foster had joined us. She wrapped her arms around him and said:

"My child, my children. You'll find us in this meadow, the flowers, the trees, the creatures that dwell here, even the fowl in the air. Remember to plant for your own girls too. Plant bluebells for Isadora and sanicle for Susannah, Foster." Those were her last words.'

Izzie reaches for another tissue and blows again.

'Usually, when they leave us, they just fade. This time it was different. It was like when we went to the Arena back in October '19.'

'What?'

'You know – the Hologram thingy – 'The Rock and Roll Dream Tour'. Remember – when Buddy Holly disappeared in a puff of lit up smoke, just as he finished *"That'll Be the Day."*? On this occasion all seven of them went together, as if Buddy had taken the would-be Crickets, and the backing girls with him. No Linda, it's not funny…'

Linda bites her lip and swallows hard:

'Izzie, sorry, but all of this has been a long journey, and I've tried to suspend disbelief every inch of the way…'

'Well you just hang on in there, for this isn't the time to falter. In truth, I suppose you have been good.'

Linda absorbs this rare compliment from her friend.

Izzie continues:

'Do you know, at that moment, the air was suffused with seven sweet scents, and that strange, fading sound I have heard down there, of a taut bow drawn slowly across an A string of an ancient fiddle. And that was it.'

The two friends drop into a companionable and reflective silence for a while. They sip their drinks, still warm. Then Izzie speaks:

'Linda, Foster and me, we've been talking. We wonder if you are willing to be Susannah's "life-guardian"? You know – the non-religious version of a godparent. We are thinking of having our own ceremony in the Gill. And a celebration, not on the scale of the last one, of course.'

'I sincerely hope not – never to be repeated. But you had Isadora done in Fewston Church – christening dress, cake, the works?'

'I know we did; Ginny was to be godmother and she insisted.'

'Right. Well, of course, I'll be delighted to be Susannah's life-guardian. I will be honoured.'

This is the moment Susannah chooses to open just one of her midnight eyes, half smiles, turns her gaze upon Linda, and with tiny right hand furled into a fist, brings it sharply into the palm of her left. This strange gesture she teams with the most penetrating caw ever heard in the Legume Café.

About the author

Stephanie Shields' short fiction, flash fiction and poems have featured in anthologies, magazines and on radio. She is also a sheep farmer in the Washburn Valley, Yorkshire.

The Strange Woman is her debut novel. It combines historical fiction with a modern love story and magical realism.

Swan Landings, a short story collection, was published in 2017.

Author's sources
and influences

Author's sources and influences

The Inspiration:

Edward Fairfax: ***Daemonologia***: *A Discourse on Witchcraft as it was Acted in the Family of Mr. Edward Fairfax, of Fuyston, in the County of York in the year 1621* with a Biographical Introduction and Notes Topographical & Illustrative by William Grainge, Harrogate: R Ackrill, Printer and Publisher 1882

Essential Works

Reginald Scot: *The Discoverie of Witchcraft*, 1584
King James VI of Scotland (By The High and Mighty Prince) *Daemonologie*, In Forme of a dialogue, Divided into three Books, 1597
The King James Bible 1611 including the 39 books of the Old Testament, 14 books of the Apocrypha and the 27 books of the New Testament
Robert Burton (Democritus Junior) *The Anatomy of Melancholy* (Volume 1) first edition 1621
Nicholas Culpeper's *Complete Herbal: consisting of a comprehensive description of nearly all herbs with their medicinal properties and directions for compounding the medicines extracted from them.* ISBN 0-572 00203 3
Nicholas Culpeper: *A Directory for Midwives: or a Guide for*

Women, in their Conception, Bearing and Suckling Their Children
J S Cockburn: *A History of English Assizes 1558-1714* Cambridge University Press. 1972 online publication October 2011 ISBN 9780511896507

The lives and the literature of the late sixteenth and early seventeenth century writers

The Elizabethan Novelists: Thomas Deloney, Robert Greene and Thomas Nashe

The Elizabethan and Jacobean Dramatists and Poets: Edward Fairfax, Edmund Spenser, William Shakespeare, John Webster, John Ford, Christopher Marlowe, Ben Jonson

The Metaphysical Poets, especially John Donne, George Herbert and Andrew Marvell

Additional Insights

Thomas Parkinson: *Lays and Leaves of the Forest; a collection of poems, and historical, genealogical & biographical essays and sketches, relating chiefly to men and things with the royal forest of Knaresborough* Alpha Editions (2019) Originally published 1882

J A Sharpe: *Witchcraft in Seventeenth-Century Yorkshire: Accusations and Counter Measures*, 1992, (Borthwick Papers) ISBN 0903857391

Margaret Baker: *Discovering the Folklore of Plants*, Shire Publications Ltd First published 1969 ISBN 0747801789

W B Crow: *The Occult Properties of Herbs*, The Aquarian Press First published 1969 ISBN 0 85030 035 5

Cynthia Wickham: *Common Plants as Natural Remedies*, Frederick Muller Limited First published in Great Britain 1981 ISBN 0-584-10475-8

Roger Phillips: *Wild Food*, Pan Books First published 1983 ISBN0 330 28069 4

Hans Peter Brodel: *The Malleus Maleficarum and the construction of witchcraft. Theology and popular belief.* Manchester University Press 2003

Carolyn Merchant: *The Death of Nature: Women, Ecology and the Scientific Revolution* Reprint Kindle Edition ISBN: 9780062505958

Silvia Federici *Caliban and the Witch: Women, the Body and Primitive Accumulation* published by Autonomedia 2004

Silvia Federica: *Witches, Witch-hunting and Women* PM Press 2018

Sherilyn MacGregor: *Beyond Mothering Earth, Ecological Citizenship and the Politics of Care*, 1969, UBC Press 2006 ISBN-13 987-0-7748-1201-6

Barbara Ehrenreich & Deirdre English *Witches Midwives and Nurses* published in 2010 by the Feminist Press at the City University of New York

Charles Bowness: *The Witch's Gospel* Clarke, Doble & Brendon Ltd, 1979 ISBN 0 7091 7619 8

B W Martin: *The Dictionary of the Occult,* Rider and Company, First published 1979 ISBN 0 09 136880 4

Paddy Slade: *Natural Magic – A Seasonal Guide* Hamlyn Publishing 1990 ISBN 0 600 57064 9

Rae Beth: *The Hedge Witch's Way, Magical Spirituality for the Lone Spellcaster,* St Edmundsbury Press Limited, 2001, ISBN 0 7090 7383 6

Francis Melville: *Defence Against the Dark Arts – Psychic Self-Protection for Practitioners of Magic,* Quantum Publishing plc first published 2004 ISBN 978-1-84573-376-6

John Gray Bell (ed): *The Trial of Jennet Preston, of Gisbourne, in Craven, at the York assizes, July 1612, for Practising devilish and Wicked Arts Called Witchcraft* (London 1612) in Series of tracts on British Topography, History, Dialects, Etc, (Leeds Brotherton Library)

Articles and Documents

Andrew Cambers D.Phil. *Print, Manuscript and Godly Cultures in the North of England, c 1600 – 1650* The University of York Department of History May 2003

Amelia G Sceats: *Belief, Influence and Action: Witchcraft in Seventeenth Century Yorkshire* 2016, The University of Huddersfield

Lesley Smith *The French Pox* published in the Journal of Family Planning and Reproductive Health Care 2006:32(4) 265-266 BMJ Sexual and Reproductive Health

Somer Marie Stahl: *Social Commentary and the Feminine Centre in John Webster*, University of North Carolina Wilmington

Relating to the locality:

Pamphlets produced at the time of Canon Peter Winstone, Vicar of Fewston

G Hardwick and P J Winstone: *Fewston Parish Churchyard*
G Hardwick and P J Winstone: *Fewston in 1621-1622*

Books

John Dickinson: *Timble Man Diaries of a Dalesman*, Selected and Edited by Ronald Harker Hendon Publishing Co. Ltd. 1988 ISBN 0 86067 110 0

David Alred: *A Pictorial Record of Life in a Dales Valley* Smith Settle Ltd 1997 ISBN 1 85825 090 0

Diana Parsons: The Book of the Washburn Valley Yorkshire's Forgotten Dale Halsgrove 2014 ISBN 978 0 85704 240 8

Catharine Pullein: The Pulleyns of Yorkshire, 1915, J. Whitehead & Son, Printers, Alfred Streer, Boar Lane, Leeds

People

My thanks to Nick Melia, Archives Assistant at the Borthwick Institute, York, for his help over records relating to witchcraft, and to Fewston church and vicar Nicholas Smithson:

- the archive of the Cause Papers in the Diocesan Courts

of the Archbishopric of York – 1300 – 1858.

- Records of the York Assizes held at The National Archives at Kew
- The Fewston parish records held at North Yorkshire County Record Office at Northallerton

Archdeaconal visitation information relating to Fewston church – 1585, 1586, 1595-6, and1613. The 1595 Archiepiscopal Visitation Court Book is the source of the reference to Smithson's resistance to the 'local custom of rush bearing'.

***

My thanks to Dr Euan Roger, Medieval, Early Modern and Legal Collections Expertise and Engagement, The National Archives at Kew, for his useful steers to Criminal trials in the assize courts 1559-1971, J S Cockburn's calendars of assize court indictments and Cockburn's History of English Assizes.
Additionally, the records of Court of Star Chamber, held at the National Archive. Herryson v Smithson, February 1621.
Plaintiffs: Thomas Herryson, husbandman
Defendants: Nicholas Smithson, vicar of Fewston, Reuben Smithson, his son, Nathaniel Smithson, Joshua Smithson, Robert Smithson
Subjects: Crime/Litigation/Religious/Religious discrimination and persecution/Sports/Treason and rebellion

***

My thanks to Bob Anderson of the Pendle Heritage Centre Museum, Park Hill, Barrowford, Lancashire, BB9 6JQ, for his help, insights, and encouragement, given on the day of his retirement from the Centre.